END TIMES

OTHER BOOKS BY THIS AUTHOR

Monroeville and the Stage Production
of "To Kill a Mockingbird"

Atlanta Pop in the 50s, 60s and 70s
The Magic of Bill Lowery

Village People
Sketches of Auburn

Lake Moon
(a novel)

END TIMES

JOHN M. WILLIAMS

SARTORIS LITERARY GROUP
Metro-Jackson, Mississippi
Sartorisliterary-dot-com

TO
Rheta and Hines
and
Edwin Gray

PART ONE
1990 - 2009

Chapter 1

Maryrell and Ramp

It was becoming painfully obvious that Maryrell (Mae-rell) was in labor, and all the moaning and groaning was getting on Ramp's nerves. Ramp, the who else could it be? father, was already pretty well loaded as he took the third-empty handle of Ezra Brooks and, grumbling incoherently, headed for the door.

Muttering something about "that snake," Daydream, their just down the road neighbor, came over to help the poor girl, which, at nineteen, Maryrell was, but nobody was surprised when not long before she died she met Cleetha Till and Cleetha smiled like she was somebody she had known all her life, and called her an "old soul."

Not even Cleetha herself knew if there was such a thing, but you knew what she meant.

* * *

Ramp, of course, was headed out Troubleneck Road to the Mud House, because aside from Rafer's, where he wasn't always welcome and which wouldn't be open now anyway, and a few other backroad places where he *really* wasn't welcome, it was the only place he had to go. And he went there a lot. You could say, it was the place where he could just let go and be himself, which sounds nice until you understood what that actually meant. His father, who used to hang him upside down from a tree limb when he was a kid and correct his behavior with a 2x4, had built it on a little piece of land along the river he had stolen from a senile farmer not quite bright enough to mistrust him. The place was a few miles upstream from the lake—a locale as remote as you can be and not be on the Congo. It was about a mile of rutted dirt road off a county road off a county road off Troubleneck Road to get there. Needless to say, it attracted an assortment of souls who had something you'd rather not think about in common.

It was called the Mud House because of its construction: chicken wire over hay bales slathered with a mixture of ground-up hay and red mud, which the Alabama sun baked into titanium, and a metal roof—and had taken eight years to patch together enough periods of semi-sobriety to build. True to his sporadic proclivity for projects that made no sense, but which impressed you with their psychotic audacity, Ramp's father had extorted the labor of a heavy equipment-owning client deeply in debt for the substances he needed to live, to bring in a 1960s-era Seaboard Coastline caboose. This fading orange museum piece had languished in the front yard of another debtor for so long the man couldn't remember how it had gotten there. A semi and flatbed trailer with an industrial-sized winch appeared in his yard one morning, and now the caboose sat permanently moored off to the side of the Mud House in a sea of poison ivy. Nobody knew why. Nobody ever went in it. Then, Ramp's father died.

The Mud House was a creepy place, with no power, no running water, no furniture, and could have served as an exhibit room for the "spiders of the southeastern United States." And more snake sightings than is comfortable. Not that any living thing stood much of a chance around there. The house perched, looking half melted, on a bluff featuring about a fifteen-foot mudslide into the river, and on more than one occasion innocent kayakers on a back to nature float trip had gotten a good dose of nature with the spectacle of a platoon of jacked-up naked mud sliding country boys.

"It brings out the 'hold my beer and watch this shit' in them," Redwine Pyle said.

Ramp, whose childhood was something he had *survived*, always said he hadn't had fun like you're supposed to when you're a kid, and had been making up for it ever since. He was thirty-two now and the thing about him was, he wasn't into hassles—in the way of people whose single greatest fear is losing their buzz. He didn't get into fights mainly because everybody knew about the eight-inch antler-handle hunting knife he kept on his belt, not to mention his nine millimeter Smith and Wesson always close to hand and with which he regularly took out his grievances against his fate on the animal kingdom, starting at ant beds and working his way up through turtles, snakes, birds, and mammals—and of course a nine millimeter and crystal meth don't really go together. Plus, after the militia chapter formed out there, he borrowed one of the AK-47s one day and in a single firestorm blew away all the dogs and cats that frequented the place, and that was something you remembered.

He had once gotten the idea from somewhere to raise hogs out there, but it turned out to be too much hassle, so he ended up butchering them all except one, which slipped by, and when somebody told him the meat in a hog over 250 pounds wasn't fit to eat, he just said the hell with it. The creature was now over 800 pounds, half wild, and could easily have starred in a horror movie. It showed up like something out of a bad dream when there was garbage at the Mud House, but other than that, nobody really knew what it ate.

Ramp stopped off at Burf's and got some dust to liven up a bud of that ass-kicking stuff from Colorado he had saved. Things were threatening to be a hassle, and it was time to nip that shit.

* * *

But, in a worst case scenario for his buzz, when he got to the Mud House the goddamned militia guy from Atlanta was holding court on the side yard. He stood on the back stoop—the cropped hair, the jaw, the muscle tee-shirt tucked into the black trousers, the sidearm on his belt—talking. The local chapter leaned against the trucks, or sat on the hoods, with beverages, listening. A flag with a snake on it barely moved in the breeze.

The man walked back and forth as he spoke. Ramp was in a highly fortified haze by that time and short on patience, knowing the man was just there for money, and was about to walk past and head on down to the river, but the guy seemed to be making a case that they were descendants of Vikings, so he slid on the side to listen.

"We are Vikings. The protectors. And as such we are the only hope of our people. The protected. Yes, we are physically strong. Nobody takes down a Viking but another Viking. But we are also superior"—he tapped his head—"in intelligence. Yes, I know you've been conditioned to think intelligence belongs to fags and weenies but that's a misnomer. Intelligence is about *survival*. And believe me, when the shit hits the fan only two things will matter: heightened intelligence and testosterone. Yes, I hate to tell you, but as the elite few of our race you will all have to take your turn at reproduction duty."

Ramp looked around him as everybody shuffled a bit and laughed at that, and thought, *If this is what he's counting on he's in trouble.*

"And I'm sure you already know this," the man continued, "but in some part of her soul every woman wants to be taken by a strong man. That's just nature, gentlemen. It works hand in hand with heightened intelligence. And what is that intelligence telling us? It's telling us that the weak are in a position of power, and the strong need to correct that. Because, gentlemen, if you don't hear anything else I say this afternoon, hear this: it's us or nobody. I'm going to be frank with you: we are at *war*. You can call it other names if it makes you feel better, but that's the bottom line: we are at *war*. Warfare to stop the decay of our civilization, people. And the ones who have used their God-given right to arm and train themselves will defeat those who are not armed and trained and who are trying to win the easy way—by taking your arms away from you. But they won't succeed because there's a network of Vikings out there. A network that's growing every day."

He pointed to the hood of his truck where a variety of nootropic supplements were displayed. "Be sure to stock up on your brain medicine," he said. "Don't get left out."

Well, this is bullshit, Ramp thought, and knowing this was the part where the dude collected the dues, he decided it was time to exit. He turned around and only then noticed Cabul Echols, in the way back, leaning against his big black Ram.

Ramp knew some of the guys worked for him sometimes— *he* had worked for him himself one time. Not quite a week. They hadn't shared the same work ethic. The man was all business.

Cabul, with an expression that said nothing, got in his truck and drove away.

The militia man watched him, and said, "Friends, you know this mission isn't for everybody—and that's okay. We only want the best. And don't let it go to your head, but we've got twenty-three chapters in three states, and yours is one of the strongest— the level of commitment, the financial support—"

The guy next to Ramp muttered, "I ain't seen a whole lot of this network he's talking about."

"Yeah," the guy next to him said, "you ain't seen it because you ain't been nowhere but your trailer and the Mud House for fifteen years."

"What the hell—Atlanta? What the hell I want to do with Atlanta? Atlanta, shit."

"The movement is growing, man," somebody else said.

"How do you know?"

"It just is."

"Shit," the guy said, and emptied his Mac-10 into the woods. Everybody turned to look, then turned back.

"Put that goddamned thing up!" the second guy cried in the

echoes that followed. "You want people down here looking for where that come from?"

"Let em come on. They'll wish they never thought about looking for where it come from. Cause I'm going to tell you something. They come looking for it, they're going to find it and a whole lot more."

"Shut the fuck up."

An inspired group was headed to town Prius-dusting, but all Ramp wanted was for everybody to get the hell away from him and quit killing his buzz.

He and Ezra headed down to the river.

* * *

Daydream was an LPN, and when Maryrell's contractions were five minutes apart she got her in the car and to the hospital. Maryrell had protested—she didn't have any kind of insurance, and Ramp—well, forget *that*—but being on the threshold of giving birth was fight enough, so she went. It was her first encounter with the medical world in her pregnancy and almost in her life except for the free shots at school. Daydream told her they had to take her in, and assured her they would set up a way for her to make payments.

* * *

What Maryrell, a beautiful girl-woman with piercing dreamy eyes, who had what Cleetha Till, because she had it herself, called a sixth sense, and could *see* the pain and sadness in people, was doing with a man thirteen years older than her and a certified piece of shit at that, wasn't really a mystery to the people around there who knew she had lost her mother which probably was all the family she had and was out on her own and how hard life could be. Maryrell had other gifts—one, more like a curse, was that she could see what people looked like under their clothes, though in truth she'd had this gift so long she was like what nudists in a nudist colony must be like: used to it. She could also see disease in people, physical and moral, like a brown stain. Some people were so far gone they looked like they'd been soaked in tobacco juice—the morally diseased of whom she steered clear of. The physically sick she generally felt sorry for, except for those for whom she sensed death would be an improvement. And when somebody was going to die soon, she could see their skull like a hologram coming into and out of focus under their face—as she had with her mother during the last months of her life, knowing it was something she couldn't do anything about.

* * *

Ramp had picked her up on the side of the road where she had run out of gas. He was stained brown, but she'd seen worse, but the main thing was, she could feel the gleam of something good buried deep inside him under all the abuse and the chemicals, but knew it would take dying to get to it. He took her to his trailer where he fed her and let her sleep on his couch. He himself passed out on the bed. The next day he took his gas can to her car and poured in a gallon which was enough to get it to the trailer.

She didn't seem to have anywhere to go back to, or to be in a big hurry to leave, and it turned out she wasn't all that sure of her destination anyway. "Atlanta" was all she knew, and the florid return address on the envelope she had with her, sent by her friend Gloria who had moved there from Douvale and found a city job and invited Maryrell to come, didn't mean anything because Maryrell had never been to Atlanta. Plus, as running out of gas five miles from the house she'd been forced to vacate, after her mother finally escaped the coma she'd been in for three weeks cavorting with spirits on the other side and hardly remembering what was over here, on a dubious trip in hopes of finding a job in a strange city would lead you to suspect, she didn't have much money.

Then Ramp learned the letter had been sent two years ago.

"You ain't heard nothing since?" he asked her with the incredulity of one who has never been around a person of faith before.

She shook her head.

"What are the chances she's still at that same place? You got her phone number?"

Maryrell shook her head again.

"You ain't got a daddy?"

"He left when I was two. All I remember is his smell."

"I ain't got one either," said Ramp. "And if I did, you could have him."

"Is he dead?"

"Yes, and he's the person in this world I'm most glad is."

That struck Maryrell as sad.

After that, Ramp kind of left off on the questions, and she didn't volunteer much, but he got the basic picture—that rather than be a *burden* on Odis and Mildra, her paternal grandparents and only relatives, who had invited her and were expecting her, she had decided to go find Gloria.

"Well, you can stay here till you get it figured out," he said.

That second night he told her she could sleep in the bed. He went to the grocery store and bought some bread and ham and cheese and saltines and pork and beans and bananas, then left, and didn't come back for two days.

* * *

Maryrell liked to read and that's what she did the whole time he was gone, looking up every now and then wondering what she was going to do when she ran out of the books she had brought—and just what she was going to do, period.

And it *was* wonder, not worry, because Maryrell never worried. All her life, everything had just washed over her like a wave, and she always had the feeling that things came and went, nothing stayed the same, and nothing that happened mattered much, and it all came around in the end. Even watching her mother die, she took in stride. Maryrell was not religious, mainly because she didn't really know what it meant to be religious. What most people call God, she called It—because nobody had ever taught her she had to turn It into an old man.

She didn't picture her mother in a "better place" or anything, she just felt that everything was fine the way it was and didn't even need to make sense because in some big-picture way it did. She trusted It. And she loved her mama, and knew her mama loved her. "You're the light of my world," she used to tell her, and Maryrell didn't see how something like dying could change that.

Knowing, of course, from what the mirror had shown her flashes of, as another mirror had for her mother, that she was going to die in exactly the same way. And though most people would be scared staying in a dirty trailer with a man of self-destructive habits and precarious emotional health, she wasn't. She knew what was going to happen there.

Of course Ramp was worthless, but he was handsome—in the way somebody who is not going to be handsome long is handsome. And he *had* helped her. She could see, as plain as if it was standing there instead of him, the mauled child inside him.

This ability had brought her plenty of sadness in her life, but she couldn't help it.

She got it from her mother.

* * *

The bed was nice and the night he crawled into it with her she could tell he was—well, just say "drunk" for short—and he— well, just say "fell asleep"—right off and started snoring like a bullfrog. Luckily, she was good at blocking things out. The next morning he was warm and kind of sweet and told her some things that made her laugh, and didn't smell too bad, and it was the most natural thing in the world. She made eggs and fried baloney for breakfast, and that afternoon he took her to Wal-Mart and let her pick out five books from the Wal-Mart book section. She looked for ones with a good story.

* * *

She got to know Daydream and spent a lot more time with her than with him, who was gone more than he was there. And when he did come, it didn't feel like somebody coming home, but just checking in. She could only hope he would be sober, but the truth was, Ramp was never sober.

"What do you expect, when that snake gets what he wants?" Daydream, who had been telling her from the minute she met her that she was a hundred times too good for him, said. But that was another thing about Maryrell: she was loyal—and for all she knew might still be standing on the side of the road if it hadn't been for him.

"Hell, an hour later and it would have been me," said Daydream, who was the kind who would have been just as happy getting into bed with her as with any man.

"He's not mean to me, and he makes sure I have food," Maryrell would point out.

"If you call it food," Daydream sneered. And she was right because she was a good cook who came home with things like asparagus and portobello mushrooms and knew all about spices and herbs, which she grew in a couple of old bathtubs behind her house.

And of course it was Daydream who brought the pregnancy test kit over. And that purple line was clear as a bell.

"I think you ought to come stay with me—for now," said Daydream, which Maryrell sort of did because once Ramp found out he really started disappearing—a week, two, three, a month— and when he did come home, and she was there, he seemed like he had lost interest in her.

Chapter 2

Jon Karl Comes to East Douvale

Maryrell knew all along it was going to be a boy, and didn't even think about girl names. She wanted something that sounded like a normal person, and she had always had a thing for "John." But she liked "Carl" just about as much, and couldn't decide. Not that she overthought it, because she knew if you left things alone, they usually worked themselves out. She didn't even ask Ramp because she knew he didn't care.

So it did work itself out when after about a six-hour labor somewhere in the hospital and a straightforward delivery, they handed the little red bundle to her and she said "Jon Karl" and she herself didn't know what had happened to the "h" or how the "c" had changed to a "k."

That's just how it worked out, and that's the name that went on the birth certificate, with the surname "Odom"—Odis and Mildra's name—and not "Cogg," which her mother had gone by, and she herself had gone by in school, because she figured it would be best to use the name of her only living relatives—which was, after all, her father's name—and that "Cogg" didn't really have a lot going for it.

The nurse who handed Jon Karl to her had a sort of smirk on her face, and Maryrell had heard a group of them snickering as they bathed and wrapped him up, and the nurse asked where the daddy was like somebody that wanted to get a look at him.

"He's not here," said Maryrell.

"I can see that. Do you know where he is? Do you know *who* he is?"

Maryrell was used to condescension and just fixed her bottomless eyes on the snide floral-smocked nurse until she looked away.

"I do."

"I bet that's the first time you said *that*," the nurse said. "*Where* is he?"

"He won't be coming." Daydream came to the rescue. "And what's so damn funny?"

"What business is it of *yours*?" the nurse shot back.

"What business is it of *yours*?"

"I'm the nurse, that's what. And we weren't laughing. We were *admiring*."

More snickering from across the room.

Maryrell didn't like that, and just wanted to go.

The hospital put together a little care package for her and wished her well.

* * *

"Forget that snake, you can just stay here with me as long as you need to," was what Daydream didn't say once they got back to her house. Instead, it was the more ambivalent "So—what are you planning to do?"

But Maryrell had already decided. She had decided once she named her son Jon Karl Odom. Everything about Ramp, including Ramp, seemed like something from long ago and not even real, like a story, which, Maryrell realized, like everything it basically was. Of course there'd been no sign of him on this momentous occasion—who, if he'd thought about it at all, wouldn't have recognized any significant connection between a little wallowing around with a girl he had picked up on the side of the road, and somebody else's momentous occasion.

As soon as Daydream went to work, Maryrell called her grandmama Mildra. When Mildra had heard the whole story, which took Maryrell, gifted with the natural pith she'd gotten from her mother, about fifteen seconds to tell, Mildra just said, *"Burden!* Don't be talking about any burden. Isn't that baby my great-grandson?"

"Yes mam."

"You got any other home besides here?"

"No mam."

"All right then."

* * *

It was what she said about not wanting to be a burden, and also a feeling that at twenty she ought to be making her own way, and not any bad feelings about Odis and Mildra, that had kept her from accepting their invitation—until now.

In fact, she had always gotten along fine with them, and loved them, and though she hadn't seen too much of them lately, she had known them all her life, which is more than she could say for her father, their son, whose name they never mentioned. They had sort of drifted apart after he left.

Leaving nothing but a smell.

* * *

Odis and Mildra were getting up in their sixties and lived in East Douvale in an old working class neighborhood in the shady bungalow they'd moved into forty years ago. That side of town had a smell Maryrell liked, maybe because it reminded her of being a little girl. Since the neighborhood was old, it had a lot of trees and flowers and shrubs smothering the houses. Over the years it had become more racially diverse—with a black area, a white area, a Latin area, with porous boundaries. Jon Karl made the drive across town serenely. He was an easy baby.

As Maryrell crossed the tracks, which cut through the area diagonally, making you have to cross them as many as four times depending on where you were going, first she saw a ragged young but old-looking man not even looking up, like he'd lost all hope, crouched on the side of the road with a cardboard sign that just

21

said "Help me." It broke her heart, who knew she wasn't but an inch away from being homeless herself, and she stopped and gave him five dollars and the bag of apples she was bringing—then when she drove off and waved bye as he looked at her like she was an alien and maybe sort of waved back, like he wasn't sure he knew how to do it, she saw a crow standing on the sidewalk up ahead like a gang member.

Maryrell noticed birds, and in some way she'd never really tried to figure out thought they meant something, especially crows, which were way smarter than a bird has a right to be. There was an obvious connection between the homeless man and the crow she knew but couldn't explain.

A dreamy sort of place, East Douvale, especially in early June with the gardenias. Past the "I Know My Redeemer Lives" church with its current sign: "Duct tape patches most things, but three nails fixed everything." An enterprising yard business: "Swings and Thing." The long-closed corner store, a relic from the era before convenience marts, with its fading Diet-Rite Cola sign: "Rich Hicks Gen. Mdse." The curious microcosm at the intersection of E Street and Silver Avenue, where Colonel Smy, retired, and Doris Ault, mortal enemies for thirty years, lived side by side.

Doris Ault was a hoarder. Every inch of her yard was choked with the treasures she daily salvaged from roadside heaps—furniture, Christmas decorations, appliances, maybe a car or two in there somewhere. Not that Doris drove or ever had. She wheeled around town on a big three-wheeled bicycle with a basket on the front in an ankle-length dress. Nobody had ever caught her in the act, but a mannequin on her front porch was dressed in different clothes every day. What was *inside* the barely-visible house was anybody's guess, since no one besides Doris had ever been in it.

"Except one time," Redwine Pyle told it, "when this new meter reader couldn't find the meter and knocked at the door and didn't hear nothing and took the liberty of stepping inside. He called out 'Anybody home?' but nobody answered. You could barely walk in there, he said, for all the junk piled up everywhere, and it was moldy-smelling—but that wasn't the main thing. He kind of squirmed his way down to the end of the hall, because he was curious as hell now, to the last door standing open and got the shock of his life. That woman's sister, which nobody even knew there *was* a sister, had been living all those years there in that house. That ol' boy said it was like a little girl's room, even if it was all moldy—all pink and frilly, dolls on the bed, clown pictures on the walls, and her sitting there in a rocking chair with a bow in her hair—in her fifties, easy—reading a picture book. He blew out of there faster than gossip."

Colonel Smy, retired, was known to be an eccentric and rumored to be a hoarder himself, though nobody had ever set foot in his house. They just saw the UPS truck drive up pretty much every day, with an endless stream of boxes going in. He didn't seem to have any family, and a lot of people thought the same thing: that's going to be one hell of an estate sale if he ever dies.

"But he *did* have a daughter," said Redwine, "and it had gotten out that she, who apparently had consulted a map and picked out the place farthest away from him she could get and moved there, had hired a lawyer to keep herself out of the will."

Colonel Smy's front yard was full of the holes he was constantly and for no known reason digging, a labor responsible for several impressive rock piles which had struck the Baptists as satanic or pagan or something, and brought them out there in numbers to stand along the street with crossed arms mouthing some chant. Colonel Smy put a pretty quick end to that with a BB gun.

"Doris and the Colonel threatened to kill each other pretty much on a daily basis," Redwine said, "and it had been years since 911 had acknowledged any of her calls claiming he was trying to poison her—which, it wouldn't surprise me if he *was*—seriously, she would stand there on the edge of the yard with a pad and pencil making lists of his transgressions which she would put in his mailbox. He put a little barrel right by the post where he would burn them on the spot, spit toward her house, and go back inside—which I'm sure made it to the next list. I've heard it suggested they were faking mental illness to get out of working, but everybody knew they didn't need to fake it."

And then there was the gentleman on the edge of the black section Maryrell had never known to be absent, still there, sitting in a plastic chair in what she assumed was his yard waving at every passing car.

She waved back.

When she got to Odis and Mildra's house, Food Stamp, their wiggly more or less boxer dog, met her at the door.

"You should have just come here to start with," Mildra mildly scolded.

"I didn't want to be a burden."

"I told you to stop saying that. Look at this sweet thing!" Mildra gushed, taking the bundle in her arms. "He's—you sure it's a he?"

"Yes mam."

"He's so *pretty*!"

"I'm going to pay our way."

"What, go off and work at Burger King? Hell no. You need to be with this baby. All the time."

Mildra was just saying what she knew. She and Odis had worked non-stop when all four of their children were growing up. She couldn't even remember it, and look how *they* had turned out. Especially their youngest, Maryrell's daddy.

"In name only," Mildra would point out.

Odis was sitting in a chair, *his* chair, in the living room, his rubbery face gurning a smile, and just said, "Looka here, looka here." It hadn't been terribly long since Maryrell had seen him, but she could tell there was a little something missing from whatever "all" meant when you said "all there." Maryrell glanced at Mildra, who just shook her head.

He had always been funny—joking, laughing, picking at people, teasing the children, making faces (a talent nature had well equipped him for). And had a way of saying then taking back bad words around children, whom everybody knows you can't take things back around.

"He was a real son-of-a-bitch—"

"Odis!"

"Excuse me, bad person."

"He pulled out his peter—"

"Odis!"

"Excuse me, his pee-pee."

"That gal's all tits and ass—"

"Odis!"

"Excuse me, she has a nice figure."

He had been instrumental in the subliminal education of an entire generation, but now something seemed to be coming up a little short. He had recently retired after forty years of the daily grind, mostly in auto parts, an event he had looked forward to all his life, only to realize he didn't know the himself who didn't work anymore, but whoever it was, it was in the house with nothing to do all day.

* * *

Which, second only to needing the money, was the main reason Mildra was still working. Fortunately she liked her job, she liked having something to be absorbed in, and after thirty-something years she was real good at it, and had her own office and didn't need to be around people. Her title was "Head Bookkeeper," which, frankly, she was proud of, for Dawes Properties, the multifarious empire of Spruill Dawes, which was more or less real estate, but included anything he could find to make money. He had so many side deals going even he could hardly keep up with them.

But Mildra could. She had, just in the natural course of events, made herself indispensable. And if the job required her to make a few creative accounting moves here and there, so be it—the world's a tough place—and she loved Mr. Dawes, a shrewd but jovial man, a people person, and born businessman. Her affection didn't extend to the current Mrs. Dawes, the third of that name, who at half Spruill's age had just presented her husband with what would be his seventh, and last, child, and the delight of his late years, Millard—but never mind that. Mr. Dawes had gone out of his way through the years to show his appreciation to Mildra, and nobody but an outright Puritan would find it hard to get along with somebody who felt that just about any way you could make money was fair game while treating the people around him like royalty, and throwing a big Fourth of July barbecue on the Square every year for the town.

"What you need to do," Mildra told Maryrell, "is spend every minute you can with your son. That's something no amount of money in this world can buy. Just like your mama did. She was special, sugar, and so are you. And I got a feeling this little fella is too."

Food Stamp had been staring adoringly at Maryrell and now, emboldened by her glance, came over and put his head on her lap.

See? Things worked out.

* * *

Maryrell gravitated to the front porch where ceiling fans kept the heat from being too bad, and enjoyed all of her favorite things: looking after Jon Karl, reading, watching the world pass by on the shady street, hearing the trains just out of sight a few blocks over and trying to picture them, with Food Stamp on his rug beside her.

In the afternoons she got into the habit of taking Jon Karl on walks in the stroller to the park a couple of streets over where the mill kids had grown up playing but now the mill was closed and the place was weedy and worse for the wear but still had an old ballfield with a backstop, some swings and monkey bars, and a bench or two and was nice and shady—even if jacked-up trucks parked in formation on one of the corners sometimes where there were no trees, like they were bluebirds that needed to see all around, and sat there with their doors open while their young owners stood around doing whatever they did, which to Maryrell didn't look like much.

Great-grandmama Mildra adored Jon Karl and had gotten the stroller and a nice playpen at a yard sale, and he seemed to have the instinctive knack for being able to entertain himself—with the various bright-colored things floating around in his playpen, or with his toes, or whatever he could get in his mouth, which would bring Maryrell to her feet.

"Baby, don't put that in your mouth—you could choke."

In fact, she talked to him constantly, held him, nursed him, read to him, took him inside to change him and make sure Odis hadn't turned on QVC, but usually he would just be sitting there staring at nothing.

When Jon Karl slept, she read the books she got from the library every week, looking up occasionally to watch the cars and loud trucks go by. That's usually when Food Stamp would take a turn in the yard, doing his business and checking things out. Every morning, while it was still cool, she waved to the older couple out for their walk, pushing a stroller. She figured they were grandparents doing what the parents couldn't, or wouldn't, and she was touched. She couldn't see the baby in the recess of the stroller, just a lump and a piece of a bonnet. In the afternoons a bald middle-aged man with a surprised face came by in an orange safety vest.

"Ed Butts' mildly retarded son," Redwine explained.

Maryrell found that touching too, that they let him have some freedom, trusting him to stay out of the street and all the crazy drivers not to hit him.

"You can't say 'village idiot' anymore," said Redwine. "You can't say you're going to Texaco because that might offend Shell—you can't say anything—I don't know where we're headed—but anyway—whether you can *say* village idiot or not, that's what he is, and you know every town is proud of theirs and think their village idiot is a better village idiot than yours. Anyway—his name is Dunstan, and everybody knows Dunstan is what you'd call gifted in the downstairs department, not that you'd really *want* him reproducing, and every now and then a group would get him in the back of the barber shop or somewhere for a look, which he was proud to do anytime anywhere, and every time somebody would say something like 'I bet you drive the girls crazy with that thing,' he would answer the way somebody told him to a long time ago—'aisk your wife'—and you could tell he knew that was funny but didn't really know why. My friend Lucille Bass got a look at it one time behind the Biscuit Stop and said 'You could have put a wristwatch on it!'"

"He got in some trouble a few times, looking in people's windows. He got fixated on this one gal and would go into her house when she wasn't there to smell her shoes or go through her bathroom trash can. They caught him in the act one day, and when they told him they were taking him down to the jail, he asked if he could take her shoes with him. When they emptied his pockets they found about twenty used Q-tips."

About once a week Maryrell would hear the familiar rumble from down the street, and the motorcycle man, who lived down there somewhere, would pass by in full regalia on his spotless bike, then about an hour later come back. She suspected he was retired.

Time melted and hid its tracks, and by the end of the summer Jon Karl was crawling and she let him out, Food Stamp in attendance, to explore the porch, keeping a close eye on him, except for those times when she would get lost in one of her reveries where little scenes played out in her head and she wondered who the people in them were—then would look up and not see Jon Karl or Food Stamp and have that feeling like somebody whose face you never saw pushing you out of an airplane, and the scene would change to him falling off the porch and hitting his head, or something involving electric sockets, coyotes, snakes, crazy people, aliens, all in one second, and she would leap to her feet and find him behind a chair, with Food Stamp temporarily diverted by something needing investigating.

The first cool night didn't come till late in October, when Jon Karl was about six months old. The center of operations moved indoors, which was harder, with Odis in there, who was falling deeper and deeper into his own private little dark place.

"What's wrong with Odis?" Maryrell asked Mildra one day.

"I think he's reverting."

"To what?"

"To whatever it is you revert to."

That seemed like a good enough explanation, but whatever place it was, there had to be *something* going on in there because he would interrupt his silence from time to time with a statement like: "Grandpa Belcher ran off with a young girl."

Or, "Daddy had a whole box full of naked pictures." Followed a minute later by: "They was all stuck together."

Or, "They said it was an accident, but that Tullson boy held him under."

Or, "That woman in the Care Center got ahold of Aunt Zena's credit card."

Or, "That girl next door had a titty with two nipples." Followed a minute later by: "She charged you a quarter to see it." Then a little later: "One time was enough."

Or, "It set down in the road right in front of my truck, and all that thing that come out of it wanted to know was what year we called it."

Or, "There was a lot of 'bachelors' in that town." Followed by: "Everybody knew he was queer but him."

That sort of thing. Mildra said to just ignore him.

She was right about that, just like she was right about how important it was for Maryrell and Jon Karl to spend so much time together—because all that first year, as Mildra worked and came home and worked, and worked and came home and worked, and it was obvious she loved having this other busy meaningful thing to do, Maryrell, even though she did keep the house straightened up and clean, and looked after Odis, spent so much time with Jon Karl and grew so close to him, she lived in a constant state of charm and gratitude.

Their bond, even more as she began, with some pride, to feel him pulling away and becoming his own little Jon Karl, was too ordinary for her to be in awe of it—and she didn't like to think how little of most people's lives they got to do what they really loved—partly because she felt sorry for them, countless nameless and faceless though they were, and partly because she knew she and Jon Karl were part of each other and had only these fragile moments themselves.

"You're the light of my world," she would tell him. And always hear her own mother saying it when she did.

The days passed by in idyllic succession, and she began to know his personality, and sense his future, which mystified her. He was playful, with a sharp gleam in his eye, and teased her, learned her buttons and how to push them. He loved it when she held him down and tickled him, and got her to do it by pretending he didn't want her to. He was so smart she didn't hardly have to do anything except love him.

Chapter 3

Ramp, One More Time

That second summer they got back in the routine of going to the park on nice afternoons, always taking something to give the man with the "Help Me" sign on the way. Maryrell would sit on the bench, as Jon Karl found endless ways to amuse himself. Sometimes another mother or two with toddlers might show up, and in that lifelong affinity of the like-aged for their own kind, Jon Karl was drawn to these other newly-formed creatures, and seemed to think those were appropriate times to pull down his pants and Huggie.

"Jon Karl!" Maryrell would call, then hurry over to pull them up. Sometimes the other mothers were amused, sometimes not. Those episodes were particularly awkward because Maryrell had never cut Jon Karl's hair, and he was so pretty people would just stare at him and think he was a girl.

Until the Huggie came down. Then one day toward the end of the summer, Ramp showed up. They were at the park, and from her bench Maryrell saw the ancient banged-up camper van pull into the little grassy parking area across the field by the backstop. Jon Karl was by the monkey bars playing in the dirt with a little girl his age.

A few seconds passed, enough for Maryrell to have a full novella play out in her head, as the mysterious driver parked and got out. He looked familiar, but it took her a minute to remember who he was. As he walked toward her, it all came back.

She figured he was on something but it was hard to tell. The year and a half had not been kind. He wasn't even thirty-five yet and looked a good ten or fifteen years older. Maryrell, because she couldn't help but feel for people, felt a little wave of pity for him.

He had been good-looking, but he was also, she knew, completely worthless. And knew it. "I know I ain't worth nothing," she could hear him saying, "except maybe a baby or two."

She didn't know how he had known where to find her. Daydream wouldn't have told him—but it probably wouldn't have been that hard to figure out. She hoped he wasn't going to try to claim Jon Karl somehow — but then he would have to pay for him and she knew that wasn't going to happen. Plus, one look at him and she knew he wasn't long for this earth.

"I don't even hardly remember you," Maryrell said as he stopped a few feet away from her bench.

"I don't either," he said. Then: "I've applied for disability."

"Okay."

He looked toward the toddlers digging by the monkey bars.

"I was thinking it was a boy."

"It?" she said.

"The baby." He stared. "Which one is it?"

"The one with the bucket."

"That's a girl."

"No. It's not."

"It's a boy?"

"Yes," said Maryrell.

"It looks like a girl."

"Well, he's not."

"Let me see."

"Just take my word for it."

"You say he's a boy — that makes him my son, right?"

"Yes."

"Then let me see my son."

"I told you to take my word for it. You just need to go away."

"I ain't going anywhere until I see what's underneath them britches."

"A Huggie."

"I mean what's underneath that."

"You don't have any right —"

"I didn't say I did. I just want to know. What's its name?"

Maryrell wasn't sure that was any of his business and didn't answer at once. Ramp waited. "Jon Karl," she said at last.

He turned and called out: "Jon Karl!"

Jon Karl, the little girl, and the little girl's mother all looked up in unison.

"Pull down them britches!"

"No! Don't tell him that!"

Jon Karl, grinning as he sized up this strange man standing by his mother, didn't have to be told twice.

As Ramp's whoop echoed across the playground, the little girl matched her friend, and they stood there looking at each other and drooling with laughter at the hilarity of it.

The other mother shot them a murderous look, rushed over and scooped up her daughter and fled, spewing gravel.

Maryrell walked over to pull up Jon Karl's Huggie, giving it a quick motherly check, and pants, and Ramp followed her.

"I'm going home," she said. "You just need to go back wherever you came from."

"I just want it one more time."

She stopped. "What?"

"You know what."

"Are you crazy?"

"Yes. But I'm being serious — that's all I want. Just one more time. It don't get no better than you, and I know that. Then I'll go away and you won't never see me no more."

She tried to look stern but could see the brown doom all around him. She wondered what a life like his meant. She felt sorry for him.

"You promise?"

"I swear to God on a stack of Bibles."

Maryrell realized it had been a while since she'd done anything even a little crazy.

"If you've got any guns or knives or anything that could hurt him, get it out," she said as they got ready to stash Jon Karl up front in the van.

"I sold all my guns," he said. He opened the glove compartment and took out a knife in a scabbard. "All I got is this hunting knife that was my granddaddy's. The handle is made out of a deer antler." He handed it to her. "I want you to give it to—" he nodded toward Jon Karl—"him."

"He's too young for a knife," said Maryrell.

"I mean for when he's old enough."

She paused, looking at him, and realized he wanted Jon Karl to have a piece of him, and this was all he had. "Okay," she said.

Ramp opened the back. It didn't smell too good in there—with a mattress, some nasty blankets, an ice chest, and clothes everywhere.

"Are you living in here?" she asked.

"I'm having to for a while."

"Good Lord. Make it fast."

* * *

When she got home, Mildra was already off work.

"Good heavens, child, where were you?"

"I was with Ramp."

Mildra looked at her and her face went through a succession of outrage, fear, and pity. She had never met Ramp, or even asked much about him, more or less lumping him together in the category that included her son, and was sure she knew all she needed to know.

"Oh baby baby baby," she said. "Am I too late?"

"Yes mam."

"Oh sweet child—"

"He's gone for good."
Mildra just shook her head.

Chapter 4
Barber Balch

Then Odis went missing. He wandered off while Maryrell was on her afternoon walk a few days later. He had spent nearly six hours somewhere before a policeman answered a call about an elderly man in somebody's backyard eating what looked like a hoagie sandwich and scattering crumbs for the birds that had gathered around him.

When they went to the police station to get him, Maryrell saw his skull and told Mildra she didn't think they'd have him much longer.

"I know, sugar," said Mildra. "He needs a haircut."

For forty years nobody had cut Odis's hair but Barber Balch, as he was called. That was actually true for a good portion of the white men—black men had their own barbers—in Douvale, white collar and blue. Mildra called him and told him it wasn't easy to take Odis out, so Barber Balch said for an extra ten dollars he would come over to the house and do it.

For some reason Barber Balch drove a big powerful immaculately clean white crew-cab truck. A lifelong bachelor with no known relatives, he drove from his secluded rat and cat infested house that nobody had ever been in by a stagnant pond on Lorona Drive to his barber shop downtown, and to a store or two where he scoured the reduced-price bins, and nowhere else. He had bought the truck new three years ago, with cash, after talking the salesman out of most of his commission, and had yet to break 8000 miles. Nor hauled anything in it but grocery bags in the passenger seat.

When he came in the house Maryrell saw brown, smelled something like beef broth, and instinctively took a step or two back, as Food Stamp growled and retreated to a corner.

"That cur's not dangerous, is it?" Balch asked.

"I don't think so," said Mildra. "You might not want to make any sudden lunges."

Balch gave her a glance. "I'll try not to," he said.

"We appreciate you coming over," said Mildra.

"Ten dollars is ten dollars," he said, not quite succeeding in making it sound light.

Of course, everybody knew there had been money in his family, and he was an only child. So the rumor mill had fantasized about bags of cash hidden in his house, but most people knew he was too smart for that.

Maryrell couldn't help but notice his face had two halves—not left and right, but up and down: the bottom, a firm set jaw, slightly working like on a last little piece of peanut, a permanent scowl, and an overall impression that he had learned how to adjust his mouth muscles to various expressions from a manual; and the upper, close-cut white hair, a pair of reptilian eyes behind tortoise-shell glasses, taking in, assessing, everything. So while you were focused on the lower half, the upper half was watching you.

Being able to visualize people under their clothes had never been a talent Maryrell wanted, and most of the time she didn't even think about it—but as Balch raked his eyes over her she felt the full curse of that gift—not because she could visualize him, but because what she saw confused her.

Something cold went through her blood, and when he stuck his eyes like leeches on Jon Karl, it froze.

Because it wasn't lascivious, that look. Just cold.

The same look he wore in his volunteer work with the eu-thanization unit at the Animal Shelter—where Food Stamp, watching like a cobra from his corner, had come from.

"She's a pretty little thing," Balch observed.

"He," corrected Mildra.

"Oh," he said, tilting his head back. "Mm."

But at least you could say he was a good barber, and got Odis looking respectable, then as he was leaving said something about that "pretty head of hair" and tried to reach down and stroke or pat or something Jon Karl, but Jon Karl's stare made him think better.

He drove off in his big white truck.

"Don't ever let him near Jon Karl," Maryrell told Mildra when he was gone, in a voice that sounded like it came from somebody else.

* * *

Several times the next day they had to get Odis up from the floor where he was trying to hold onto the furniture until at last they got him calmed down in his chair where he said, "I just hate it for the squirrels," and drifted asleep. Sometimes when you walked by there he would be breathing heavily, sometimes his eyes would be open, and then his head fell forward, and they let him sleep as long as they could until they realized the reason he wasn't moving was that he was dead. When they lifted up his head Maryrell was relieved to see that he didn't look crazy, just spent.

Only a handful of friends dropped by, when word got out — the pocket change at the end of a life, and Mildra, doing the math, realized that if you lived long enough there wouldn't be any. She couldn't think of anything sadder than that.

Fortunately, one of those paying his respects was Spruill Dawes, who counted for about ten.

Maryrell, living her sheltered Jon Karl-absorbed life, had never met him, but she'd heard Mildra talk about him often enough. Now when, with little Millard in tow, he came in the house it felt like somebody had opened all the windows. He didn't just enter a room, he became it. Food Stamp wriggled over to him.

"I bet you're Maryrell, aren't you?" he said. "And, Jesus on crutches, you don't even have to tell me that's John Paul I've been hearing so much about."

"Jon Karl," corrected Maryrell.

Spruill laughed. Jon Karl cut his eyes to him, then back to what they'd been fastened on since he came through the door: Millard. And vice versa.

"Holy spumoni, this kid's going to be a handful and a half, I can tell by looking at him."

"He's no trouble at all," objected Mildra, mostly relieved that Leela, Millard's mother, hadn't come.

"I said going to be." Spruill laughed. "Mark my words."

It wasn't that he was nervous, just eternally ready for the next thing, Maryrell observed, the way he was never quite still, shifting his weight from one leg to another, always moving his arms, turning his head from this to that. He was one of those people that everything he said was like setting up a funny story, and seemed always on the verge of a punchline. And when he held forth, you could tell he expected everybody to pay court. But, looking at him, Maryrell could sense another picture: him alone, brooding, plotting against his enemies, working on the intricate puzzle pieces of his master plan.

But not today.

"I sure am sorry," he said, "I'm going to miss ol' Odis. You let me know anything—and I mean anything at all—I can do"—then, that said, stayed as long as his nervous system would let him, not long, as Jon Karl and Millard checked each other out and Jon Karl brought out his second-favorite truck—then slipped something into Mildra's hand as he tore a not ready to leave Millard away and headed for the door.

"Oh, Mr. Dawes—"

He just shook his head and frowned. When he and Millard were gone it was like somebody had flipped a switch and turned off the juice.

Chapter 5
Spruill Dawes

Spruill grew up on the family farm with the gnats in south Alabama, the youngest of five kids. His daddy had a hundred acres—with fruit trees, a pecan orchard, row crops, and a tobacco allotment. It was in his young years that Spruill learned to hate not just farming, but physical labor in general.

Unlike his two older brothers, who seemed to be in line to keep it all in the family, and had worked themselves into indispensable roles in the little agri-empire, branching out into landscaping, hardware, and an all you can eat restaurant, and who spent most of their combative energy competing with each other, Spruill had no ambitions of ever being involved in the family business—in fact, his dream was to escape it: move to a city where he could create his own empire, a world away from dirt and sweat and forever-breaking down machinery.

As for his two older sisters, even by their high school years they both exhibited a sure instinct for getting the one thing that mattered in their lives right: securing a man they could more or less stand who could give them the affluent lives they craved.

Being successful in this, they got what they deserved.

All of which left only the role of black sheep for the baby—the role Spruill had been born to play.

The lovable black sheep. Because Spruill was a sweet rogue, charming, non-threatening, and he got along fine with his siblings, and with his lenient father and affectionate mother, all of whom took some secret family pride in his shenanigans: the scrapes, the wrecked cars, a couple of narrow escapes with country girls, both of which had been handled by a confidential meeting of the opposite fathers, and a sum of money changing hands.

Spruill had walked away from everything if not smelling like a rose, at least untamed. It seemed to be his particular gift.

He never forgot where he came from—he just didn't want to stay there. Nor was he, in spite of his aversion to manual work, lazy. He was just fortunate enough to figure out at an early age— as though his parents' generation had saved the best for last—that what mattered was not how hard you worked—because he saw people all around him working themselves to death for no discernible gain—but how smart. He was fascinated by stories of big money, easy money, smart money, and couldn't bring himself to invest one joule of energy in anything that didn't pay.

He carried that ethic with him into his first job, as a teenager, working as a delivery boy and all-around gofer for Clayton Horne, who owned a drug store, more like an old-time general store, and dabbled in real estate. Well, more than "dabbled"—he owned several rental houses, a rectangular row of concrete block apartments, and had friends who had steered him into various investments over the years that had, with a couple of exceptions best forgotten, turned out well. Everything Mr. Horne did, Spruill thought, studying him keenly without really knowing that he was, was smart.

* * *

The hurricane, which hadn't been of a mind to let a coastline stop it, had been devastating, and certainly the victims deserved his thoughts and prayers, but Spruill couldn't help seeing the opportunity. The Dawes themselves had suffered some serious damage to the house and barn, and lost some trees, but they would rebuild, replant. All around them, thousands of acres lay littered in damaged and uprooted trees, and Spruill, at seventeen, rode out every day to watch the salvage operations and to pick the brains of the workers when he got a chance. When he found out the money to be made in timber and wood fiber, he looked into the market for used trucks, skidders, forwarders, and came up with a plan. Buy some used equipment, hire people to run it, make a ton of money while the getting was good, then sell the equipment when the getting was over.

He did the research, wrote it all up, and asked Mr. Horne if they could have a talk.

Mr. Horne agreed, and Spruill laid out two options: help him borrow $150,000, or go in halves with him.

"Good God, son," Mr. Horne laughed. "You don't know anything about salvaging timber and neither do I."

"It'll work. I know it will," said Spruill.

"It might, but I don't think you have any idea of the headaches you'll be dealing with."

"That comes with it, right? You hire people. You handle it."

It was the first time Mr. Horne had seen the magnitude of his young delivery boy's ambitions—seventeen years old, for Christ's sake—and he was impressed. Amused. And, like the old lion, a little wary. But mostly he felt inspired to help him.

Years later, when Theotis Fields said, without a trace of blame, that Spruill couldn't help being who he was, and just took the white man's path, it was moments like this that he meant.

"What about your family?" Mr. Horne asked Spruill.

"I don't want to do it with them. I want to do it on my own," Spruill said. "Or with you."

Mr. Horne turned it over in his head for a minute. "Tell you what," he said. "I've got an idea for something that might be a little more manageable."

And that was the seed that would flower into Majestic Estates, a mobile home park for migrant loggers and construction workers, destined to be a permanent fixture of the town.

* * *

Unlike his siblings, who saw no need, Spruill went to college. The mobile home park back home was, more or less, a success— it wasn't paying *big* money, but it was paying enough to live on, maybe a little more, even if it was also costing a lot of money.

They hired a manager, a smart, hardworking Mexican man who could handle the tenants, and Spruill tried to keep the problem-solving trips back home to a minimum. The first thing he did when he got to the college town was buy two used trailers, one to live in, one to rent to make the payments on the $2000 loan his father had co-signed. He paid it off in two years.

"That's how you establish your credit," his father noted proudly.

As in high school, Spruill wasn't particularly good at being a student, but he excelled at student life. It was a pretty wild time. He somehow survived until his junior year, the time when he had to declare a major, and several things happened.

First, though Business would have been the expected choice, he didn't think it was *his* kind of business, and he didn't like the people, and after he heard about the Baldwin Duggar Scholarship for budding foresters, endowed by a timber magnate, though he had no interest whatsoever in Forestry, he selected Forestry. The scholarship went to a rich, well-connected kid, and that was the last time Spruill had any illusions about the world giving you anything. There was only Taking. And with Taking his new lodestar, he quit wasting energy plotting revenge on an entrenched and unchangeable system, and began thinking about the Big Picture.

* * *

He had gotten in the habit of following the housing market in the college town, vaguely thinking of finding a house to flip, and knowing the local barons would take all the low-hanging fruit, he scoured the margins. He found what he thought was the perfect house, in a moderately respectable cul-de-sac. He had gotten to know the son of a local contractor in one of his favorite bars; they'd hit it off and become drinking buddies. Spruill took him out to look at it, then they went back to the bar where the buddy did his best to talk him out of it.

"There's no way to make money flipping houses," he told him, "unless for some reason the land value is going to go way up. Or if you can get something condemned cheap."

But Spruill had done his homework. He felt sure he could get it for ten, put eight in it, and sell if for twenty-five or thirty.

"That's a lot of work for five grand," said the buddy.

But Spruill was itching to do something. He wanted to jump in, learn. Fuck college, *this* was his education.

Again his father had co-signed the note, for eighteen, and he ended up putting ten into it, not exactly doing the deluxe job he had envisioned, with everything that could possibly go wrong going wrong, and in the end he broke even.

As in, didn't actually lose anything.

Which, just on the general chutzpah, impressed his buddy, who had watched the entire debacle compassionately, because he knew the damn thing was a recipe for losing your ass.

It was right about then that the young woman Spruill had been spending most of his time with told him she was pregnant.

The news awakened something in Spruill at twenty-one: his desire to be the patriarch of a dynasty—the big family, the big house, the whole bit. He had not really, until then, thought seriously of marriage, but suddenly liked the idea.

He dropped out of school, sold his trailers and made a few thousand dollars, and married the young woman in her home town, Douvale.

"Douvale?" his drinking buddy said when he heard the news. "That's where my uncle lives."

"Small world," said Spruill.

"Smaller than you think."

"Like your dick."

And that's when his buddy told him about something that might be an opportunity to make some *real* money. "I was thinking about a partner," he said.

His uncle, a county commissioner, had told his brother (his buddy's father) about the likelihood of a mall being built on what were then the outskirts of town. On a nearby side road, a Gulf station run by the same man for forty years was for sale.

"You want to run a gas station?" Spruill asked.

"Not even a little bit. I just want the land, and whatever other land I can get on that road."

"Just because it's near the mall?"

"No, because I hear there's a chance—a pretty good chance —that side road could become a main road."

It wasn't for certain, things could change, but would Spruill be interested in sharing the risk? They could buy options from the landowners willing to sell, and see which way the wind blew. They would need to raise a few thousand dollars.

Spruill felt his heart pounding, sort of like sex but more exciting. That deal would work like a charm, and when the city did re-route the road, destined to become a commercial thoroughfare alongside the mall, they made their money back tenfold.

In the meantime Spruill and wife moved to Douvale, he got his real estate license, and soaked up everything he could learn about doing business in a growing town. He figured most people must be blind, because he saw nothing but opportunities everywhere he looked. Which was an important step in his continuing education: understanding that most people *were* blind, or chicken: the fruits of the earth were there for the seizing, but only by those who could either beat everybody else there, or push them out of the way.

The three children came in quick succession, but by the time the third one was born, Spruill was already spending most of his time with soon-to-be wife number two, as wife number one was with soon-to-be husband number two.

Spruill was thirty, and making money like most people make small talk.

Chapter 6
Redwine Pyle

Redwine Pyle had a real name, but except for his mother, nobody had called him Albert for fifty-plus years—and she had been dead for fifteen. Redwine had now crept over the border into his eighth decade. He owed his nickname not to his love for red wine, but the opposite. The one and only time he had tasted it, at nineteen, he had made the mistake of thinking you could drink it like Kool-Aid, and pulled an empty-stomach all-nighter. He was cracking his fifth bottle as the sun came up. He got sick, very sick, and wanted to die. The hangover lasted three days, during which he wanted not to live—a slight improvement.

"I peed purple for a week," he would tell you. "Or maybe it was my eyes."

The experience was so miserable he would drive fifty miles out of the way if he thought he might even catch a whiff of the stuff, and had never gone down the wine aisle in a store once it became legal to sell it there. He drank no spirits either, only beer—Michelob Ultra these days—daily and generously. "Come on over," he would say, "and have a beer or twelve."

When he paid a call an hour or so after Spruill, Food Stamp whined and came over for an ear massage. "This dog is proof that being friendly makes up for a lot of ugly," Redwine observed. "Come to think of it, so am I."

He had been to the grocery store and brought in a couple of bags of "Quick Sale" produce and a rotisserie chicken.

"That was sweet, Redwine," said Mildra. She had known him for fifty years, and he and Odis went back even further than that.

When Mildra introduced him to Maryrell, he said, "I didn't know it was legal to be so pretty."

Maryrell smiled, and Jon Karl stared at him with great interest.

"Now this little feller—he looks straight out of the Jungle Book," Redwine said. "You think the world is going to be ready for him?"

"It needs to be getting ready if it ain't," said Mildra.

Redwine didn't stay long—only about three stories—and as he was leaving he asked Maryrell, "This boy ever been fishing?"

"No sir."

"Good God a'mighty, don't go sir-ing me. That's just one step away from helping me out to my truck. Y'all come out some afternoon and we'll wet a hook."

"He's only two, Redwine," said Mildra.

"The younger you get started, the more of it you get to do," said Redwine. "And that's true of everything. Right now I believe I'll run by and see what Doug and them's doing, maybe have a beer or twelve."

"Thanks for coming by, Redwine."

"Well, I'm going to miss the ol' boy. We was young-uns together. He was as strong as an ox and could bite a ten-penny nail in half back in the day. Did I ever tell you about the time we had a double date in my '58 Chevy? I guess it's a double date if it's the same girl."

"You might have tried."

"Well, I'll save it for this little tyke—what'd you call him?"

"Jon Karl."

"Jon Karl. I like that. I'll save it for him—when he's older. He'll get a kick out of it. I'm going to run on now. If you get to missing me, just call. And here's a little something to help out—"
He handed Mildra an envelope.

"Oh, Redwine, I don't expect you to—"

"It don't matter if you expect it or not—I want you to have it same reason men's got tits. Just in case."

* * *

Two days later, the funeral: the tent in the cemetery where there was a double headstone with Mildra's name already on her half, just missing the one date. Then within a few days they had settled into the new territory of life beyond Odis. Because, as Maryrell knew, death comes and goes, but life goes on and on.

Chapter 7

Summer Arrives for the Odoms

This time, after Maryrell missed her period, it was Mildra who brought home the pregnancy test kit. As it had been with Jon Karl, the purple line was decisive.

"He's just Mr. Silver Bullet, ain't he?" said Mildra.

Which was all she had to say about him. She went straight into "new baby coming" mode and didn't give another thought to Ramp. Neither did Maryrell.

It must be true that if nobody thinks about you, you aren't really there.

About eight months later Maryrell went into labor again. But no emergency room this time—Mildra and Spruill Dawes, who'd seen to it she'd had a doctor, saw to that too. The floral arrangement Spruill had ordered from LaKay's Blooms By Design, with tropical fruit worked in, attracted admirers from all over the hospital.

A girl this time—born about suppertime after a routine labor.

Maryrell named her Spring Summer, after her two favorite seasons, and said she would be called "Summer."

Jon Karl was two and a half.

And Ramp kept his promise. Nobody ever saw him again.

He either was, or soon would be, dead, Maryrell knew. But she also knew that death isn't always a sharp line, but can last a while, like a deep bruise that settles in and isn't going anywhere in a hurry.

* * *

God—if unlike Maryrell, who sometimes said Fate or Nature but mostly just It, you'd learned to call it that—had decreed that they would have three years. God always had a thing for three.

Three years of love and plenty and togetherness. You could say they didn't fully appreciate it because they didn't have anything to compare it to, but what is appreciation anyway but just thinking about something rather than the something? But it is true that you don't really know how good things are until you've had a taste of how bad they can be. That's a gift from God too. They say all evil comes from Satan, but they should think a little harder.

Over that blessed island of time, Jon Karl would grow to five and a half, and not long after he turned five they enrolled him in kindergarten.

Jon Karl had a way of withdrawing into himself when he was concentrating on something, to the point of not even hearing people talking to him, and would go off by himself when all the noise and confusion became too much, and could be quite irritable when he wanted to be left alone, but when he was in the mood he socialized well. The boys and girls had separate swing sets, and he liked to swing with the boys for a while, then go over to the girls, though he wasn't supposed to. Ms. Wigelia Ditmore, the teacher, was lenient with him, maybe because he was the only boy who did that, and maybe because he had gotten nothing but prettier as he'd grown, and most people who saw him still thought he was a girl. But he wasn't, as the girls, all but one or two of whom were drawn to him—the lovely thing about children, and dogs, they can't fake it—learned when he pulled down his pants in front of them one day. Ms. Ditmore snatched him up and took him inside and told him he was *not* to do that again, as he smiled the biggest smile. The truth was, he had Ms. Ditmore, who might have looked Methuselan to her charges, but was twenty-three, wrapped around his finger and knew it—without of course knowing he knew it. He was just, in his five year old way, smitten with her himself.

Jon Karl's best buddy was Tyler Gass, an adventurous rascal who, if he could have in any way worked it, should have stayed five because, sadly, for him, son of an alcoholic sometime preacher and a crystal meth mother who never left the house, there was nowhere for anything to go but down. But, happily, neither Tyler nor Jon Karl had any way of knowing that in those days of the alphabet and numbers and log-sized pencils inside, and seemingly endless play periods outside. Jon Karl had a much easier time with the inside stuff than Tyler—in fact, he loved and devoured it—but outside Tyler was in his element. They built a not so secret fort in the little patch of woods by the railroad tracks that no one else was allowed to enter—strictly enforced by Tyler—and played pirates and gangsters. Pirates Jon Karl already sort of knew about, but he learned about gangsters from Tyler, even if he didn't really understand what they were—actually true of Tyler too.

Yes, the railroad tracks ran just behind the kindergarten, separated by the strip of trees and brush and a fence, and Jon Karl was ever alert to the whistles, and never missed one that went by—two, or on a good day, three—by the time they got out at two o'clock. Tyler was oblivious to trains, but for the rest of Jon Karl's life the sight and sound of a train would bring the taste of orange-ade and graham crackers and the smell of paste and Ms. Ditmore's lotion into his mind.

* * *

On the home front, Mildra kept working, paying the bills, and Maryrell devoted the same time to Summer as she had to Jon Karl. As two o'clock approached every weekday, Summer, sneaking up on three years, would start looking out for Jon Karl. It was one big lovefest around there, but her affinity for her brother was supreme. In a way it was as though when he walked in the door her life could start back. She wanted nothing but to be near Jon Karl, and Maryrell and Mildra would laugh about it. "You and me don't count for nothing," Mildra would say. Summer believed everything Jon Karl said, and had no doubt the moon was up there because Jon Karl put it there.

Jon Karl naturally fell into his role of mentor and protector for his little sister. He had great affection for her. Outwardly diffident, energy churning within, she was an extraordinarily alert child. The default state of her eyes was wide open. She seemed to be constantly drinking the world. Her face, with those luminous olive eyes, like Jon Karl's, and elfin ears sticking out of her straight brown hair, shone with its own peculiar light.

But for all the light and love, there was the shadow, the brown one, creeping up on them,that no one but Maryrell knew about. Or maybe Mildra sensed it too—maybe the children did—but if so, they let it stay a shadow. Of course it was the secret Maryrell had known as long as she could remember, the knowledge that her road would diverge from the people in this life, and she would have to return to something she knew but couldn't remember. It wasn't fear she felt, not even now as the shadow had made it to the yard, the porch, the house, and now her room, only solicitude for Jon Karl and Summer. But she knew Mildra would take care of them. For as long as she could anyway. A shadow for another day.

But no fear—just the knowledge, a gift, that she had to make sure she poured all the contents of her deep pitcher into her babies, because she knew if she did that, everything would be fine.

She thought a lot about her own mother, safe inside her, during those days.

And Food Stamp never left her side.

* * *

One day she asked Mildra, "Can you take me to see Cleetha Till?"

Mildra, a little surprised, studied her earnest face. "I guess so, sugar, if you want me to."

Maryrell knew who Cleetha Till was. She'd heard Mildra's stories about her. She'd heard Redwine talk about her. Cleetha was in her seventies now, and for half a century it had been the

53

custom of high school seniors and soon to be marrieds to go for a reading. Of course in both cases the clientele turned out to be almost exclusively female. Boys tended—or pretended—to look down on the whole business unless a drowned body or missing truck was involved—even though the sheriffs of fifty years, including the current, Spruill Dawes' good friend Ulmer Cubbage, had regularly consulted Cleetha, who had helped solve a many a case.

When something disappeared, Cleetha could tell you where it was. She could see it in her head and describe the place, even if she'd never been there herself. Sometimes the person would know where the spot was, and sometimes not. On occasion people would come to her with nefarious motives, but she would always know, and say something like, "Here's your dollar back. You're dishonest and I don't want your money and I don't want you in my house." A dollar in the old days, five dollars now. "I hate to charge anything," she would say, "but it takes so much of my time and I've got to live." A business license, a little crooked in a cheap frame, hung on the wall behind her. There was no such thing as fooling Cleetha Till. But her specialty was drowned bodies. She'd never been wrong. She'd send you right to them. Even if what you'd find when you got there would rarely be pretty. You wanted to check in with Cleetha pretty early in a suspected drowning. But of course sometimes it took them a week or two to surface.

She lived a few miles out of town in what had once been a farmhouse, but now with the farm sold off, just a house, a big, airy, tired clapboard house with a sloping front porch, rusty roof, and in need of the paint job it would never get. Cleetha had been unable to keep it up in the twenty years since her husband Ethan had died. When Mildra and Maryrell got there, three cars with three out of state license plates sat parked in the yard under a big oak tree, and they had to wait their turn.

Inside, the house was sparsely furnished. Cleetha lived alone. Ethan slept in the little cemetery, where she knew she would soon sleep too, beside the church just around the next bend. Her four grown children were scattered around the county. They looked after her, but she insisted on earning her own way, and the five readings she limited herself to a day (no weekends, except in an emergency) was way better than the egg money of her younger days.

She had a strict policy of not telling you anything about your death, especially not when it would happen, but when Maryrell walked in the door, her face said it all. Cleetha saw what was so near, and in the same instant saw that Maryrell knew it too. It wasn't exactly that Cleetha felt she had known her before, though she did—more like they recognized themselves in each other.

"Well?" asked Mildra when Maryrell came out after almost two hours.

"She said she could see a drowned boy."

Mildra stared at her, alarmed. "Jon Karl?"

"No mam, she said it was somebody else."

"Mercy," said Mildra.

"And she said I was an old soul."

"Beats being an old woman," said Mildra.

Chapter 8

The Brown Shadow

When the shadow made it to armslength, Maryrell took to her bed in her room that didn't feel morose because she insisted on having the shades up and the windows open, blurring the boundary between the illness within and the spring days full of sunlight without. From her bed she could see the bird feeder hanging from the oak limb, and watched the action for hours. Jon Karl became the bird feeder filler, always with Summer in rapt attendance.

Mildra tried to keep the children quiet, but Maryrell said she hated it when they were quiet, so they played in there and watched the birds and got in bed with their mother where in the evenings Mildra would read to them all, including Food Stamp, not exactly in the spring of life himself, on the rug with his head between his paws and his eyes looking up at his humans on the bed. Unless he was *on* the bed. They all became co-conspirators, bound and inseparable, in this adventure that was headed somewhere.

Maryrell said she didn't need a doctor, being sick was bad enough. But Mildra called Dr. Rumus anyway and asked him if he could come look at her. He made clear *that* wasn't going to happen, but did send his nurse practitioner over who checked her vital signs and said they were normal.

But when Maryrell went to the bathroom she could see in the mirror, vital signs or not, the true state of things.

And that was how—Jon Karl six and a half, Summer four—their mother passed into myth. Jon Karl saw a vertical black rectangle, a doorway, and told Summer to look, which she did, with all the concentration she could muster, and thought she saw it too. With Jon Karl there wasn't much of a line between the power of suggestion and reality. If, indeed, they are different.

But they had to stay behind as their mother headed out of town, along the shady streets. Of course a train was passing through, and she floated by, past Ed Butts' mildly retarded son, Colonel Smy digging a new hole and Edith Ault spying on him through the fence and taking notes, the couple pushing the stroller where from above Maryrell could see, with a surge of affection, that the "baby" was an ancient Scottish Terrier in a bonnet, the man with the "Help Me" sign whose head she reached out to touch, bringing an astonished look to his face, the gentleman in the plastic chair who looked her in the eye with a smile as he waved goodbye.

* * *

Spruill Dawes came through again. He took care of the funeral and wasn't stingy with the checks he wrote. And even though every time Mildra said, "Mr. Dawes, I can't accept this," every time she did. She had learned a long time ago when Mr. Dawes decided he wanted something to happen, there was no force on earth that could stop it.

This time there was hardly anybody to come by the house because nobody had really known Maryrell. Her life had been full and centered right here. Except of course for Mr. Dawes who brought Millard but, again, mercifully not Mrs. Dawes.

"Where'd your mother go?" Millard asked Jon Karl.

"She went through a door."

Summer stared at them both with her big eyes and got up the nerve to say, "I saw it too."

That didn't impress Millard, who had brought his Game Boy with the Legend of Zelda, very much.

Later that afternoon, Redwine Pyle came by with a box of fried chicken, a wedge of watermelon, and a twelve-pack of some kind of grapefruit flavored beer. He gave Jon Karl and Summer each a bolo paddle and an American flag pinwheel. "When the little ball breaks off, and I hate to be a party pooper but it's going

57

to sooner or later, you can use the paddle to give your great grand-mama a good paddling when she don't act like she should."

And to Mildra, at the door, he said, "Call me if you run out of beer," which after knowing her for forty years he still hadn't quite got it in his head she didn't drink. And added, "I sure am sorry. I guess somebody that sweet and pretty just ain't meant for this world."

Chapter 9

Life Goes On

About a week after the funeral, which was really just a small gathering at the Odom plot in the cemetery, attended by Mildra, who couldn't help see—it was right there—the neighboring headstone with her name and the blank date space that most people, if it was them, would probably find dismaying—Jon Karl, Summer, Redwine, Spruill, Millard, Zadie (Spruill's daughter from his second marriage), and, because how could she not? Mrs. Leela Dawes, groomed to a tee and exuding the hauteur Mildra knew was, you might say, added on, a bill for $500 arrived from Dr. Rumus. When Mildra showed it to Mr. Dawes he just said "Give me that goddamned thing," and that was the end of that.

Then, a month later, when the first grief had worn off, Mildra decided Summer should have her own room.

Summer didn't like the idea, but didn't resist—she was unassertive and let Jon Karl do all the resisting, if any was needed, except for when it came to the canned spinach casserole Mildra made with sliced boiled eggs on top that turned green from the juice, and watermelon, the seeds of which filled her with horror after Redwine told her if she swallowed one a watermelon would grow inside her, triggering the nightmares she had off and on until she was twenty and giving her a phobia of pregnant women. Mildra gave her Maryrell's old room figuring she would get over her obvious discomfort in there and appreciate the privacy. But Summer had no interest at all in privacy, and even after Mildra had it repainted and new Goodwill furniture put in, she only *said* she liked it, which you could tell by the fact that she never went in there. After Mildra tucked her in at night, it took her five minutes at the most before she tiptoed down the hall and, careful not to stumble into gray-faced Food Stamp on the rug, got into Jon Karl's bed.

Jon Karl didn't mind. He knew she was scared.

Of course Mildra was aware of the covert goings-on, and could hear them whispering in there, but found it so touching she let it be. She had no way of knowing that Summer couldn't go to sleep until she heard a train.

They would wait, staring above the bed into the space where the sound would be.

"I hear a whistle!"' Jon Karl would whisper.

Silence—Summer not sure if he was telling the truth or not. Then, after a minute, "I hear him too!"

And they would listen as it came closer, roared past, and gradually disappeared.

Summer would quickly fall asleep then, as Jon Karl listened for the last faraway whistle, almost not separate from the night air itself. Jon Karl would try to picture the people where the train was then, to whom it was at that moment as loud and close as it had been for them five minutes ago—back when those other people were hearing it from far away.

Sometimes Summer would ask for a riddle first, even though she was afraid of riddles—a fear that was at least half fascination. It was the same compulsion that made her look right at a worm.

"What follows you all the time but you can't touch it?"

"Boogey man!"

"I told you there's no such thing as the boogey man. Anyway, you could touch *him*."

She thought deeply. "I don't know."

"Your shadow."

That, being profound, cast her into even deeper thought. "Shadow," she said.

"I hear a whistle!"

They had always taken their baths together, and as time went by, Mildra, bone tired at night, continued the practice. It saved water, gas, and time. She let them play with their flotilla of toys for a while, keeping an eye on them, before getting down to the washing. Actually, Jon Karl, at almost seven, could wash himself, but Mildra had to help Summer, at four and a half, and she did all the hair washing. Jon Karl's hair had yet to be cut, and after Mildra rinsed it with her little plastic bowl, a rope went down the back of his neck. Summer's, never cut either, did the same thing, just not as long.

They grew up in plain sight of each other's bodies. Sometimes Mildra thought, maybe that's not the best idea, but she was too tired to change. Along with having to fill two bathtubs, it would mean keeping Summer in her room, a battle she didn't have the energy to fight. The time would come, of course, but Mildra figured she would know it when it did.

Their bodies were not exactly the same.

This fact had never registered on Summer, until one day it did. When she asked Jon Karl about it, he cleared it up.

"I'm a boy, and you're a girl."

That was another profound thing, but Jon Karl obviously knew what he was talking about, so she was satisfied.

* * *

First grade had come for Jon Karl, and now second, and Summer started kindergarten. Mildra was getting more tired all the time, but being kids, they didn't really understand that. They just got used to the fact that after she cleaned up the kitchen and sat down in her recliner in front of the television, her swollen ankles on the foot holder, she would almost immediately start snoring.

She told Jon Karl not to let her stay there all night, so about eight o'clock he would tap her arm. "Mildra?"

"What? What? Who?"

"Time to go nigh- night."

"Oh. Thank you, sweetheart. Y'all go put yourselves to bed."

"Yes mam."

* * *

At five, Summer was skinny awkward self-conscious and shy. Kindergarten—exiled from her secure place and cast into this jungle of new personalities—was traumatic for her. The other girls all seemed to know each other and were mean, and the boys were rough and absorbed in their own world. They played in their sandbox with trucks. Trucks trucks trucks! Her habitual stance at play period was off to the side by herself, against a tree. The truth is, she would never quite shake this attitude all her life. Something imprinted at that age never really goes away. All those girls talking about Mama-this and Daddy-that. Luckily, Ms. Ditmore was still the teacher, and she had by no means forgotten Jon Karl, for whom she retained great affection, and it carried over to Summer with her big olive green eyes and her sense of wonder and her natural grace, which Summer was completely unaware of. Which is what made it natural grace. Ms. Ditmore had noted Summer's love of drawing and painting, the only times she seemed happy, and also noted how her bold productions stood out, not at all like the other children's. And there had been more than one occasion when, everyone stumped, Summer had shyly directed them to the hiding place of some lost or misplaced object, including, one day, Ms. Ditmore's keys which had fallen from her pocket on the playground and were buried in the clump of grass she led her to, but after a few such instances when her only reward was drawing suspicion and enmity to herself and an even deeper isolation, she kept what she knew private. Ms. Ditmore was ever on the lookout for a suitable friend for Summer, maybe a kindred spirit, but so far nothing had taken.

But of course Summer had love at home—soft-touch, long-suffering Mildra, and the center of gravity of her life, Jon Karl, who felt her pain as though it were his.

And, in their time, the fragrance of gardenias, which Summer loved more than almost anything. A smell that could bring tears to her eyes all her life.

Chapter 10

An East Douvale Childhood

Jon Karl had two main friends—Tyler and Millard—from two different worlds.

Tyler lived a few blocks over in a house in East Douvale not too different in style from Mildra's. But the similarity ended there. Where Mildra's house was cushioned with shrubs and flowers and shaded by very healthy oaks, Tyler's had one dying tree in a bare scraggly yard. The same difference continued on the inside. Mildra's house was cozy, full of furniture and *stuff*, in the way a house that has been lived in for forty years has no choice but to be. But Tyler's house, where the restive Gasses had only been for a couple of years, echoed with emptiness and with the lassitude of people who lack the means or initiative to do anything about it. It was not cozy, and Tyler's room had only a bed that was more like a cot, his few clothes in boxes on the floor, and one askew Metallica poster tacked to the wall. His dad was almost never there, and on the few times Jon Karl had ever seen him, he'd tried to give the boys a drunken Bible lesson. Tyler's mother was usually in the kitchen, where there was no food, with her little paraphernalia—red-eyed, emaciated, pocked with sores—who gave you the feeling she was trying to be sweet and friendly but just couldn't pull it off. She seemed always to want the same thing: for them to go outside and play.

Which they did.

But if you were talking about best friend, that would be Millard. The boys had connected from the first time Spruill brought him to the house, when Odis died, and Millard started asking his father to bring him back from that day. Which Spruill was happy to do—even if it was rarely him but somebody who worked for him, usually Rodolfo, who did the hauling—because Spruill had taken to Jon Karl at first sight. Spruill had escaped his growing-up years on a prosperous farm in gnat-ridden south Alabama without a trace of snobbery. Leela, who had grown up poor and been homeless when Spruill found her and pygmalioned her into the third Mrs. Dawes, didn't think Millard going over to East Douvale accorded with their status, but Spruill would have none of that. Plus, whatever Millard wanted, Millard got.

"That Leela's an odd bird," Redwine would tell you. "When *her* mother died, Elmore Korn at the funeral home told me she sent the body back four times before she was satisfied. She didn't look lifelike enough. Which, of course, how could she? she was dead. You didn't hear that from me."

There was a creek, years ago full of sewage, and some woods on the other side of the tracks that were perfect for nine year olds. Tyler was a fort builder, and possessed of a colorful imagination; they peopled the woods with a variety of scary creatures and bad people mostly of his invention. But later, after Mildra's rheumatism got so bad and Jon Karl realized it was Tyler stealing her pain pills, and then one afternoon high as a kite he tried to slide his hand under Summer's panties, Jon Karl whacked him between the shoulder blades with the back of a shovel, knocking the air out of him and buckling him to the ground. After that, the Gasses moved somewhere and they lost touch. But the truth is, even before that trashy backstabbing behavior they had been growing apart because of Tyler's other trashy behavior of smoking and drinking and doing every drug he could get his hands on, including stealing not only from his friend's great grandmother, but from his own mother, taking the hobbling next door dog's fentanyl patch, and going around the neighborhood stealing the copper from heat pump units to sell to the "salvage" man with the junky yard down by the lake, and sniffing the freon.

As for Millard, Jon Karl didn't know him in school because Millard didn't go to public school, but to the Academy. They were friends anyway. Millard much preferred to come over to Jon Karl's house, because it was different and something of an adventure, and in those woods back there they could take off their clothes. That was Millard's thing, not Jon Karl's—for some reason he was into that—taking your clothes off in broad daylight outside. "*Damn*, man," Millard said the first time they checked each other out. He said what they needed was a girl and when Jon Karl told him about Bonnie Stinchcomb, who lived a few houses down, he begged Jon Karl to invite her to come play in the woods, which Jon Karl wasn't very comfortable doing, but like his daddy, Millard was persuasive.

It paid off.

Spruill had a few simple rules for success—one of which, kin to "get there firstest with the mostest" was that everybody was waiting on everybody else to do something, so the key to winning was to do whatever it was first.

So once they got Bonnie Stinchcomb in the woods, Millard initiated the proceedings by promptly shedding every stitch—and then, prodded by Millard, Jon Karl, who could see that Bonnie was only pretending to be shocked and embarrassed but was actually getting an eyeful, did too. There was no stopping it—she followed suit and they studied one another thoroughly. Even if it was nothing that Jon Karl didn't already know.

That went on for about a year until Bonnie's mother smelled a rat—then no more Bonnie.

Jon Karl himself, not surprisingly, preferred to go to Millard's house. Sometimes Mildra would drive him out there, but usually somebody on Theotis's crew would come pick him up.

It was a big house on the edge of town, with a winding drive out front, and horses, and a swimming pool in the back. Millard's room seemed almost as big as Mildra's entire house, and full of every amusement conceivable, all of which naturally Millard was completely bored with. He had a cache of dirty magazines hidden in the back of his room-sized closet, and a little how-to pamphlet he had snuck from his mother on breastfeeding, that they examined most studiously. Millard thought it was really funny, and then showed Jon Karl how you could squeeze the udder of their collie, Maggie, who had just had a litter of puppies, and milk would shoot out, which he found *hilarious*.

"You look at those pictures, you may think they're tits, but that's not what they really are," he explained to Jon Karl.

"I know what they are," Jon Karl informed him.

Chapter 11
Theotis and Billy Reuben

By the time they were eleven their base of operations had shifted almost entirely to Millard's house. They had basically outgrown the fort thing, and the truth was, once you were no longer going out in the woods and taking off your clothes with Bonnie Stinchcomb, East Douvale didn't really have all that much to offer. The only problem, for Jon Karl, was Summer, in the third grade now, who had only one friend, Wady Carothers, whose father kept a tight rein on her and had a long list of chores every afternoon for her to do, so Summer was left alone which made Jon Karl sad. Maybe you couldn't blame Mr. Carothers—his other daughter, some years older than Wady, had been in a bad car wreck in which she had suffered severe brain and spinal cord injuries and gone into a coma. Seven years later she was still in it. In a nursing home. Summer had gone one time with Wady to see her, and told Jon Karl you couldn't tell how old she was. Anyway, even though Millard thought things were better without Summer, usually he would let her come and she would follow them around.

Of course Millard, cute as they come with his dark bushy hair, dark eyebrows, a permanent rakish smile, and the cheeky ways of the privileged, had no idea of the fascination he inspired in the skinny nine year old girl following him and his buddy around. Nor would he have recognized himself in, nor understood the impulse behind, the dozens of secret drawings he inspired— zestful whirlwinds of hair and feral eyes in technicolor landscapes.

Those drawings confused Mildra, who would just say something like "Mercy!" but they had a suction effect on Jon Karl. To peer into them was to peer into the mysterious heart of the riddle who was his sister. Summer herself had no interest at all in those drawings once they were done, but Jon Karl began tacking them to the walls of his room.

Millard had four-wheelers, a dirt bike, two go-karts, with all kinds of trails out in the woods, and a lake where, if Theotis was around, he would fix up their poles and then later clean whatever fish they caught—usually for Luthelma, his wife, to fry since Leela thought eating catfish and bream out of a pond wasn't befitting their status like getting red snapper and orange roughy the average person couldn't afford from Kroger was. Leela hardly ever went outside and was the only person Jon Karl ever knew who had to have a TV on in every room of the house. Summer loved the whole drama of fishing—getting a nibble and catching a fish to her always had a bit of "See? I can get good things too" about it, even if she felt sorry for the fish. Jon Karl did too, but not enough not to do it. Millard had no such compunction.

Usually, on afternoons when they went fishing, Theotis's grandson Billy Reuben would go too. In fact, unless he had work to do, he hung out with them most of the time. Billy Reuben was smart and funny and, following in his father's footsteps, could do damn near anything. He was small, compact, and fluid, constantly in motion. He met life elastically and made you want to look where he was looking because he was always grinning. Just being around him made everything okay.

"Pure mischief," said Theotis.

Theotis worked him hard—Billy Reuben's specialty was the garden which he planted, putting a little fish in each hole, and tended—but on weekends and when things were slow, Theotis would let him off and usually he would meet up with Millard and Jon Karl and they would ride the four-wheelers, or steal plums and peaches or a watermelon from Mr. Autry's orchard.

Billy Reuben was fanatical about not letting Theotis see the evidence.

"He'll think I be done stole it."

"You *did* steal it," said Millard.

"That's what I'm saying."

They also shot cans and bottles in the creek with Millard's .22, or sometimes, with his Glock—another activity Billy Reuben begged them to keep secret from Theotis, who had no truck with handguns of any kind. Many afternoons they took the canoes out on the lake. Especially if Summer was around, they would ride the horses.

You could tell Billy Reuben loved horses and knew how to talk to them and handle them. And they loved to see him coming— usually with apples. He would tack them up and they would ride on the trails in the woods. Summer had been scared at first, but gradually got over it, especially after she bonded with Myrtle, the sweet chestnut mare with a sense of humor she always rode. Those rides were her happy time. When they got back to the stable, she and Jon Karl would help Billy Reuben groom the horses. Millard didn't bother with any of that.

Billy Reuben had, you might say, a greater preference for investing his energy in fun than work, but as Jon Karl would come to find out, that didn't mean he couldn't do the work.

"Just have to stay on him," Theotis would say.

That was less true for Billy Lirenzo, Billy Reuben's older brother, who looked like he might be in line to take over for his father when the time came. He had a baby and ran with an older, rougher crowd.

But they all knew how to let go. On Sundays.

That was the day when the extended family and friends and usually Jon Karl and Millard would gather at Theotis and Luthelma's house. Theotis had built a big barbecue pit and stainless steel fish fryer in the back yard, and he would have one or the other, occasionally both, going all day. Everybody brought something to eat and there would be a tub full of ice with sodas and beer.

These gatherings were loud and you could hear the music and laughter a good ways off.

"This here what life all about," Theotis might loosen up enough with a few beers to observe. Then pick up an ear of corn and say, "I'm fin to eat this from the tuti to the fruiti."

"You going to be like your granddaddy when you grow up?" Jon Karl asked Billy Reuben one day.

"Where the rule say I got to grow up?" Billy Reuben said.

"You just do," said Millard.

Billy Reuben drew his head back, his rubbery features incredulous. "*You* telling *me* about having to grow up?"

Millard laughed. "You're funny."

"*You* funny," Billy Reuben returned. "I don't want to be like my granddaddy, I want to be like Oscar Philpott."

"Who the hell is Oscar Philpott?" Millard asked.

"Man be getting all that boot."

"Good luck with that."

"Shit, gone get me some this weekend."

"I don't believe it. Who with?"

"I can't tell you."

"Why not?"

"Cause then you be spying on me."

"Why would I spy on you?"

"To see how it's done."

"*Shit.* I know ten times more than you."

"You don't know half of what I know. Them little girls you run around with just after your money. Girls I know after *me*. Ain't that right, Jon Kar?"

"I wouldn't know," said Jon Karl.

* * *

Summer loved the swimming pool, though she looked like a baby bird in her thrift store bathing suit. Billy Reuben was only half comfortable in the water, but Millard could swim like a fish and had more or less taught Jon Karl. Summer didn't know how to swim, and in fact never did learn how her whole life. Fortunately Spruill forbade anybody to get in the pool unless an adult was there. The real danger, however, was not Summer getting drowned, but Summer doing the drowning—because even though she stayed on the shallow end most of the time, if she ever did try to follow Jon Karl out to where it started to get deeper, she would panic and entangle him like an octopus, taking them both under. So after one particularly close call when Jon Karl thought *this could be it*, he ordered her to stay on the shallow end and *never* do that again. She obeyed, the only exceptions those times when she would daringly float over the terrifying *deep end* in an inner tube. She was in her thirties before she realized an inner tube was something from a car tire.

Chapter 12

Time Does Its Work

At home, Mildra was going down. The cooking and house-cleaning were taking a back burner to her time in the recliner.

"I'm just worn out, sugar," she would say to Jon Karl or Summer when they asked her what was wrong. She was climbing up in her seventies and still working, and that's where most of her energy went. She was still indispensable to Spruill, and he didn't know how in the world he would ever replace her. She understood him and his businesses so well she could figure out an entire plan of action from a raised eyebrow. But as he repeated over and over—she could retire any time she wanted to, and he would help her.

The secret truth was, she liked working and didn't want to stop. She thought about Odis, a lost soul without a job to go to in the morning and complain about at night—and she had seen the same thing in her own mother and many of her friends. She had no hobbies, unless you counted baking but that wasn't a hobby, it was just something you did. Or trying to stay awake, which she wasn't very good at. Watching television?

"How much of that bullshit can you stand before your brain starts leaking out your ears?" Redwine would say.

Obviously it wasn't a hobby, but proof that you didn't have one.

Good kids, both of them, Jon Karl and Summer had stepped up and were taking care of the house. Summer swept and dusted and vacuumed, and learned how to do laundry, and Jon Karl started cooking, absorbing everything from Mildra, and bringing home cookbooks from the library and reading on-line. Even though she had ascended the steep learning curve of the washing machine, sorting and detergent and bleach, and the dryer, delicate permanent press and cotton, Summer just didn't take to cooking and, like swimming, never did. Years later, during her one brief stint as a waitress, she got in the habit of eating and/or taking home uneaten food on patrons' plates—shocking sometimes—rib eyes with just one bite taken out of them, intact salads, barely touched platters of Firecracker Shrimp, ignored baked potatoes in their silver foil. Why not? They were just going to throw it away, and it was illegal to give it to the homeless people.

Nights, Mildra did well to make it to eight o'clock, and Jon Karl would never forget that lonely feeling, in the summer, of somebody going to bed while it was hot and *still daylight*. Like their mother, Jon Karl and Summer both liked to read and didn't really like television or being on-line. Jon Karl once explained to Summer that he liked doing something you could stop and look up from and think about, and Summer smiled because as always he was exactly right and she had never thought about it like that. Of course, when Jon Karl made the same point to TV-addicted, game playing Millard, he just said, "You never heard of a pause button?"

Summer and Wady Carothers had officially become "best friends," which made Jon Karl happy because he knew what those brats in her third grade class thought about her—that she was a nobody—the same thing his sixth grade class thought about him. He was thicker-skinned than her, and knew how it bothered her, who didn't deserve it. Sometimes he pictured a Chinook helicopter with a giant net scooping up the lot of them in a bus and dumping them in the ocean.

Why nobody thinks to take pictures of people and places while they still can, unlike those who take too many, is a mystery, but Jon Karl and Summer had only three pictures of their mother. One was from grade school, when Maryrell was eleven, and Summer thought she was beautiful, without being aware, as Jon Karl was, that she looked just like her. Summer thought herself skinny and ugly.

"I hate to tell you, you're not ugly," Jon Karl would tell her.

"You're just saying that."

"Yeah, because it's true."

The other two pictures of Maryrell were snapshots—one with Odis and Mildra and a dark-faced Food Stamp on the front porch, and another with her sitting in a chair holding baby Summer, with little Jon Karl alongside.

For Summer, there was no greater mystery in her life, no greater absence, no greater tectonic force, than her mother. The mystery, the absence and the force of her. All her life in her own mind she was the girl without a mother, without a normal family, without a real life. Not to mention without a father—but he didn't count, he had no chance to be real, maybe because there were no pictures of him, only those three of her mother. Those, Summer had looked at so long and hard she couldn't really see them anymore. Which itself had a way of undermining the reality of her existence.

She had two or three little memorial gleams floating in her head, but those too had just frozen, like the actual pictures, into something too habitual to really see anymore. But still, she clung to those gleams, which were the only thing that allowed her to say "Yes, a little bit" when somebody asked her if she remembered her mother.

She depended on Jon Karl. Even if she couldn't help feeling some jealousy that he remembered her and she didn't.

"She was real sweet," he would tell her. "She was pure love."

She would just lie there, wide-eyed, listening.

"I remember Odis too," he would say. Which, for Summer, flirted with the Paleolithic.

Jon Karl would be sitting in the chair in the den, and she would be lying on the couch, facing away from him. She didn't need to see him, just hear his voice. The pictures materialized in the airy theater above her.

"What did she look like?"

"Just like you."

"She couldn't look just like me, I'm eight and a half."

"That doesn't matter. If you look like somebody, you look like them."

"What color were her eyes?"

"Same as yours. And she used to walk around holding you saying how sweet you were and how much she loved you."

"You're making that up!"

"No I'm not. I remember it."

"Did you really see her go through that door?"

"I did. And you did too. You just don't remember."

"I hate not being able to remember."

The truth was, Jon Karl *was* making it up. The details anyway. Doing what he instinctively knew was the necessary work of remembering—maybe fabricating, even he didn't know—the idea of their mother. And at the same time protecting his own fragile little gallery of memories. Sometimes, after Summer was asleep, Jon Karl would look at the photographs alone, almost seeing, hearing, smelling her, and when his eyes started burning he would put them away. And, if he was lucky, hear a train on the lay-by track a few blocks over, the giant grumbling engines as soothing as a lullaby.

* * *

Usually when you think you've got things pretty well managed, something comes in from your blind side and ambushes you. In the case of the unconventional Odom family, it was the sudden decline of Food Stamp.

Well, he *was* thirteen. But still.

First, he just didn't seem to have any energy, and could only look at you with those sad brown eyes that said, "I'm so sorry I'm in pain but please help me." He hardly moved, he couldn't get up. Then the next night, Sunday, after showing no interest in food, he started panting. Mildra said she hated to bother Dr. Breeding on a Sunday night—they'd take him in the morning—and went to bed. Things didn't get any better. The panting turned into wheezing. Jon Karl and Summer brought their blankets and pillows out to the den and snuggled against him, petting him as he lay on his side and kept wheezing.

It was a long night.

First thing in the morning they got him in the car and took him to Dr. Breeding. It didn't take Dr. Breeding, who had grown up in south Georgia with a dream of becoming a veterinarian, and now had a thriving practice and a thirty-acre farm, long to issue a diagnosis. "He's just wo-urn out."

Like a car. Or a washing machine. Or a pair of shoes.

Jon Karl had heard the phrase "put to sleep" before, but it was Summer's first time, and from that point the expression took on, for her, it's sad and suffocating tone.

"It's the hardest pa-urt of my job," Dr. Breeding said.

Spruill got Theotis to send some of his men over to dig the grave just this side of the fence in the back yard. A truck with "Dawes Properties" on the door towing a Bobcat with a backhoe showed up, and Rodolfo drove it to the spot they had selected and made short work of the task. Jon Karl and two handy Guatemalans stood to the side, while Mildra watched from the back porch, and Summer, feeling the love as grief and the grief as love, half hid in the shadow of the big red oak, watching stoically. Then Jon Karl and the men lowered the worn out old body in his favorite blanket into that sad cavity and covered him up. Jon Karl knew he had to act brave.

Food Stamp was only in one picture. The one with Maryrell and Mildra and Odis on the front porch. When he was fully alive. In his prime.

* * *

Spruill waited a week, then came by with Millard and picked up Jon Karl and Summer and drove them to the Humane Society shelter.

"You don't want one of these inbred snoot-dogs, I don't care how many papers they've got. You'll find the best dogs in the world right back there." And instructing Millard to "let Jon Karl and Summer pick it out," said he had some phone calls to make and went out to the car.

They found a dog, a just-weaned female yellow Lab-looking thing, even if it was actually Millard who first noticed her, which Jon Karl and Summer didn't mind since the whole process was heartbreaking for both of them. There were two things Jon Karl never forgot about that day, which was the last time either he or his sister ever went into an animal shelter: the look in the eyes of the dogs wanting to be picked but who weren't, especially after Millard told them: "They kill the ones you don't pick."

The other was a man, who came out of a door in what could only be called a uniform, sort of medical, sort of military, apparently unique to him, and stood there looking at the young trio, his jaw frozen in a dour frown, barely grinding his teeth, his eyes flicking over them like lasers.

Most of the dogs started growling, or retreated to the corners of their pens.

Volunteer Euthanist Balch.

"Well now," he said, his mouth barely moving, his eyes bright and busy. "Look who's here. You looking for something?"

Jon Karl and Summer were silent, maybe instinctively feeling that to exchange words with him was to open some portal into yourself. Summer visibly shuddered, and Jon Karl felt the quiver run up his own spine. But Millard was bolder.

"None of your business," he said.

Balch just turned his eyes to him with no visible emotion, just a subtle sense that the day would come for him to deal with that cute impudence and he would be ready for it when it did and was in no hurry. Then his eyes came back to Jon Karl.

"Never seen such a head of hair. You look more like a girl all the time," he said. "You need to let me shape that up for you."

"I like it the way it is," said Jon Karl.

Balch just kept looking at him, with that almost subliminal grind of his molars, and didn't reply. His eyes did all the talking. Jon Karl tried to look at him but couldn't. Not those eyes. Like the eyes of a fish you caught.

* * *

With a sweet yellow puppy sprawling all over the still inconsolable Summer's lap, they drove away.

"He's going to kill those puppies!" she sobbed.

"Try not to think about it, sweetheart," was all Spruill would say. He could have said, "They'll find homes for them, don't worry," but he didn't like to lie if it wasn't a business deal, especially not to children.

All the way home they read signs trying to come up with a name for the now sleeping puppy. One church sign said: "Suicide Awareness Brunch and Bake Sale Friday." "Bake Sale?" But it was kind of in the same vein as "Food Stamp," and they didn't even like to hint they were replacing Food Stamp. Then another church sign said: "Get an Afterlife!"

So by the time they got to the house, "Afterlife" had settled on the lucky girl, who would never know she was a lucky girl, for good.

Mildra gushed over her, and Summer's portrait of Food Stamp, three-fourths eyes, with the green world below and blue heaven above, went up on Jon Karl's wall.

Chapter 13

Growing Pains

At thirteen, Jon Karl took over the cooking completely, while Summer, approaching eleven, did all the house cleaning and laundry. Mildra mostly slept. Summer was troubled by what she could almost see behind her face, but didn't mention it to Jon Karl.

Without knowing it, Maryrell had instilled a love of the library in Jon Karl—the corner with the magazines, the VHS shelves, the excitement of looking through the books and picking one out— and he had transmitted that love to Summer. They still went once a week. Summer leaned toward the Young Adult section, Jon Karl non-fiction. Most of the books Summer picked out had plucky heroines, a term she had learned from cover copy, and a label she fantasized for herself. Lately Jon Karl had been reading everything he could find about the cuisine of different lands, always bringing home new books, and poring over recipes. Abundant garlic, and strange herbs—basil, thyme, rosemary, fennel—began to appear in the kitchen, along with such oddities as Shiitake mushrooms, Chinese vegetables, artichokes, leeks, proscuitto, ginger, and buckwheat noodles. Mustard thyme vinaigrette replaced Thousand Island. Mysterious marinations were almost always going on in the refrigerator.

Mildra ate perfunctorily and sometimes didn't seem aware of what she was eating. Whatever it was, she always told Jon Karl it was "real good," though once or twice she had let it slip that nothing really tasted right anymore. Summer was pretty finicky, but she usually liked what Jon Karl made and was starting to show some early signs of "filling out."

After dinner—bath time. Then Summer did homework—Jon Karl, who never did homework, got engrossed in his various pursuits—and Mildra began to leave off the layover in the recliner and take a direct flight to bed.

She didn't have anything to do with their baths anymore, and her prediction that when the day came for them to stop bathing together she would know it, proved true.

She walked past the open door of the bathroom as they were getting ready one evening, looked in, and with that glance the day had come.

She immediately ordered Jon Karl to put a towel around himself and take his bath after Summer. From then on. And said they had to stop sleeping in the same bed too. Jon Karl just said "Yes mam," but Summer cried, her eyes pleading. She already felt lonely, but that made her feel ten times more lonely. She didn't throw a tantrum because she didn't let anything out, she gathered everything within. It wouldn't have done any good in any case: Mildra was adamant.

"I'm sorry, sweetheart," she told her, "but y'all have gotten too old to be taking baths together."

All at once Mildra seemed to notice for the first time the dark shadow on the upper lip of Jon Karl as he closed in on fourteen— maybe because it matched what she had seen down below—along with what else she had seen down there.

I'm too old to be raising children, she concluded—and until that moment children is what she had been thinking they were. She just thought, *That was fast.*

She decided to check on them a little later, after their separate baths, and walked by the open door of Jon Karl's room where they stood drying off, talking to each other. Okay, maybe they looked as innocent as two people who had never heard of clothes—but *mercy*.

* * *

Jon Karl at fourteen. Eighth grade.

He got along with most everybody, was neither ostracized nor accepted. The jocks were more inclined to ignore than pick on him, maybe because he just didn't respond in the right way to that stuff. A few of the jocks, the future med school types, even befriended him. He belonged to no group, fit in no drawer, was self-confident in the way of one who didn't recognize that was a thing, so he achieved by default the coveted status of being tolerated as the weird-oh he was. Yes, he was different and defied all norms—but, that was just Jon Karl.

Plus, everybody knew he was buds with Millard Dawes and went out to his house all the time.

With notable exceptions, such as the viperish Ms. Boyle, who responded to Jon Karl's charm with straining neck tendons and bulging eyes, his teachers liked him. He was smart and made decent grades without studying, and had learned somewhere along the line that everything you needed to know was in the textbooks, all of which he read cover to cover, and everything else was just babysitting—and without, of course, being aware of it, he was not unknown, in fact in some cases he played a leading role, in the reveries of some of the younger teachers. At least one or two, such as the voluptuous Ms. Palmer, had weighed the risks of making a cougar move, but no one had yet dared anything more than keeping him after school so they could look at him. Girls in general—he inspired something in them, something confusing, and they didn't know what they wanted to do with him. Put him in his place, punish him, make him drool, sit on him, lead him around with a leash, go out behind the gym with him, turn him in to the police—*something*.

Not surprisingly, Jon Karl didn't care for the term "pretty" but that was the word most people used to describe him. His chestnut hair, straight and fine, had still never been cut, and he wore it in a long ponytail down his back. Half the girls in his class envied it, and they all said it wasn't fair, but—that was just Jon Karl. He was compact, a bantam-sized guy, but he had that Adonis thing which you either have or you don't.

He hated PE. The showers. All those guys looking at him. Making him feel like a freak. He just wanted to get dressed and get out of there as soon as he could. He wasn't paying attention the day Virgil Smoke snuck some pictures with his little spy camera. The giggling and the looks started with the girls, then spread to everybody, and finally a guy in American History class showed him the pictures messages that had been going around.

Some shower shots, then full frontal, drying his back, along with a full backal, drying his front.

He felt the obligatory outrage and embarrassment at first, but that didn't last. A fatalistic attitude soon took its place. *Everybody in this school has seen me, and there's no way to ever get rid of those pictures,* he thought. *The worst is done, I've shown my ass, there's nothing else they can do, screw it.*

There was freedom in that. And not only that, but power. The power of the guy with nothing to lose. That look he was getting? It wasn't condescension or mockery. More like awe. *They're* the chicken shits.

Millard thought the whole deal was hilarious. *"Dude,"* he gushed. "You're famous, bro. I'd get a camera and pay those fuckers back, every one of them, if I was you."

"I would never do that."

"Why not? You could start a whole new section in the back of the yearbook!"

"Naw."

"Come on, man. Golden Rule: do unto others what they did to you."

"*Huh?*"

"Who cares? Pay them back."

"I don't even know who did it."

"Hell, everybody knows who did it. Virgil Smoke."

"How do you know?"

"Everybody knows that. I know it, and I don't even go to your school."

"I couldn't do it. It would embarrass him."

"Well—*yeah*."

Spruill thought it was hilarious too. "Damn, boy, you take your warrior to school with you, don't you?"

When he showed Summer one of the pictures she just gave it a glance and frowned. "That was mean," she said.

Chapter 14

Evelyn

It was the moment Jon Karl realized there were a lot of girls everywhere—that they were, in fact, half the population (how did the population know?)—some in full bloom, some just about to be, and almost all of them sneaking looks at him. At first it was just a sensation of plenty, with nobody standing out—and he thought, *how does anybody ever pick one?*

He certainly never considered he might be a hot topic of conversation in the hen house. Nor suspected the mothers were already afraid of, but, like their daughters, fascinated by, him—and had set out on a communal competition to outdo each other in outrage. It wasn't enough just to paint him and his kind as the lowest sort of trash, they had to bring in divine censure. Clearly Satan was involved in it somehow, and it was their duty as good taxpaying Christians to put such wickedness and perversion in its place. They *forbade* their daughters to have anything to do with him, knowing full well his low-caste status was a major part of his allure—the feeling that you could do whatever you wanted with the hot little jungle boy. In the shadow of their mothers' sham outrage brewed an unspoken competition among the more advanced girls to be the first to nail him. Any such thing as that *really* never occurred to Jon Karl, who was not interested in any of them in what you would call a romantic way. He was only fourteen.

But nature had been busy, and he was curious.

And then—it took him a while to realize it—there *was* one, who seemed to have appeared out of nowhere and whose eye he kept catching. A tenth grade girl. He had yet to make the observation that nothing, except the universe itself, ever really appears out of nowhere.

The middle school and high school were next to each other and shared a lunch room. In true adolescent spirit, the territories were strictly segregated, but occasionally high schoolers who couldn't find a seat were forced to migrate to the edges of middle school land. She was one of those. It seemed like every time he looked around, there she was.

Little by little she crept into his thoughts.

She seemed shy, sort of by herself, but when their eyes met she kept looking at him a bit longer than you might expect. He was touched by what he construed as her exclusion from the higher circles on the other side of the room, and drawn to it. She was pretty, but probably not the kind of pretty that everybody would agree was pretty—not generically calendar pretty—but soulfully, uniquely pretty: dark, sad, secretive eyes, long black hair gathered in the back with a clasp, a hint of freckles across her nose and cheeks, smooth slender arms with a whisper of dark down.

He knew nothing about her so his imagination was free to work. And of course she, like everybody else, had seen him naked.

Then one day as he was crossing the parking lot after school, she appeared in his path.

"Excuse me," she said, "I'm having trouble getting my car started, could you help me?"

Her voice was smooth, half an octave lower than he had imagined, and he just stared at her for a second. She smiled.

"I'm not really a mechanic," he said.

"Would you mind giving it a try?"

Not a mechanic but, yes, at fourteen already an experienced driver, used to running errands for the exhausted Mildra who told him to just sit on a pillow, try to look like he knew what he was doing, and come straight home.

An older Camry—he got in behind the wheel and it started right up.

She smiled a hard to read smile. "What did you *do*?"

"I didn't do anything."

"Well, of *course* if you ask somebody to help, it won't do it."

"Maybe it was just flooded," Jon Karl said, because he'd heard Theotis say that.

"Well, maybe it's okay now," she replied. "But please let me at least give you a ride home for your trouble."

Jon Karl shrugged. "Sure. I guess. Thanks."

He didn't notice, but she did, a group of girls watching from the side door of the Band Room.

"I bet you don't know my name," she said as they drove along.

He shook his head, lying, because he had looked her up in the yearbook.

"Well, I know yours—it's Jon Karl—so you're probably thinking it's not fair."

Jon Karl, who wasn't thinking that, said, "I guess it's not."

"I hate my name," she said. "I may change it."

"Why?"

"I'm named after my grandmother—"

"What's wrong with that?"

"Nothing, if it doesn't sound like a grandmother name."

"I bet I'll like it."

"Do you want me to tell you?"

"Well—"

"It's Evelyn."

"What's wrong with Evelyn?"

"You don't think that sounds like a grandmother name?"

"Not as much as Myrtle."

"That's my middle name!"

"Oh, I didn't mean—"

"Silly, I'm just kidding. It's not Myrtle."

"My friend has a horse named Myrtle."

"Figures."

"So what *is* your middle name?

"I'm sorry, I can't divulge that information. That's where I live," she said, gesturing toward a house just ahead. She slowed down.

A fairly ordinary rancher a few blocks the good side of East Douvale.

"Oh. I just remembered I have a dresser I wish somebody would help me move." She didn't quite look at him. "Do you have a few minutes—"

"Well, I—"

"There's nobody home. They don't get here till late."

He was looking at her. And now she turned rather decisively to him. She looked incredibly pretty, but there was something in her expression he didn't understand, something sad. Also something, in that moment, in charge.

It wasn't until they went into her room and she closed the door and turned to face him that he understood, and then all at once a wave of excitement unlike anything he had ever felt roared through him. His face got hot and he didn't know how to turn to hide what was going on in his pants.

"You're blushing!" Evelyn cried. He saw some color rise in her own freckled cheeks.

"I just—where's the dresser?" he asked, trying to figure out what to do with himself.

"Over there," she said. "Actually it's fine where it is—you're not like other boys, are you?"

Not sure what she meant by that, he just gave her a puzzled look.

"Going around thinking they're all that just trying to get what they can all the time. Only to end up a bald insurance agent."

"I don't know—" He was hardly breathing.

"Do you think it's weird that I'm in tenth grade and you're in eighth?"

"Not really—"

What's weird, he was thinking, *is that what's been living in my head is standing right here in front of me and it's not the same.*

"I don't care what anybody says. I don't care what they think." She started unbuttoning her blouse. "Do you?"

"I—I—"

"I didn't think you did." She reached behind her and unfastened her bra, freeing that which it's amazing half the human race takes for granted considering the effect on the other half.

She walked over to him, a couple of inches taller, and unbuttoned his shirt.

"You're not like other boys, you're different," she whispered as she kissed his ear. "It should be ten years from now."

You only get that afternoon once.

Later, she asked him if it was not too far for him to walk home from there, she wasn't sure she could drive, and he said no. Leaving her in tears that completely mystified him, he walked home, seeing her face, her hair splayed on the pillow, smelling her, astonished.

Around him the same world looked different. By the time he got home the thrill had faded and he could tell the feeling wasn't going to be permanent.

Summer was standing there waiting for him when he walked in, and fastened her wide eyes on him.

"What?" he said.

"I was just wondering why you were so late."

"I had some stuff to do," he said, and feeling her loneliness, avoided her eyes and headed for his room.

Because by then his thoughts had been hijacked by anxiety. Hey stupid!—that's how you get *pregnant*! Obviously something that felt like that couldn't be free.

** * **

The next morning he woke up terrified and thought about skipping school, as if that would protect him. But he went, then almost chickened out going to the lunch room. He both wanted to, and was afraid to, see her. How could you just chat with somebody you'd done that with? How could married people, who did it all the time, even look at each other? He was partly relieved, partly disappointed, that there was no sign of her.

Yeah, because she's at the doctor, pregnant as hell!

Could you tell in just one day? Jon Karl didn't know.

He didn't see her the next day either. Or the next. In fact, as he stopped seeing her altogether, he realized she had indeed been in charge—she had engineered the whole thing, and was engineering it still, out of some inscrutable design or need of her own and he was just the eighth grade doofus kid standing there.

If so, maybe she could engineer not getting pregnant too.

After a week, Jon Karl didn't mind being the eighth grade kid standing there, but couldn't quite remember what she looked like. Other girls, hundreds of them, were swarming in his vicinity all day long, and had diluted the juice.

But his body remembered perfectly well. If she *didn't* get pregnant, maybe she'd want to do that some more? Wherever she was.

He considered going over to the high school side and looking for her—that is, for the one second it took him to picture himself parading through their ogling ranks—*hey, it's the naked boy!*—like some kind of trailer park victory lap. And she, back with her quarterback boyfriend, knowing he wouldn't dare.

But after two weeks of not seeing her he became convinced she *was* pregnant, and her father, probably a lumberjack, or her brother, or, God forbid, the quarterback boyfriend, was going to show up at any moment with—what?—a shotgun? axe handle?

the FBI?—or just his big fists, and kill him and take Mildra's house and all her money—

But none of that came to pass. And as the school year wound down and the whole thing began to feel like something he had dreamed, she settled inside him, more the myth she had become than the person she had been, if she had been real at all.

Then one mid-May afternoon he came home from school and Summer handed him an envelope.

"What is it?" he asked.

"It was in the mailbox."

No address, no return address, no stamp. Just "Jon Karl."

"Did you see who left it?"

Summer shook her head, her bottomless eyes looking into him.

He didn't take the envelope into his room but opened it right there.

Jon Karl,

Fate is funny. Not that I really feel like laughing. There is no one like you. I wish I could be all the women you will have in your life but I won't be. Only the first. I can live with that. I will never forget you.

    Evelyn

Summer was looking at him.

He lowered the letter, sighed, and looked back at her. "I had sex with a girl," he said.

She stared. "You did?"

"Yeah. I did."

Her eyes were wide with wonder. "Did you like it?"

"Yeah," he said, nodding. "I did."

"I'm going to have sex one day."

"Yeah, I'm sure you will."

She couldn't look away from him. Oh, the mystery of it all.

* * *

In June, on one of his many drives by Evelyn's house, he saw a moving van backed in the driveway.

Turns out fate *is* funny. He never saw her again. In his life.

She's still the only girl I will ever love, he told himself, not really understanding what that would mean if it were true.

But started looking around him all the same.

Chapter 14

More Growing Pains

Summer at twelve. Sixth grade.

In her own eyes she was shy, awkward, and ugly, and when she covered up the mirror in her room, Mildra said nobody had died and made her uncover it. So instead she just didn't look—except for the accidental glance every now and then—and she would think, *who is that?* There was still the occasional night when something scared her down the hall and into Jon Karl's bed, but not so much anymore. The truth was, she was beginning to appreciate her privacy and had some personal things that weren't meant for sharing.

As always, she assumed, wrongly, that everybody saw her as she saw herself.

"You're pretty and you don't even know it," Jon Karl would tell her.

"No I'm not."

Mildra, too, saw Maryrell in her.

Summer was lithe, and seemed taller than she was because of her litheness. Of course she thought herself clumsy and mousey, but what she felt as self-conscious and inadequate was expressed in her innate nonchalance and femininity, as she moved about like a willow, with her own rhythm, not yet grown into her feet.

She was still technically best friends with Wady Carothers, but Wady was so boy-crazy that was all she thought or talked about. She had arranged all the sixth grade boys into a pecking order of hotness in a special notebook that she was constantly re-arranging, and she kept, in another notebook, a who's who of the hot boys of the upper grades too, boasting an especially thorough knowledge of the senior boys, the sports they played, the clubs they were in, the cars/trucks they drove, their girlfriends—especially those, as Wady calculated it, who had gone *all the way*. She claimed she could see it in a girl's eyes. She was fascinated by high school girls who put out, while at the same time looking down on, and savoring, their trashiness. You might say, she was a pretty likely candidate of becoming one herself one day.

Summer realized one day how boring Wady had become, and the thought made her sad.

Boys, who didn't even notice or care, had stolen her best friend. And she didn't know how to find another one. In a way in her innocence she was as naked as Jon Karl had been. How far are you going to get in this world without deceit or guile or affectation?

It wasn't that she wasn't interested in boys herself—it's just that they seemed so distant and impossible to her it's like they weren't real, and she missed having a girl friend she could talk about certain things with—as she had with Wady back in happier days, before the hormones hit.

In fact, though Summer would never have used the word "crush," certain boys had singled themselves out in her mind and reigned there for fleeting periods before giving way to the next. She couldn't help pondering them, wondering what they did at home, what they did for fun, what they talked about in that most mysterious world of all, just guys, what, if anything, they thought about.

You could call those fantasies, but they weren't sexual. She didn't really think about sex—it was just what it was, something that came with the boy, like it or not, rather than something about the boy. Her fantasies centered around what was about the boy, the story she wove around them and featuring the true object of her lust: normality and status. She brooded endlessly over the idea of a good family, a mom and dad, money, a nice house, good clothes, ski trips and cruises. When Wady told her about Colt

MacGregor, the SGA president everybody said would be at least governor, and who had a closet full of expensive clothes, including a long row of starched and pressed shirts that he would rip off the hangers and throw to the floor until he found the one he wanted, she was enthralled.

"He's a dick," Jon Karl told her, which, okay, he probably was, but she couldn't get the picture out of her head. Those starched shirts like little tents on the floor for the maid or somebody to come along and hang back up. Unless that was enough to require another washing and pressing.

Not that she had any interaction of any kind with such creatures, who she knew had no more awareness of her existence, except maybe as the naked guy's sister, than of the pimply girl handing them their breakfast biscuits. Maybe it was envy, what she felt for those boys, but she would never have thought of, or used, that word. Nor would she have used "pity" to describe her feelings for the other class of boys, who *were* real, and accessible. Feel sorry for them, yes, but not pity. You had to be somebody to have pity.

At lunch those garrulous, challenge-hungry, math-problem-solving wraiths gathered around her, and though none of them knew it, their table was by far the most interesting in the room: Summer, ears sticking out of her long straight hair, and six or seven outcast boys—Hispanic, Asian, black, white—laughing with their mouths full, and doing what separated them from everybody else there—not talking about other people. Unless it was something funny Mr. Allison, the calculus teacher, had said.

Wady wouldn't have been caught dead within a mile of them.

* * *

Jon Karl and Millard were still best buds, however.

Maybe because they weren't in competition with each other. Social status and nature had settled all that.

Of course Millard got everything he wanted, that's just who he was, with one exception. When he turned fourteen he wanted a

95

Ninja crotch rocket, but Spruill put his foot down on that one. His favorite cousin had been killed on one of those goddamned things, when he was fifteen, and Spruill hadn't even allowed the word "motorcycle" to be spoken around him since then. Millard had pitched the obligatory tantrum, extremely unconvincing, and even Leela knew better than to take his side.

Jon Karl didn't tell Millard about Evelyn. It was the only thing he had ever not told him about. He knew Millard would want to know all the details, and he didn't want to talk about it. About *her*. The love of his life. Who had selected *him*. Awakened *him*. It was, as some things are, private, and in his mind she was already well on the way to beatification.

Jon Karl knew Millard hadn't yet done with a girl what he had done with Evelyn, because he wouldn't ever have stopped bragging about it, but in everything else Millard was ahead of the curve. He drank, with a preference for dark rum and fruit juice, he smoked reefer, he always seemed to have a variety of pills, and now his latest: magic mushrooms.

"It's abso-fucking-lutely in-fucking-credible," he told Jon Karl, and started trying to talk him into it.

But it was a tough sell. Jon Karl didn't do any of those things. Anybody who knew Jon Karl knew that about him. Actually, it would be more accurate to say he had done them all once, which in each case was enough to keep him from ever wanting to again. Alcohol made him sick, reefer made him paranoid and overly conscious of himself, the pills, uppers and downers, made him feel crazy and out of control—and though, yes, some were fun, what you had when they wore off was worse that what you started with. Jon Karl hated the sensation of coming down worse than anything he had ever experienced, and would rather not go up at all.

"But shrooms are different," Millard had persisted. "It's about alternate reality, man. It's about the other side." And hadn't let up.

In the end they reached a deal: as with the other stuff, Jon Karl would do it this one time, and Millard would never try to talk him into it again. The mushrooms grew in cow patties in Mr. Autry's pasture which connected to the back end of the Dawes property. They'd had a good rain a couple of days before. They rode the four-wheelers out there, climbed over the fence, and with the cows watching them curiously, it didn't take Millard but about ten minutes to find eight nice-sized ones.

"How do you know they're the right ones?" a scowling Jon Karl asked him.

"I just do. Would I give them to you if I wasn't sure?"

"Probably."

"Yeah, but it just so happens I *am* sure. I mean, I'm *pretty* sure."

"*What?*"

Millard laughed. "I'm just jerking you. Let's go make some smoothies."

Jon Karl thought the stuff was going to make him gag, then they got back on the four-wheelers and headed to the lake. For about thirty minutes he was pretty sure the whole thing was bull-shit. Then he felt a little tingle.

Years later, after Jon Karl indeed had never done them again, he would admit that for three or four hours, or whatever three or four hours was in that time signature, it had been exhilarating. And, yes, like a visit to the other side by confirming his lifelong intuition that something else than the obvious was going on. Just as obvious in its own way. The dissolution of his sense of self created a portal into another plane of being, visible without that film of ego. The luminous colors. The patterns in the pasture grass, and on the surface of the lake. The visible and musical waves of the air. The hyper awareness of everything, the sense of watching everything with awe and love—part of, and not part of it. The miracle of Millard—a sprite with the cosmic loan of a body, for whom he felt overwhelming affection and trust.

Then at some point, the sensations shifted and he could feel himself drawing more into himself. There was a big chunk of time he couldn't account for. He remembered being invited somewhere in that radiant void to ask *the question*. Which he had done—and though he didn't remember what the question was, he would never forget the answer, because it was suddenly standing before him, looking at him.

Himself.

He had never seen himself, and himself had never seen him, and they just considered each other for a while. And he was pierced with the truth of it. *The answer.* To everything. Simple and obvious. After a while the answer reduced itself into an aching violet glow and floated away from him—off in the distance—there but without a where.

During that long sojourn, sitting alone on the grass by the lake, Jon Karl had lost track of Millard, and when he emerged from wherever he'd been, and located him again, he was aware that the effect was fading.

Coming down.

Back to the old Jon Karl.

He thought about Himself. *What about him? Does he get to stay?*

He went home and closed himself in his room for the rest of the day.

Summer sensed something, but knew better than to bother him. She knew he would eventually tell her—and when he did, she, having guessed he'd had sex again, just listened with her big eyes, absorbing it. Nothing Jon Karl ever told her *really* surprised her.

"Do you see the glow now?" she asked him.

"No," he answered. "But it's there."

* * *

Jon Karl's mustache, and now his chin, were making progress, and he had taught himself the rudiments of shaving. His two little patches. Summer marveled at his armpits and didn't believe him when he told her girls got hair there too. She inspected herself in private. Nothing.

On the last day of school the girl appeared at his locker with an enigmatic smile—a female smile, the kind that says there's something here, if you're a real man you'll figure it out.

And in the event you don't, I'll fill you in.

He didn't, and by asking him if he wanted to go swimming, she did.

He was pretty sure he had never seen her before—an eleventh grade girl this time, and they never quite made it swimming. She parked the car on a piece of dying road about halfway to the creek, and though this didn't feel like love at all, he got pretty excited.

He quickly discovered her body wasn't like Evelyn's exactly, the first step in his realization that bodies were like the people they housed: each one different.

On the way home they hardly talked, and Jon Karl was thinking, *I'm already used to this.* Summer saw the girl out the window as she parked on the street to let him out—before getting the hell out of East Douvale.

She was staring holes in him as he came inside and sat down. Afterlife jumped up on the couch beside him. Jon Karl didn't offer anything, he just sat there, petting that rapidly growing affectionate hound.

"Does it feel good?" Summer asked him.

He nodded equivocally. "Yeah."

"For the girl too?"

"It must."

"What's it like?"

"It's good," he said, and shrugged. "It's not *that* good."

Summer contemplated that. "Do you think people would still do it if it didn't feel good?"

Jon Karl laughed. Speaking of not ever knowing what was going to come out of somebody's mouth. "You know, that's a good question. I'm going to say no. Considering how insane it is. Just enough to make new people."

"Do you think people would cut their hair if it hurt?" she added.

He laughed again. "I'm going to have to go with no on that one too."

Mildra was "lying down" in her room, which is mostly what she did these days. "I'm just worn out, sugar," was her answer to any and all questions. At first Spruill had let her go to half days at work, then down to three of those a week, for the same pay, then to just one while she was training a new woman.

At first it was Leela's unemployed sister, after Leela had begged Spruill to give her a chance, against his better judgment, which had been confirmed when, after a frustrating week, Mildra, in private with Mr. Dawes, had pronounced her a complete idiot. Even when a more promising candidate arrived, Mildra realized that nine-tenths of what she had learned in forty years she couldn't even remember, let alone teach, so she didn't even try.

She was worn out.

* * *

Girls, with a summer at their disposal, began to appear at the oddest times and in the oddest places. Jon Karl would never have believed that thirty years hence, for a group of middle-aged women, tipsy at class reunions, he would be a bragging right.

There were quite a few. He wasn't sure how many, they sort of merged together. They wanted to devour him. He liked the thrill, but hated the depression that followed each encounter. He didn't want to remember them.

He knew none of those randy queens gave a flying shit about him. As Evelyn, he refused to believe otherwise, had.

He always ended up thinking of Evelyn.

What was Evelyn?

Because Millard like his father just naturally had eyes and ears everywhere, plus he was around Jon Karl most of the time except for those mysterious absences and wasn't stupid, he had a good idea of what was going on, and Jon Karl confided in him.

"*Damn*, man, you're a hound dog," Millard said, and wanted details.

But he soon learned that Jon Karl didn't remember, or more often had never really been sure of, their names, so Millard couldn't picture the girl, which took the fun out of it. Not to mention that Jon Karl didn't distinguish any episode from the others.

"You're no fun," Millard said.

"It's just boring to talk about. And most of the time it's like they're getting something but I'm not."

"You're getting a piece of *ass*."

"Yeah, I guess."

"I'd call that even. And shit, man, you ought to be making *money* off it."

"*Money?*"

"Hell yeah, money. You've got something they want. Didn't you know having something people want is how you make money?"

But money wasn't really in Jon Karl's mind. Evelyn was.

Chapter 16
Redwine Pyle

What I heard, and I ain't going to tell you where I heard it, is that boy was making money on this computer off his clothes. And I'm not sure if he was doing it just for the money, or for something else, because all he had to do was look pitiful, which he'd gotten down pretty good, and his daddy would give him damn near anything he wanted. On *top* of his allowance, which was two hundred dollars a week, is what I heard. A fifteen year old boy without the first bill to pay. What's he going to spend that on?

Well, it turns out there's a long list of things, not too many of them what you'd call healthy, or legal, and he burned through that money like a five-alarm fire. So maybe he needed some extra, I don't know, but he was always a little bit what you might say on the wild side so maybe he was just doing it for the thrill.

You know that mansion out there has got these damn big closets, more like room themselves, and what I heard, he had fixed up a little place in the back of his where he had a computer and he'd sit on his chair with the camera on him, and I guess there'd be ten thousand people watching him—hell, I don't know—and he'd say, come on, people, let's get the bidding started—and people would send in ever what it was, a credit card or some kind of funny money, I don't know, and it'd get up to a hundred dollars or something like that, and he'd take off his shirt. And it would just go up from there. Next it'd be his britches, and they'd be sending in money left and right, and then he'd be setting there in his damn drawers saying, come on, folks, I've got bills to pay, I'm trying to save up for college, open up them wallets—it was damn near enough to bring you to Jesus—and these people sitting out there with I guess *absolutely nothing* to do just forking out the cash he'd got them so hot and bothered. And if it got up high enough to suit him, he'd pull off his drawers and go to playing with himself. And if they kept sending in the money he'd keep going.

They'd be so afraid he'd stop, he could make five or six hundred dollars in a half hour. And then turn around and spend it right back watching somebody hisself. It was girls and boys both that done it, take your pick.

I think they called the one he was on Clicks for Dicks, or something like that. But I grew up in the country. There ain't a damn thing in this world that surprises me.

Chapter 17

Cue on the Square

That summer was the first time in almost thirty years that Mildra missed Spruill's Fourth of July Cue on the Square. She was seventy-eight and hardly leaving the bed now. Spruill had arranged for a sitter to help her with getting up and down, sponge baths, and so forth. She had taken to observing: "We're all here for a purpose, and once we've fulfilled that purpose, that's it." And would add a little pttpt.

Cue on the Square was an elaborate production—three different barbecue trucks that had been there since the day before, smoking away, triangulated around the fountain, handing out free rib and sandwich plates with slaw and beans and iced tea. What was in people's personal coolers was up to them. The free-mealed attendees voted on their personal favorite of the three, and the winner got a trophy. Those businesses took the competition very seriously, and losers packing up and stalking away grumbling accusations of cheating were not uncommon. A big banner over the Square said, "Happy Birthday, America! from DAWES PROPERTIES," with a picture of Spruill and Leela and Millard. Sheriff Ulmer Cubbage patrolled the grounds as the token peace officer, telling jokes and handing out campaign cards listing his solid law and order credentials and his fit-to-print accomplishments. Whose office do you think masterminded the street-blocking plan for this event every year?

The Cue on the Square was Spruill's way of saying thank you to Douvale. At dusk the crowd would migrate two blocks over to the amphitheater, where the City put on the big annual fireworks show.

Spruill didn't do anything by halves, and liked to say he never spent, but invested, money, as Mildra would be the first to corroborate. It might look like he was throwing money around, but he wasn't. It was more to it than that. People from remote reaches of three or four surrounding counties would tell you that Spruill Dawes was one of the finest men walking the earth. *That's* investment.

Greeting Cornell Hargett on the way in, Spruill, with Leela, Zadie, and a smattering of the rest of his three-marriage brood, along with Theotis, Luthelma, Luthelma's niece Miriam and her husband Grady, Billy Lirenzo and his wife Sherica in tow, handshook and backslapped his way to their table. Millard, high on something, Jon Karl, and Billy Reuben were all over the place. Summer had found Wady Carothers, but she was so absorbed in her meticulously detailed observations of the important boys there, she was no fun and Summer went off to find Jon Karl.

That youthful cadre finally came to light at the table, Jon Karl and Billy Reuben with plates piled high, Summer with only a funnel cake, and Millard with just tea, which he had spiked from a flask in his back pocket. As always, Jon Karl caught Miriam looking at him with her sad, soulful eyes, and smiled back, just as Zadie patted the empty place beside her, and he sat down. Catching his eye, she gave the air a little kiss which Jon Karl pretended not to see. She would graduate to licking the sauce off her lips for his benefit, but he would pretend not to see that too.

"A hell of a day not to be hungry," Spruill scolded not-eating Millard.

"Why's it always my fault?" Millard pouted back.

Spruill looked away with a scowl, but Leela consoled him with an indulgent smile.

"There go Pruet Echols," said Theotis.

Spruill turned his head just enough to see the man, dressed in seasonal leisure, on the far side of the Square with Bettine, flashing her big fake smile, and Brenleigh, fresh out of rehab.

"He has to put in an appearance," Spruill said.

Jon Karl vaguely knew who Pruet Echols was, some kind of businessman, like Spruill—

"*Not* like Mr. Dawes at all," Mildra would have corrected you right there. "Don't even mention him in the same breath."

Jon Karl glanced over at the collegial-looking man talking and laughing in a little group of country club types, with what had to be his big-hair tanning bed wife and cleavage-showing hottie daughter, whose eyes were locked on, of all people, himself, then, colliding with a nasty look from Zadie, looked back at Spruill who had turned his attention elsewhere.

* * *

After a while, because he couldn't put it off forever, Pruet led the little Echols entourage over to the Dawes table.

"Here he come," said Theotis, and Spruill made an effort not to make any effort as he waited.

"Good to see you," said Pruet. He was a pretty thick guy, looking like the one-time fullback he had been, bald on top. Bettine looked older the closer she came.

"She's had plenty of work," Mildra would explain later. "After she had her lips done and her eyebrow implants, I ran into her one afternoon and she looked like a Neanderthal. I thought, they must not have shown her the after picture."

Millard nudged Jon Karl and surreptitiously pointed. Dog shit on her shoe, which apparently no one else had noticed. She caught them stifling a giggle and fake-smiled them. My, things were awkward already. If there was anything Bettine couldn't stand, it was cute boys—they just pissed her off. She wished they could be put in work camps. The only thing she hated worse—her eyes grazed over Summer—was unfake girls. She didn't buy it for one minute.

"Glad you could come," said Spruill.

Of course they all kept their seats as the visitors stood.

"Douvale enjoys your little party," said Pruett.

He wore two buttons on his patriotic polo shirt. One, a red white and blue campaign button that said GUIN, and the other— he must have been feeling a little sportive today—a stylized waist-up crucifixion image with the legend: "This Blood's For You."

You could question a lot of things about Pruet Echols, but not his faith.

"Hope you enjoy yourself," Spruill replied.

Jon Karl could feel, at closer range, Brenleigh still looking at him with about the same heat as he could feel Zadie looking back at her. Those two were more Bettine's type.

"Say hello, David," said Pruet to the sprucely dressed eight year old boy standing beside him.

"Hello," David said.

Their own little late-life surprise which, considering what had to have caused it, beggared belief.

"It's the daughter's," Mildra would clarify later.

"Good to see you," said Spruill.

"Mam—" said Theotis, but Bettine didn't hear him.

Another little group of young people had walked up to join them. One, what could only be, and was, the twenty-five year younger version of Pruet, Pruet, Jr., a former fullback/linebacker himself. Jon Karl caught his eye and it was like looking at a pit bull. An out of place-looking girl stood ignored by his side. His stuff. The other guy was crisply dressed and toothy, mid-twenties, wearing a GUIN button like Pruet's on his shirt.

"I don't know if you've had a chance to meet Todd," said Pruet, and gestured toward the young man. "Todd Guin. He's running for the County Commission, District Four."

"I thought I would jump in, get my feet wet," Todd cheerfully explained.

"He's a fine young man from a good family with a solid business-friendly platform. We hope you'll give him a look."

Todd Guin beamed his smile. "It's awfully generous of you, Mr. Dawes, to regale the community with such a fine patriotic event. We're all so deeply grateful to you for this colorful event every year."

Spruill just eyed the fellow, nodded, but didn't say anything.

He colored slightly, but held his own.

"Ma'am—" said Theotis.

"Where's your other son?" Spruill asked, bypassing the hopeful commissioner.

"Oh, you know Cabul," Pruet replied. "Always working. I tell him he needs to lighten up, have a little fun, but he doesn't listen."

"He's so *serious*," Bettine added with a high-pitched laugh.

"You're looking at doing some expanding, I hear," said Spruill.

"We're considering some options," Pruet replied.

No secret that Pruet was planning to expand the Glorious Light Turnaround Center. His little cooperative detention venture with the City.

"Which direction?"

"East."

"Towards Hargett Hills?"

"Yes. In that direction."

Spruill held his eye and nodded. "And I assume this expansion won't be a City or County project, but—private?"

"That's right," Pruet said. "Private."

Spruill nodded again. "Everything working out okay?"

"We're encouraged."

"Good. They say the poor will always be with you. I guess it's just a matter of where."

"I guess so."

"Ma'am—" said Theotis.

At last Bettine realized she was being addressed. She must have tried to keep her expression from turning ugly as she recognized the source, but didn't quite succeed.

"Yes?"

"I believe you stepped in something."

She looked down—her face turned frantic. "Oh!—" she gasped.

"Just wipe it off," Pruett snarled. "You'd think they'd keep it a little cleaner around here. We need to be going." He turned to Spruill. "I'll say one thing for you—you don't skimp on the barbecue."

"I don't skimp on anything," said Spruill.

Though in truth, Pruet didn't skimp either. Maybe he didn't put on a barbecue for the town, but those billboards at the north and south entrances to town, with the Scandinavian quarterback-looking Messiah standing with outstretched arms and the legend—"Ready or Not, Here I Come—Jesus"?

You could thank him for those.

Chapter 18

Pruet Echols

One day when Pruet Echols was young, he heard the voice of God. God promised him a kingdom, and said his seed would be scattered over the earth. It had only been that one time, and no drugs or alcohol were involved. Pruet never heard the voice again, but I mean, it was *God*. God doesn't need to repeat himself.

As his father had been, and his first son would be, Pruet was athletic, but like father and son, he topped out at about 5'9", which had made him too small for big-time college football, but three times as mean as he would have been at 6'2". He had gone to a Division II school where he'd had some playing time, and a couple of moments, but when he graduated he found himself traversing the dark valley of incertitude. It was his forty days and nights in the desert, his dark night of the soul, as he later saw it. People looking at him today would never suspect that he had known a season of youthful dissolution and rebellion. But those people wouldn't know much about God's circuitous ways. Pruet, having hair then, had grown it out, gotten a couple of tattoos, and given himself over to partying and hell raising, drinking and, yes, other things. His father wanted him to join him in business, but would accept law school. Pruet hadn't been thrilled by either of those prospects, and had remained rudderless, entertaining a sequence of crazy ideas—touring the country on a motorcycle one day, joining the Marines the next. He came back to Douvale wanting only to be somewhere else.

So off he went to law school.

Hated it.

Then his father surprised everybody by dying.

And God spoke.

Pruet dropped out of law school and suddenly realized, with his father gone, Douvale wasn't all that bad. The old man—well, actually he had only been fifty-three—had left everything to him. Pruet came back, and started trying to figure out what to do, hardly aware that his father had once been in the same position. Well, minus the headstart.

In the Sixties, when the elder Echols had been the same age as Pruet then, mid-twenties, he had smelled the potential of a growing town on a river and an interstate, with a strong tax base and the slogan—painted on the water towers—"Open for Business," and moved there. He joined everything, and set about learning how the local politics worked. Corrupt as hell, but if you want to play, you learn the rules. He figured out who to pay for what, and started buying up crummy houses—not for the houses, but for the lots, though he rented out plenty of the crummy houses for years, ignoring the tenants' complaints about anything short of a hole in the roof, and even those he had usually handled with a blue tarp. Then he acquired a couple of buildings downtown, built Echols Plaza, one of the town's first strip malls, then in the seventies forced out the residents of a low-income housing project, at low dollar, leveled the place, and put Camelot Armes in its place. As he became more adept at the politics, he was able to coax the growth of the rapidly spreading town toward his holdings, and cashed them in one by one at a turnover many times his investment.

Yes, the old man had been a crafty and ruthless businessman, but had he heard the voice of God?

Pruet thought not. As *he* had. He could see his path like a lamp unto his feet.

Once re-established in Douvale, his father safely tucked away in the cemetery under an elaborate monument, he sold the strip mall to an Atlanta group for a killing, just ahead of the dot-com explosion, sold the apartments to another group for a mini-killing, and most of what was left of the lots, holding onto just two or three prime ones with "McMansion" written all over them.

Pruet had vision. He saw opportunities where no one else did, which is what happens when you follow the voice of God. He arranged a meeting with the politically appointed president of the local Baptist Junior College, and when he came out he had a private contract to run the campus police force. All three members. Dealing with rowdy adolescents, keeping undesirables off campus, and detecting and bringing to account ideas that weren't consistent with God's plan.

It might not have looked like much to the casual observer, but it was a start and, like God, he had a plan.

That plan was much facilitated at that critical point in his life by two positive developments: his marriage, and his religious conversion.

The marriage had made him a family man overnight, and though he liked others, and himself, to think he had pursued and won this prize, most others, and on bad days he himself, knew it had been the other way around. Bettine Schotts was a recent divorcee who knew a little about plans herself. She had moved to Douvale a few years before, maneuvered her way into the Country Club scene, and then, like a hawk spotting a hapless rodent on the ground, had zeroed in on Clive Barksdale, sole scion of the trucking company his father had built into a Douvale-based fleet, then passed on to Clive, who would expand the business, so the man could finally, after forty years, do some fishing. At the divorce five years later Bettine forced a sale of the company, took the lion's share of the proceeds, and went on the hunt again.

Thank God for religious conversions. Pruet's, certainly, hands down, was the greatest event of his life, and he had thrown a gala spectacle at First Baptist to celebrate it, a piece of local theater surpassed only by the staging of his Homecoming in Heaven some years later, with actors portraying the welcoming Jesus and the angels pulling the phaeton-like carriage, in which he sat in a white robe, across the Fellowship Hall amid flora provided by his tenants in Newsome Flower Shop. The event had made an impression and inspired numerous imitators.

The impetus behind his religious zeal owed to an encounter with some advanced thinkers, and his realization, in his thirties, that white western Christian civilization was under assault. That the lower races were breeding out the higher and, do the math, on track to supplant them, taking the law, the financial structure, the civilized church, and every other decent institution with them.

It was time to fight back. Nothing could be clearer or plainer, and he had no doubt, not a smidgen, about the utter rightness of his thinking. So he went in whole hog, and in short order became one of the pillars, the titans, in the First Baptist Church. The wealth and influence that he enjoyed he had no doubt were God's way of rewarding him.

Because God takes care of His own. Why couldn't people understand something so simple? Reveal it to children, hide it from the "wise." It was all about knowing how God operated.

Pruet's first idea, inspired by the work of the Cultural Impact Team he had joined, and building on the solid base of what had proven to be the *very* successful Baptist Junior College police force, was—frankly, he didn't like the word "police," and insisted on simple uniforms—a police-like squad deployed by the church.

He recruited the members himself, whose job it was to ferret out belief systems and ideas that weren't in keeping with Scripture, the kind that "manipulate people's senses and reasoning ability and destroy minds and families," both in the church itself, because as Pastor Bulborn said, not everybody came to church for the right reasons, and in the town at large and, especially, in the pubic schools. Of course they weren't really *police*—they couldn't arrest you or put you in jail, but they could put your name and whatever wrong thing you had thought or said up on their LED marquee for everybody to see, and on their website.

It was only natural that Pruet's taste for law enforcement would lead eventually to an interest, both financial and spiritual, in for-profit detention and, yes, rehabilitation, and that's where he got the idea for the Glorious Light Turnaround Center: a straighten-them-out boot camp for the wayward young, opiod addicts, the sexually confused, and other deviants. The sign over the entrance proclaimed "The Rebellious Dwell in a Dry Land." Like all his other ventures, it had been a great success, with a cadet population nearing a hundred, and constant inquiries from all over the country. Yes, inspired, at least in this, by his father, he was looking into expanding and had designs on Hargett Hills, the trashy "ethnic" subdivision that stood in his way and over which all the puzzle pieces of court-appointed receivership, condemnation, and razing hadn't quite come together.

All well and good—but his major contribution to the community, now in its tenth year, sprawled on a tract of land he had pounced on with the death, *finally*, of a nonagenarian widow in a big pecan orchard-shaded, soon to be plowed under, antebellum house out by the interstate: Scripture Land. He had brought in experts, biblical scholars, archaeologists, and so forth, and built replicas of select biblical scenes—the Garden of Eden, a crowd favorite, where groups would be let in to stroll through the blooming foliage until an angel with a flaming sword (a rip-off light saber) appeared and thrillingly chased them out, Moses's burning bush (ceramic with gas jets), the Ark (not to scale), Jacob's ladder (staircase to nowhere, with a viewing platform at the top, overlooking the interstate), Daniel's lion den (with the drugged real thing); scenes from the New Testament—the Nativity (least favorite for the actors, just sitting/standing there), the Feeding of the Multitude (with a snack bar selling fish sandwiches), the Sea of Galilee (where an actor walked across a just-submerged concrete walkway), Lazarus's tomb (coveted role among the actors), The Wrath to Come (where God Himself stormed out with a whip—a plum, King Lear-like role for an older actor), and of course Golgotha (with crucifixions on the hour). Also a small play area for the kids (where Jesus would appear and let them come unto him). People poured in by the busload. Pruet paid off his debt in five years, and now was making money hand over fist.

And doing God's work.

Are you maybe seeing a connection there, people?

The only problem was that God's work had led Pruet, on several occasions over the years, to butt heads with Spruill Dawes. Who now, he had a feeling, had his eye on the same acreage that he did.

Chapter 19

Redwine Pyle on the Hargetts

Cornell is Rufus Hargett's son. He runs the real estate agency his daddy started—which is mostly Hargett Hills, along with a few other houses scattered around and some apartments and whatever else he can find—and the colored funeral home over by the Cleyton Street water tower. I think he makes more money out of that than anything else. You can always count on people to die, but you can't always count on them to pay the rent.

Rufus built Hargett Hills back in the sixties—it's that little subdivision I guess you'd call it out there behind the discount bread outlet off Fenton Road. The sign is still there but most of the letters are gone—like you just turned on Wheel of Fortune. It's twenty or thirty houses in there. Rufus was real proud of it—it wasn't easy for a black man to do something like that back in those days, and for a while there it was kind of a prestigious address for the black folks, you know. Maybe it still is, even if it's got to where it's a little bit what you might call rundown.

I haven't run across too many in my life like Rufus. He died a few years back, and to be honest none of his children has turned out to have the full package, so to speak. Cornell tries. I guess they do all right. But Rufus got things done. He was a businessman, an entrepreneur, a contractor. He built that subdivision, and owned some buildings and a little shopping strip on his side of town, and sold insurance on the side, and usually had about ten cars for sale on the side of his house. "Always Fair Auto Sales," the sign said. Him and Theotis were real tight. They grew up together and went to school together, even though neither one of them ever finished high school. Theotis had to work, and after Rufus got hurt playing football he said the rest of it was a waste of time and dropped out.

That was back when there was a white high school and a black high school—Douvale High and Fraser High. After integration they made Fraser into a middle school, then finally tore it down. Back in the day, folks—white folks—used to call that whole area over there Frasertown. I know it's hard for you to picture all this but that's the way it was.

When I was coming along, we used to get up a carload, pack a cooler in the trunk, and go over to watch the Fraser football games on Friday night—on account of they were a whole lot more fun than the Douvale games. I never cared two cents about football, and still don't, but I've always been a people-watcher, and there was just way more to watch across town. We didn't cause any trouble and the folks over there were nice to us and we cheered on the team. And when it came to the halftime show, there was just no comparison. John Philip Sousa in one, James Brown in the other.

That "stadium"—it was just a piece of pasture with some rickety seats and lights on each side—has been gone for years. You couldn't really say they "tore it down"—all's you had to do was walk away from it and six months later you couldn't even tell where it had been. And the team wouldn't even be wearing the same uniforms or helmets—they just had to make do with whatever they could find—and it was the same for the other team so it was hard sometimes to tell who was who.

The same thing was true for the band, but when they come out there at the halftime, buddy, it didn't matter what they were or weren't wearing, I'm talking about it was *showtime*. That drum major was *in charge*, and bent over so far backward his big hat had grass stains on it. He'd rare back and come down that field and all the girls would squeal. The band wasn't the best one you ever heard, but from the drum major and them damn majorettes you got your money's worth and then some, even if it was only a quarter to get in there. Good God almighty, those majorettes. Us damn country boys had never seen nothing like that. If our mamas had known we were going over there they would have chained us to the bedpost on Friday night.

I don't know if you know this, but Theotis was a good athlete back then, kind of like my wife—started out a tight end but ended up a wide receiver. If he ever got in front of you, you could forget it. Couldn't nobody catch him. I remember one night he got tackled pretty hard and he was down on the field. I don't think it would have been any better on Broadway. *Everybody* came out there—the coach, the team, the cheerleaders. One of the other players escorted his mother out to the field, along with his daddy. They covered him up on the field with a blanket and were kneeling all around him with the coach squeezing him and asking him what his name was, which they said for a few minutes he couldn't come up with—then after a little bit of what you might call suspense he threw off that blanket and *refused* to let anybody help him, and got to his feet with everybody still trying to help him, but he *refused*, and limped around a little bit, then he took off on a little sprint down the field—then sprinted back—and, buddy, Jesus healing a cripple and him throwing down his crutch and doing some dance steps didn't have nothing on Theotis that night.

And Rufus was an even better athlete—one of the best that ever came out of there. He was a fullback and he was a damn bull. It took a minimum of three people to get him on the ground. Everybody said he was going to Grambling, but he messed up his hip and always had just a little bit of a limp from then on. I think it was one of them famous blessings in disguise because it motivated him—I believe he went into business because he wanted to do good at something. And he did.

His daddy died right about that time. He was one of the best brick masons and concrete finishers in town and he always had work. But he didn't live to see Hargett Hills, which was his son's dream. He had bad kidney stone problems all his life, and this is something you can't repeat, and you can't ask how I know it, but they were checking out his kidney and found out his adrenal gland was eat up with cancer. They knew he didn't have much money, and no insurance of any kind, so they didn't even tell him about it. Just gave him some pills and sent him home.

I mean, they didn't bust their ass going to medical school and all the rest for fifteen years just to work for free.

Chapter 20

Mildra in Decline

In better days they would have brought Mildra a plate from Cue on the Square, but Mildra was hardly eating anything now. Certainly not barbecue.

Along with implying that her purpose in life, whatever it was, had been fulfilled, Mildra was saying things like: "All this"—with a feeble wave of her hand—"ain't but just the tip of the iceberg. This room, and this furniture, and the whole world out there—the trees and the wind and the birds and everything else—ain't even in it." She also claimed that "Momma and Poppa" were right there, she talked to Odis every day, and Maryrell was watching over Jon Karl and Summer.

Which all pretty much added up to she was headed for the door.

Jon Karl and Summer had speculated about what Mildra's "purpose" had been.

"It's a riddle," Jon Karl provocatively said.

"It's *not* a riddle," riddle-hating Summer protested, then to prove it, made bold to ask Mildra, who answered rather vaguely that love was all that mattered, or something like that.

You could say that was a mystery, but it was *not* a riddle.

"I think it was to take care of us after Mama died," said Summer.

"Like all the years before that didn't count?" Jon Karl said.

Summer had to think about that.

"And why does there have to be just *one* purpose?" he added.

"Because that's what she said: everybody has a purpose. *A* purpose."

"I'd say one big purpose with a lot of parts," Jon Karl said. "Like making it so we could have a house."

Summer stared at him. "What house?"

"What house do you think? *This* house. Except they probably won't let us stay here."

"I want to keep living here," said Summer.

"Me too," said Jon Karl. "It beats the alternative."

"What is the alternative?"

"Me in one foster home, you in another one—maybe in California or somewhere."

"I would never do that."

"It doesn't matter what *you* want. It's what the judge says."

"Mr. Dawes wouldn't let that happen."

"I hope not."

"Was Mama's purpose just to have us?" Summer asked him.

"What—like *she* didn't count for anything?" Jon Karl said.

Summer was confused. "Did I say that?"

"In a way."

She thought it over. "What do you think our purpose is?"

"I'd say we each have a different purpose."

"What is it?"

"I don't know. Something."

"How can you know if you fulfilled it if you don't know what it is?"

"I guess you have to figure it out."

"Are we orphans?" Summer asked.

"Where'd you hear that?"

"I've read it a bunch of times."

"Do you want to be an orphan?" he asked her.

"No."

"Then don't say it."

* * *

Jon Karl was almost sixteen, and Summer was thirteen and a half.

One day he said, "Let's go see Cleetha Till."

Her expression turned a little dark. "What for?"

"Just to see what she has to say."

"You aren't scared of her?"

"What's there to be scared about? Redwine goes to see her all the time. Mama went to see her."

"Did she tell Mama she was going to die?"

"She won't tell you that."

"What *did* she tell her?"

"You're not supposed to tell what she tells you."

Summer thought a minute. "Why not?"

"It's personal."

Chapter 21

Cleetha Till

Cleetha was a small woman to begin with, but age had shrunk her even more. Jon Karl went first, and when he entered the room where she did her readings, he found a little old lady with wire spectacles and pale blue eyes sitting behind an old handmade wooden table just barely smiling.

"Sit down, sugar," she said.

There was one other chair in the room, on the other side of the table, and not much else. Jon Karl sat down. The tall curtainless windows stood propped open but without admitting much breeze and it was a little warm in there.

Cleetha held a piece of blue satin ribbon in her arthritic hands and was running it absently through her fingers.

"I knew your mama," she said. "I was real sorry when she passed."

"Thank you, mam," said Jon Karl.

Cleetha's smile had bloomed a bit. "I don't see too many that's getting too *much* love," she said.

He could pretend he didn't know what she was talking about—but this *was* Cleetha Till, and it didn't seem like a good idea to be dishonest with her. And he *had* paid five dollars.

"I don't think it's love," he said.

"It's not," she confirmed.

"It's just lust, isn't it?"

"Well, you can call it all kind of things, but it just is what it is, sugar, it's just nature, and you need to remember everything is a gift from God, and if God has given you a gift, you'd be wrong not to appreciate it."

That was hardly what he had expected to hear, but he didn't argue.

"Did you have anything you wanted to ask me?" Cleetha said.

"I know you don't tell people when they're going to—pass," Jon Karl said, using her word, "not even for twenty dollars—"

"All my readings is the same, sugar."

"But I'm just wondering—you're not seeing something way off for me, are you?"

"No, baby, I'm not."

"I'm not either."

"You've just got to live the life God gives you."

"I know. But—do you think I'll ever get anywhere?"

She smiled. "Get there, or get back there?"

"Are they different?"

"Well, they're both just wanting to get somewhere. It's all a circle anyway. It ain't how long you live, sugar, it's what you do with the life you're given. It's the love you have in *here* that matters," she said, touching her heart.

"Is love all that matters?"

"That's what God is, baby."

"That's what Mildra says."

Cleetha smiled her little ghost of a smile again. "I'm sorry about her, sugar. It's just her time."

"I know." A little silence, Cleetha stroking the ribbon and gazing steadily at Jon Karl. "I'm just wondering what's going to happen to my sister and me."

Cleetha smiled. "Yall feel more like one thing than two." Jon Karl looked back at her quizzically, then she added: "Good people have made plans for you."

That, too, was a little cryptic. "A place to live and all?"

"Yes, sugar. But you need to know there are other people who don't wish you well. Bad people that you can't trust, that will try to take advantage of you or hurt you."

"What can we do?"

"There's nothing you can do about bad people. I wish there was. Except learn how to recognize them and stay away from them. Don't let their voice into your head—you might get to where you can't tell it from your own."

He digested that. She stroked the ribbon. "Was there anything else you wanted to ask me?"

"What about our father? Will he try to get us?"

"Your father is not on this side, baby."

"What happened to him?"

"A bad man killed him."

"Did they catch him?"

"No, baby, they didn't. It was—" she looked off, seeing it— "deep in the woods—with nobody else there."

A vivid image appeared in his mind. He shuddered.

"Why did he kill him?"

Cleetha narrowed her eyes. "They had an argument." That seemed to be as far as she wanted to go.

"And he just got away with it?"

"Nobody gets away from God's judgment, sugar."

Jon Karl thought for a minute. "All these girls—it's a sin, isn't it?"

"Sugar, sin ain't my department. I ain't sitting here in this hard chair all day to pass judgment. God is the only judge. I'm just here to tell you what I see—if you're of a mind to hear it."

"None of it means anything, does it?"

"I ain't here to tell you what nothing means neither."

"Sometimes I'm just tired of it."

"I know, sugar. You and all the rest of us. Sometimes."

"What about love—for me?"

"Baby, you got love in you you don't even know about."

"I mean one—person."

"Some has one, some has many, some has none at all," she said. "Everybody just has to follow their own path."

Well, that wasn't really an answer, was it? Jon Karl shrugged. "You mean figure out my own way to live."

"That's right, sugar. Figure out your own way to live. As long as God's happy, nothing else much matters." She looked at him frankly. "You've got a tender heart. Which opens a lot of doors. But some of them would do better to stay closed."

* * *

Summer was so nervous she was hardly breathing. If Jon Karl hadn't been there to almost push her into the room, she probably would have chickened out.

"You look like your mother," Cleetha said, smiling at her so disarmingly Summer managed to seat herself successfully. "And you're like her in other ways too. Aren't you?"

"I don't know," Summer practically whispered. "I didn't know her."

"You were so young when she passed. I know it's been hard. But she knew you. Get comfortable, baby, you don't need to be afraid of me." Summer adjusted herself a little. "I just mean the way you feel what other people feel, which is a gift from God, but it can be a hard gift. Was there anything you wanted to ask me?"

Summer looked down, then back up. "Will I ever be normal?"

Cleetha allowed herself a little laugh. "Why in the world would you want to be that?"

"I—"

"You're still so young. Remember that sometimes the best way to get what you need is to not find what you want."

Summer's eyebrows dipped. "Is that a riddle?"

"Baby, I don't talk in riddles. It's just something that's true that a lot of people don't understand."

Summer's eyebrows relaxed a little. "I mean like—"

"A husband? Oh, you'll have your husbands."

Summer looked at her, alarmed. "Not just one?"

"No, baby, you'll have more than one. Some do—and some have just one, and some none at all."

"I figured I'd be a none-at-all."

"No, sugar, that's not who you are. A lot of men are going to want to be with you. You just need to be real careful, and remember, some things that smell like a rose is not a rose."

"And a family—"

Cleetha nodded, with her faint smile. "Yes, baby."

"Will I always be unhappy?"

"You'll have your share, sugar, like everybody else. But don't forget, we're put on this earth to learn. As long as you keep learning, and have love in your heart, you haven't wasted your time."

Summer looked at her hands, a little disappointed.

"What I'm telling you's good news, baby. And like I told your brother, you've got some good people watching out for you. God has more ways than you can imagine."

"Sometimes I worry about—" she faltered.

"No, baby, you won't always have him. But that time's a ways off."

Chapter 22

Worn Out

The Hospice nurse explained where Mildra was in the process. Right at the end. And everything she said to expect, happened. The woman was so kind and professional—somewhere *up here*, above it all, but right in the middle of it too. She didn't say "Mildra"—she said "we." Like it may not be your or my turn yet, but it will be. She left a deep impression on Summer.

For a while Jon Karl secretly thought, she's dying too early, but he thought about Cleetha Till, and God's love, and the way pieces fit together, and everything that was still to be, and he remembered what he already knew: that death has its own logic and doesn't care about your logic, or your plans, or your purpose, or anything else, and Mildra did in fact die.

Spruill Dawes, who had been keeping a close eye on Mildra's steady decline, and had arranged for the around-the-clock Hospice care, was there the afternoon the nurse came out into the living room, tight-lipped and shaking her head.

He stood up and held out his arms for Jon Karl and Summer, embracing them as tears ran down his cheeks. Afterlife, who maybe understood, maybe didn't, watched it all with a little whine.

"She's one of the best people I ever knew," said Spruill. "Maybe the best." He swallowed, collecting himself. "There are some things to talk about," he went on. "But first thing: I'm going to take care of all the arrangements here—you don't have to worry about any of that."

"Thank you," said Jon Karl.

"You're welcome."

After the ambulance came, and the Hospice nurse had bade an emotional goodbye, they went out into the back yard and sat in the patio chairs. Afterlife sat on her haunches, alert, watching them curiously.

"I'm sure you don't know this," Spruill began, "because there's no reason for you to know it, but your great-grandmother and Odis made a will a few years ago, with the first one dying leaving everything to the other one. And that's what happened when Odis died. As to what is going to happen *now*—well, that's what we need to talk about."

They stared at him, wide-eyed. Millard was doing something on his gadget.

"About six months ago we updated the will, and your great-grandmother made me executor, and gave me power of attorney. She left everything she owned, mainly this house, to me, because that's what we decided would be best to do. Your great-grandmother knew I would make sure her wishes were honored. She *trusted* me—" He looked from one to the other, making sure they understood the weight of that remark. "And when somebody *trusts* you, you know you would go down into Hell itself before you broke that trust. They say God sees everything, which I'm sure he does, but you damn sure wouldn't want him seeing *that*. Your great-grandmother and I had an understanding. This house, and all her assets—her car, and there is a little money—will be yours when Jon Karl reaches majority age at eighteen. Until then, I will be your legal guardian."

Except for a few birds, the yard was silent—just two expectant pairs of eyes locked on Spruill, and Millard clicking away on his gadget.

"What does that mean?" Jon Karl asked.

"It means I'll take care of you."

"Can we stay here?"

Spruill gave Jon Karl a wry smile. "Is that what you want?"

"Yes sir. We can already take care of ourselves, and if we lived here, we could figure out our own way to live."

Spruill laughed, admiringly. "Without your great-grandmother?"

"We'll still have her in our hearts," said Jon Karl.

That was about too much for Spruill. He dabbed away a tear and said, "You know how fortunate you are your mother brought you here, don't you?"

"Yes sir."

He sighed. "I was thinking you should move in with us—"

Millard looked up. "Yes! I want them to move in with us!" Then returned to his gadget.

"But y'all are so independent—I'm not sure what the best thing would be." He didn't mention the reception that idea had met with at home. He studied Jon Karl. "You're Millard's age, aren't you?"

"I'll be sixteen next month. Then I can drive us where we need to go. I can take us to school, I can buy groceries, I can cook—" No need to mention he was doing all that already.

"I can clean the house and do the laundry," said Summer.

"I know you can, sweetheart," he said to Summer. Then to Jon Karl: "Aren't you going to need a job?"

"Yes sir, I can get a job."

"Well, fact of the matter, I've been thinking about that too. I'm going to hire you to be Theotis's assistant. But I want you to understand, Theotis does a lot of work for me—he stays real busy. The man can do anything, and that's no exaggeration, and he does everything *right*. Nothing sloppy, he doesn't cut corners, he doesn't have a speck of half-ass in him. He'll work the ever-loving daylights out of you. I'm just telling you."

"I like Theotis," said Jon Karl.

Spruill sighed. "Any time you have to put down the address where you live, put down mine."

"Yes sir."

Chapter 23

Redwine Pyle

The next morning, Redwine was the first to call. He came in with two bags of groceries and an envelope that he left on the kitchen table. "For the pantry fund," he said. "I understand you will be staying here."

"I hope so," said Jon Karl.

They sat in the living room. Afterlife came over to check him out, seemed to remember him, and lay on the rug. "Y'all can offer me something if you want to, but it's too early for beer and I'll go ahead and tell you, I'm just fine, I don't need a thing."

"Oh!" said Jon Karl. "Can I offer you something?"

"No thank you, I'm just fine."

A brief silence.

"I'm going to miss that lady," Redwine said, "I'm sure going to miss her."

"Us too," said Jon Karl. The other half of "us," sitting up straight on the couch, blinked.

"Back in the day when I was married, we had some good times. Used to get together and have a beer or twelve. Odis was a mess, but your great-grandmother was solid as a rock. Always was. Damn if it don't seem like all the good ones is dying off." He coughed. "Feeling a little puny myself."

"It's too bad people have to die," said Jon Karl. "But I guess they do."

"Damn if I ain't starting to see a pattern myself," replied Redwine. "Of course, my grandaddy, my daddy's daddy—he was in the Great War—the only thing I remember about him is him saying the best thing would be never to have been in the first place. I've never been sure how you would manage that, but I've often thought he had a point. Y'all figure y'all can run the show around here all right?"

"Yes sir," said Jon Karl.

"Yes sir to you. And I will say this: you two ain't like nobody else I've ever met, especially as young as you are, and my money's on you."

"Thank you."

"You're welcome. Mr. Dawes has sure been looking out for you, hasn't he?"

"Yes sir, he has."

"If you keep saying 'sir,' I'm going to go ahead and pick out a casket."

"Sorry."

"He's done more good around here than the next fifty people. I'm not going to sit here and say everything he's done has been right by the book, which is not a complaint, just an observation, but he's give more than he's took. A durn sight more. And now, danged if he ain't stepped up to be your daddy."

"Cleetha Till said our real daddy was dead," Summer interjected. "She said somebody killed him. And whoever it was just got away with it."

"Well damn," said Redwine. "I'm sorry. I wish I could tell you that kind of thing don't happen, but I can't."

"Do you think it's true?"

"If Cleetha said it, that's the way it was."

"How does she know?" Jon Karl asked.

"Shoot, son, she couldn't even tell you. Folks just call it a sixth sense. Which is the beginning and the end of what they know about it. But I'm going to tell you something. She sits in that house day after day, people coming from six states to hear her tell them where their teeth's at, and she would tell you she's doing the work God give her to do, but she'd way rather somebody else did it."

"Really?"

"Hell yeah."

"You've known her all your life?"

"Son, I'm on the other side of eighty—'all my life' covers a lot of ground. She and me's the same age, and we both grew up in the country around here. We was in school together but I didn't really know her when we were little. But everybody knew *about* her. She told Lem Coker, the sheriff back then, where this poor woman whose sorry-ass piece of shit husband beat her up and strangled her's body was. They couldn't prove it, but everybody knew he'd done it—Cleetha wasn't but about fifteen—people said she was just trying to get attention, till they went and *looked* in that dried-up well—and from then on, ever sheriff that's stole his way into office has paid good taxpayer money for her services— even if there was a whole lot of people—mostly these ignorant country people, the kind you have to slow down when you drive by their church so you won't run over snakes—that was scared of her and would cross the street if they met her in town. I guess she was about fifteen or sixteen when we got to be friends—wasn't nothing romantic about it—she was nineteen, I think it was, when she married Earl Till, a farmer out there, he was about thirty—I think her daddy took the first offer just to get shed of her. This was before she started doing her readings, which she did a while for free—but it got to where it took up so much of her time, and she was a farm wife, ended up raising four children, with her husband out there beating his brains out in them fields from first light to last every day—I tell you, them dirt farmers just wore theirselves out back then—you were old at fifty, and more times than not didn't have nothing more than you started with to show for it— anyway, she had to start charging. She said when she was little her dreams would come true and she would dread going to sleep."

"Really?" Summer whispered.

Jon Karl just stared at Redwine.

"She could tell you where a cow was caught in a fence, when a mare was about to foal. She could find eggs, tell you where something you lost was, and *forget* about playing hide and seek with her, but she'd also come out with "Uncle Luster has been going to see a colored woman," or point right at the mayor on the sidewalk in town and say "That man is stealing money," that kind of thing, and her daddy especially didn't want anybody outside the family knowing about it. But of course everybody did know, and people used to spit on her in town, and cross their arms when they saw her, but mostly they just disappeared because of what she might point at them and say. The preacher—the damn preacher—called her a witch and wouldn't let her in the church. Her aunt, her mama's little sister, said she never had children because she was afraid that curse might run in the family."

A lull, as they absorbed that.

"I feel sorry for her," said Summer, deeply moved.

"Everybody's got their cross to bear," Redwine reminded her.

Chapter 24

Barber Balch

Word got around pretty fast, and folks started coming by, bringing food, paying their respects. Spruill was there all day with Jon Karl and Summer, and being a natural people person, took the pressure off them. He seemed to have an inexhaustible supply of Mildra stories. Like the time Ruthie, who had helped her mother when Mildra was growing up and she'd known all her life and loved her just like her own mother, died and Mildra sat in the wrong funeral for thirty minutes—and you know the brothers and sisters can get a whole *afternoon* out of a funeral—then finally asked the man sitting next to her whose funeral it was and he said "I don't know, I'm just here for the fucking"—(not in front of Jon Karl and Summer)—and laughter echoed through the house. You might say, the concluding sound of a life well lived.

Everybody had loved her. And the people who loved her the most were the ones who had known her the best. That could have been her epitaph. She was one of those it takes a funeral to unearth all the stories of generosity and big-heartedness and love because everybody had thought it had been directed just to them.

Then Afterlife started acting cagey, with a low-grade grumble in her throat.

Balch entered a room with his eyes. Even though he was a barber, physical contact was not his thing, and since childhood he'd had a habit of disinfecting his hands after contact with anybody. People spoke to him, but cursorily, then moved away—a win-win—a protracted interaction unthinkable. Balch's eyes would be busy elsewhere, and he would acknowledge these evanescent greetings with a barely perceptible moving of his lips.

He seemed to be examining the pictures on the walls, the froo on the shelves, the books in the bookcase, until a rare lull formed around Spruill, and he slipped in. His eyes took in Jon Karl and Summer, lingering a bit on the former, and he sort of said to Spruill, "I don't know when somebody's going to give this boy a haircut. And a shave." His throat made a funny sound, and his hand made an odd finger-snapping gesture, or something, toward Jon Karl, then sort of petered out. Jon Karl just stood his ground, staring at the man.

Summer, creeped out, kept her distance and checked on Afterlife every few minutes.

"I think he's gone past the point where he *can* cut it now," said Spruill. "We're all wagering on how long it will take it to reach the floor."

Balch just kept looking at Jon Karl, his jaw working.

As for the shave, it was only those whiskers on his upper lip and chin that he himself dealt with every three or four days.

"Will these kids be going to a home or—" Balch ventured.

"They've *got* a home," said Spruill, "so they won't be needing to go to one."

"I was just wondering. I could help—especially with this one—" nodding toward Jon Karl—"help with entertainment— take him places—or I thought he might want to learn about barbering—you can earn a good living—"

"That's very nice of you," said Spruill. "We'll keep it in mind."

Jon Karl glanced at Spruill, and just caught his eye.

The moment of "please accept my condolences but I need to be going" came and went, and Balch just stood there. Then, as though it were the finale of some inner conflict he took out his wallet, and turning slightly away, fingered through what appeared to be a pretty well-provisioned cache and, after a micro-debate, surgically extracted a twenty dollar bill. He just held it at first, then, to the accompaniment of a low growl from the corner, almost did, didn't, almost did, did proffer it to Jon Karl.

"Here's a twenty dollar bill for you. Twenty dollars was a lot of money in my day. If you spend it wisely you can make it go a long way. Or if you're smart you'll save it. Start a little nest egg."

An awkward moment—the bill suspended in the dubious space between them. Not knowing what else to do, Jon Karl reached for it, but when he tried to take it, Balch held it tightly. Then expressionlessly let it go.

"Thank you," said Jon Karl, holding it like a dead mouse by the tail.

Chapter 25

Farewell, Mildra

At the graveside the first thing Jon Karl was curious about was whether Mildra's half of the headstone would be filled in.

It wasn't. It seemed improper to be putting her in the ground with the final date left off. But then, it had been pretty improper to have her name on there at all while she was still alive. Jon Karl pictured some Grim Reaper type sitting there with hammer and chisel in his long bony fingers, waiting. He found out later from Spruill that it would be at least a week before they could get to it. As it turned out, it took two. And only then did everything seem to be in order.

The second thing he was curious about was actually more curious about him.

Zadie Dawes Gight. Giving him the eye.

She was twenty-two. She had a marriage, a brief one, behind her, and was back living with her father. She was one of the three offspring from his second marriage, matching the three from his first. Zadie wasn't living in the house—you could say she and Leela "didn't get along" and leave it at that. She had taken up in the loft above the garage and came and went as she pleased. Yes, Daddy was helping her a little, which infuriated Leela, since it was *Zadie*, not her, who had gone out and got herself knocked up, then married the loser, who—surprise!—had proved about as loyal as a snake slithering across your yard, then had an expensive abortion.

"Is she even looking for a job?" Leela asked one day.

"I think she's put in some applications," Spruill answered. "What I want her to do is finish her school."

She had done some work toward her Associate Degree at the junior college.

"I won't be holding my breath."

"She's my daughter. It hasn't got anything to do with you. She's just staying here until she gets on her feet."

"When will that be?" Leela wanted to know. "She's just running around spending your money."

"So, are you saying I'm depriving you?"

Leele dropped her eyes. "No."

"You're my sweet potato, aren't you?"

She raised her eyes back. With that look. And nodded.

Which marked an official end to the audible phase of the conflict.

Zadie wasn't bad looking, she just hadn't gotten the memo about how to dress for a funeral. Or maybe she had—the one from her brain stem. The one for funerals where that hot little piece of ass gypsy boy was going to be.

None of Spruill's children were what you'd call bashful when it came to the opposite, or in a couple of cases, the same, sex, but Zadie had snakes in her head.

"I can't even remember when I wasn't fucking," she would later tell Jon Karl. She had asked him about his first time and he had lied and said he couldn't remember, and she had told the truth and said she couldn't either.

Zadie liked anything that had sugar in it—don't even talk to her about a custard bismark, unless you're ready to go get in the car—and the only exercise she ever got was pouring big bowls of Cap'n Crunch. "Better be quick," Redwine would have said, "while you can still find it."

Not that Jon Karl had any such plans. Mr. Dawes' daughter? No sir.

The look she gave him as they left the cemetery said something else.

Chapter 26
Daryl Pays a Call

Two days later, the condolences spent, the new normal in place, Summer was drawing in her room, and Jon Karl was sitting on his end of the couch by the lamp, with a book on his lap and Afterlife beside him under her blanky. His mind had drifted—he had been listening to a group of people he didn't know in a room somewhere discussing something he couldn't remember—when Afterlife suddenly lifted her head alertly.

Jon Karl bestirred himself. "What is it, girl?" he asked.

A minute later a sharp rap sounded at the door.

Afterlife jumped down, half dragging her blanky, and started barking—and Jon Karl went to answer it. He opened the door to find a compact-sized man standing there. He wore a frown, his eyes locked on Jon Karl, and Jon Karl felt an electric tingle in his nerves. Behind the man, parked on the street, an old ratty Toyota with a woman in the passenger seat looking straight ahead smoking looked like it might start up and drive again, and it might not.

"What are you doing in my house?" the man asked.

A moment to process that. "What do you mean, your house?"

"The bitch did croak, didn't she?"

"What are you talking about?"

"You know what I'm talking about."

Then he pulled open the screen door and came inside. Afterlife growled and backed away.

The man looked around, an expression on his face like he smelled something, and his eyes came to rest on the couch.

"You let that goddamn dog on the furniture?" he asked.

"That's not any of your business—"

The man spun on him. "It is if I *make* it my business." He scowled at the upside down book in the circle of light cast by the lamp. "What are you doing—*reading*?"

Jon Karl looked at him—a dissolute air and a paunch despite his small stature, his hair, going gray, in a ponytail He looked rode-hard, so his age wasn't easy to guess. Maybe late fifties? His face had good features, handsome even, but was deeply lined and he needed a shave.

It was his eyes that froze Jon Karl. His familiar eyes.

And a smell.

"Who are you?" Jon Karl asked him.

"No, the question is, who are *you*?" the man returned. "Reading your *book* in my house with a goddamn filthy dog on the furniture."

"I live here," said Jon Karl.

"Correction: you *used* to live here. This is my house."

"I think you've got the wrong address—"

"You think I don't remember the goddamn house I grew up in? I'll give you till five o'clock to get out of here."

The pin-drop silence from Summer's room clearly said she had her ear to the door, listening.

"This is our house—"

"Our? Who the hell is '*our*'?"

"Me and my sister."

"Your sister? You ain't nothing but a damn kid. I'm going to start bringing some things in. And I ain't going to be sleeping on no goddamn couch neither. Especially one a damn dog's been licking its ass on. He's going to be the first thing to go."

"*What?*"

"You heard me. You got anything to eat in here?"

"No," said Jon Karl.

"We'll see about that."

The man went out to the Toyota and Jon Karl tapped on Summer's door. Her saucer-eyed face appeared in the crack. "Who is that?" she whispered.

"I don't want to tell you who I think it is. Call Mr. Dawes and tell him."

* * *

The man had brought in two or three boxes of clothes, some small appliances, tools and assorted crap, while the woman, a very skinny woman, had moved from the padding-spewing seat of the Toyota to a chair on the front porch, smoking a long cigarette, looking half strung-out, half disgusted.

"You too good to be giving me a hand with this shit?" the man said.

"It's just going to be going back," she said in a weary, raspy voice.

"The hell it is. I told you this is my house. I got a will." Then to Jon Karl he said, "Where's this damn sister you're talking about?"

"In her room."

"*Her* room? There ain't no *her* room. There's only *my* room, which is whatever room I say it is. And I need to get a good look at this sister, because I know I can damn sure do better than this thing I'm keeping alive."

The woman hardly reacted, as though it couldn't reach her anymore.

* * *

Ten minutes later, Spruill scorched to a stop behind the Toyota with a sheriff's car right behind him.

The man in the orange vest stood on the other side of the street, watching. The couple with the stroller had just passed, and they too paused a few houses down, looking back.

Spruill stormed up the walk, past the woman on the porch, the deputy clambering to keep up with him, then straight into the house.

He stopped six inches from the man's face.

"You've got exactly three minutes to get the hell out of here," he said. "And if you ever so much as show your face here again, I'll have you arrested for trespassing."

"You can't arrest me for being in my own house."

"You're right, I can't. If you had one. And if you do I'd advise you to go back there because this one is mine."

"Yours?"

"That's what I said. And it will stay mine until I decide it's time to deed it over to this young man and young woman. In perpetuity. As their great-grandmother wished."

"Their great-grandmother?" The man's surprised eyes cut from Spruill to Jon Karl and Summer.

"That's right. Their great-grandmother. And there's no time in that entire process where you will be welcome here."

"I got a will that says it's mine."

"Even if you did, which you don't, it would be superseded by the one drawn up, signed, and notarized six months ago and on file in the probate office."

"My mother said one day this house would be mine."

Spruill laughed. "That's your *will*?"

"I wrote down what she said. Signed by two witnesses."

"I'm guessing that was before you stole three credit card applications from her mail and maxed out three cards in her name, then stole her car and slinked away for thirty years."

"I don't know what you're talking about. I'm talking about I got a will."

"Maybe on the planet where you're from that would be considered a will, but not on this one."

"I can get a lawyer."

"So can I. And you'll need a good one if the District Attorney decides to prosecute, even if all that would mean is the taxpayers would have to feed you from now on. And don't even talk to me about your 'mother', when you didn't even bother to show up for her funeral."

"I didn't hear about it."

"Is that right? Then what brings you here?"

"I didn't hear about it in time."

"That's right. You didn't hear about it because you haven't had anything to do with your mother since she disowned you thirty years ago."

"Well—she's dead, what difference does it make now?"

Spruill could only sear him with his caustic stare. "You've got a fucking nerve. Deputy, this man is trespassing. Do your job."

Summer stood in Jon Karl's shadow in the hall, both of them listening intently.

The weary woman on the porch was overwhelmed with un-surprise.

Chapter 27

Wondering Who They Were

When Jon Karl and Summer walked into the Piggly Wiggly, people couldn't help but stare at them: the pretty boy with the long ponytail walking ahead, shadowed by the radiant waif who seemed connected to him by some invisible tether. She, spindly at fifteen, with her elfin ears, stood an inch taller than her older companion, and moved with her own peculiar grace as her eyes absorbed all the novelty around her. Though he was clearly the chief of this two-person tribe, anyone eavesdropping might have been touched by his deference to her input in all decisions of what and what not to buy, and the frugality of their deliberations. How could anyone look at them and not wonder who they were?

Chapter 28

The Library

Usually on grocery days they stopped by the library, that cool grotto that shut out the noise of the world and lured its introverts. They felt at home there.

Summer would find an empty table in the Young Adult section, sampling the wares and occasionally doodling little sketches of the funny people she had seen in the grocery store and were in no shortage in the library.

When they got home she would enhance and color them, and pass them to Jon Karl. Even when they looked like spiders, or penguins, or aliens, or were embedded in elaborate blooms or water towers or clouds, Jon Karl could tell who they were. "These are more than just crazy," Jon Karl, who got no end of delight in consuming every last detail of them, would say. He would even attempt a few himself. Since he couldn't draw, they were terrible—terrible, but funny. Summer would laugh silently and so hard tears would roll down her face. She would recover herself, dab her eyes with the bedsheet, then go on to the next one. Could the unsuspecting people around them, going about their ordinary errands, ever have guessed what characters they were in the alter-world of that curious pair?

Like a light, Summer also conjured one or more of the awkward moths that tended to flutter around her. One in particular, Leonard, always seemed to know when she would be there, as evidenced by his being there too. He was oblivious to the cues of indifference in her as he expounded the plot of the latest science fiction novels he devoured. Summer herself just felt sorry for him.

Meanwhile, Jon Karl would prowl the non-fiction aisles—psychology and philosophy, religion, social sciences, natural science, history—searching for the (he was pretty sure) faded magenta, or maybe violet, book, possibly with water splotches on the spine and, you would think, glowing, that he had once, and only once, held in his hand. On that day, a couple of years back, he had selected the book at random, taken it to his table and read a paragraph somewhere in the middle—then, stunned, looked up and said out loud: "Wow."

So simple, so clear.

Then Summer had beckoned to him from her table across the room, and still blinded by that gleam of revelation, he went over to look at the photograph of a python ingesting a fawn she wanted to show him. When he returned to his table, the book was gone. Another patron had picked it up? An aide had reshelved it? He would never know—but his search for it began that day and continued to this. He kept the faith that he would someday find it, and have in his hands again the answer to the vital question he couldn't remember.

The modus operandi of his search had evolved. Now he just went down the aisles, touching the spines of the books, waiting for one to give him the right feeling—and when he convinced himself one did, he would take it to his table and delve into its secrets. Sometimes he would lose interest, take it back and find a replacement, sometimes he would just scan it, sometimes he would be drawn into reading long sections, and sometimes, if it really grabbed him, he would check it out and take it home. But always, he would know it wasn't *the book*. The one that answered everything. Still, he had learned about a lot of things that way: plate tectonics, Genghis Khan, the history of garlic, the communication of trees, quantum entanglement, spirit animals, the heat death of the universe, and so forth.

He had grown to appreciate the state of not knowing what he was looking for.

Chapter 29

The Gazebo

Leela had always fancied a gazebo.

Nobody in her family or anybody she knew had had a gazebo when she was growing up. But she had seen them in the yards of better-off people and in home and garden magazines.

"A gazebo," Spruill repeated, tasting the word as though not quite sure what it meant. "Are we talking about the same thing?"

"I don't know," she said. "And I've decided the perfect place for it."

A flat spot just off the path from the house to the lake.

She had found some examples in her magazines but she didn't want just an imitation, she wanted her own personal touch.

Spruill showed the pictures to Theotis. He studied them silently, with an expression that might have been thinking about being a frown, then exhaled and looked up at Spruill.

"That fancy stuff, have to pay somebody with a scroll saw," he said.

"You couldn't do it?"

"I *could*—"

"How much would they charge?"

"I have to find out."

Spruill nodded. "You can build something like that?"

"Yeah," said Theotis. "I build it just fine. But it ain't gone be overnight."

"How long, do you think?"

Theotis shook his head, uncertainly. "It's hard to say. I have to figure it all out and draw up the plans for it. That take a while. Then cut everything and put it together. Paint it. A month or two, at least."

"Can your guys cover you?"

"About would have to."

"Maybe you could work half days on it."

"Might could. Might not go fast enough to suit Miss Leela."

"I'll worry about Miss Leela."

"I have to have some help."

"You've got Jon Karl."

"Yeah—he probably be some good. Might need Billy Lirenzo too."

* * *

"This here some sensuous work," said Theotis.

"Sensuous work?" Jon Karl asked, puzzled.

"Yeah—since you was here, why don't you do this too?"

Jon Karl laughed, and Theotis said, "You gone be any help to me?"

"I learn fast," Jon Karl replied. "If you just show me what to do."

"Don't know how much time I have for *showing* while I'm busy *doing*. You just have to be *watching*, and do what I tell you."

"I can do that."

"And I'm gone tell you something. That hair hanging down to your butt, and the kind of work we do, don't really go together."

Jon Karl absorbed what he was saying, and in a sudden epiphany realized that his hair was, and for a while had been, a pain in the ass. He nodded. First time for everything. The only thing he knew was he wouldn't be going to Barber Balch.

A gazebo. His first job.

Chapter 30

Theotis

Everything Mr. Dawes had said about Theotis proved to be true—except he left out, as resumés do, the soul of the man.

He did indeed work Jon Karl hard, he was indeed exacting, but Jon Karl loved it. He loved the feeling that he was *doing* something, and from Theotis—a master carpenter, plumber, electrician, mechanic, who could figure anything out, fix anything—he absorbed everything he could with great relish.

Jon Karl was still in school—bored, wasting his life as he saw it—and usually managed to skip out after lunch and spend the afternoon with Theotis. For the first week or so Theotis was at his drafting table, in the mornings anyway, designing Leela's gazebo to the sixteenth of an inch. If Theotis was tied up, Jon Karl would work with Billy Lirenzo and Billy Reuben.

And Mr. Dawes was paying him twelve dollars an hour.

* * *

Spruill owned rental houses and office buildings all over town, and two large apartment complexes. The maintenance was endless. Theotis had a competent crew of Guatemalan underlings to whom he relegated much of it, unless some serious figuring-out was needed. Jon Karl had never known, let along worked for, anybody like Theotis—who could look at a situation, listen to it, smell it, and cut right to the bottom of it. "I believe the problem is—" he would say, then finish that sentence with a working hypothesis that ninety-nine percent of the time would be dead-on. The rare times he was stumped would energize him like someone bent on revenge.

At night, Summer would listen to tales of the man's ingenuity.

Theotis's grandsons, Billy Lirenzo and Billy Reuben, worked on the crew and though quite skilled, were not their grandfather. Maybe one day they would be, but not yet. Billy Lirenzo was twenty, with a baby, and Billy Reuben was in tenth grade. Jon Karl, who could learn more in one afternoon in the library than in an entire year of school, was a most uncommitted and bored high school senior. After just a couple of weeks of working with Theotis he started to think about dropping out of school. Really, what was the point? He kept this ambition private for a while, and then finally one day mentioned it to Theotis.

The intensity of the man's reaction took him by surprise.

"Here I was thinking you had some sense," Theotis said, a look of bewilderment at such stupidity transforming his usually placid face. "You ain't got but half a year left and you talking about dropping out? Just talking about dropping out, period, no matter how much you got left."

"But I'm not learning anything and I've found what I want to do."

"Tell you what, I'll check back after a roof job or two in July about *that*. And whether you learning something or not ain't what it's about—it's about having the piece of paper to show The Man. Boy, don't you know, all these rich people out here, that's exactly what they want you to do: drop out, just take whatever handouts you can get, and not even *try* to run with them? Don't you know that's the one thing they been trying to get you to do since day one? Get out of the way? Both my sons, and then Billy Lirenzo and Billy Reuben too, said the same thing. Mon drop out. Shit, drop out. I told them, I said, you drop out, I'm done with you. I meant it too. We didn't fight all these years to get education just to piss it away. I ain't worried about what happen on the other side of the door—the fight is getting *in* that door. I look around here at all these young people going to waste, got their butt hanging out their pants, like going to prison gone get you somewhere, dropped out of school, ain't got no job, ain't got nobody to look up to, everywhere they turn another door slam in their face, always looking for some shortcut to get rich—drugs, usually—like somebody ain't even *on* the bench, they *behind* the bench, watching everybody else play the game. Most of them ain't got a chance anyway, but they damn sure ain't got a chance without education. I tell you when you finished—you finished when you quit trying. What you call somebody drop out of school is a *fool*."

"I could get a GED."

"Yeah, you *could*. But you too young to understand how life trick you into a rut fo you know what hit you. How you get into habits, and them habits eat you up. Every day you live make it that much harder to change. You get your education when you young or you ain't got a chance."

"Did *you*?"

"Not all the way. I didn't have no choice, I had to help my daddy. But that was a different time and I got lucky. It ain't like you find a Mr. Dawes under every rock out there."

"What about Billy Lirenzo? He finished high school and he's working for Mr. Dawes. It didn't do him any good."

"But what if something better come along? What if he decide to go to that junior college like Sherica?"

"What's she studying?"

"Something about computers. You think you ain't got to know about computers out there, you ain't paying attention. And Miriam too."

"Yeah, Miriam. I think she's your—niece?"

"She is."

"She's—"

"My brother's daughter. And I'm gone tell you right now, she's as fine as they come."

"Her husband?—"

"Yeah. Her *husband*. You probably ain't never heard me use the expression 'worthless piece of shit'."

"I don't believe I have."

"That's because I don't use it unless there is one. That's all I'm gone say."

"Okay," said Jon Karl, and that was indeed all he said. He pressed on. "Billy Reuben doesn't like school either, and he said he didn't want to go to college."

"Billy Reuben like you—ain't nothing but a boy. Don't know his brain from his butt. You think what he gone want today same as what he gone want tomorrow, you crazy."

"He works hard."

"Yeah, he work hard because I stay on him. Minute I let up, good luck finding him. What he gone do if something happen to me?"

"Billy Reuben will do good."

"*Do* good, or *be* good?"

"Come on, he's your grandson."

"Yeah. He my grandson for sure. Pure mischief."

"Nothing wrong with a little mischief."

"Yeah—if you white. If you black, it don't do you no good around here."

* * *

Whatever design Theotis came up with, a succession of them, wasn't quite right. Leela would frown apologetically and say it was nice, but not quite what she had in mind. What *did* she have in mind? Well, that was the problem. So as usual Theotis found himself in the frustrating position of trying to figure out something exact for somebody who had only a feeling.

"You know, kind of frilly on the sides with some kind of doo-dad on the roof."

"This on *top* of everything else I got to do," Theotis had once let slip to Jon Karl.

153

Jon Karl shook his head. "She didn't want me and Summer living with them."

"You blame her? Hell, I don't want you living with *me* neither."

Finally Spruill had to step in.

"Baby, I love you, but I can't spare Theotis on all this," he told Leela. "Just decide on something so we can go on and get it done."

How unfair! Did he honestly not know how much it meant to her?

Honestly, he did—but he also knew it was time to build the damn thing and be done with it.

"Ain't nothing to do but just do it," Theotis told Jon Karl. "Even if you know no matter what you do she ain't gone like it."

Jon Karl scowled. "Mrs. Dawes—I don't know about her. She's—"

"Just stop right there. Don't even think about finishing whatever it is you about to say. Mr. Dawes crazy about that woman. That's all you need to know."

"I know you respect Mr. Dawes."

"Son, if you don't know how much I respect Mr. Dawes, you don't know what respect is. You'd be sitting here a long time if you tried to list everything that man has done for me."

"You've done a lot for him too—"

"And I plan to keep on doing it too. Mr. Dawes all but give me that land for my house—"

"But *you* built the house."

"Yeah, where you think I got the *opportunity*? I strike down the first man say something bad about Mr. Dawes around me."

* * *

Jon Karl was averaging thirty hours a week working with Theotis. It turned out he *did* learn fast and had an aptitude for the work, and after a couple of months he had done a little of everything, digesting and trying to remember it all, and had become a valuable toter and gofer. The first time he hit his thumb with a hammer, Theotis just commented, "Do it again, I didn't feel nothing," and repeated it every time after that until Jon Karl stopped.

Theotis was easing him into power tools, even if not near fast enough for Jon Karl.

"You talking about something take your hand off before you blink your eyes," Theotis said. "I don't believe in getting in a hurry about nothing, but you *damn* sure don't want to get in a hurry with nothing you got to plug in."

The foundation, floor and wiring of the gazebo were done, with lattice around the bottom, and Leela came down to look at it with crossed arms and a bit of a glower—then a major plumbing emergency at Orchid Pointe had taken all the manpower, and work on the gazebo had languished for a while.

Three hundred and sixty dollars a week under the table was good money—enough for gas and groceries and bills, and even a little rainy day savings account. Jon Karl kept up with all that, but Summer liked to see the account register where the interest of five or six cents was added every month. The sum had gotten up to about eight hundred dollars. She just stared at it and felt rich.

Jon Karl loved working with Theotis, and though he still seethed about it sometimes, had resigned himself to finishing school. He was a marginal presence there—just a couple of what you'd call friends in the whole place, a tolerated freak to everybody else, belonging to nothing, attending nothing, doing the absolute minimum in the dreary classes.

Only one thing kept the experience from being pure Hell: Ms. Quilliam. His English teacher. Jon Karl knew, because he asked her, that she was twenty-four years old. He also knew, because it was obvious, that she was fond of him. She was pretty, with sleepy eyes, and he would stop by her room sometimes in the afternoons, and they would talk. She was the one person who wasn't telling Jon Karl "You need to go to college!" because she said not everyone needed to. Yes, she herself had gone, and it had gotten her this job, but most days she felt like she'd been tricked. People who did no real work except create useless work for the people who did, made most of the money.

Jon Karl loved to hear her talk about her dreams: she wanted to travel, she wanted to see where all the famous writers lived, she wanted to *do* things. And what was she doing? Grading these stupid papers day after day. When she asked about *his* dreams, Jon Karl was surprised to realize he didn't really have any. He just wanted to make enough money half the day to do what he wanted the other half. And he wanted Summer to be happy. Ms. Quilliam was touched because she could tell he meant it. And that he knew it might be a bit complicated. Jon Karl wondered if Ms. Quilliam had seen the photographs of him, but since everybody had, he figured she probably had too. Funny thing, he didn't care anymore. And she never even hinted at it.

The novelty had long worn off.

Girls never acknowledged him in public, but still found ways to approach him in private. He kept finding himself lured into trysts, thrilling enough, but he didn't tell anybody, and only hinted to Summer, how humiliated they were making him feel. Every time, he would end up thinking about Evelyn, even though he couldn't really remember what she had looked like. What memory he could conjure was starting to look a lot like Ms. Quilliam.

Summer, meanwhile, approaching sixteen, was beginning to bloom—"filling out" as women innocently say—men have more colorful expressions. The days of her sneaking into Jon Karl's bed had long gone the way of bathing together, and she had become more private, naturally, but not really modest. Insecure as she was about her social status, her abnormality, she had never been and never would be shy about her body. Neither was Jon Karl. Of course, living together, having grown up together, they were aware of, but immune to, each other's physical selves—but one day Jon Karl walked by Summer's open bedroom door to see her standing there after her bath, and seemed all of a sudden to see her. She looked at him.

"I'm not a little girl anymore," she said.

"I can see that."

Chapter 31
Making Money

Jon Karl took her to school every day where, unlike himself, having no distractions, she delved into the work and obsessed over her grades. He was still driving Mildra's thirteen year old Taurus, and even starting to give Summer some terrifying lessons on the weedy softball field in the park. The Taurus was a decent car, which along with every other car in the world Jon Karl had never really thought about, then abruptly one day did, and began to notice other cars. Just like that, the idea of getting a different vehicle wormed its way into his head. He said something to Mr. Dawes, who told him he doubted they could get more than a few hundred dollars for Mildra's car, if that, and when the time came, he would help Jon Karl get a bank loan that he would have to make payments on, and that cooled him down a little.

Millard had *his* heart set on a Lamborghini and lobbied relentlessly.

"No Lamborghinis," Spruill said.

"I never get what I want!" Millard cried.

Which of course wasn't true, but Millard knew how to plant seeds.

In the meantime, the black Jeep Wrangler served just fine.

Jon Karl got to looking at cars more and more. He liked most all of the newer cars he was, as it were, seeing for the first time, but had nothing particular in mind. Something appropriate for a family. Because, as he saw it, that's what he and Summer were. He started checking into the figures, got ten thousand dollars in his head, and one day he told Millard he might need to make a little extra money on the side somehow.

"You could make a fortune on Clicks for Dicks," Millard said. "I'm just telling you."

"I'm not doing that," Jon Karl said.

"Whatever," said Millard. "I do know of another option."

"What?"

"Let me see if I can get the ball rolling first."

* * *

"How long will you be gone?" Summer asked.

"We're going somewhere on the river, so probably a couple of hours," Jon Karl told her.

Afterlife always knew when he was leaving and sat there looking despondently at him. "Give Afterlife some hugs," he said, and sneezed. Afterlife just kept looking at him.

"When you sneeze, how does a dog know you sneezed and weren't mad at him?" Summer asked.

"You got me," said Jon Karl.

When Millard came by in the Wrangler to pick up Jon Karl, Zadie got out of the passenger seat in tight white shorts barely doing their job, a low-cut green mesh almost-see-through blouse, and a floppy cowboy hat.

"Hey, Jon Karl," she smiled.

Jon Karl's eyes said "What's she doing here?" but he didn't say anything out loud. Millard caught his drift.

"Zadie's cool," he said. "She wants to show us something."

"There's all kind of things I want to show you," she said and got in the back seat so Jon Karl could get in the front.

Summer and Afterlife watched out the living room window.

They headed out Troubleneck Road towards the lake. Jon Karl watched the rural world drift by, reflecting how you tended to see the same things when you were driving, but saw other things, like another version of the world, when you were riding. He liked driving, but it was nice to ride sometimes when you didn't have to watch the road and could see the sights.

He noticed, for example, past a crimson clover filled ditch, a little house, closer to a shack, with a toy and junk cluttered yard, a sagging badminton net, and several dubiously functional vehicles—the one squeezed, apparently in another geological era, into the rickety added-on car shed, certainly not. Some canna lilies tried to survive in the dust around the sagging front porch, and over on the bare side yard a tall shirtless white teenage kid was shooting hoops on a plywood goal. All the times Jon Karl had come by here and he'd never noticed the place. The kid was knocking them down, and Jon Karl's mind spun a quick fantasy of him working hard, becoming a basketball star, buying his hardworking mother and bedridden father a new house, seeing the infirm man raising himself up in his bed with tears of gratitude . . .

And a smell. Both strange and familiar. What *was* that?

On the other side of the lake they headed north, following the river. After a couple of miles Millard said, "Along in here?"

Zadie was leaning forward, looking. "Yeah. I'll know it when I see it."

Millard slowed for all the side roads, and then about a mile later Zadie exclaimed, "That's it!" and Millard wheeled them onto a dirt road disappearing into the woods.

After an oblivious mile Millard said, "You sure?" and she said "Pretty sure," and after another mile, a carbon copy of the first, they came upon an overgrown driveway, and a just visible roofline a ways back from the road, and she said, "This is it." Millard pulled into the overgrown driveway and they got out.

All abandoned houses have their own mystique—an idiosyncratic mystique written by time. A place where *is* has surrendered to *was*, and the people to ghosts. Jon Karl stood there taking the place in, hearing the distant whistle of a train, and feeling a mysterious attraction: a good-sized brick ranch house, still more or less intact, though the roof shingles were buckling, and some delinquent shrubs blooming cluelessly around it hadn't heard the news—all of it, in fact, content to be what it was and apparently unconcerned with or unaware of what it had been—and he couldn't help but imagine the place in its people-time, the house maintained, painted, the grounds groomed, kids playing, Mama cooking supper and calling out the back door wanting to know what was the matter with little Grover, Dad down in the chicken houses.

Because, as three long, parallel, now roofless buildings testified, this had been a chicken farm.

Had been. But hadn't been for some time.

"Who lived here?" Jon Karl asked.

"Tamela Johnson's grandparents," said Zadie. "She owns it now. Nobody else in her family wanted it."

"Imagine that."

"Oh, its days aren't over," she said. "We've got plans."

"You going into the chicken business?"

"Not chickens."

Jon Karl looked at her, standing there oozing out of her clothes, smiling conspiratorially.

"I'm confused," he said.

"It's just a matter of time before it's legal," Millard offered.

"Recreational and medical," Zadie added.

"It's like everything, dude," said Millard. "It's all about who's ahead of the curve when it gets here. Which, I can tell you, it's coming. Sooner than you think."

"You talking about growing dope?" Jon Karl asked.

"Yeah, but not this jackleg shit you get around here. High quality shit. The best."

"Oh," said Jon Karl. "You know how?"

"I've read some stuff," said Millard.

"So have I," said Zadie. "And Tamela knows a lot. She grows orchids. I mean, like, you know, for her house. Is that not cool?"

"I guess."

"You said you wanted to make some money," said Millard.

"Yeah? What would I have to do?"

"We need somebody out here."

"What—you mean live here?"

"No. Just two or three times a week. There's shit you got to do. And go in on the seeds. And equipment."

"How much are the seeds?"

"Five hundred bucks—"

"*What?*"

"That's nothing, man. We're talking Petunia Death Dream. Straight from Colorado. There's nothing like that around here. Not even close. I already have a guy who will buy all we have. Five hundred plants, with these fucking buds—unbelievable—you can get a pound per plant—five hundred bucks per pound—you're talking half a mil."

"I don't believe it—"

"Believe it. And is this not the perfect place?" He swept his arms around. "Middle of nowhere? Can't see it from the road? Nobody living within a mile?"

"What equipment?"

"The usual shit. Some buckets. The well needed a new pump. Tamela got some guy to do it."

"How much was that?" Jon Karl asked.

"Well, it was a couple of grand—I covered it," said Millard. "You can pay me when we get paid. We had to get a generator too, to run it."

"How much was that?"

"Don't worry about it. I can jack off four or five times for my fans and make that."

"You're such a *pervert*," said Zadie.

"*I'm* a pervert?" Millard cried, then turned back to Jon Karl. "I'm telling you—the money's going to be crazy. Nobody's going to give a shit about a couple thousand dollars."

"Did you already get the seeds?" Jon Karl asked.

"That's where we're headed now," said Millard.

"Which would be—"

"The Mud House."

"What's the Mud House?"

"Come on. I'll show you."

Chapter 32

Mud House Again

He took them a few more miles north, not too many people living out there, most of them giving you the impression they weren't interested in company. What was with all the country churches? They passed at least ten. What kind of per capita ratio would that be? Concrete dinner on the grounds tables under the shade trees. Maybe a church van parked under a metal car shelter. Where would a country church van go? Disney World? No, probably go out and round up the righteous and afflicted on Sunday mornings. Cemetery usually on the side. Several spots along the road where there were just little cemeteries, by nothing. But well maintained. You're real as long as somebody remembers you.

From one county road to another, and after a few turns Jon Karl realized if he had to find his way back out here, he'd be shit out of luck. The final road, where you had to go around a gate, was barely one, just wide enough for a car, badly rutted, with a few stretches of what looked like permanent mud, and extemporized bypasses through the woods. At last they tumbled out into a sort of trashy yard with six or seven muddy trucks and a few little shit-cars parked around a bizarre-looking house, and off to the side, a caboose. A flag with one angry eyeball showing drooped listlessly on a pole. And the thud of some serious country rock.

A skinny guy, maybe in his thirties, in shorts, a ball cap, and barefoot, his lower arms and neck tanned deep bronze, his skeletal chalky torso bright with sunburn, approached them, a beer in one hand, a cigarette in the other.

"You looking for somebody?" he asked.

"I'm Millard, man."

The guy squinted. "Oh. Yeah. I remember you."

"Is Herschel here?"

"He's out in the river."

Their voices shrank in Jon Karl's mind as he stood there looking around. The house. The caboose. The sounds from the water below. The smell. A quiver ran along his nerves, and he seemed to step across some crevice of time. Not déjà vu exactly, but a feeling that time had unfolded to the end and made it this far back. It was not until Millard took him by the shoulders, and his familiar smiling face came into focus, that Jon Karl realized somebody had been talking to him.

"You okay, man?"

"Yeah," said Jon Karl.

"You took a little starship cruise, dude. We're heading down to the river."

The path there was basically a muddy slope with sapling trunks embedded across it for traction. Treacherous nonetheless. The surrounding woods teemed with poison ivy, beer cans and garbage, a rotting johnboat, a couple of busted canoes, and the wheelless remains of some ancient motorcycle. The bluff to the left could only be a mudslide, but no sliders. Everyone seemed to be out on the water.

The river split there, the deeper channel on the far side, the shallower on the near, and rocks and a sandbar island in between. The first thing Jon Karl noticed, no doubt the first thing anybody would have noticed, was a 300-pound gal in a Confederate flag two-piece, chugging a beer shin-deep in the water. She finished and tossed the can downstream.

"Don't throw the goddamn beer can in the river!" someone yelled at her.

"I'll throw the goddamn beer can anywhere I want to!" the girl returned. "Including up your ass!"

Laughter.

Fifteen or twenty people altogether, a few in camp chairs on the sandbar, the rest in the shallow water. The women, exhibiting the spectrum of body types, looked okay from a distance, but even from there Jon Karl could see the ravaged faces of some. At the edge of the water a little group huddled around a pipe. One guy with a spinning rod stood on the far side of the sandbar casting toward the bank. The pounding music was coming from somewhere out there.

"Herschel!" Millard called.

It took a couple of tries. Finally a bearded guy with wet hair to his shoulders, sitting in the shallow water, looked up to the bank.

"It's me!"

The guy gestured and finished his beer. Then he stood up and started looking for his shorts and another beer.

An emaciated fellow, also with crazy hair and a stringy beard, came with him as they dog paddled their way, beers aloft, across the narrow channel to the rickety and chaotic collection of tree trunks that served as a dock, and pulled themselves out.

"You know Zadie," Millard said.

"Everybody knows Zadie," said Herschel.

"And this is Jon Karl."

"Hey, man," said Jon Karl, but he was fixated on the other guy, who was fixated on him.

"Jon Karl?" the guy said, and it was his voice that did it. Because he sure didn't look the same.

"Damn, man," said Jon Karl. "Tyler?"

His last memory of him, trying to grope Summer, dissipated in the presence of this current creature, just as did Tyler's of Jon Karl, wielding a shovel.

A complete severance of then and now.

Sores on his face, tracks on his tatted arms, maybe ninety pounds of him, his legs like sticks falling out of his cavernous shorts. A couple of strategic teeth missing, the others looking starkly separate.

Something like a nod acknowledged Jon Karl. Whatever he mumbled didn't quite make it to words. Jon Karl almost asked, "How have you been?" but it seemed like a stupid question. Neither of them could think of anything to say.

"Come on inside," said Herschel.

They headed for what looked like the only door, Tyler limping. It was cool in the Mud House, so apparently mud and straw walls were good insulation. But dim too. No electricity. Against one wall a row of assault rifles were locked in a metal frame. Over by one of the windows Herschel unlocked the padlock on a wooden box, fished out a Tupperware container and opened it.

"Five hundred Petunia Death Dream," he said. "Feminized, hand-selected. Guaranteed."

Jon Karl took a peek at the bounty of fat, dark seeds, and something about it seemed a little exciting. He just glimpsed Millard passing Herschel a wad of bills.

Back outside, Herschel said, "Want a beer?"

"Yeah, I'll take a beer," said Millard.

"Me too," said Zadie.

"No thanks," said Jon Karl.

Herschel looked surprised. "You don't like beer?"

"Not really."

Herschel blinked a couple of times, not sure how to take that. "You want something else?"

"He doesn't drink anything," Millard intervened. "He doesn't like it."

"Damn," said Herschel, and lit a fat roach.

Jon Karl waved it away.

"You don't smoke either?" Herschel asked him.

Jon Karl shook his head.

"Damn," said Herschel, and turned to Millard. "You didn't bring a spy, did you?"

Millard laughed. "He's my friend."

"I can't understand somebody that don't like to get high," said Herschel, not belligerently, just genuinely puzzled.

Jon Karl shrugged. "I just don't."

"He's cool," said Millard.

"Let's go swimming," said Zadie.

As they headed back down the slippery path to the water, Jon Karl and Tyler held back. Zadie looked over her shoulder to Jon Karl. "You coming?"

"Eh-h," he said noncommittally.

Tyler had lit a cigarette and stood there smoking. Jon Karl turned to him.

"You're looking at it," said Tyler.

"How come you're limping?" was all Jon Karl could think of to say.

"I had a bike wreck a couple of years ago. Messed up my leg. Hurt like fuck. My old man got pissed off and said he wasn't going to pay for anything. I should have had it operated on—it was about to kill me—but I didn't. I had to go to about five doctors before I found one who gave enough of a shit to help me. Percocets. Then after about six months he said he was 'releasing' me and I was going to have to find a new doctor. He recommended this guy and I went to him and he cut off the Percocets and wouldn't prescribe nothing. On the street I could get two for ten dollars. Forty bucks for oxycontin. Forget that shit. Or I could get a spoon for five dollars. When you ain't got shit you notice that five is less than ten."

Jon Karl felt hot standing close to him. "It still hurts?"

"Yeah it still hurts."

"Are you living out here?"

"Sometimes. When they start doing that militia shit I get the hell out of here."

"What militia shit?"

Tyler gestured toward the flag. Jon Karl could see a snake head on it now. Open mouth, fangs, flared nostrils, malevolent eyes.

"Oh, man," he said, "don't ask. These fuckers come from Atlanta. They got rules about needles and fags. I get sick of being out here anyway."

"You go home?"

Tyler laughed. "Yeah. Home. My old man kicked me out. Said don't ever come back, then decided to go ahead and croak. It was about time. He's probably about medium-rare in Hell by now, waving his Bible around. I now know it's possible to die of being a hypocritical son of a bitch."

"What about your mother?"

"She died too. Goddamn, that woman didn't stand a chance. Sometimes dying is the only thing you got. I'm not going to stand here and say I don't understand that. Being sick of the whole goddamn thing. Just fucking sick of it."

Better never to have been in the first place.

* * *

When Jon Karl got back to the riverbank, Millard had shed his clothes and was splashing some squealing girls in the shallow water. Zadie, on the sandbar, had debloused and was just stepping out of her shorts. Still in her hat, she waved to Jon Karl, gestured "Come on!", jiggled for him, then headed for the water.

She could lose a few, but next to the girl in the desecrated Confederate flag, she didn't look too bad. At least Big Mama didn't take her bathing suit off. Like that roadhouse outside Tarville Redwine had told him about.

"There were these, I guess you'd say, strippers, in there. They made all their money from the men paying them to keep their clothes on."

Jon Karl had one desire at that moment: to not be there. That familiar feeling of being out of step with everyone else. The ones who had brought him were having fun, and he just wanted to go. He looked back where Tyler had disappeared around the back of the house, as though he might join him. But the feeling Tyler had given him threatened to suffocate him. Something more than depression—but just call it depression for short.

He didn't follow the others to the water, but ventured back to the yard—no sign of Tyler now—and navigated carefully through the poison ivy and refuse, scanning every footfall for snakes, to the caboose. He mounted the steps onto the rear platform. The doors on both ends stood open and he could see all the way through and up into the cupola. He picked his way through the broken glass and crumpled beer cans and debris, and stepped inside. Mostly gutted, but a bunk area, kitchen, little desk. His mind wandered—he was the caboose man in the time of its working life, the fields and woods going by the windows—lonely being stuck back there?—the long dull unchanging hours.

Just fucking sick of it. Universal human fate.

How long had it been a working caboose? Twenty years? Thirty? Now enjoying the peace that passeth understanding amid a sea of poison ivy in a broom closet of the universe.

A yelp from the river reached him, but felt far away. Irrelevant. *I'm still me*, he thought. *There are the woods, the mosaic of the sky through the trees, the air, the clouds.*

Same as always. Me.

Chapter 33

More Growing Pains

Millard wanted to bring the seeds back home, but Jon Karl made him drop them off at the chicken farm house. No need for a key. Millard shoved the front door open, and they went inside. Most of the windows were choked with vines and overgrown shrubbery, and it was dim, musty, and cool in there. Heart pine floors, wavy linoleum in the kitchen. The shredded remains of a rug or two. Peeling wallpaper. A few water stained blotches on the ceilings. Eerily, several pieces of apparently unwanted furniture, including a ravaged upright piano and on old busted-out TV. A few utensils on a table in the kitchen, a bathrobe hanging on a nail in a bedroom closet. Some lonely coat hangers on the rod. In the bathroom a framed print of a big-eyed girl with a swan.

Did they leave in a hurry or something?

Were the Huns coming?

In one of the bedrooms a big black Hefty bag, stuffed with something, hulked in one of the corners. *There's not enough money in the world*, Jon Karl thought, *to get me to open that.* Askew in the middle of the room a listing broken-legged bed frame with only the gnawed boxsprings provided a haven for rats. And of course, where there are rats—

But Jon Karl wasn't really afraid of snakes. They eat rats, not people. Millard was still holding the tub of seeds as they reconvened in the kitchen.

"Creepy," said Zadie.

But Jon Karl was feeling that outside of time feeling again, and a profound sense of repose. The place exerted an odd attraction.

"Where do you want me to put them?" Millard asked, like somebody speaking from a tunnel.

Jon Karl looked at him. "Put what?"

"The seeds."

"Put them in the refrigerator," suggested Zadie.

Would it even open?

It would. Only a few condiment jars in there. Luckily sealed.

* * *

When they pulled up in front of Jon Karl's house, a mo-ped with a helmet on the seat was parked on the front walk.

"You've got company," said Millard.

Jon Karl looked curiously. "Hm."

"I'll call you tomorrow."

"Bye, Jon Karl," said Zadie as she wiggled into the front seat.

* * *

Afterlife was whining at the door as Jon Karl walked in. Leonard was standing in the middle of the room, awkwardly, like he had just stood up. Summer stood a few feet away. All three pairs of eyes, one pair a little dreamily, were focused on Jon Karl as he stood there massaging Afterlife's ears.

"I was just leaving," said Leonard. "I mean I was just—going."

"Okay," said Jon Karl.

Leonard lingered uncomfortably for a few more seconds then, looking down, hurried out. Jon Karl watched him, then looked over at Summer.

"Hey," he said.

"Hey."

"What's going on?"

"Nothing. Leonard came to visit."

"I see that. Excuse me, I've got to take a leak."

As he headed down the hall he heard the mo-ped try a few times to start, then catch. The buzzing sound disappeared down the street.

Coming back up the hall, Jon Karl glanced in Summer's room and saw the tousled bed.

He returned to the living room and Summer was still standing there. She hadn't moved. Her big eyes followed him. "Did y'all eat?" he asked. A pizza box sat on the coffee table.

She nodded.

"I guess I'll fix something."

"He only stayed for a little bit."

"I don't care how long he stayed. I want you to have friends come over." They looked at each other. "What'd y'all do?"

She looked like she was about to say something, but didn't. Then she said, "I'm sixteen."

"I know how old you are." Another silence. Then, "Summer, I don't care what you do. Your life is your business." He studied her face. "Do you like him?"

"He's real good at math."

Jon Karl laughed. "I asked if you liked him."

"They get those good jobs, don't they?"

Jon Karl laughed again. "I guess. I don't know. But you still haven't answered my question. Do you like him?"

"I feel sort of sorry for him."

"I don't think that's the same thing. I know plenty of girls I don't like or feel sorry for either one."

She didn't say anything, just kept looking at him.

"You know that's how you get pregnant, right?"

Now her expression changed. "You must think I'm stupid."

"Summer, I think you're a lot of things, but one of them is not stupid."

"Which one?"

Smart ass, he thought.

"He put on a thing," she added.

"Good."

She frowned. "I don't think he did it right."

"What? Put the thing on right?"

"No. Just—it."

"He may not get any better."

"I don't care, I don't want to do it with him anymore."

"There's plenty of others."

Summer had discovered a little taste of power. How much something so simple meant to boys.

"Me, I don't know what I'm getting into," Jon Karl said with a sigh. Summer stared at him, waiting. "I may get into growing some pot with Millard."

She stared. "Isn't that against the law?"

"Yeah, but Millard said we can make a lot of money. I want to get a different car."

Chapter 34

The Chicken House

Tamela Johnson and Millard came up with several hundred plastic buckets from somewhere, and after that it became all Jon Karl. Millard wasn't kidding when he said they needed somebody "out there." Jon Karl read and watched videos in a crash course on what proved to be a complex and labor-intensive process. But, of course, he learned fast. And he didn't mind because he loved being out there. He felt free.

He germinated the seeds, transferred the sprouted seeds to peat pots on long tables in the first chicken house, open to the sky, and finally transplanted the seedings to the buckets. As he had learned from Billy Reuben, he put a fish in each bucket. He and Millard had spent several afternoons catching as many little bream as they could and taking them out there.

The feminized seeds were as fertile as advertised, and after natural winnowing he had about four hundred and fifty healthy plants. He studied soil—he figured he had fertilizer covered—pruning and watering, and the chicken house protected the young cash crops from most varmints.

By May he had gotten into the routine of going out there every third day. The only way he could do that, and show up for Theotis in the afternoons, was to skip school after dropping Summer off. Nobody cared. He was almost a ghost in the place anyway, so close to graduation nobody dared jeopardizing getting rid of him.

Maybe it was the TLC, maybe it was the fish, but the plants were thriving. One morning he was watering and a healthy looking black dog with tan jowls, eyebrows, and lower legs, not quite

Afterlife's size, appeared on the periphery and Jon Karl knelt and tried to call him/her over.

"Come here, bubba." He clucked his tongue. "I won't hurt you."

But the dog, though tempted, was wary. It took half of the sandwich Jon Karl had brought to get the creature close. She (Jon Karl confirmed) licked her lips and looked like she wouldn't mind a bit more of that, so Jon Karl gave her the rest and resumed watering. She stayed close and Jon Karl filled up a bucket with water for her, and she promptly made a mess of that. He didn't succeed in getting her close enough to touch, but she didn't leave either.

The next time he showed up, she came bounding into the yard at the sound of his car, and he realized she had been looking out for him. Needless to say, this time he brought dog food.

Jon Karl had been spending some time cleaning up the front room of the house, and a few days after that he brought an old rug, his inflatable mattress and sleeping bag, a butane stove, lantern, ice chest, a ten-gallon Igloo water cooler, some books, and a deep sense of secret thrill, and prepared to spend his first night in what by then had become an almost enchanted place. A place where the world and its endless troubles just didn't seem to reach. The newly named Chicken House Dog trusted Jon Karl completely now, and spent the night on the rug. As she would many nights after.

"Are you going to move out there?" Summer, who had never been to the place and had no desire to go, asked him, her brow furrowed in concern.

"No, I'm not going to move out there," Jon Karl assured her. "Just sometimes. Chicken House Dog has gotten attached to me."

"That's not fair to Afterlife."

"I'm not abandoning Afterlife. I'm just going out there sometimes. Plus, she's got you."

"You're not scared out there?"

"I'm not. I'm really not. It's a million miles from everything. I love it."

"I'd get lonely."

"I've never been lonely," Jon Karl said. "I'm not even really sure what that means."

* * *

On evenings when he had tended the plants, make a little supper, and fed the renamed Big Chicken House Dog (Big Chic), and Little Chicken House Dog (Little Chic), the lap-dogsized Jeff to Big Chic's Mutt who had apparently heard the news of Big Chic's good fortune, and checked in—he would sit down in the splendid isolation of the rural evening in a chair on the feral patio behind the house, facing east. Jon Karl realized he had never really thought about what happy meant, but this must be it. He would often think of Maryrell then—here, not here, real, not real, the fount of life. Like God, everywhere and nowhere. Or Evelyn. Who, even more than Maryrell was less person than idea. And too much idea for one person.

He loved the view. Woods to the north bordering a rolling pasture that had become a field in these fallow years, stretching eastward to a pond and distant line of trees. That view could easily have stood in for eternity, and on the clear early evening when the Flower Moon rose over the line of trees, it did feel eternal. If you define eternal as complete, which he was beginning to.

Sometimes deer emerged from the woods into the field. Hawks cruised overhead, or found a perch with a view, divebombing at intervals for some take-out. A couple of times he had seen eagles. The vestige of an old road skirted the edge of the field, and often he took walks, with the two dogs in attendance.

He wondered if they were previously acquainted, they seemed so accustomed to each other. The thought worried him a little. Neither wore a collar, but he could almost see the deranged coot from whose trailer they had disappeared coming to look for them. That wouldn't be good. More likely the coot didn't care. Dogs came and went. If one ran off, another one would show up.

There weren't too many candidates for the coot. The nearest house—and though it was set back from the road and obscured by trees, it was clearly a house not a trailer—was about a mile down the road. A few times Jon Karl had seen a late-model red and gray pickup out on the road going or coming. Too far away to see the driver. And he hoped it would stay that way.

When Jon Karl sat on the patio, the dogs reclined on the weedy grass just at the edge, a few feet apart, like guard lions, scanning the pasture, smelling the scents, and at any sound from Jon Karl each would turn an ear his way like a periscope, then back. Jon Karl looked at them sometimes and thought, *It sucks being at the top of the food chain—we don't have any gods to hang out with. Look at them, they just take it for granted. No awe, nothing "sacred," they don't "worship," and they're not afraid. They just have a heart for these big creatures that give them food and shelter and affection, and don't have to put on a big show of being grateful, because they just are.*

What's my god? Jon Karl sometimes thought. No being, no person, nothing regal or flashy, he concluded—just the end point of intuition that couldn't be distorted into a character. About all you could say was It. Anything more than that and you're making it up. *We're* the characters. In this sublime story—sublime for all its pain, sublime because it has to be the longest shot imaginable, and is anyway.

Jon Karl had a way of getting lost in his thoughts, and often dusk would sneak over the place before he realized it. Sometimes a far-off train whistle would bring him back. One of the two railroads that threaded through Douvale skirted the lake and crossed the river at Frog Eye, heading off to the northwest, and the familiar, distant sound comforted his soul. Besides the trains, he never lacked for company, with all the activity behind his eyes. People he didn't know, places he had never been, endless talking. Often he would come to himself convinced he had been loitering in another dimension, where he was loitering in this one. Sometimes he would hear the sound of someone just getting up from a chair, or feel the absence of someone who had just left, people he knew, though they didn't exist, leaving a hollow place and a smell. Or he would feel something radiant just to his side, and would turn to look but see only the breeze in the leaves, and the feeling as in a lost dream that something meaningful, now irretrievable, had been there. He would let the thoughts go, like a puff of smoke, then watch them float away and dissipate.

He enjoyed the anticipation of who would show up next.

Anybody but himself.

Inside, by his lantern, he would read.

He didn't think about women except to be glad there weren't any there.

* * *

After Jon Karl had noticed the little house on Troubleneck Road with the lanky kid playing solo basketball, he could never not notice it again. The next time he passed by, the kid was out there, in the rain. *Is he ever not there?* Jon Karl wondered. Couldn't blame him—he was pretty sure he wouldn't want to be inside that house either. Then Jon Karl had cut his eyes and seen the second house. Until then he had been so focused on the boy it hadn't been there. But now it was: reality is where you're looking. It sat fifty yards away, a similarly modest dwelling of an equally haphazard but different design—if "design" wasn't going a bit far. Some banged-up toys lay scattered across its hardpacked grounds too, and Jon Karl's mind telescoped ahead: Basketball Boy knocks up next-door Susie, ensuring that the cycle would go on and they would be trapped there. Basketball Boy would abandon his dream and get on at the plant. Jon Karl didn't like the drift of that thought and shook it out of his head. He knew, with certainty, that he himself would never reproduce. At least he didn't plan to.

It took a few more trips for him to notice the third house. The one behind and below the other two, crouching in an effusive thicket with only the top half visible. A small plain box, radiant in the late sun when he first saw it, and often saw it after, with the suggestion of open space behind it.

Well—a little community, they seemed—a cosmos all their own, all but invisible on the side of the road. He asked Redwine about those houses and he wasn't even sure which ones he meant.

Chapter 35

Graduation and Beyond

Somehow, Jon Karl successfully completed the prescribed necessary requirements of Douvale High School and was in line to have the diploma conferred upon him with all the rights privileges and responsibilities thereunto appertaining. He had waited for this day, and there was only one thing he would miss. He went by to see her on the last afternoon of school.

Ms. Quilliam was at her desk. Her smile as he walked in turned oddly despondent.

"I get it," she said. "This is the life of the teacher. You get close to them and then they go away."

"That's sort of everything, isn't it?" said Jon Karl.

"I hope not."

They talked, but not for long, and then she had to excuse herself and hurried out of the room.

Unceremonious to the core, Jon Karl skipped the formalities, with only mild protestations from Mr. Dawes, who gave him $500 for a down payment on the seven year old Chrysler Town and Country he had located and said was a great deal. Saying no to Mr. Dawes just wasn't an option and Jon Karl's newer dream car would have to wait. Summer cried when they dropped off Mildra's Taurus at Bob Hauer's Auto Barn, but cheered up a bit when they rode away in their roomy new van. Spruill, of course, because he knew everybody, knew Bob Hauer and worked a deal. Payments on the two-year loan, after the trade-in and down payment, were only $120 a month.

"I think you can afford that, can't you?" Spruill asked him.

"Yes sir," Jon Karl assured him.

"You can't be missing payments. You're building a credit history."

"Yes sir, I know."

The day of the non-commencement, the white pick-up pulled up in front of the house. Barber Balch had come, bearing a gift. Which turned out to be a crisp new $20 bill, which as before he held demonstrably out, as though the *New York Times* were there to document the occasion, before relinquishing it.

"You're pretty," said Balch. Jon Karl shuddered. "You must have cut your hair yourself—or maybe got that sister to do it." He attempted a sardonic smile. "You'd look better if you let me shape it up for you."

He stared, working his jaw.

"I'm good," said Jon Karl.

* * *

Millard's graduation present was a little more interesting.

A couple of months before Commencement Day—which in Millard's case *was* illustrious, with Leela going whole-hog when she got her hands on the regalia catalogue for the Academy, both she and Spruill choking up a little at the sight of their little man in full plumage—Spruill asked him what he wanted for his graduation present, and Millard handed him a magazine opened to a photograph of—no, not a Lamborghini, but a customized van.

Spruill studied it with furrowed brow. "You want *this*?"

Millard nodded.

"Is it for sale?"

"You always told me everything is for sale."

"That's true, but—" In spite of himself Spruill's head was already spinning with figures, tactics, haggling strategy. He couldn't help it, it was what he was born for. "Why don't you see if you can get in touch with the people—"

"Me? It's my *graduation present*! Why should I have to do it?"

"All right, all right."

* * *

Theotis had gotten back to work on the gazebo, and keen to be done with it, had poured all his energy into it. Jon Karl had to leave off his morning trips to the Chicken House to be either in the shop where they cut out all the pieces, or on-site, at seven a.m.—and had to put off checking on the plants until after work. Theotis couldn't spare Billy Lirenzo around town, but enlisted Billy Reuben for the duration.

Jon Karl loved working with Billy Reuben, even if he became basically a different person. The clowning and gleefulness and frenetic energy migrated to another dimension somewhere, and as he measured, cut, joined, attached, his face was all concentration, his body still.

He never hit his thumb. He never made a mistake.

When they were finally finished, Spruill threw a party there. What Theotis had come up with was unique and original for sure, and even though Leela couldn't quite reconcile this all too solid, ornamental, purple and green (her selections) hexagonal structure sitting above the lake on a pad of newly sodded red clay with the phantasmagorical photographs of the magazines, she let it go, as an impressive gathering enjoyed the punch and heavy hors d'oeuvres the caterers had laid out on the round table in the middle.

Spruill, however, was dazzled. Goddamndest thing he'd ever seen in his life, and Theotis had just come up with it out of the blue.

"How many people do you know, if you just said 'build me a gazebo' could have come up with something like this? I've never seen anything like it on the face of the earth. The man's a genius."

Spruill was in his element, going from one semi-circular micro-audience to another, everybody hanging on his words and laughing. Jon Karl stood off to the side with Summer, who had

183

insisted on attending, and Billy Reuben, watching the people, including Zadie, who was working the food table like a predator and shooting him looks. That, the mosquitoes and gnats, and the TV Leela had installed down there and set on some home improvement channel, were driving him insane, and as the celebrants popped the champagne, he and Summer left.

It's true, when you think about it, there's not a lot to do in a gazebo, and in fact Jon Karl never saw Leela, or anybody, in it ever again.

Like most acquisitions: only causing pain when you didn't have it, giving no real gratification when you did.

* * *

Millard hadn't shown up for the party, and Jon Karl wondered a bit, but not much, about that as he headed up the hill. Millard did what Millard wanted. Then he heard a long deep train horn, startlingly out of place, and he looked toward the drive to see a miniature diesel locomotive heading their way. Another loud blast.

Every head turned.

Jon Karl could see Millard in the driver's seat, and some girl riding shotgun.

Because it wasn't really a diesel locomotive, but a retrofitted van that was an exact replica of one, in green and white Southern Railway livery. To a fine degree of detail. A sign on the side said: DAWES PROPERTIES.

* * *

With the gazebo finished, Jon Karl went back to working with Theotis in the afternoons and heading out to the Chicken House every other day after work. He had taken to leaving out food for Big Chic and Little Chic, who were usually there when he drove up.

Very happy to see him.

The other partners were scarce at the farm. Tamela and Zadie had checked in a couple of times, only to discover there was a lot of work to do, which was all it took to keep Zadie away. Millard never came, just got periodic reports.

"Cool, man, cool. You're doing great."

The scarcity actually was welcome to Jon Karl. The less traffic out there, the better.

Then Zadie found out Jon Karl was spending some nights at the place. It was only a matter of time.

She showed up late one afternoon in her signature tight shorts, cowboy boots, and deep-V tee shirt. She had come to "help."

The plants were growing rapidly and Jon Karl was in the process of topping them. He had been studying this procedure carefully and was working his way slowly and methodically through the crop that had turned the open-roofed chicken house into a miniature forest. Zadie just followed him around and watched, which suited Jon Karl, who didn't want anybody messing with his babies. He did let her help a bit with the watering, closely supervised.

When it was time for her to go away, Jon Karl was dismayed to see her produce a pizza in a warming bag from her car. They ate on the patio, Big Chic and Little Chic alert for windfall, as the long summer twilight faded to dusk. After the fifth or sixth ignored hint, Jon Karl said:

"It's getting late. I'm tired. Shouldn't you be getting back?"

"I thought you might invite me to spend the night."

He was silent. Then said, "I've just got this air mattress—"

"I know," she said, and closed her eyes, humming.

Goddamn, he thought.

Everything was telling him—*not her*. Not Mr. Dawes' daughter. One voice said, "It's the only way to get rid of her," but another said, "It's the surest way to get stuck with her." Yet another said, "No good will come of it." He had no rubbers out here, and wondered what if anything she used. He didn't want to even hint at it, because then *it* would be real. Plus, he hated rubbers.

Then she stood up, took off her tee-shirt, and said, "It's so *free* out here. Nobody to bother you!"

Easy for you to say, Jon Karl thought. Followed by: *This is my fucking place. Mine!*

Then she was facing him, hands on hips. "Don't act like you've never seen them before!"

"I wasn't," he truthfully said.

Leaving her boots on, she likewise relieved herself of her shorts, soaking up the freeness and unbotheringness.

"I like being out here by myself," Jon Karl said.

"I know that," said Zadie, swaying now to her own private rhythm, looking like some roadhouse go-go girl. "I don't want to move in. I just want to fuck you."

* * *

The next morning he slipped off the mattress before her, thinking of Evelyn/Ms. Quilliam. He always thought of that composite heartbreaking creature when he was with another woman, because she could only exist when somebody wasn't her.

Zadie, thinking of the heroin rush of warm Krispy Kremes, didn't stay to "help," and then he didn't see her for a while.

* * *

A couple of days later he stopped by the Dollar General on Troubleneck Road for some bread and cheese and milk. On the bread aisle he ran into a girl laden with chips, cookies, and soft drinks, having some trouble adding a box of Little Debbie cakes to her armload.

Their eyes met. God, what a look. Wary and beguiled all at once. Jon Karl could see she had been gnawing on her fingers— and she was pretty. A bolt of protective affection surged through him.

"Can I help you carry some of that?" he said.

She seemed unsure of her dominant emotion. "Well—"

"You must be going to a party."

"Not really."

He let her go first at the checkout, and put the Little Debbie cakes on the counter for her.

She paid, and as she gathered up the bags, their eyes met again.

"Thank you," she said, hesitated a second, attempted a smile, then was gone in the way they're always gone.

A potential lifetime walking out the door on a Tuesday afternoon.

Jon Karl watched her go, thinking a wistful thought. He had never gotten a girl. Never been the hunter, always the prey. Never flirted, never chased. He had never had to.

The thought made him sad.

Chapter 36

Dinner with Millard

Sometime after that, he got off a little early and stopped by the library. He cruised the aisles, but nothing called. Still, he picked up a few books, flipped through them, but none of them grabbed him until he found one about dreams that he checked out. On the way home, Millard called and asked if he wanted to go get something to eat.

"Eh, I don't know," he demurred. In his mind he was already settled into the couch.

"I really think you should," Millard said. "Just saying."

"Summer too," said Jon Karl.

"Yeah, sure."

When he got home, this time it was a Volkswagen parked out front, and the pimply bespectacled boy was Marvin.

"I was just leaving," he said.

When he was gone Jon Karl asked Summer, "Did you already eat?"

She shook her head.

"Good. Millard is coming to get us."

Her features turned quizzical. "To go out?"

"Yes."

"To eat?"

"Yes. To eat. Where do you want to go?"

"I don't care."

Jon Karl looked out the front window where the Volkswagen was making its comical exit. "Do you like *him*?"

"I feel sorry for him."

He slowly nodded. "Did he use a thing?"

"Yeah."

"Was he better than the last one?"

"Not really."

"It would be a lot better if it was somebody you actually liked."

"There isn't anybody I actually like."

"Well then, wait till there is."

"*You* do it with girls you don't like."

"Yeah," said Jon Karl. "I know. But that's different—"

"How's it different?" she demanded.

"I don't know. It just is."

"No it's not," she said, then as her little flash of anger passed, she cut her eyes down. "I like Millard," she said softly.

"No, Summer, not Millard. Please."

She frowned.

"It would ruin everything. Trust me. And he would break your heart. He would *crush* your heart. He wouldn't mean to. But he would."

Her face went through a series of expressions, but she didn't say anything.

"How about Boca Loca?" he asked.

"I don't care," she said, then looked up at him. "What do you do out there?"

"What do you mean what do I do out there?"

"I mean, like, what do you do?"

"I take care of the plants."

"You're not going to get caught, are you?"

"I hope not."

"But I mean, when you're not taking care of the plants."

"Do I have to *do* something?"

Summer considered the opposite possibility, with no luck.

"Yes. You can't just not do something."

"What qualifies as something?"

"Everything besides nothing."

"Okay then, I do something."

"What?"

"I watch myself do whatever I do."

"That doesn't make any sense."

"I do whatever I feel like."

"Do you service yourself?"

Jon Karl laughed. "Where did you hear *that*?"

"It's not like I don't hear things."

"What kind of question is that?"

"I was just wondering. I do. Sometimes."

"I don't really need to know that."

"So you're not going to tell me?"

"You already know, so why bother? But it's not what I *do* if that's what you're thinking."

"I wasn't thinking that. I was just wondering."

"Wonder no more."

And then a loud locomotive horn sounded from the street.

* * *

People on the sidewalk had stopped to stare, and a little crowd had formed on the corner. Some kid pumped his arm, and Millard blasted the horn again.

Jon Karl and Summer came out like celebrities and got in.

They created a sensation driving across town. On the parkway, some kids in a muddy jacked-up Toyota pick-up came around them, gawking, and with a blast of his horn, Millard floored it. The van had a V-8 and it lurched ahead with a throaty roar and the race was on. The van was no match for the truck, but Millard made it interesting. They were coming up to a light just turning red, and the truck raced through with a victorious blare of its horn as Millard braked and turned right with a farewell toot. Jon Karl looked back at Summer, holding on with both hands, eyes wide as saucers, eating it up.

* * *

Jon Karl didn't like Boca Loca, but then he didn't like any restaurant. He had come to realize he didn't like being around large groups of people—like more than three. Unfortunately it was Fajita Night, and the place was packed.

But he did like their flautas, and Summer liked their sopaipillas, which with a Dr. Pepper would be her meal. Millard would get beef fajitas, but more for the sizzling table show than the taste. He would eat only a few bites, and walk off and leave the rest.

"Did you get a haircut?" Summer asked Millard.

"No," said Millard, "I got them all cut."

You would have to know Summer to know she found that hilarious. Summer's eyes did the laughing.

Jon Karl, who would never have noticed unprompted, looked at Millard and concluded that, yes, he seemed to have had a trim.

"And I don't know what you did to get Balch all excited," Millard said, "but he told me to tell you you needed his services." He grinned.

"Jesus," said Jon Karl.

"He wants to get his hands on you, bud. But then, who doesn't?"

"They'll be selling Sno-Cones in Hell before that happens," said Jon Karl. "Why do you go to that creepy fucker?"

"I don't like him," said Summer.

"Shit, nobody *likes* him," Millard said. "Who cares? Dad goes to him. I've always gone to him. It's no big deal. Twenty bucks and he just squeezes your biceps and rubs your shoulders a little bit, that's all."

"Ew-w," Summer shuddered.

Jon Karl scowled. "He's nasty," he said.

"Yeah, just ask his cats."

"Stop!" cried Summer.

"What cats?" said Jon Karl.

"I heard he lives with a bunch of cats. I don't know what goes on in there."

Summer started to push herself up from the table. "I mean it."

Millard laughed. "Oh baby," he said, "don't leave. You're the only thing I can stand to look at in here. You want to sneak out to his house sometime and spy through the windows?"

She paused for the microsecond it took to consider the idea of going somewhere with Millard, then said, "No!"

The waitress appeared.

"Took you long enough," said Millard. "But that's okay—we don't have anything better to do than sit here all night."

The poor girl looked mortified. "I'm sorry, I—"

"Don't listen to him," Jon Karl said. "He's just being a butt."

She tried to smile back.

Oh God, he saw what she was, he saw her future, all in one heartbreaking vision. She couldn't have been more than eighteen, pretty, luscious as a ripe peach, vulnerable, awkward, and Jon Karl knew she appeared to the leering eyes of men how a plump mouse must appear to a hawk. And it was instantly obvious she was almost over her head in this job. Somebody had forced her to get out there, make some money, after that disastrous episode at Walgreen's—instructed her to act friendly, servile, to get the good tips, but it was painfully hard for her. She was afraid of most people, she didn't understand them, and was never sure what they were laughing about. She wasn't witty or quick or smart. High school had been terrifying for her. She fit nowhere. She had dropped out and no force on earth, not even her cruel and feckless father or her wasted mother—herself in twenty years—could goad her back to that place. So here she was, socially helpless, overwhelmed, struggling to act friendly. Trying to make a living, for God's sake. Always screwing up—the job was so hard!—she hated it when Mr. Rodriguez yelled at her. She was cursed with universal sex appeal—here in the flickering moment of her bloom.

What man wouldn't want to see her on her back? The world is going to chew her up and spit her out, Jon Karl knew—and there would be nobody to help her.

He understood. Oh God. He looked away from her, and caught Summer looking at him. And only then noticed the trio at the next table: two humorlessly staring at the poor girl, the third a lounge-dressed young man maybe in his late twenties, smirking with eyes locked on Jon Karl. They were an odd assortment, apparently having some kind of business discussion, files stacked on the table: the roving-eyed young lizard, showing some chest hair and some gold, but not as much as the large ugly man with shoulder-length hair, bulbous features, and baseball glove hands—a Neanderthal; and a worked-over fiftyish woman with extremely blonde hair, garish jewelry, and a look like you really wouldn't want to play poker with her.

The waitress fumbled with the chips and salsa, got a little flustered, then forced a smile and said, "What do you want—I mean, what would you like—for your—I mean, to drink?"

Charmed, Jon Karl smiled encouragingly at her.

"You. On the rocks," said Millard.

God knows she was used to it, but still her face radiated confusion and helplessness.

Jon Karl shot daggers at Millard.

Tea, Dr. Pepper, and a Megarita. Her eyes narrowed in concentration as she squeezed the pencil and laboriously recorded the order.

"What?" Millard said when she was gone.

"Jesus, man, don't hit on her," said Jon Karl. "Can't you see how hard it is for her?"

"Is that my fault? And I wasn't hitting on her. I was just playing with her."

Summer looked pained.

"Just—have some class," said Jon Karl.

"*Class*," Millard sneered. "It's not my problem she's not the brightest bulb in the box."

"All the more reason."

* * *

The food was slow coming, and about halfway through eating, Jon Karl started to feel panicky. He was good for about thirty minutes in a crowd, and they had passed that. He looked around the room. The trio were going through their files, studiously. The lizard looked up, as though waiting for his glance, and smiled that oily smile.

Good God.

Some assholes at another table were skewering the young waitress. *"Jesus Christ—it's an order at a half-ass Mexican restaurant, it's not rocket science!—"*

Elsewhere people were laughing, drinking, shoveling in food. *Americans*. Gross, fat, arrogant, stupid.

Get me the fuck out of here, Jon Karl almost said out loud.

Millard was paying. "Give her a big tip," Jon Karl said.

"Yeah, I'd like to give her a big tip," Millard replied.

"Goddamn, Millard."

On the way out they passed the trio, who were a little guarded with their files. The lizard leered at Jon Karl as they walked by. The Neanderthal and the woman were talking. Jon Karl caught a snippet.

" . . . the kid's got good wood and he lasts . . . "

The waitress was carrying an overloaded tray, powerless to keep the desperate look off her face. Jon Karl gave her a smile, and she tried to give him a brave smile back.

Cradle to grave in this sick world, everybody in a different seat. Destination the same.

Chapter 37

Ms. Quilliam

When something lives a secret life in your mind, and you round the corner onto the Piggly Wiggly spice aisle and there it stands reading the label on a little jar, it gives you a start.

In this case, more like a surge of voltage. Jon Karl himself was holding a plastic bag with two artichokes.

Ms. Quilliam stood frozen—then her face bloomed into a smile and she gave the nose bridge of her glasses a little nudge.

"Jon Karl!" she cried.

"Hi, Ms. Quilliam."

"You like artichokes?" she asked him.

"Yes mam."

"Listen," Ms. Quilliam said. "You're all grown up now. Can you spare me the 'mam,' please?"

"Yes ma'am."

"All right now—I don't want to have to put you in Detention."

Jon Karl smiled. "That'd be okay. If you were the monitor."

"I thought you would prefer Ms. Boyle."

"Oh my God—"

"Sorry. I'm bad." She checked out his cargo. "You know how to cook artichokes?"

"Yes m— Yes, I do. Me and my sister like them."

"I like the hearts," said Ms. Quilliam. "But the rest of it always seemed like too much work."

"We think it's fun."

"Yes," she said. "You would." They stood there. "Do you know anything about cardamon?" she asked.

"Not really."

"I don't either. It's supposed to be good for you. Your heart or something."

"It probably is."

"So—are those—" she nodded at the artichokes "—for to-night?"

"They are."

"What else are you having?"

"I was thinking Cornish game hens."

"Cornish game hens! Wow. Are you the cook?"

"I am."

"I'm impressed."

"Come eat with us sometime," said Jon Karl.

She skipped over the invitation. "You're still living in a house with your sister?"

"Yes m— what am I supposed to say if I can't say 'yes mam'?"

"Just say yes."

"Yes."

"Are you sure you're not supposed to be twenty-one or something to do that?"

"We're doing it."

She laughed. "Yes mam, I guess you are."

"I'm eighteen," Jon Karl said.

"I know you are. And she's—"

"Sixteen. Anyway, Mr. Dawes is our guardian."

"He's not *living* there?"

"Oh no. Just us. And Afterlife."

"Ah. The dog."

"Yes."

"Well, you and your sister are out of the ordinary, I'll say that."

"We're just us."

She smiled. "Anyway—congratulations. You made it through high school."

"How, I don't know."

"I put in a good word for you."

"You did? Thanks."

"I'm *kidding*, Jon Karl. Do you think they'd listen to anything I said?"

"They should."

"No, actually they shouldn't. So—what are you doing with yourself this summer?"

The thought came from nowhere: *why's she asking that? She's working for the police! How did they know I'd come down this aisle?* Followed immediately by: *Jesus, that's insane.* "Just working," he said.

"For Mr. Dawes, right?"

"Yeah, I work with Theotis."

"That's his foreman, I think you said?"

"Something like that. He does everything."

"And you help him."

"I do."

"That's good."

Then they hesitated for several odd seconds, Jon Karl holding his artichokes, Ms. Quilliam her jar of cardamon seeds. Finally Ms. Quilliam said, "I'm going to miss you."

"Yeah," said Jon Karl. "Me too."

"You're going to miss you too?"

"No. *You.*"

Something was going on in her face. Jon Karl read it as embarrassment. Being seen talking to her juvenile student. Well, *former* student. And not exactly juvenile.

"Good luck to you, Jon Karl."

"Thank you, mam."

"No *mam*."

"Thank you."

Her smile seemed a little strained. "You take care."

"You too."

Well, that was the last he would ever see of her. It made him feel lonely.

* * *

Except it wasn't.

She was waiting with her little shopping bag, discreet by the rack of hanging ferns for sale in front of the store, as he came out.

"Jon Karl," she said.

He jumped. Then his face bloomed in a smile. "Oh—"

"Look, I figure this is it or nothing—so I'm just going to put it out there. I want you to come see me sometime. I'll cook for you."

"Me and Summer?"

"No. Just you."

So. Maybe that hadn't been embarrassment.

He returned her very direct look. "I don't know where you live."

"Willowcreste Apartments—you know where those are?" He nodded. "Number 119. And—you've graduated—so—I don't think it's an issue—but I'm not sure. So it might be better if—nobody knew."

Her look was so frank and unguarded he felt a rush of affection for her. "Probably would be," he agreed.

"I'm pretty sure they would fire me if they found out."

"They'd be sorry."

"Jon Karl—people like me are a dime a dozen. I don't even know if I want to be a teacher. One more year maybe."

"What else would you want to be?"

"That's just it. Listen—the apartments have these little patios in the back—and wooden fences in between. My place is on the corner, so if you came through the woods on the—" she was no good with compass directions, or just directions in general, so she motioned with her arms "—you know, if you're facing it, the right side—"

"Yeah—"

"—you could come in—I know this sounds dramatic—the *back*."

Jon Karl laughed. "It sounds fun."

She smiled. "You're a good sport. I have a blue light—you can't miss it. Do you like salmon?"

"Sure. So—when?"

"How about Saturday?"

"Okay."

"What do you like to drink?" she asked.

"Ginger ale?"

"Ah," she said, "I remember you told me you were a teetotaler. I admire that, actually." She shook her head slowly, smiling at him. "You really aren't like anybody else, Jon Karl."

* * *

Summer was intrigued. "What are you going to do?"

"Eat, I guess."

"What else?"

"Talk."

Summer mulled it over. "She's really pretty."

"Yeah," Jon Karl said. "She is."

"She's not like any other teacher."

"No," said Jon Karl, "she's really not. But I don't think she's going to keep doing it. I mean, not forever."

"What else is she going to do?"

"I don't know. *She* doesn't know. I think she wants to travel."

"Where?"

"Well—anywhere. See some different stuff."

"You have to have a job to do that," said Summer.

"Yeah. Unless you're rich."

"Is she rich?"

"I don't think so."

"I think she's lonely," Summer said.

"You think?"

"You only see her at school," said Summer. "When she's busy."

"Not anymore," said Jon Karl.

* * *

He parked at the Sunoco station and ducked into the little stand of woods left by the bulldozers. When he got to the edge, there were about five blue lights. But one of them was on the end.

She said the corner apartment, Jon Karl told himself as he darted across the opening and onto the patio. Some potted plants. Unbussed table—a couple of wine glasses—a few dishes—one chair. Shielded by the wooden fences on either side, he walked to the sliding doors and saw her within—not doing anything, just standing in the narrow kitchen with a glass of wine. He tapped on the glass.

She tried to modulate her excitement at seeing him, but there was no hiding it. It was as palpable as the smell of salmon cooking. She was a little tipsy—just a little—and they had an awkward few seconds of maybe embracing, but refrained. "I'll get your ginger ale," she said and headed for the fridge. Jon Karl watched her.

He sat down on the sofa, and a not-scrawny orange tabby cat jumped up beside him.

"That's Saskatchewan," said Ms. Quilliam, setting his ginger ale on the end table. She herself sat propped forward on the adjacent chair. Jon Karl stroked the purring cat.

"Are you hungry?" Ms. Quilliam asked.

"Yeah. Pretty hungry."

"I hope you like it—oh, what the hell, it's just salmon, how can you mess that up?"

"You can overcook it."

"Yeah, you can at that. I made a dill mustard sauce. I hope it's okay."

"Sounds good to me."

"And a surprise—you want to see it?"

"Okay."

His lack of nervousness excited her. But she'd had some wine and didn't care.

Two artichokes simmered in a big pot on the stove. "Cool," he said. "But you said you didn't like them."

"I'm taking one for the team."

He laughed, and glanced around the kitchen. A bit of cooking messiness around the stove—but mostly neat, clean. Coffee maker with one cat-themed mug beside it. Some apples and desiccated tangerines in a bowl on the breakfast nook table. Refrigerator with tidy magnet fodder—photograph of her and another young woman standing in front of maybe Mayan ruins. Some kids—nieces, nephews? No handsome young man.

Back in the den, another glance seemed, unfairly, to disclose little truths of her life: the cat, the polite work clutter on the dining table, the laptop, the TV, the books and magazines, all the contours of her presence. *The same would be true for me,* he reflected. Not so different.

"Ready to eat?" she said.

The salmon, as it turned out, was excellent, and they dipped their artichoke leaves in the bowl of melted butter she put between them. Well, she realized, it *was* sort of fun. Fun work.

When they were done, she didn't sit in the chair, but on the couch. They turned three-quarters towards each other.

"Jon Karl," Ms. Quilliam said. "I appreciate you coming over—"

"Sure."

"And of course you can go—but—I was hoping you'd stay."

"I can stay."

"I mean—the night."

"I can stay the night."

Nothing fazed the boy! She laughed. "I thought I was going to have to talk you into it."

"You just did."

"But I mean—the thing is—I'm the one taking the risk. You've got nothing to lose. I'm sure they would fire me. And maybe I don't even care if they do—except I know how it would look. It would follow me. The *cougar*. All that."

"To me you're not a cougar, or a teacher, or anything. You're just you."

She looked at him affectionately. "Bless you. You're pretty much the only person in the world who could say that and I would think they actually meant it." She touched the corner of her eye, smiled. "But doesn't it feel like we're in this secret place and we can do whatever we want and nobody can see us?"

Well, you had to like the sound of *that*. He nodded his head, shifted around, needing to situate himself a little better. He rubbed the tops of his legs, and she took off her glasses—then scooted toward him. He raised his arm to make a hollow for her.

"I don't even have to say I'm depending on you not to tell anybody, do I?"

"I won't."

"Not even Summer?"

"Well—Summer—we don't have secrets."

The simple honesty of that stopped her. "You're very close, aren't you?"

"We are."

And it seemed a beautiful thing—the way men and women need each other.

* * *

The first thing Jon Karl did the next morning as he awoke in the cool, dark room was remember. Then he rolled over from his solitary fetal position hoping it would still be there—*please*— ah, yes. He burrowed against the soft warm sleepy creature where he'd left her, as the morning light threatened the cracks in the drapes.

"Thank you," he whispered, his lips just at her ear.

"Jesus," she murmured. "Thank *you.*"

Chapter 38
Zadie

They remained burrowed in the cocoon of the apartment all day Sunday, curtains and shades tightly drawn, and didn't look, let alone venture, outside. The thought that Ms. Quilliam had been the author, he the character, was there in Jon Karl's thoughts, but not very potent. What had she said—a secret place hidden from all eyes? Jon Karl imagined God on his throne up there, looking over his holdings, unaware of his furtive little couple. It would seem logical to suppose that when God wasn't thinking about you, you didn't exist. If so, you had to admit, not existing was the time to get things done.

They ate a bit, talked a lot, watched a couple of old movies, exchanged amateur massages, and time seemed to ooze. The only intrusion was a phone call from Ms. Quilliam's mother, which Ms. Quilliam took into the bedroom for about thirty minutes. When he recounted the day later for Summer, that was what stood out to her—and it did indeed seem like a rare luxury. A phone call with your mother.

But as the afternoon aged, Jon Karl began to think more and more about his babies out at the farm. It was a curious sort of anxiety he felt when he had been away from them for a few days. Of course he didn't mention that to Ms. Quilliam—there just wasn't any reason for her to know about it—and as he grew antsy she let him go easily enough. But with a promise that he would be back.

Easy promise to make.

He stopped off to check in with Summer and Afterlife, and grab some things, then headed out to his other life. No basketball boy on this afternoon—in fact, no people at all in the little roadside community, just their pell-mell effects in the bare yards. The houses sat there, looking contemplative in the lonely afternoon— maybe people in there, maybe not—the top half of the introverted third one radiant in the aging light.

Big Chic and Little Chic bounded out to meet him as he drove up. Maybe they didn't exist either, until he returned, but hung suspended in some timeless dimension out of the flow of events, like off-stage actors—even if their smoky odor belied that little daydream.

Late July. The buds on the plants were fattening nicely. Jon Karl had bought a magnifying glass, and made his rounds, watering, and looking for the signs he had read about on the internet, Ms. Quilliam mentally accompanying him less as a person than as an easiness in the nerves.

When, just about dusk, he heard the crunch of car tires in the driveway, he looked around at possible avenues of escape, thinking of making a run for it. But it was too late. Zadie came clomping down the path in boots, hot pants, and that fucking cowboy hat.

She had brought her usual pizza, but Jon Karl had his own stuff and didn't care for any.

"Okay, be that way," she said. "More for me." Which she validated by eating three-fourths of it.

Jon Karl was thinking, *You better keep your damn clothes on.*

But this was Zadie, who needed only the flimsiest provocation to take them off anywhere she could get away with it. By the time the sun had slipped behind the western trees, she was swaying like a sea fan, unencumbered, on the patio, and Jon Karl had such a vivid image in his head of a walrus he couldn't shake it.

Things got worse as she polished off her bottle of wine, sucked a few times on the amber-stained half a doobie she had brought, and started closing in.

"Look, I just want to be by myself tonight," Jon Karl said. "Okay?"

"That won't get you anywhere," said Zadie.

"Actually, it will."

"You're not getting rid of me *that* easy, pal."

"I'm not trying to get rid of you, I just want to be by myself."

"What the hell's the difference?" she demanded. "Look, bud, when a woman throws herself at you, it's not a good idea to say no."

"It is if you're not in the mood."

"Not in the mood? What the hell is that about? Here I am. *I'm* in the mood. Fuck me."

"I don't want to."

"What the shit, you little piss-ant? What—I'm too fat?"

"No."

"Do I smell?"

"The same smell as always."

"Whatever the hell *that* means. You're not thinking you're too *good* for me, are you? You're *above* me?"

"I'm not thinking anything."

"Because that would be pretty funny, coming from *you*. Jesus, you little shrimp piece of shit—what the hell are you? A dick with a white trash teenager stuck to it that my daddy for some reason decided to save from the orphanage."

"Mildra saved us—and you daddy came with her."

"I'm going to tell him."

"Tell him what?"

"That you don't appreciate the way he helped you—"

"That would be a lie."

"What makes you think you're too good for me all of a sudden?"

"I never said I—"

"You're not too good for anybody, prick!"

She was breathing heavily now, standing there furious and

naked, hands on hips with a cowboy hat, and it was like the adolescent fantasy—those glasses that let you see through people's clothes—with a vengeance.

She looked him up and down. "You're fucking somebody else!"

"What the hell business is that of yours?"

She panted, staring at him, not really sure how to answer that. "It's my business if I'm getting the leftovers. I don't do leftovers, pal."

Jon Karl laughed. "You don't have any claim over me."

"Christ, here I am, dancing around. I got naked for nothing."

"So I'm just supposed to be ready and waiting when you are?"

"Don't act like you don't like it. I know better."

"I just want to be by myself."

"Fuck you, asshole."

She got dressed and, taking the rest of the pizza, spewed away, screaming something out the car window on the driveway that he couldn't make out.

Well, that wasn't good, he thought.

But at least she was gone.

* * *

He spent the next three weekends at Ms. Quilliam's apartment. Her dining room table was littered with new school year stuff. Gradually the situation became routine—yet still felt like one of those things that would just go on forever. That it wouldn't, or couldn't, was a thought—more than a thought, a certainty, a sad one—far more present in Ms. Quilliam's mind than in Jon Karl's.

Fall semester began. They missed a weekend. Then for a while she didn't return his calls or texts—part of him accepted it, part of him didn't like it. Finally she answered him after four tries one day and reassured him that she was just very busy, and invited him to come over on Sunday.

She hadn't cooked, but had brought home some Vietnamese take-out.

As they sat in the den after eating, he on the couch, she in the chair, Jon Karl had the odd feeling that he was seeing her for the first time. She was the same, but different. It was like her close but not exact twin sister had swapped places with her. They sort of fell into making love but it never really got comfortable.

He felt distracted and cheerless, without understanding why.

She woke him up the next morning, dressed and ready, her backpack stuffed and waiting on the dining table, and told him she had to leave in ten minutes. In other words, he had to leave in nine.

Which he did.

Chapter 39

E Street and Silver Avenue

September.

Back in the routine: farm every other morning, Theotis in the afternoons. Not having to go to school was one of the best feelings Jon Karl had ever had. But he thought of Ms. Quilliam in there, and what was that—jealousy? Entire new classes of kids. Maybe a new Jon Karl bored on the back row.

Gradually their communication dried up to the occasional forced-cheerful but brief text. Somewhere along the line, the heart emojis stopped.

Most of the time when he thought about the whole business, he felt foolish. There were days he wasn't sure it had actually happened. But of course there were days when the itch was bad.

He made an effort to spend more time with Summer, just starting eleventh grade. They went shopping, drew pictures, watched nature documentaries, worked on Summer's hair-raising driving lessons, spent long Sunday afternoons at the library.

On one of those afternoons Jon Karl was absorbed in a book on bird augury at a table when he felt a presence. He looked up just as a young man crossed by, looking sidelong at him with an expression that only looked like a smile.

Their eyes met. Jon Karl quickly cut his eyes back to his book. The man passed by, and Jon Karl looked over toward Summer a couple of tables away. She was watching the man too. After a couple of minutes Jon Karl walked over to her.

"Did you see that guy?" he asked her. She did. "Why did he look familiar?"

"He was in the restaurant that night," she said, "at the table with those creepy people."

His mind made a couple of moves, and there it was: that hopeless young waitress in Boca Loca—and the guy, who gave him such a crawly feeling, looking at him from the table with the same leer.

"Yeah," said Jon Karl. "I remember." Mr. Lizard.

"He was at the Piggly Wiggly the other day too."

"He wasn't at the Piggly Wiggly—*I* didn't see him."

"He was in his car."

"Really? Are you sure?"

"Yes."

"You *saw* him?"

"Yes."

"Did he see you?"

"Yes."

"What was he doing—hiding?"

"No. I don't think he cares if you see him."

"Ew," said Jon Karl.

"I think he's stalking you," said Summer.

* * *

A couple of blocks from home, four or five people were gathered on the sidewalk. Jon Karl slowed down and as they inched closer they saw a police car round the corner.

"It's those crazy people," said Summer, craning her neck to see.

"Let's just go home," Jon Karl said. "They probably got in a fight or something."

"No!" Summer said. "I think something happened. I want to see what it is."

He obliged her. Just as he parked the car along the street, an ambulance, no siren, passed them and turned the corner.

They got out and walked up behind the onlookers.

"What happened?" Jon Karl asked.

One of the onlookers was Doris Ault, who turned to him with her wild white hair and a look so unreadable—stricken, confused, energized, lustful—you would just have to call it insane. "I've been telling them for three days he was dead! Don't you smell that?"

Yes, there was a smell.

A young policeman was standing a few yards away. "You wouldn't listen!" she scorched him. "I called 911 and you didn't listen, you didn't care! I told you he was dead but you wouldn't listen to *me*! He's dead. And I didn't kill him!"

"Nobody thinks you killed him, mam."

"I wouldn't be too sure about that," the man standing beside Jon Karl with his hand over his nose murmured.

"Nobody listened!"

"Well, we'll take care of it now, mam."

"And he told me to tell you I had first rights to everything— before anybody else. That's what he told me to tell you."

"There's no way he said that," the man, pinching his nose now and sounding like he'd taken a hit of helium, said.

"How do you know what he said?" Doris roared back. "You weren't there!"

"They couldn't stand each other," the man explained to the policeman.

That young officer, what they call heavy-set, and no stranger in the gym, tugged on his elaborate belt and stood there. "Sir, I don't have anything to do with that. Detective Grissom is in the house—he'll handle all that. I'll let him know if you want to make a statement."

"*I* want to make a statement!" Doris screeched. "That crazy man said I had first rights to everything in his house!"

"He didn't say that," the man calmly repeated.

"Shut up! You're an idiot! He *did* say it! Right there by that fence!" Back to the policeman: "I called for three days and you just ignored me. I knew he was dead. I knew it before I even smelled it. The minute you get him out of there you need to let me in that house so I can start going through everything."

The steam seemed to be going out of her.

"Mam, I'm going to have to ask you to stay away from the house. You can talk to Detective Grissom when he gets a chance."

"Let's go," Jon Karl said to Summer.

"I want to see the body come out," Summer said.

"That could take a long time. Let's go home."

"Go ahead. I'll walk. I want to see it."

"He said I had first rights," Doris said, but limply now, with a voice that had taken on a note of woe, and an expression like that of a lost soul.

* * *

That night Summer had a wealth of material: the creepy guy in the library, the crazy woman, the comical policeman, the shrouded body coming out on the gurney with the masked paramedics, the mannequin on the crazy woman's porch in an officer cap. The drawings were like visual renderings of a shriek, with slashing lines, fierce colors, and swirling eyeballs.

Jon Karl marveled at them but, for once, they were almost too much. He slipped onto the back porch to watch the shadows engulf the yard, and the birds at their evening buffet. Cardinals, sparrows, wrens, finches, some doves on the ground, hummingbirds chasing each other off the feeders hanging from the eaves.

Then a single crow, a big one, flew onto a low branch near the feeders, scattering everybody else. He cawed distinctly three times, maybe a crow's way of saying *watch this shit*, then flew to the ground where he had the entire place to himself. He ate at his leisure, giving the impression he didn't particularly want it, he just didn't want you to have it. At least not while he was in town. Then he flew back to the same branch, tarried long enough to make his

212

point, and finally disappeared in a graceful muscular swoop, cawing a final warning, into the woods.

* * *

This time, it was the beans and rice aisle, and she had company. The guy was her age, maybe a little older, clean-cut, preppily dressed, with hipster glasses and an eager, toothy smile. Handsome, but in a youth minister way, which Jon Karl feared he might actually be. Surely not a fellow teacher—the thought was just too dreary. Ms. Quilliam, who clearly would have preferred that this encounter not take place at all, introduced them: "Trent," and "one of my favorite students, Jon Karl."

Current?

No, he had graduated.

Jon Karl could see in her altered face the transaction she was navigating, and could almost feel her mother's warm approval.

That was a wonderful dinner, Mrs. Blah-de-Blah.

Thank you, Trent.

Jon Karl was depressed for two days. But only two days. Then the grace that always follows trauma, like theft.

"She probably wants children," said Summer.

Good luck with that guy, Jon Karl thought. *More likely a different life.*

Well, who doesn't?

Chapter 40

Redwine on Barber Balch

Balch's family was from off. He didn't grow up around here. When his mother died—this is years ago—he was eighteen, nineteen, something like that—an only child—he moved here with his father, who was a banker. Daddy got involved in several businesses around town, this and that, real estate—plus, there was just some money in the family. Actually, more than just *some*.

Balch and his father didn't see eye to eye—it wasn't like they got into fights, at least not in public—they just didn't care anything about each other—after Balch had been so close to his mama. I think it was cancer. Anyway, the boy was what you might call a little bit odd—and he got it in his head he wanted to go to barber school. His daddy thought that sounded about right. Get him out of the house anyway.

So that's what he did. Then he graduated, or whatever you do from barber school, and came back to Douvale and started working in Norman Sagweede's barber shop, the only one in town at that time. Maybe his daddy had something to say about that, I don't know. Plus, he had a certificate, which is something most of those barbers back then didn't have. He had it framed on the wall by the mirror, just behind his chair. It's still there to this day. And none of them had a uniform, if that's the word, like he wore, either. Brass buttons and a bow tie.

Then his father died. Kind of sudden—they said a heart attack. I'm not going to sit here and say I know any different. So maybe it *was* a heart attack. They didn't spend a lot of time looking into it—said they didn't suspect foul play. Okay. I don't know and I don't pretend to know. I just know the old man had more money than friends, I'll just put it like that. And who got every penny, all the properties, a dry cleaning business, a drug store, and I don't know what else? But except for one office building up-town, Balch wasn't interested in any of that, he just wanted the money, which it turned out he didn't want to spend, just have. So he sold everything off, except that one place, and if I was a betting man I'd bet nobody he sold it to got what you'd call a bargain.

I'm sure I'm not the first person to wonder just how much he's worth. He sold his daddy's house and bought the place off Lorona Drive and all them acres. It had been a dairy farm way back, and that's where he's been for forty years. I can pretty much guarantee you nobody in this town has ever set foot in it. Or anybody from any town. He never married. No children. No family. I don't know if you've ever gone by there—creepy goddamn place. You can't see it from the road—just pieces of it in the winter. Got this nasty pond off to the side. I bet you could walk across it on water moccasins and never get wet. Maybe that was Jesus's trick—I bet the goddamn Baptists never thought of *that*. And let's just say, he didn't do yard work. Balch, not Jesus. Though come to think of it, Jesus didn't do a whole lot hisself. And all those fucking cats. People used to talk about things going on in there, but you know how people are, they never let not knowing shit about something stop them from telling you all about it. But I think most folks figured everybody has a right to prefer what they prefer and it was better to just not think about it. I mean, you might prefer something a little funny yourself.

Then, not long after he moved in, Norman Sagweede got sick. Not a single doctor could figure out what was wrong with him. Then he was in the hospital, then he was dead—with all these medical bills. Anyway, use your imagination—that's how Balch got the barber shop. And it didn't take him long to move into the bottom floor of that building he had kept uptown, where he still is today. He was, you might say, thinking ahead.

But here's what you need to remember about Mr. Barber Balch. Well, one, he's sitting on more money than God—doesn't hardly spend anything, doesn't go anywhere, nobody to leave it to—and when you've got a situation like that, people try to stay on your good side. But, two, the men, the white men, who run this town have all been his regular customers all through these years. You better believe he hears it all. To the point where, if you need to know what's going on with something, you go get a haircut. He knows who did what to who, and when. He knows who's planning what, who's got it in for who, who owes who, who's shacking up with who, and he knows who knows what and how they found out. He decides not just what to tell, but how much of it and to who, and he knows how to let you know without telling you.

He's been cutting my hair for forty years and I know what I'm talking about. He remembers everything and never forgets a goddamn thing.

Chapter 41

Night Mission

It was a mission. They had done careful reconnaissance, and made a plan. On the chosen night they put on dark clothes, and Jon Karl and Millard blackened their faces and hands. Billy Reuben could skip that.

"I been trying to tell you black was better," he said. "One day you a wish you had some mellow-nim."

"What's mellow-nim?" asked Millard.

"Pigment," said Jon Karl.

"I never heard of it," Millard said.

"Don't even start making a list of the things you never heard of, or we be here all night," said Billy Reuben.

* * *

Lorona Drive was a twisty road, basically a right angle L at the corner where Grantham and Buckhalter Roads intersected. One of the secret places in town you drove by and never saw, like another dimension hiding in a crease of our own. The left side had houses—split-level and the like, with big yards and a swampy feeling out behind them. Those houses had been built in a single flurry half a century before, when the right funeral finally happened and the licensed buzzards showed up. The right side, however, was untouched, a bank of thick woods fronting about fifty acres sixty or seventy years removed from their days as a pasture. Somewhere in there an old dairy barn had choked to death. The property was still enclosed by what used to be a fence. There were no roads, no access—except for the almost invisible driveway about halfway down, barred by a metal gate and a couple of No Trespassing signs.

They were in the Wrangler, and parked on a little dead-end dirt road off Grantham Road, and picked their way through the dim woods.

Billy Reuben had been hard to convince, at first, because he had heard that Balch let snakes out in the woods all around his house to guard it. It was also rumored he could see in the dark.

"How are you going to make snakes stay around a house?" Jon Karl asked him. "And nobody can see in the dark."

"You can with night-vision goggles," said Millard.

"You think he's standing there all night watching the woods with night-vision goggles?"

"He might be."

"What else he got better to do?" asked Billy Reuben.

Which, actually, *was* the question. What did the man *do* in there at night?

"Probably surfs the dark web," Millard speculated.

"What's the dark web?" Billy Reuben asked.

"Ha!" Millard snorted. "You don't know what the dark web is?"

"Why would I be asking you what it was if I *knew* what it was?"

"You don't want to know."

Fifty yards or so in, they came across another, unused, dirt road, or the vestige of one, that angled off the driveway to the right, behind a densely wooded ridge. On the other side lay the house.

They made their way, upright, up the slope—some scruffy undergrowth and no shortage of wait-a-minute vines on the ground. Billy Reuben tripped on a particularly healthy one, got tangled up and tore his pants getting free.

"Granddaddy gone *kill* me!" he fiercely whispered.

"Shh!" hissed Millard. "I'll buy you some fucking pants."

"You always *say* you gone do something, then nobody hear another word."

"I'll *do* it. Be quiet."

Nearing the crest, they dropped to all fours. The low-lying, single-story house came into view crouching beside the pond, visible in the moonless night only because it was white, with only a couple of dim lights burning within. The pond, a symphony of croaks and bleats and chirps, provided the perfect soundtrack. Patches of a window behind a mass of shrubbery on the far end of the house glowed in sickly yellow light. Bedroom? What went on in *there*? The only other light leaked from the wide picture window in the front center.

The drapes were three-quarters open, presumably for the cats, about seven or eight of which crowded the window sill. Against the far wall, barely illuminated, stood a vaguely human figure— except it wasn't moving—at all—which put the hypothesis of it being human in question.

"Let me see the binoculars," said Jon Karl.

Billy Reuben unslung them from his neck and handed them over.

Jon Karl had a look. "Ooh. Creepy," he said.

"What?" said Millard.

"It's a mannequin. In some kind of military uniform."

"What's a mannequin?"

"Like in a store."

Millard gleefully digested that. "Let me see!" he said.

"Keep your voice down," Jon Karl whispered.

Millard raised the binoculars and had a look. He was beside himself. "Man, that's *sick*!" he gushed. "You want to see?" he said to Billy Reuben.

Billy Reuben declined. "Naw man, this getting too creepy."

"Come on, let's get closer," Millard insisted.

"Hell no!" returned Jon Karl. "This is close enough."

"We can't see anything. Billy Reuben, do you want to sneak down there with me to that window and look in?"

Billy Reuben stared at him.

"Look!" Jon Karl whispered.

A figure had just slipped into view behind the window, walking in slow, delicate steps across the opening.

"What the fuck?" Millard exclaimed.

Did the figure pause and cock its head?

Maybe. Then resumed, and passed out of sight.

He was dressed in some elaborate get-up, a maybe dead cat cradled in one arm, a fancy staff in his other hand.

"Ooh!" grinned Millard.

"It's the fucking Pope!" said Jon Karl.

"What's the Pope?"asked Millard.

"The *Pope*, man. He was dressed up as the Pope."

"Is that a church thing?" asked Millard.

"Yes."

"We don't go to church," said Millard.

"Well, that's who he was dressed up as."

"Ooh—*sick*, man," said Millard, in high spirits.

"What's he doing with that cat?" asked Billy Reuben. "I'm getting out of here."

"No—*wait*," pleaded Millard. "Let's go down and look."

"Shit, I ain't going down there," said Billy Reuben.

Just then, the Pope reappeared, no longer holding the cat, only his ferula, his mitre disappearing overhead. He stopped—then turned his head toward them and instead of eyes they saw two glowing blue circles.

Billy Reuben gasped. "He *do* have night vision goggles!" he exclaimed. "I'm outa here!"

"No!" Said Millard. "Wait!"

But Billy Reuben scrambled to his feet and took off.

Jon Karl was right behind him.

"Shit!" said Millard, and followed.

* * *

As they made it back to the Wrangler and blew away from there, the first thing they discussed was whether they should tell anybody.

No, they decided.

Except Billy Reuben said, "If my granddaddy ask me, mon have to tell him. He know if I be lying."

"That's all right," Jon Karl said. "Theotis won't tell anybody."

The second topic was a briefing from Jon Karl.

"The Pope," he said. "The head of the Catholic Church. The *Pope*. They have the Pope and all these cardinals and bishops and shit. They walk around the Vatican—"

"What's the Vatican?"

"It's their palace, where they walk around in silk slippers and get manicures. And they have jewels all over them, and these altar boys standing around—which is something you don't want to be—and they're all men. Men surrounded by men. Everybody there is a man. The secretaries. The assistants. The dude standing by the desk with a pad. Nothing but men."

"Just like Balch," said Billy Reuben.

* * *

When they pulled in to drop Billy Reuben off, Theotis was sitting on the porch in the shadows, and came down the steps. He walked over to the Wrangler.

"I knew you was up to something. Why you got that stuff all over your face?" he asked Millard.

Millard was slow answering, so Theotis said, "So couldn't nobody see you. I don't want to have to talk to your daddy. Y'all ain't stole nothing, have you?"

"No—we didn't steal anything," said Millard.

"Tore nothing up? Hurt nobody?"

"No, we were just checking something out."

Theotis looked at Billy Reuben though the back window. "You done tore up your pants?"

"Millard said he get me some more."

"You get your own pants. Don't even think about lying to me—where y'all been?"

"We went to that man's house," said Billy Reuben.

"What man's house, boy? Don't you be playing no games with me."

"I ain't playing. That barber's house."

"Barber? You talking about Balch?"

"Yes sir."

"What you be spying on him for? What's wrong with you? Don't you know that man crazy? I wouldn't put nothing past him. I bet you that house full of guns, and all he got to say is y'all was trespassing—which y'all was."

"He didn't see us," said Billy Reuben. "We was hiding in the woods."

"Except he might have had night-vision goggles," said Millard.

"What the hell you talking about?" Theotis demanded.

"Nothing—just—he might have had night-vision goggles."

"This batshit crazy enough without that," Theotis said. "I just want to know what y'all *doing* there."

"Just to see if what they say is true," said Millard.

"What they say?"

"That he crazy," Billy Reuben answered.

"I done told you that—"

"And have all these cats."

"What business that of yours?"

"Just curious."

"Curious get your ass killed."

"We won't be going back," said Jon Karl.

"You damn sure won't," Theotis said, then stood there a minute. "You see him?"

"Oh yeah, we saw him," said Millard. "He was dressed up."

"All right. That's enough right there. I don't want to hear nothing else."

"It was a whole bunch of cats," said Billy Reuben.

"And a mannequin," Jon Karl added.

Theotis turned to Billy Reuben. "What you saying?"

"I'm just saying it was cats in there."

"No, you saying something else." Billy Reuben kept silent. "You saying he was doing something with a cat? Tell me the truth, boy."

"Naw, we didn't see nothing. Just him walking by the window. Dressed up."

* * *

When Jon Karl got home, Summer got a full report.

Wide-eyed, she hung on every word.

"Like—*the* Pope?"

"Yes," said Jon Karl. "Him."

Chapter 42

Billy Reuben

Billy Reuben preferred to go frog-gigging when storms were in the forecast, because everybody knows if a snapping turtle gets you, it won't let go till it thunders.

He also preferred a new moon, and a hot humid night in mating season—late spring, early summer. But they'd had some luck in September before, and they decided they wanted to go one more time. The frogs were still there, just not croaking their brains out, and you had to know where to look. And for that you needed Billy Reuben, because when it came to frog-gigging, he was the man.

They went out on the pond just after dark in two canoes: Millard and Billy Reuben in one, Jon Karl and Billy Lirenzo in the other. They paddled toward the shallow end, Billy Reuben and Billy Lirenzo kneeling in the bows of the canoes with LED headlamps, and gigs ready.

"Right in there," Billy Reuben directed Millard, and he slid him into the hydrilla under the willow trees.

"Watch out for snakes," said Millard.

"Don't you be talking about no snakes. They listening to every word you say."

Billy Reuben raked the bank with his light. Billy Lirenzo and Jon Karl were a few yards down.

"Little more that way," Billy Reuben pointed, shining his light into a little nook in the cattails. Then: "There he go! Get in closer!"

Deadeye Billy Reuben struck, and didn't miss.

"All right!" Millard cried.

Pretty good size. He went into the bucket.

Billy Lirenzo didn't like it when his little brother scored first. His directions to Jon Karl grew more terse and urgent. Within about forty-five minutes Billy Reuben had three and Billy Lirenzo still none. The latter started blaming the canoe, the time of year, the wind (of which there was none), the barometric pressure, the way Billy Reuben was getting into all the good places and blocking them, but fell short of blaming Jon Karl.

Then, just when they were about to give up, his headlamp caught a pair of eyes—Jon Karl slid him in closer, and he threw a strike. That broke the tension. They had four. All pretty big. Not enough to feed a family—but eight meaty legs for Luthelma to fry up.

* * *

Later, the sequence of events would melt into uncertainty as the three young men told three versions of what happened, and even they grew to doubt what they remembered. But all remembered Millard—or had it been Billy Reuben?—shouting "Snake in the boat!" and then Millard paddling them madly away from the overgrown bank, rocking the canoe, and Billy Reuben fumbling with the gig and trying to keep his balance.

He wasn't successful. The canoe kept rocking wildly, almost out of control, and it didn't help when Millard started hacking the bottom of it with his paddle. Later he would say there hadn't been a snake, but a little bream that had flopped somehow into the canoe, or maybe there *had* been a snake, but in either case he hadn't gotten a good look at it. Jon Karl was paddling towards them, but neither he nor Billy Lirenzo was too keen on the idea of a snake in a canoe—but it didn't matter. The canoe capsized and spilled its contents into the murky pond.

"Was it a snake?" Billy Lirenzo wanted to know.

"I don't know." Millard was wheezing. "It might have been."

Billy Lirenzo shone his light over the scene. A half-submerged canoe on its side, two paddles floating, and a plastic bucket. Nothing else.

"Where's Billy Reuben?" Jon Karl said.

Billy Lirenzo kept raking his light over the whole area.

"Where's Billy Reuben!" Jon Karl cried again.

He was just gone.

"Billy Reuben!" His voice echoed over the water.

Then Billy Lirenzo: "Billy Reuben!"

Jon Karl stood up and almost capsized that canoe as well as he jumped into the water. He didn't care about snakes or snapping turtles or anything else.

The pond was about eight feet deep there. Jon Karl took a gulp of air and dove, clawing himself to the cooler water on the bottom where the canoe had flipped. Nothing! Where did he *go*? He groped madly for him—how could he just disappear? He had to come up for air.

"I can't find him!"

Billy Lirenzo was kneeling in the canoe. "Where'd he go down?"

"Back a little bit," Millard said, holding onto the canoe.

Billy Lirenzo jumped in, this time succeeding in capsizing the canoe

Jon Karl took another gulp of air and went down again. His hands brushed against slimy limbs and other submerged debris from the making of the pond, half buried in the mud, and he felt madly for something solid. Nothing. This time when he surfaced he had to come over to Millard's canoe and hold onto the side, heaving to get his breath.

"Aren't you going to help me?" Jon Karl said.

"I don't know what to do," Millard said.

"Dive down and try to find him!"

"I'm not sure where to look."

Billy Lirenzo had surfaced now too, his headlamp still shining. "He probably up there on that bank," he said, and shone his light that way, but it wasn't strong enough to reach.

"Billy Reuben!" Jon Karl cried. No answer. Then to Billy Lirenzo: "Could you see anything down there?"

"It's cloudy—can't see much."

Jon Karl went down again. He realized he only had the air for a few seconds of groping around the sodden trash on the bottom before he had to go back up.

He went down again and again, only able to do a few seconds at a time—no longer sure if he was even close to the spot, or if he was just feeling the same crap over and over.

Billy Reuben, goddamnit, where are you! he screamed to himself. How could he just vanish like that?

He was exhausted. Maybe Billy Reuben *had* made it to the bank. And then in a panic took off running. It had to be that.

Billy Lirenzo was calling him, frantic, exhausted.

Then the light on Theotis's back porch came on.

* * *

Spruill got Sheriff Cubbage out there, with a johnboat, and they paddled over the area with a bright light, but they couldn't really see into the murk. His deputies searched the woods and pasture all around. A team from Atlanta arrived just after daybreak.

The search didn't take long. Jon Karl, Millard, Billy Lirenzo and Sherica, Luthelma, Miriam, Spruill, Sheriff Cubbage and a couple of his deputies watched from the bank. They found him as the sun was clearing the trees, tangled in debris with a swollen bruise on the side of his head. Jon Karl had never felt, and would never feel again, the mortal blow he felt as he saw the diver come up with that body.

Luthelma shrieked. Miriam wrapped her arms around her and tried to turn her away from the sight, but Luthelma wouldn't let her. "My baby!" she cried, words that would echo in Jon Karl's head from that day on.

He came over and embraced her, inconsolable, then saw Miriam's face so distorted with pain he let Luthelma go and enveloped her in a hug.

"I loved that boy," Miriam whispered.

"I know you did. I did too."

A sound he had never heard before escaped Theotis, and Jon Karl could hardly bear to look at him.

When he did, he saw a look on his face he had never seen before. A look that would never really go away.

PART TWO
2009 - 2012

Chapter 43

Dreams

The pond hadn't wanted to kill the boy, it just wanted to be left alone. It got its wish. In one fell day it found itself severed from the world, isolated and haunted. After the hasty construction of a memorial made of a plastic flower festooned cross with Billy Reuben's hat, his favorite sneakers, tools, his frog gig, and various other effects of his stolen life, no one ever went there. No one ever looked there. It lost its place in waking reality and became something more akin to the dark caverns that breed bad dreams.

* * *

The next day, for the first time Jon Karl had ever known, the old gentleman in the plastic chair was missing. The chair remained, but the man, who apparently wasn't a permanent fixture after all, was gone. Then and now, no one else ever seemed to be around the house, and the empty yard offered no explanations.

Had he died? Who found him? *Had* anybody found him, or was he in the house, melting back into the ocean of peace and oblivion? Either alive or dead, like Schrödinger's cat.

* * *

That night, Jon Karl had his first taste of what in various forms would become recurrent dreams: alone, walking along an overgrown, rusted, barely discernible railbed, in suffocating hot air, going somewhere, unable to remember where, knowing there was nowhere, really, to go, with the woods looming on both sides, blocking out the sky, and the sounds of huge coyote-like creatures and feral cats just out of sight. Fighting each other.

For now.

A view of the lonely ocean—a huge sailing ship approaching, covering a wide swath of the horizon, from which many small

231

boats would be calving soon. In dread, he headed inland, wanting to get as far as he could, thinking of places to hide.

* * *

Spruill had given Theotis all the time he needed, but as it turned out, he didn't need much. The only hope for him was to get back to work. Jon Karl went back to work with him, but it all felt different. Theotis got through most days in almost complete silence, his only words the compact little orders he couldn't avoid—something so full and tight inside him the words came out like blood from a pinprick. He wasn't funny. The Sunday gatherings got left off for a while, but for a long time after they resumed they too were something less than they had been.

Theotis still did everything he had done before, but as though Theotis himself wasn't there. Jon Karl couldn't quite name what was absent, and imagined a world where everything proceeded exactly the same, but without the absurd complication of consciousness and souls—a mechanical replica of the one we know. And though that world would have no love, no laughter, no joy, neither would it have self-loathing, grief, or regret. And death, like everything else, would have no meaning.

Sometimes Jon Karl tried to remember the old Theotis, but one of the slyest tragedies of our human fate is that our traumas bar us utterly from the world before them. Memory is just a bad dream.

Something in the air changed after Billy Reuben died.

Jon Karl and Theotis never talked about Billy Reuben, but one day Jon Karl made a wrong cut—he just muddled the number in his head, knew he should double check but didn't, and because of a half inch, they lost a twelve-foot two by eight. Theotis showed no emotion—he didn't trot out the "measure twice, cut once" adage, or tell Jon Karl to go find the wood-stretcher, the one with the yellow handle, not the red—he just absorbed it.

"Billy Reuben would *never* have done that!" Jon Karl said impulsively.

Theotis's reaction was instant. His face transformed, and everything he was holding back threatened to overwhelm the dam. Jon Karl saw a flash of something desperate.

Tears streamed down Jon Karl's face. "I'm sorry, Theotis—I—"

Theotis struggled to re-pack his emotions, but there was no getting them back in the trunk. A pair of his own tears ran over his cheekbones. He let them. "Naw, man," he said. "You good. I don't think he would have either."

The moment, for all its pain, offered some unexpected relief.

They could say his name now.

Chapter 44

A New Shadow

Jon Karl came around the potatoes in the Produce section, and stopped. He was standing there. Looking at him. Waiting for him? It wasn't the half unbuttoned pink shirt, the gold, the tight pants, the pointed shoes—but *him*—that look in his eye, that froze Jon Karl's steps.

No one was around, except a woman, her back turned, looking through the salad packages in the upper corner.

The man had strong features—some might say handsome, but that wasn't the right word. Something more predatory about his beauty, with his full lips and black eyeliner. Maybe he didn't even understand, he certainly didn't *have*, any modesty—he radiated the arrogance of one who got what he wanted.

Jon Karl realized he was tired of him.

He approached, watching the man's eyes flicker up and down his body. "Okay, who are you?" Jon Karl said.

The man mockingly feigned a look of surprise. "Well, good *heavens*," he exclaimed. "Where did *that* come from?"

"Drop the bullshit. You've been following me."

Again that playful shock. "So bold! Accosting a complete stranger!" His eyes left off the mockery as quickly as they had put it on. "I'm not following you," he said, "I just keep running into you." He looked Jon Karl over. "I wonder why that is."

"Me too."

"Coincidence?"

"Cut the shit. What do you want?"

"Well, everybody wants the same things, don't they? And nobody ever got poor by knowing what people want."

"Good God."

"What? Am I wrong? I should say, everybody wants some *variation* of the same things. And now here I am talking to this pretty boy in the Piggly Wiggly, wondering what *his* variation is."

"Don't call me that."

"What are you going to do, wrestle me to the ground?"

"Not a chance."

"I'm guessing you're not here to pick up women. Or men. I mean, I'm guessing you're here for your stomach, not something else."

"What the fuck—"

"See? It all comes down to what you *want*."

"All right," Jon Karl said, turning to go. "Just stay away from me. Whatever it is you're about, I'm not interested."

"A fellow can't be curious?"

"About what?"

"About your preference."

"My preference in what?"

"Well, if I'm not saying it, it shouldn't be too hard to guess."

"If I'm asking, it must be."

"Hmmm," the man said, looking frankly at Jon Karl. "You're not just pretty, you're a handful. Nothing wrong with that! Guess what? I'm a handful too! And for what it's worth—I'm just saying—if you ever wanted to make some money—some *good* money—I know a way you could do that—*Jon Karl*." He smiled. "Oh dear, he knows my name! Mine's Vance, by the way. Okay—enough small talk—I've got places to be. And you wouldn't believe me if I told you where some of those were. Be good. Don't keep your handful just to yourself!"

He turned and swept away.

The woman by the salads had turned and was looking quizzically at Jon Karl.

Miriam.

Chapter 45

Redwine Pyle

Did I ever tell you the story of how Douvale got started?

I'm not sure—

Well, the railroad ran through here before the Civil War. Running east and west. There wasn't a whole lot here except a coaling tower before the tracks crossed the river—you can still see the old bridge pilings—and there had been a skirmish here before the end of the war. When I was growing up we used to dig musket balls out of what was left of that old tower—it's gone now—but anyway, one day back then a train carrying a load of mental patients they were transferring from one institution to another came through and jumped the tracks and wrecked. All the passengers ran out into the woods and hid. A couple of days later they got hungry and came out and founded the town.

I'll be damned.

* * *

Redwine lived on the lake. Actually, not *on* the lake but, as they say, back from the lake. You could see slices of the water between the bigger lakefront houses across the road.

He lived alone with his hound dog Kurly Bobo. Kurly Bobo was also the name of one of Redwine's friends when he was growing up out in Tarville, and the subject of many of his stories, so whenever he said Kurly Bobo you had to know which one he meant. Redwine wasn't a hermit or anthrophobe—he made his weekly rounds and had his places where he would drop in for a beer or twelve, and even entertained the occasional visitor, like Jon Karl—and he was a repository of a lot of information that nobody but he was a repository of. You can say that for most people—what made him unusual was that he had never harbored any elaborate fantasies about himself, but had simply kept his eyes and ears open throughout his life, and found his fellow bipeds interesting. And when it came to human nature he didn't recognize the line most people draw, somewhere, between the proper and the profane. To Redwine, it was all human and all fair game. Retired now, he was near eighty and gave no impression of wearing out. He had worked hard, at times, in his younger years, and now had all he needed, which wasn't, in the typical world view, much. His small cabin was tidy and comfortable and he wasted absolutely no energy thinking about himself or what he did or didn't have. If anyone ever asked him if he needed anything, his perennial answer, "Not a thing," was simply the truth. He was perfectly happy in the seats, watching the human comedy. And having a beer or twelve. No red wine, of course, no white or pink for that matter, but also no distilled spirits of any kind, no drugs, no medicine— an abstinence to which he credited his health and longevity. Apart from his Ultras, about the only thing he drank was water, and tea, but he kept a supply of ginger ales in the refrigerator for Jon Karl.

I've concluded, he told Jon Karl once, that you and me may be the only sane people in this town, so I need to keep you hale and happy.

Jon Karl could think of no higher honor.

Every couple of weeks Redwine would go to Wal-Mart, not because there was anything there he couldn't get someplace else, but just to see the sights.

Well, I've been to Wal-Mart, he would say, popping an Ultra and bringing Jon Karl his ginger ale.

What'd you see this time?

Well, as soon as I walked in the door, the first thing I saw was a, let's just say, good-sized gal not what you'd call young, driving one of these motorized things with a full-sized doll in her lap and a cane that she was using to rake the Cheese-Puffs and doughnuts and everything else off the shelves into that big old basket.

You don't think she *ate* that stuff, do you?

Oh no, I'm sure she donated it to the poor. But what I mainly remember was when I was standing in the checkout line, catching up on my reading. Right in front of me was a, I don't know, middle-aged woman and a young teenage boy. Mama and her son is what you would have guessed. As usual, I had picked the stupid line, so it was taking forever. The boy was toting a Slip'n'Slide box under one arm, and after a while I couldn't help but notice he had got to rubbing that woman's back and shoulder with the other—and she had on one of these, I don't know what you call it, wraparound things that just covered up the business and not a whole lot else, and of course some kind of butterfly tattoo over her whole shoulders, and a tramp stamp downstairs, and she says, *If your daddy catches you doing that again he'll beat the shit out of you.*

Jon Karl laughed. I'm not sure how to take that.

I'm not either, Redwine said, and shook his head. *Your daddy! Again!*

Chapter 46

The Bright House

Jon Karl had come to think of it as the bright house because he often saw its roof, the only part visible from the road, catching the afternoon sun on his drives out Troubleneck Road to the chicken farm. The first day he stopped was simply the day it finally came completely into focus.

Most days, basketball boy was there, playing against himself, hammering away, each fading jump shot over the never anything but imagined defender another penny in the jar of muscle memory—but not on this day. Jon Karl's fantasy decayed: this nobody kid would never get his chance—he would break his back working and need all his energy to survive—and feed all those hungry mouths that kept appearing around him.

None of the passel of younger kids were there either—the whole place sat empty, silent, not a soul of any age anywhere to be seen, leaving all the junk and broken toys scattered over the yards, robbed of the imagination of children, to be just junk.

Jon Karl entertained a flash of Lakeshore women breezing by in their gleaming SUVs seeing only an eyesore that "they" needed to bulldoze and hose down with Lysol.

On this day, as Jon Karl passed by, depressed, he noticed for the first time an insignificant little road or disused driveway a few yards beyond the second roadside house, disappearing into a tangle of privet. On an impulse he slowed, found a place to turn around, and went back.

The privet scraped the sides of the Chrysler as Jon Karl followed the little tunnel to its end, predictably enough, in what was left of the back yard of the third house, the bright house.

Why am I doing this? Jon Karl wondered as he turned off the motor and an old deep silence rushed into the void. It was perfectly obvious that no one lived there, that no one *had* lived there for a long time. Some busted furniture and pieces of decomposing appliances lay ensnarled in the privet crowding the house. Cans, bottles, an old doll, littered the grounds. The house itself could not have been plainer, a simple rectangle with a roof that, up close, showed its age, a simple back door with a stoop and some concrete steps, and windows, none covered, some broken, offering a view into the barren interior. He got out of the car, and the clunk of the closing door died in the still afternoon.

The door was unlocked but half stuck, and thinking again *what am I doing*?, he shouldered it open. He was convinced, as he scanned the lonely scene before him, that those kids never came in here, and he wondered why not. He stepped into the empty room and immediately had the vertiginous sensation that the interior space was distorted. A hallway led away to the left, lined with doorways, doors either standing open or missing—more to it all than the modest outside proportions could account for.

He stepped carefully from room to empty room—no furniture, no clues to individual people, just a feeling of something familiar, affectionate even, like a lost smell coming back.

Approaching the back room, he stopped short. An empty chair sat before a window offering a view over a broad field. The trace of a crimson clover-lined road disappeared into it. The tall grass swayed in the breeze.

Some crows off in the distance, the occasional muffled rush of a car a million miles away out on the road—but mostly an old, deep silence.

As he left, not really thinking why, he didn't pull the door shut, but left it half ajar and walked halfway across the barren yard. Then he stopped and turned around to look at the once again unassuming house. A more ordinary, a more mysterious place could hardly be imagined. How could something so mute be saying so much?

Stepping into his car, he caught the scent of gardenia, thinking of Maryrell.

* * *

That night Summer shuddered at his description.

"I don't want to go there," she said. Then added, "Did you see her?"

"No. I just felt her."

"I feel her sometimes too," said Summer. "She doesn't want to leave where she is."

Chapter 47

Summer Gets a Boyfriend

With growing anxiety, because it turned out Tamela Johnson didn't really know anything, Zadie had disappeared—forget Millard—and all he had was YouTube, Jon Karl had been going from plant to plant with his latex gloves and magnifying glass, trying to read the hairs and trichomes and crystals. He knew if you waited too long, the potency would start to diminish—but it wouldn't be at its maximum if you did it too soon.

He made the call about mid-September—cut the stems and hung the fat-budded plants up to dry. Tamela Johnson had finally shown up with a vanload of boxes of quart Mason jars, with Zadie.

"Hi, Jon Karl," Zadie chirped, then helped unload the boxes, chattering away about nothing.

She's seriously mentally ill, Jon Karl concluded.

By October all the trimmed and dried buds were in the jars, under a tarp.

"About how much, would you say?" Millard asked him on the phone.

"A pretty good bit," Jon Karl answered because, of course, he had no idea.

"When will it be ready?"

"Three or four weeks?"

"Okay, let me know."

* * *

Summer had a boyfriend. Maybe.

She had met him through Wady Carothers, whom she was seeing only sporadically these days. Jon Karl had yet to meet him. About all he knew was that his name was Logan and he came by to pick her up sometimes and take her out to eat or to the show.

From what Jon Karl had gathered, it sounded like the guy had a tendency to drink a little too much sometimes—on a few occasions he had even asked Summer to drive—which apparently he didn't know was far more life-threatening.

Summer was eighteen and had, on her third try, gotten her driver's license. Jon Karl had done the best he could, but there were some things about the process she had never really grasped, such as staying in her lane, parking, and left turns. She would grip the life preserver of the steering wheel and wobble like a needle sewing up the centerline. Parallel parking was simply impossible. You might as well ask her to take a running start and leap across the Grand Canyon. The woman who had given her the driving test had spent the entire time chatting with somebody on the phone, looking up every now and then to say "turn here" or something, followed by "Uh-huh—you got *that* right, girl" into the phone, and for the parallel parking had finally just said, "Okay, you good, just be careful." Angle parking in front of a store was possible, barely, but still traumatic for Summer—she usually ended up astride one of the lines, at a crazy angle, and most days, the whole concept was so daunting she would just pull in front of the store and leave her car askew in the fire lane. As for left turns, she simply refused to make them, and so spent her entire driving life spiraling in one big circle.

Anyway, the guy drank too much, and judging by the way, as Summer described it, he was almost catatonic sometimes, and elated others, he did some other things too much too, but he didn't try to have sex with her the first time they went out, so maybe he was okay.

"He's going to help get me a job," Summer told Jon Karl.

Well, that sounded hopeful. Summer was a high school senior and had yet to have a job; Jon Karl made enough to support them and told her she needed to concentrate on her schoolwork, but lately she had been talking a lot about having her own job, so

Jon Karl knew she just wanted to at least pay her own way, and not feel like a mooch, which he understood.

Then, finally, Jon Karl met Logan.

He came by to get Summer and didn't say anything when he shook hands with Jon Karl—not out of rudeness or arrogance, but just blankness. He seemed sober, maybe a little lethargic, and apparently just didn't have anything to say. He was lanky, dark-haired, with heavy whiskers that made his lower face blue, black-framed glasses, and big hands and feet. He must have made some kind of first impression but Jon Karl couldn't say what it was. He was just sort of there.

"Do you like him?" Jon Karl asked Summer later.

She shrugged. "I don't know."

"What do y'all do?"

"We just go eat somewhere."

"Do you talk?"

"Some."

"What about?"

"Well, really, he doesn't talk a lot. If we go to the show, he talks about that a little bit."

He liked action movies, which bored Summer, but she went along.

"Do you think he's a good person?"

Summer frowned. "He's going to help me get a job."

"When?"

"He said soon."

Chapter 48

Redwine Pyle

I know I've told you about Clytus Lamar (Ly-mur).

You might have.

Just a dumbass country boy like me. We used to run around together, and get pretty deep in the cooler sometimes. I'm not going to say he was *simple*, but he was different. He's the one that asked me one time—back when I was married—what my wife did, and I told him she was a beautician, and he said, *my wife's good-looking too*. Shit like that. And he *did* have a wife, hard to believe though that may be—you wonder how these people find each other—but like they say, there's a lid for every pot—but as for her looks, she wasn't humpbacked from toting around beauty medals, that's all I'll say.

We was sitting on his porch one afternoon and a car pulled up out front. It was Myron Grimes—lived down the road—had that functionally illiterate brother everybody called Fishhook that would walk around town asking everybody for a quarter. When he got enough he'd go over there to the cafe and get him a sausage biscuit or a hamburger. One day he went into the post office. The postmaster was L. C. Woodruff, and he caught him in a foul mood. *Give me a quarter*, Fishhook says, and L. C. just said, *Ain't got one! Now wait a minute*, says Fishhook, *you're the postmaster and your wife teaches over there in the elementary school, and you ain't got a quarter? No, I ain't. Well*, Fishhook says, *you need somebody to manage your financial affairs!* That kind of got off on L. C., and he says, *Fishhook, instead of walking around town asking everybody for money, why the hell don't you get a job? That sawmill over there always needs people—they'd hire you.* And Fishhook says, *I don't need a job—I got $30,000 in that bank* *across the street. So why don't you go get some of it and buy your own damn hamburger? I can't*, says Fishhook, *everybody else's money is on top of it and I can't get to it.*

Well, anyway, Myron stopped out front of Clytus's house and says, *Clytus, so-and-so's been down there doing something he shouldn't with your cow. Well, damn*, Clytus says, and after Myron drove off I said, *You reckon your cow's all right?* And he says, *Hell, I ain't worried about the cow—I'm just afraid to drink the milk!*

I don't blame him.

Fishhook was friends with Buster Simmons, I know I've told you about him.

Probably.

He used to work his way around town too, getting handouts, going through stuff people had put out on the curb, that kind of thing. He was so ugly dogs barked at him, and he wore these filthy old blue coveralls. Some of the people in town got to feeling sorry for him, I guess, and started bringing him some decent clothes every now and then, but he never would wear them. One day I asked him why not and he said, *if I wore them they'd stop giving them to me.*

I see his logic.

I remember once Zeke Greaves came downtown with his German Shepherd and he got loose. Zeke looked everywhere but couldn't find him. Somebody told him he ought to go out to Buster's place, he might know something. So he went out there and Buster said, *it was a German Shepherd?* It was. *Had a black patch on top of his head?* Yes, he did! *And a white patch down here on his chest?* Yes, exactly! *And was wearing an orange collar?* Yes, yes!

No, I ain't seen him.

Chapter 49

A Little Cash

Millard handled the transaction. It was people from Atlanta and Jon Karl told him he didn't want to know anything about them.

"That's smart," said Millard. He had come out and gotten an ounce and taken it to them.

"They said it was killer," he reported.

Jon Karl felt pleased with himself. It had been a learning curve, and he had made plenty of mistakes, but they'd still ended up with around 200 pounds, trimmed, dried, and cured. Millard, Zadie, and Tamela Johnson came out to help compress it into garbage bags and tape them up. The next day the propane guy stopped by in his truck and they loaded it into his accessory box and he drove off.

A week later, Millard brought Jon Karl $5000 in cash. Jon Karl looked at the money, his brow furrowed in thought. "I thought it was going to be 500 dollars a pound," he said. "That's a hundred thousand dollars."

"Well, they didn't give us that much," said Millard. "Plus the expenses."

"What, the buckets and all that?"

"Yeah, and the pump, and a lot of other shit. It adds up."

"I did all the work."

"Yeah, I know. That's just what they gave us."

"What's just what they gave us?"

"Well, it was less than twenty thousand."

"Damn."

"What was I going to do? I had to get rid of it."

"Hm."

"Five to you, me, and Tamela." He hesitated. "And I gave a couple thousand to Zadie."

"Zadie? No way! What the fuck did she do?"

"Well, she helped pack it up—"

"Give me a break! That took an hour and a half."

"Dammit, I had to give her something to keep her mouth shut."

"She should never have been in this at all. She should never have come out here."

"Well, it's too late now."

"I tell you something—if you expect me to do this again next year, we're going to need an agreement up front."

"Absolutely, man."

Jon Karl was left thinking, *I have no idea if that bastard is telling the truth. And if he is, this isn't worth it.*

All of which depressed him. He hid the money in the house where nobody would ever find it.

* * *

Jon Karl was smart enough to know he shouldn't suddenly appear at the car place with a wad of cash. He was down to the last payment on the Chrysler, and remembered Mr. Dawes had told him they would send him the title when he paid it off.

The *title*. That meant something.

He went to talk to Mr. Dawes and told him he wanted to get a car for Summer. Sharing had become hard to manage.

"You got the other one paid off?" Mr. Dawes asked him.

"Just one payment left."

"Good deal, Jon Karl. I'm proud of you. That'll go on your credit history. I'm going to tell you—something you need to remember—having good credit is the secret to success. Everybody's got ideas. They come and go. What matters is who's got the capital."

"Yes sir." Actually, he *had* told him. More than once.

Jon Karl and Summer went car shopping. Jon Karl told her they needed to find something under $5000—two or three, if they could. "It just needs to be a bright color," he said.

"Why?"

"So people can see you coming and get out of the way."

"That's funny."

They didn't have much luck at Bob Hauer's Auto Barn, or at any other car lot—everything they liked was too expensive. They were starting to get a little frustrated when they saw a silver ten year old Honda Civic in a front yard in town with a homemade cardboard "For Sale" sign in the window.

"It's not a bright color," said Summer.

"That's okay, I'm going to order flashing lights for it."

It was dinged-up, some duct tape helping the ceiling stay up, high mileage, but seemed to run okay. They guy wanted $2500. Jon Karl called Mr. Dawes.

"Don't do anything until I look at it," he said.

Which he did, that afternoon. "You've got it priced way high," he told the man, who knew who he was and was a little intimidated. "The Blue Book says $1800 if it's in good shape. Which it's not. So we're offering $1200."

When did he look at the Blue Book? Jon Karl wondered.

Summer squirmed a bit. She'd decided this was the car she wanted. Mr. Dawes was going to mess it up!

"I'm going to have to get more than $1200," the man said, shaking his head a little abashedly.

"Well, it was nice meeting you, and I wish you luck," said Mr. Dawes, and turned to leave.

He got almost to his car.

"Wait a minute!" the man called. "Make it fifteen and we'll have a deal."

Mr. Dawes stopped, then came walking back.

Shortly after, he wrote the man a check for $1300. The man wrote the bill of sale on the back of the title.

This time they got a twelve-month loan, and, as with the Chrysler Jon Karl kept a register which he would hand the bank lady each month as he came in with his payment and she would subtract it and write the new amount on the next line, so he could watch it go down. He knew it was mostly interest in the beginning, but if you stayed with it, the interest would be almost nothing at the end, and every payment would make it that much closer to being your car. Free and clear.

Jon Karl had explained his plan to Summer: take the money from his cache every month and go down to the bank and make the payment in cash.

But Summer said, "I want to be the one to pay it off."

"How are you going to do that?"

"By getting a job."

"When?"

"I've already got it. I'm starting Friday night.

Chapter 50

Sensations

She wouldn't tell him where, which made him a little uneasy. But he understood she was just trying to be independent, trying to grow up. The thought made him sad, but at the same time proud.

His little sister with a boyfriend. A senior in high school. Her own car. A job. Damn, things changed fast. You just turned around and everything was different. In his mind's eye he still saw her as about twelve, thirteen, drawing her crazy pictures. She wasn't drawing them so much anymore. Her prehistoric art teacher in school, who knew what a *picture* was supposed to look like, had throttled that. At least for now.

On Friday morning Jon Karl was making a Wal-Mart run, and as he drove past Sensations, something caught his eye.

The place had been a series of lounges or clubs—a "sports bar" once, with out of proportion amateur paintings of soccer, baseball, basketball, football players on the plywood covering the windows—just enough out of town on Lawrence Road to be shady, just enough in it to pretend to be respectable, and now was enjoying an apparently prosperous life as a low-grade strip club, the plywood now lavender, a sagging roof, a single entrance door under a tattered awning, and a portable roadside sign that said: "Sensations. Girl's"—the latter with a backward "s." Jon Karl had never seen anything close to an overflow crowd there, usually just a smattering of pick-ups and cars that told the story all too well of the caliber of the clientele. There were fights, and every now and then a shooting.

What Jon Karl saw on this day was two men standing by the entranceway, talking. One, in a seasonable orange shirt with a gold-pattern blazer and tight white pants, looked like—could it be?—*was*—Vance. Goddam, was he *everywhere*? The other, in blue jeans and an untucked white shirt, managing to convey, even across the parking lot, the impression that he had just woken up, was Logan.

Logan?

Jon Karl went ahead to Wal-Mart, then out to the Chicken House where he was planting a winter garden, like Billy Reuben used to do, but kept thinking about that sight all day long. He had planned to spend the night, but toward late afternoon his uneasiness drove him back to town.

Summer wasn't answering her phone, and when he got home, her car, and she, were gone. He looked around the house for some clue, and found it in the make-up bottles and a hand-mirror on her nightstand.

Okay.

Red flags were flapping in the wind. It was just after six.

He got in the car and drove out to Sensations. He parked in the front lot and walked toward the building. Then he saw the Civic, at a weird angle on the side of the place. Summer was sitting in it. Giving her a start, he appeared at her side window. She didn't seem to be eager to talk to him, and he had to prod her with gestures before she lowered the window.

"What are you doing here?" Jon Karl asked her..

She was very nervous and looked at him for several seconds without answering. The make-up looked wrong on her.

"I'm getting ready to go to work," she said at last.

"*Here*?"

"What's wrong with here?"

"Jesus, Summer—"

A side door opened and Logan walked out. He headed their way with a scowl. "Is there some kind of problem?" he said. He was dressed better now.

"As a matter of fact, there is," said Jon Karl.

Logan stopped and stood there, his arms slightly flexed at his sides. He was a sturdy guy, a head taller than Jon Karl.

"What problem would that be?" he asked.

"My sister being here."

"She's here of her own will. Nobody's making her."

"I sure hope not."

Summer's eyes flicked from one to the other.

"Why?" Logan said. "Is there something you're planning to do about it?"

"Yeah, there's something I'm planning to do about it. I'm planning to take her home."

Logan took a step closer. "Look, buddy, she applied for a job here, and she got hired. She's coming to work. She's late right now," he said, then looked at Summer. "Come on, Summer, let's go."

"She's not going in there," said Jon Karl.

"We have a *contract*," Logan persisted, taking another step.

"I'm calling the cops," said Jon Karl.

Now another man came out the side door. Jon Karl immediately recognized him—the Neanderthal man from the restaurant.

"What the fuck?" the man growled.

"This guy's trying to keep one of our employees from coming to work."

"She's not one of your employees," said Jon Karl. "She's my sister, and she's not working here."

"Look, buddy, just get the fuck out of here, okay?" said Neanderthal. "You don't want to get messed up in something over your head."

"Over my head? Jesus, I'm calling the police." He pulled out his phone.

Both of the men came closer. "Put your goddam phone up," said Neanderthal.

"Why should I?"

"Because we don't need any fucking cops out here."

"I bet you don't."

"I'll tell you something, buddy. You're about to get yourself in an unpleasant situation."

"I just want my sister to get away from here. To come home with me. That's all I want."

Summer, whose opinion so far nobody had asked, watched the goings-on anxiously.

"Summer," Jon Karl said, "did they tell you what this job was?"

"Yes, we told her what the fucking job was," said Neanderthal.

Jon Karl ignored him, looking at Summer. She nodded.

"What?"

"Dancing," said Summer.

"It's dancing with your clothes off. Did they tell you that?"

Her eyes, pretty with the make-up, overwrought though it was, seemed about to bulge out of her head. "They said exotic dancing."

"Yeah, it's *exotic*."

"We told her what the job was," Logan confirmed. "She's here of her own will. Ask her."

"Her will is to come with me. Jesus, Summer, you don't even know what this place is. Scoot over."

The two men stood there, watching. Jon Karl pulled out of the parking space, or the one where the majority of her car was, and drove down to the Chrysler. Neither of them said a word. Mascara-streaked tears were running down Summer's face. "You go first," he said. "Go straight home. I'll be right behind you."

* * *

Later that night, after Summer had spent several hours barricaded in her room, she emerged.

254

Jon Karl was on the couch, with Afterlife, reading. He looked up.

"Was that really what it was?" she asked.

"Yes, Summer, that's really what it was."

She took that in, nodded, then went back to her room and closed the door. She started that night on a drawing frenzy that lasted two days. Then, finally, on a mid-afternoon, she went to bed and slept until about the same time the next day.

The episode was recorded and filed away. While she was sleeping, Jon Karl slipped in her room and took the drawings, then on the couch pored over them like a connoisseur.

Later, when at last he headed back to the Chicken House, he took his favorites with him.

Chapter 51

A Wreck

The wreck was a hot topic on TV-39, Douvale's community station. The story featured several titillating elements: the son of Spruill Dawes, a smashed-up van that looked like a diesel locomotive, a girl of dubious character, and a brush with death.

The van, which the son of Spruill Dawes had lost control of on a back country road fooling with a pipe, had centered a tree and was totaled. Luckily, the overgrown ditch had slowed their speed before the impact. Millard himself had walked away from it with only a headache from his head hitting the steering wheel.

The girl of dubious character, Paisley, who lived with her drunk father in a small house in that gray world neither this side nor that of the tracks, and was the kind who had been known to give the floorboards of her car, in the periods when it was functional, a quick vacuum in the driveway when she got home late at night, wasn't quite as lucky. She had been thrown against the dash at an awkward angle and knocked unconscious, and was only semi-conscious when the paramedics got there. They had strapped her to a backboard.

Millard, of course, using the whiny tone of a victim, had called his daddy first, who had said, "If you've got anything in the car you shouldn't have, get it the hell out of there. Where are you?" Millard told him, and Spruill said, "What the hell were you doing out there?"

"Just riding around."

"If you're not sober, *get* sober," Spruill said and called 911. Then he called Ulmer Cubbage.

* * *

A deer had run in front of the van, causing Millard, who had a stellar driving record—only three speeding tickets and not really an *extensive* amount of minor incidents—to swerve and lose control of the vehicle. When Paisley regained consciousness, the first order of business was to inform her of that story—though it was well known, in the event she remembered it differently, that spinal injuries had a way of boggling memory.

Later, Redwine would claim that the deer council had convened in the woods and issued an official condemnation of the false and defamatory charge, and of the general unconscionable scapegoating of their species.

Notwithstanding, that was the gist of the Sheriff's report.

Spruill's main objective was to keep the ambulance-chaser on all the billboards, or some lower-grade version of him, if you can, in fact, go any lower, out of the picture. He accomplished this by sending his attorney, Samford Grimsley, to meet with the girl's father, a fragile unassertive man who was sober enough to understand that Mr. Dawes was offering to pay his daughter's medical expenses, along with some generous compensation for the inconvenience, just sign here.

Millard, who, if *anybody cared*, had endured the hellish pain of a minor concussion, was not only back driving his boring Wrangler two days later, but had driven out to Misty's Flea Market, where they had local wrestling every Saturday night in a barn, looking into having a go at the sport himself with a cute bad boy persona and checking to see if the name "Kid Demon" was taken, and never got around to visiting Paisley in the hospital. Happily, she recovered her speech and movement and was able to go home after a week, with several months of painful rehab ahead of her.

They told her she was lucky, and she tried to believe it.

Jon Karl and Summer *had* gone to see her in the hospital, where she looked terrible, a lot like the punched in the face van now moored behind the Dawes' barn, but were pleased to see her looking much better when they visited her a couple of weeks later at her house. They could hear the muffled TV from behind the closed door of her father's room.

Her mother had died of cancer a few years ago. The house was small and dirty, with a mama dog in a cardboard box on the front porch nursing eight puppies. There wasn't much inside and they could tell that Paisley, in a neck brace, was embarrassed for them to come in. They were living on the portion of the old man's disability that he didn't drink up.

She's got nothing, Jon Karl thought. Thank God she's going to be okay, and get on with her life, get the hell away from Millard, maybe get a new start, leave some bad habits behind. But later, Summer, her eyes welling with tears, said that the accident had weakened her inside, in a way that would be waiting in later years. She could see her in pain, and her tears were for the poor girl—so unfair—but also for herself, cursed with having to see it.

Mr. Dawes would not speak of the incident. It was over. As if it had never happened. Theotis wouldn't talk about it either, except to make one comment: "You looking at the difference between the white man and the black man right there." Nothing else.

And the next time Jon Karl saw Mr. Dawes, he saw him in a light he had never seen him in before. A man with the means to get out of anything. That's what he bought, year in and year out. *Credit*. They weren't evil people—*look at how much he's helped me and Summer*—just people in their own particular situation, playing their parts.

* * *

That night the coyotes and feral cats were barely out of sight in the woods. And the rusted tracks just went on forever, nowhere.

Chapter 52

Redwine on Pruet Junior

What they call the way of the world, said Redwine.

All you got to do is open your eyes. There's plenty of examples around. Spruill Dawes is just being Spruill Dawes, and I've told you before he's done enough good to make up for whatever else. My guess would be he worked something out with the insurance company, but he paid for the girl and at the end of the day he was just protecting his boy.

And himself.

That's true. But different from somebody like Pruet Echols—that's a different kettle of fish. Spruill Dawes I would trust with my life—he may be as slick as they come, but you get down inside of him, he's got principles. Pruet Echols I wouldn't trust any further than I could spit. He's got the kind of principles you have to turn off three-fourths of your brain to have. I'll tell you something, if anybody ever invented something that could reactivate that part, he'd be a rich man, and this country might have a chance.

Pruet Junior has been *accused* of rape three times. God knows how many times he's been guilty of it. And all three times you never heard a word about it, so don't ask me how I know. Pruet's got this lawyer out of Atlanta that could talk the paint right off the wall—he also represents some of those crooks in the State House, if that tells you anything—and he goes to talk to their lawyer who of course already knows there was no witness, no way to prove it, and make sure the girl knows they know some things about her she would rather not hear on Channel 39, and Junior's walked away every time.

I will say this, he was a damn good football player—in high school. He was just pure mean. He was the kind—he still is—that went out looking for fights, and if he couldn't find one, he'd go somewhere and conjure one out of thin air. He got a football scholarship to Troy State, but his freshman year the coach played another boy ahead of him—black kid who was about four times better, so like everything else it comes down to which pond you're in. They played him some at linebacker, and he made some tackles, but anybody that could throw over the middle ate him up, because he ain't that tall and just wasn't that good at pass coverage. If you ran right at him he would flatten you, but why would you do that? You didn't have to be but kind of a smart coach to take him out of a play. He was easy to fake.

So it was his wake-up moment, you might say, when you look around you and realize that being a bad-ass just ain't really going to take you but so far, and he got all flusterated, and what did he do? What you'd expect—he quit and dropped out of school and came home to Daddy.

He's supposed to be working for his daddy some way or other, but I don't believe he's done any work the last five or six years but chase pussy and drink. He's real good at both. There's a crowd he runs with, but I'm not sure that's really what you call friends. There's no such thing as getting along with him. I was getting a haircut one afternoon and he was in there too, looking about half crazy like he always does, telling some story about whooping somebody's ass or getting some pussy. I don't remember which, probably both, though for him they're not all that different—and his phone rang. He yanked it out of his pocket and made it stop, then went back to telling his story, but you could tell it had agitated him being interrupted with nobody's ass to whoop to make it better, and he got a little crossed up—and then it rang again. This time he yanked it out and threw it like a goddam grenade right into the mirror behind Barber Balch's chair, taking the mirror, and three or four bottles, not to mention the phone, with it.

Of course, Big Pruet took care of that. The one that got the short end of the stick was that other brother.

Cabul.

Yes. Cabul. Two years younger. Their daddy used to tell them that Junior was the Alpha—he had got the alpha sperm—and Cabul the second-place sperm, and when they were growing up would make them fight and just stand there and watch, pulling for Junior, who of course would beat the shit out of him. Cabul didn't play football—he didn't play anything except tennis, which his daddy didn't even recognize as a sport. He had one girlfriend in high school and ended up marrying her. He did everything he could to be different from Junior, and I'll tell you something— that fucking Pruet never bailed *him* out of a goddam thing. And never let him forget he wasn't the jock. The stud. Pruet terrorized all of them, but especially Cabul, with that Baptist shit, and when Cabul rebelled, he sent him to a camp to cast out his demons. What I heard, they had a way of going about it that would make Parris Island look like a picnic.

He went off to college, but dropped out after two years—said it was a waste of time—and started his own construction company. You've seen that compound out there—he's built it into a major operation, building shit all over the world. And he did it without one bit of help from Daddy.

By the way, speaking of getting a young lady on the road to motherhood when that wasn't your intention, did I ever tell you about Bum and Buck Hester and that country girl?

I don't believe you did.

Well, she was kind of a natural girl, if you know what I mean, and these two brothers were just taking turns, bringing it to her, and she couldn't get enough. So, sure enough, she comes up pregnant, and Buck says, *What are we going to do?* And Bum told him, *Ain't no problem, we'll fix this.* So they had this not really a friend but this other boy they knew out there: Floyd Dudley—his mother had been my third grade teacher—and told him all about this hot to trot country girl they knew, and it didn't take long before he got to hammering her too, and one day she tells him she's pregnant with his child. *Now wait a minute*, he says, *how do you know it's mine? Because when you did it, I felt it*, she told him. And he's thinking, *damn, I didn't know the woman could feel it take*, but she made a persuasive case and he was a good man and he claimed it. They got married, and ended up having about five more, and stayed married for forty years.

Ain't that sweet?

Chapter 53

Miriam

"Well, look who's here," said Miriam.

Theotis had sent Jon Karl to the house to get his keys to the shop.

"Walked right off and left them," Theotis said. "Getting where I can't remember nothing." And indeed Theotis was starting to show little signs of forgetfulness and carelessness so un-Theotis-like it made Jon Karl uneasy.

"Where's Luthelma?" Jon Karl asked.

"She's out doing her business," said Miriam. Mason jars covered the kitchen table and a couple of big pots were boiling on the stove.

"Looks like you're putting some stuff up," said Jon Karl.

"Me and Luthelma. She be back in a little bit."

It was October, still warm, with only a few nights so far to remind you, after that endless hot and humid summer, that the season would in fact change like it always does. But this sunny fall day had that quality that such days have—the illusion that there had never been anything else and it would last forever.

"I saw you talking to that man in the store," said Miriam.

"I saw you," Jon Karl told her.

"Do you know him?"

Jon Karl shook his head. "No."

"You looked like you did."

"I don't know if it looked like I did or not, I'm just telling you I don't know him."

"I was just wondering. I didn't think you was that way."

"What way?"

"The way he is. You know what I'm talking about."

"I think he's a lot of ways I'm not."

"I was just wondering—because all the girls like you."

Jon Karl shrugged. This was a long way from his favorite topic. "If you say so."

"And you like some too."

"Yeah. I like some too."

She put her arms behind her back, extended her head forward, and pursed her lips.

"Come over here," she said.

"Why?"

"Just come here."

"What do you want?"

"I want you to come here." She waited.

"Why?"

"Because I want you to."

Jon Karl took two steps and stopped. "What do you want?"

"You know what I want." She touched her lips with a finger. "Right here."

"Oh, come on, Miriam." He looked around.

"Luthelma at the store. She ain't been but ten minutes gone. Ain't nobody here. Just you and me." She touched her lips again.

"You're crazy."

"*You* the one crazy. Right here," she repeated.

"I can't."

"Why can't you?"

"Because I just can't."

"Because I'm colored and that's not good enough for you?"

"No."

"Then come here."

"Miriam—"

"Because I'm married?"

"Well—yeah."

"You think he don't grab a handful of everything that walk by? Where you think he at right now?"

"I have no idea—"

"Just don't say *work*, because that man ain't worked long as I known him. He over there on Porter Street standing around doing nothing—less you count drinking and buying scratch-off tickets— with all the rest of them. Used to, they worked you to death, now they just let you do nothing. They end up the same—one just take longer. Like Luthelma say, they used to call it slavery, now they call it welfare. He ain't a bit different from them—except for me keeping him alive."

"Maybe you ought to divorce him."

"He'd kill me."

"Then kill him."

"I ain't the kind. It ain't in me to kill nobody. And even if it was, what you think happen to me? They send me off to prison, or maybe the electric chair, and everybody be saying, there go that woman killed her husband—got the devil in her—and nobody ever know nothing about it. Is it because I'm too old?"

"No, you're not too old."

"I ain't but thirty-four."

"You're not too old."

"Maybe you find out I'm just right."

"I'm sure you are."

"Why don't you find out for yourself?"

"Oh come on, Miriam, it's just not possible."

"Why ain't it? You ain't told me yet."

"It's just not."

"You think I ain't been with a white man before?"

"How would I know?"

"Well. I ain't. You ever been with a colored woman?" Jon Karl shook his head. "I think you scared."

"I'm not scared."

"Yeah you are. You just scared."

"Scared of what?"

"Scared of me."

"I'm not scared."

"Then come here."

Jon Karl took another step.

"Right here," she said, tapping her lips, closing her eyes.

"Would you please stop? Theotis is waiting on his keys. I've got to—"

She opened her eyes. "I thought I had a real live man on my hands, but now I see it's just a little boy."

"I'm not a little boy."

"You just acting like one. You think I ain't pretty?"

"No. You're pretty."

"I ain't sexy?"

"No. You're sexy. You're nice. You're everything—"

"You just chicken."

"I'm *not* chicken."

"Then come here."

She had blocked every way out and left him no choice.

He kissed her and she put her arms around him and pulled herself to him.

"When you gone take me to your house?" she asked.

"What do you mean?"

She pulled back and looked at him. "Why you want to act like you don't know what I mean? I got something I want to show you."

"Miriam. Why are you doing this to me?"

"To *you*? You think I ain't taking a chance? What you mean, why? Is that the way you do, go around asking why all the time? Everybody else be making love, and you be asking why?"

"It just doesn't seem like—"

"A woman say she like you and you got better things to do? It ain't like I'm trying to kill you. I just want to make love with you. What's so bad about that? What kind of life you think *I* got? Everybody see me, the way I always smile, the way I act happy, and nobody ever know that's what it is—*acting* like it. I lost the only baby I had—now I'm pose to take care of all *his* children and drag myself into that nursing home every day—pose to plan my whole life around what people don't even appreciate me want. Life so cruel sometimes—I even say most of the time. I'm tired of not having nothing good in life. I'm tired of living for somebody else. I wake up every morning and think, Lord, how I'm gone get through this day? And at night I think, if I could just keep on sleeping. The only time my husband sleep with me is if he can't find nothing else, and then he be drunk and wallow on me like a big old pig, and he stink. I hate him. Maybe I *will* kill him."

"Don't do that."

"Why not? Which prison the worst? Ain't nothing say I can't make my own way."

She was crying. A very pretty, very sad woman with some kind of hope not dead yet. A mile deep. She wanted to feel valued. Like everybody. Jon Karl held out his arms and she pressed herself tightly against him. He could feel her sobbing against his chest.

* * *

The property Pruet Echols wanted for the expansion of his Baptist Correction Camp was now infected with Hargett Hills, a low-rent neighborhood of small houses poorly built in the sixties and in varying stages of disrepair, some abandoned, a canker of putrid rot in the town. As Pruet saw it. His mission was to get the entire property condemned, and basically steal it. Then bring in the bulldozers, wipe it from the face of the earth, and put an eye-catching detention facility in its place that would be an economic boon for the town.

And get the government to pay for it!

267

The only thing stopping him was the Daughtry-Knowles Management Consortium, whose agents were resisting every move he made. Arguing that the property was clearly salvageable and it was wrong to drive all those people from their homes. What kind of bullshit was that? Whover was behind it was invisible, but you didn't have to be a bloodhound to smell Spruill Dawes.

In November, Todd Guin won the election for County Commissioner, District 4, and if you had to pick an adjective to describe him—and this had been the mainspring of his campaign as well—it would be "business-friendly." He was the youngest person to ever hold the seat.

Fucking Dawes, thought Pruet. Pure spite. There was a special oven in Hell for his kind.

But as he always reassured himself, "God's got this."

Chapter 54

Barber Balch

Balch knew that nothing in the world was what it looked like. He didn't know why everybody put up a false front and lied to everybody else, he just knew that they did, and left it at that. Take love. Everybody knew there was no such thing—people just pretended there was, to get what they wanted. Or foreign languages. All those crazy people in the world obviously faking it couldn't fool *him*. In fact, he didn't really believe there *were* all those crazy people in the world. He knew most of what you saw on TV was just actors.

The truth is, he didn't really watch TV—he had his own materials. And a good imagination. Someone who has lived alone his whole life tends to develop one. Yes, he had his little fantasies, some better left unmentioned, others involving the blade, that silver and pearl mainstay of his craft, sharp as a wasp sting. Oh. The clean, surprising slice, the red bloom. He felt it down *here*.

No one, and there were many, would want to know the life they unwittingly lived in Balch's mind. The full-crotched pretty boy was only one. But no way around it, a favorite.

Balch had a fetish about papal bulls. He fantasized over the idea of issuing them, telling people what to do and what not to do, condemning them, devising punishments.

Because, if it happened that someone wasn't to your liking—and people *do* have their little spites and jealousies, do they not?—you could issue a papal bull denouncing them. Issuing papal bulls—that was his greatest lust—okay, maybe except to use his mouth on that pretty boy and then to be mounted by him like a papal bull, without mercy. And then: the clean slice, the aghast surprise of the subject, taken unawares and discovering all at once where the true power lay. Then the treasures in his hand. Not such a little stud now, are you?

He composed his papal bulls at night, dated them carefully and kept them in a locked filing cabinet that would be easy to crack open when he died and—who knows?—maybe the authorities would see their necessity and enact them at last. That would be good.

But not the pretty boy. *Him*—clearly a heathen libertine—he would have no choice but to imprison in his own special place. Many nights his last waking thoughts were of the punishments he would be bound by duty to inflict on the little sinner. Yes, his *duty*. He would look up sagely and seriously from his writing into the empty house around him, his jowls sagging in a papal frown— maybe examining those photographs again, those gym photographs, that he had issued many a papal bull over, you can be sure.

Balch was, in those moments, at least in his way, happy.

Even if he believed everybody was faking that too.

But he himself wasn't faking anything tonight—he was savoring a piece of genuine good fortune. With an uncommonly sizable gesture of support, he had persuaded Pruet Echols to appoint him—he didn't demand a high salary—Head Jailer in his correction camp, a position he had long coveted. Claiming he had "some medical training," he had told Mr. Echols that he would be happy to help out with the medical exams of incoming cadets, for no additional salary, but Mr. Echols said he had it covered.

Maybe later.

For now, he had a uniform to design.

Chapter 55

Jon Karl and Summer

"Everything reminds me of something," said Jon Karl.

"What?" asked Summer.

"You mean, what I mean, or what does it remind me of?"

"What does it remind you of?"

"That's what I'm trying to figure out. Not what it reminds me of, but why it reminds me of it."

"What does that mean?"

"It means the thing it reminds me of is the same thing as why it reminds me of it. And that's what I wonder about."

"Oh," said Summer.

"Sometimes it seems like there isn't anything else to do," Jon Karl said.

"There's a lot," said Summer.

"Yeah, I guess there is. Even if it is just something else. Do you ever wonder if everything has already happened?"

"I don't know how you could wonder that."

"I was just wondering. I want you to come to that house with me."

Summer frowned. "I don't like it. It scares me. Gardenias bloom in June."

"I didn't say they were blooming, I just said I smelled them."

"That's even worse. And crimson clover blooms in April."

"I don't think that place pays any attention to time."

"You can go there if you want to—I don't want to."

"What are you afraid of?"

"I'm not afraid—just all the pain there."

She had felt it driving by. She shook her head contemplatively. These days it seemed every time Jon Karl looked at her he saw someone herself out of time—older, somewhere remote.

"Dreams are bad enough," she said.

"I think you inherited something else from Maryrell," he said. Even though neither of them could really picture Maryrell, they both knew Summer looked like her.

"I don't want it," Summer said.

"Well, I can't blame you. But most people would call it a gift."

"That's because most people don't have to have it."

"That's true, I'm just saying—if you do have it, maybe you should just go ahead and have it."

"I'm getting another job," she said.

"Are you going to tell me about it this time?"

"Not yet." She smiled.

"No new boyfriend this time?"

"No. But I drew a picture."

Jon Karl's face brightened. "You did? I want you to keep drawing pictures."

"I drew this one."

Jon Karl knew, but nobody else would have, that it was Logan and the Neanderthal man, gashes of red peering through black, like a smoldering fire—black hair, black glasses, grotesque red eyes, and noses like animal snouts, the air filled with something like wasps with hair-do's. The picture, her masterpiece of that episode, *said* something—you couldn't say what, and it didn't matter. Jon Karl smiled at her.

She was smiling back.

"I'm framing this," he said.

* * *

That night he dreamed they were out in a boat on a lake—the kind of lake a doomed soul would dream—fishing. He hooked one, and saw a flash of a green and silver fish, reeled it in, but when he pulled it up from the water it was more like a dog, thick white coat and waterlogged, sad and hopeless. The line disappeared down its throat and he told Summer to get the hook out, but she quailed and couldn't do it, so Jon Karl reached into the apologetic creature's mouth and ripped out the hook, then heaved the wounded thing overboard, where it sank, its eyes slowly descending, swallowed by the black water.

* * *

The stupid line—*again*. I can pick the line with one person buying a pack of chewing gum, and when I get there, the cashier has to call the assistant manager, or the receipt tape runs out, or the customer's debit card won't work, take your pick—and this fella's there—I don't know, about forty-something—talking on his phone—got this hangdog face and he's talking in kind of a deep voice—real matter of fact:

Somebody stole Mama's car again . . . No, we don't know who . . . yeah, she's gone be mad.

Redwine shook his head.

Again!

Chapter 56

Live Wrestling

"Are you a good guy or a bad guy?" Summer had asked.

"Kid Demon—what do you think?" Jon Karl said.

"Yeah." Millard grinned.

"What does that mean—you have to always lose?"

"No, I win sometimes."

"Even if you're bad?"

"So they can get revenge."

"Oh. Are you going to win or lose tonight?"

"You'll just have to come and find out." Devilishly.

Misty's Flea Market sprawled on an acre out from town off U.S. 99—an expanse of long wooden tables with rickety roofs, and a broad parking area. Vendors and buyers converged on the place every Saturday, keeping the ocean of bric-a-brac in constant circulation. Misty was in her eighties now, but her progeny kept the place running, and had added various other enterprises over the years—the Haunted Barn in October, U-Pick-Em blueberries and strawberries and peaches in their seasons, and for the last seven or eight years the inspired and instantly popular spectacle of live local wrestling on Saturday nights.

It was five dollars to get in, and the competitors split the gate and a tip bucket by the door. It cost twenty dollars to participate, but you could still make seventy or eighty on a good night. Though a couple of the younger guys, trying to find their way in life, harbored professional dreams, and invested some effort in costume and image, mostly the warriors were older guys with bulging guts willing to put on tights and Wal-Mart masks. In it strictly for the beer money.

Millard had novelty in his favor, and decided to just be himself: a kid, average-sized, with curly hair and a surplus of gall. Kid Demon. His persona of the cute lippy brat made him easy to hate and impossible to take your eyes off of. He did it for the thrill—he didn't need the beer money.

Jon Karl and Summer got there early and got good seats near the ring where the kids congregated to goad the villains and cheer their heroes.

"You're just a big stupid turd!"

The old guy in black leotards and a homemade mask, finishing his last cigarette before battle, wheeled toward the audacious urchins. "You shut up!"

"*You* shut up!"

He feigned a lunge. "Shut your stupid little mouth or I'll come down there and slice your gizzard out!"

"Ooh!" went the crowd, and then watched the poor old man, since he was a bad guy, after a few scares, be slammed onto the foam padding and neutralized in a scorpion death lock. Then howled derision at him as he strode unvanquished in spirit, through the crowd, giving as good as he got, to the exit.

He would be back.

It wasn't until somewhere in the second match, basically indistinguishable from the first, that Jon Karl noticed Brenleigh Echols eyeing him from across the way. Kind of surprising to see *her* here—but then again, maybe not. As he looked around, he saw a few other faces he recognized, but the patrons had come mostly out of the cracks and crevices of the hinterland.

Kid Demon was the third match, and he came through the crowd in his black trunks and boots and a purple mask with his crazy hair spewing out from it to a raucous reception. It was mostly jeering, which Millard lustily provoked, but also a kind of electric thrill. The boy had charisma, you had to give him that. He milked his entrance for everything it was worth, stopping along the way to strike menacing poses, some with scandalous pelvic thrusts, to the crowd's delighted outrage.

His opponent was another specimen of the sack of guts on stick legs with a roly-poly head somewhere past his prime type—which gave him a catchy look in red trunks, mid-calf red boots, red cape, white tights and a hood.

"I'm going to take you out!" Millard roared as they faced off.

The spectators howled.

"Eat shit and die, spawn of Satan!" roared Big Daddy.

Millard had been working apparently, and had learned some spins and locks and holds, and what his performance lacked in technique, it made up for in bravura. With virile shouts he managed to get Big Daddy pinned, for the victory—and then with the man wincing in pain and Millard strutting to the roaring displeasure of the crowd, suddenly Big Daddy's brother, somebody apparently having sent Lassie to tell him, burst down the aisle, took a little more time than was convincing to pull his way into the ring, and made short work of the cocksure lad, locking him by the jaw and hair, the coup de grâce a much deserved spanking—privileged little shit—to thundering cries of glee.

Jon Karl looked over at Summer. She didn't like the result, or maybe she did—all the same, her face was radiant with excitement.

A couple more matches, dull by comparison, and then the referee/emcee, one of Misty's seventeen grandchildren, announced a special guest—Mister Maniac.

Mister Maniac burst through the barn door into the arena with a savage screech. All heads turned and followed his terrorizing progress through their midst. He seemed to be of the opinion that dressing up was for girls, one of the two things—well, three, if you counted feeding him—that girls were good for—and had made no attempt at showmanship—just a tight pair of gray gym shorts, revealing his many scars, with his playing number, 27, on his butt, one digit to a cheek, and a cheap Zorro mask—which, as with Zorro, did nothing to conceal his identity. At twenty-six, he was past his peak but still in his prime, even if the beer was maybe catching up with him a bit—still compact as a dump truck and mean as a water moccasin.

Pruet Junior.

You knew he wasn't in it for the beer money either, and you couldn't help but worry a little about what that left.

His opponent, who had an uneasy look in his eye, was from the same gene pool as most of the others, maybe a little younger, forties maybe, and heftier—but the sagging had started, and his low-dollar tattoos were going out with the tide, and you would assume he wished he could get a do-over with *that* episode. But fuck it. He was all in red white and blue with American flag trunks and an Uncle Sam hat his daughter had found on ebay, which he rather ceremoniously doffed prior to battle, entrusting it to the safekeeping of his crew, and was obviously a crowd favorite. He watched Junior, whose malevolent eyes were now locked on his own, stride ringward, and he didn't have a good feeling. Junior had been a self-invited last-minute addition to the bill, and they hadn't had time for any kind of rehearsal, only a brief verbal run-through, and Junior hadn't seemed a particularly attentive student. Now or ever.

When the bell rang, Junior came at him hard, catching him up high and trying to muscle him down, but Uncle Sam back-stepped and neutralized him. Jon Karl and Summer could hear him issuing instructions but couldn't quite hear what he was saying. Just the frustrated urgency in his voice, since Junior obviously had no idea what he was doing. They kept grappling, Uncle Sam kept backing away, and the crowd registered the increasing tension. The bell rang, they returned to their corners, and you could hear Uncle Sam complaining to his people. Junior had no people, and wouldn't have listened to anybody anyway.

Jon Karl looked around the barn. Brenleigh was staring directly at him, her lips parted, and that *look*. Jesus.

As the second round started, Junior came out like "enough of this shit," and calling on his football training, went low. He tackled Uncle Sam, much to Uncle Sam's surprise, daring the referee to do anything about it, then fell on his hated enemy and tried to pin him. Jon Karl heard the man squeeze out "I'm supposed to get on top of you and pin you!" but with Junior that shit wasn't going to happen. Jon Karl glanced at Summer, her eyes feverishly bright—she had heard it too. As had apparently quite a few of the other spectators, who started to boo. Gas on a fire. But Uncle Sam knew a move or two and got Junior's left arm in a lock which drew a yelp from him and poured several more gallons of gas on the fire. Enraged, Junior reacted like a pit bull—freed his arm and began punching the man's face savagely like a jackhammer with both fists.

The ring was suddenly flooded with men trying to pull the maniac off his now prostrate and bleeding prey. Junior tore himself from their grip, got to his feet, only then facing the howling booing crowd on theirs. He leapt from the ring and threaded his way defiantly through their ranks. The attendant deputies tried to contain him but he started slugging them too, so one of them tasered him, and they lugged him out and took him to jail.

That was it for wrestling that night. Jon Karl looked around—good God, Brenleigh again! Her face red, energized by the violence, her eyes crawling over him like scorpions.

He grabbed Summer's arm and they got the hell out of there.

* * *

Junior's one call, of course, was to Daddy, who came and bailed him out, threatening to sue over the tasing. Maybe Junior's going into professional wrestling hadn't been such a good idea.

Jon Karl was pretty sure, Millard or no Millard, that he'd had enough of the sport as well.

Chapter 57
Summer Joins the Work Force

Summer was one of those, you leave in the morning she's a skinny, gangly, self-conscious girl, and when you come home that afternoon she's a beautiful young woman. Just that fast. Or maybe the fast was Jon Karl's, who being so much with her he couldn't really see her, then saw her all at once. She made him proud—and uneasy. He knew what was swimming around in that water out there.

Eighteen and in full bloom, Summer was not feeling particularly challenged by her senior year in high school. When she got the lead on the job at Scripture Land, she ran it by her brother.

"You don't really need to get a job," Jon Karl said.

He was still making good money with Theotis, and had taken her out to the Chicken House and shown her the $5000, which had lit her up like somebody seeing Jesus and she was afraid to touch it—but he hadn't shown her where he hid it.

"I don't want to depend on everybody—I want to do my part," she argued.

"Your time will come," Jon Karl said.

"I want it to come now."

"Well, you know who owns that place. You'd better ask Mr. Dawes."

Which she did. And he had surprised them both by saying, "If that's what you want to do, I don't see anything wrong with it. I think it's good for you to have a job—start learning something about managing your money and building up your credit."

"We thought you might not twant her working for—"

"A job is a job," said Spruill. "If there's any kind of problem, you just let me know."

* * *

She had to buy an Israelite woman costume for seventy-five dollars, but she saw it as an investment, and then found out the job description included some janitorial work after hours. Which was only right, she thought, since being an Israelite woman was mostly just standing around, which because of the boredom was harder than it looked. She honestly looked forward to her turn to carry water jugs from the well, and help bake the unleavened bread, and she got pretty good at all of it.

At no point in the process had she had any interaction with or even seen Pruet Echols, which was a relief: even though she didn't know him she was afraid of him. She knew he could walk in at any time, but he never did. Her supervisor was the Director of Scripture Land, Abdiel Eubanks, who had seen something in Summer from the first day, and taken her under his wing.

Abdiel was a serious man. What some might call "spiritual," others "humorless." He never laughed. He was too busy believing wholeheartedly in what he thought of as the *mission*, as opposed to the business model, of the thriving tourist destination: bringing the truth to whoever had ears to hear and eyes to see. Plus, he was just naturally serious anyway—devoid of laughter in himself and suspicious of it in anybody else. Maybe you heard laughter—he heard Satan at work.

His first and only wife, and what drove her to it you can imagine for yourself, had left him quite a few years ago, and he was somewhere in his forties with two grown children he didn't particularly keep up with. His once dark, now salt and pepper, hair he wore in a country bouffant style that forced him to avoid wind, paired with a sharply trimmed goatee. He walked like somebody attempting smoothness in too-tight clothes, a little pigeon-toed with some mid-age midsection spilling over the boa constrictor of his belt. Summer was a little embarrassed by the special treatment Abdiel, which he insisted she call him, showed her, and could tell that the other Israelite women resented it and talked about her behind her back. She was used to it. She had never really gotten along with other girls, with the exception of Wady Carothers, for a while anyway, and had always been more comfortable with boys. One of whom, a centurion, had caught her eye.

And she had caught his. His name was Jackson Fitch, and he had come right up to her the first day. She was so taken with his big blue eyes she hardly registered anything else about him, though she did notice Abdiel looking none too happy, watching them askance from the camel stalls.

Well, special attentions or not from the boss, by her third day she was in love. For the first time in her life with a boy who wasn't just something in her head. And Jackson seemed just as smitten. He would bring her little surprises on breaks—a Granola bar, a Dr. Pepper—and one night had even helped her scrub the toilets, though technically he didn't have to—in Echols land that was women's work. Jackson's after hours work was tending to the sheep and camels and goats—men's work.

When Summer told Jon Karl about Jackson, she gushed, and cerulean-eyed drawings began appearing. Maybe, Jon Karl thought, he actually was a good guy—the real deal—exactly what he knew Summer wanted and needed—but he hadn't met him yet, and reserved judgment. She had a way of latching hold to some oddballs.

Summer tried to keep the budding love affair hidden at work, but there was no hiding anything from Abdiel. One day after closing, when she was getting ready to start on the bathrooms, he asked her to step into his big air-conditioned office.

She saw the other girls watching them, and avoiding their eyes she followed him apprehensively into his executive lair. He had landed here at Scripture Land after a career of mostly successful business projects, some with his friend Pruet, over the years, and had reached a point where he wanted something more ful-filling. A large framed matinee idol-looking Jesus with—damn!—blue eyes, tousled hair, and a garment open at the neck, hung on the wall behind his desk.

"I suppose you could say it's none of my business," Abdiel began, "except the welfare of my employees *is* my business, just like the welfare of the flock is the business of the shepherd." One inquisitively raised eyebrow said, "Right?"

She nodded.

His hands did an up and down on his desktop and she seemed to notice his rings for the first time. A pretty big diamond in one, and a green stone in another. Was that an emerald? She had never seen an emerald, but was pretty sure he wouldn't have a fake one.

"I don't know how familiar you are with the Bible," he went on, then attempted a smile, even if the muscle memory was a little dubious, "but I would be honored to serve as a *guide*, to use the popular phrase, in your studies of God's word, if you were ever of a mind."

She practically whispered, "Yes sir."

"Please don't call me 'sir'," he said. "I know I am a bit older than you, but we're both God's children, equal in His eyes, so let's be equal in each other's."

"Yes—"

"Anyway, I'm sure you're familiar enough with God's word to know the expression 'patriarch.' Abraham, Issac, Jacob—whose other name you may not be aware was 'Israel.' Also Moses, though he was you might say more a prophet than a patriarch, per se. Both, really. They all reflect the fatherhood of God."

Summer stared. Where was *this* going?

"Those patriarchs had wives—Sarah, Rebecca, Rachel, the list goes on—but the truth is, and this was part of God's plan too—you remember his promise to Abraham to scatter his seed over the earth?—the patriarchs often had more than one wife in those times, and relations with other women—I'm sure you've heard the term 'concubine'."

Puzzlement came over her face. "Like a farm machine?"

"No, no. It just means another woman in his household—not quite the status of his wife. Usually younger," he said, then hastily added, "equal in God's eyes." He held her eyes.

She didn't know what to do with hers.

He waved the off-the-subject business away. "Well, anyway, I just mention all that—well, to remind you of the nature of God's plan—"

He wants to make me a columbine! thought Summer.

But then he added, "It's natural for us to be attracted to people near our own age—but maybe that's not always the wisest course, because we just don't have the *experience* with human nature when we're young to see the difference between what people appear, and what they are."

Oh, she thought, *it's about Jackson*. That wasn't so great either.

Sure enough: "Again, it's none of my business, but I have noticed that one of our young men here has been showing you some attention."

She stared at him, wide-eyed, and couldn't think of any response.

"Were you aware that he travels to Atlanta every weekend to gamble at cards?"

Well, she *wasn't* aware, but still couldn't think of anything to say. She sort of shook her head.

"I've just found out about it. Apparently it's been going on for quite some time. I don't have *firsthand* evidence—but I know it on pretty good authority." He was looking evenly at her, but she just couldn't meet his eyes.

"I judge no one!" His bejeweled hands went up and down again on his desk. "My motives are pure," he assured her. "I just want to be sure you have the information you need to make good life choices."

She murmured something.

"Will you pray with me?"

Chapter 58

Abdiel and Jackson

By the time she got out of there, the other girls had finished their chores—their bitching voices seemed to echo in the room— and were gone. The place felt deserted. She went into the break room to get her jacket and lunch tote-bag and, her back to the main door, she froze.

An icy shudder ran through her. She didn't know what "it" was, but she felt it. She turned around.

There, just inside the door, stood Pruet Junior.

"Hey," he said, and took a few steps toward her. She seemed to be seeing him through a dirty filter—he and the air around him were stained. Brown. She wrinkled her nose at a smell like hospital food.

He took a couple more steps.

She didn't know a lot about levels of drunkenness, but she could tell he was at a pretty advanced one. Nothing playful about him—he meant business. She stared at him speechlessly. He advanced a bit more. "You're here kind of late," he said. "You're not stealing anything, are you?"

Her expression turned baffled. "*Stealing?*—"

"Are you getting smart with me?"

"No, I—"

His eyes weren't sharp, but filmy, and like the rest of him, brown, and he wasn't quite focusing on her eyes, swaying a bit. The shirt he hadn't quite managed to button all the way down gaped open, revealing his swollen belly and hairy navel. His thick, scarred arms hung at his sides.

"I think you and me need to have a talk."

Behind him, Jackson appeared in the open door. Junior saw her cut her eyes, and his own narrowed, and then in no big hurry he turned his head. His face took on a *Who's this loser?* sneer.

"Who the hell are you?" he asked.

"I—work here."

"What the fuck you want?"

"I came to get Summer."

"She's busy."

"I'm giving her a ride home."

"No, *I'm* giving her a ride home."

"I think she needs to come with me."

Junior laughed and took a couple of steps toward him. "Since when do *you* get to say what *she* needs to do?"

"It's what she wants to do." Jackson looked around him to Summer.

Junior didn't like that, and something seemed to be working up in his face. "*Goddam,*" he said. "What she *wants* to do is come have a talk with me, and the sooner you get the fuck out of here, the sooner I don't beat your fucking ass."

Abdiel stepped into the open doorway. "Pruet," he said, trying to sound friendly. "I'm going to take the young lady home—" Jackson glanced at him, and Junior spat out a "Shit!"

"It's for the best."

"The *best*?" He slung his arms around. "I own this fucking place. I say what's for the best."

"I don't want to have to call anybody, but I will."

"What—call the sheriff? Goddam! You can't deal with a situation yourself so you call the fucking sheriff? So they can tase me again? Fuck that!"

"I don't want to see anybody make a mistake, that's all."

The swaying was back, and Junior didn't seem completely focused. He had grown a darker brown and exuded doom. Summer tried not to see what was coming into and out of focus behind his unstable features, but it was impossible not to see.

"Summer," said Abdiel. "Come on. I'm going to take you home."

She stood frozen.

Then suddenly Junior laughed—an unhealthy laugh with a note of *Fuck it* in it. "Go ahead, bitch. Tonight's not really the night anyway."

She didn't move.

"Go on!" he barked.

Nothing sudden—she slowly started across the room in a wide berth around him. He laughed again, at her timidity. "Just don't think it's because of either one of these piss-ants. I've decided I'm not in the mood. But I will be."

The blood had left his face. He now looked like he might be sick, but nobody was interested in hanging around to find out.

* * *

Outside, Jackson said to Abdiel, "I can take her home."

Abdiel's face said *That's about as likely as a pig flying to Mars*, but his voice only said, "I'll handle it."

Jackson had only a second when Abdiel turned his back to point to himself, make a steering wheel gesture, and point to her.

He saw a faint acknowledgment on her face.

Junior's banged-up Silverado was parked at an angle like a broken arm just at the entrance.

As they drove away, Abdiel said, "I'm going to make sure that situation never happens again. Don't worry."

She nodded, holding her lunch bag, thinking of Jackson.

Then Abdiel called the sheriff's office. He told them Junior was in there, and please run by and make sure everything was locked up.

Silence for a few seconds. Then the dispatcher said, "The deputy wants to know how they'll know when he's gone."

Abdiel shook his head, and exhaled. "His truck's out front," he said.

* * *

Summer and the compass were mortal enemies, but she knew Abdiel was taking a strange route, not heading for East Douvale, but crossing town and turning into Lakeside, where McMansions sat on broad wooded lots. He stopped on the street in front of one with a gable-cluttered roofline and a turret, set back from the road, with a circular drive.

"I think it would be a good idea for you to stay here tonight," Abdiel said.

"This is where you live?" Summer asked.

"Yes," said Abdiel, "this is where I live." He smiled. "I've got plenty of room. You'll be safe here. And tomorrow you can relax by the pool and get yourself together."

The pool.

"I'm together now," she said. "I want to go home."

* * *

Jackson was indeed a betting man and, watching from an empty lot down the street, he bet that Abdiel would wait ten or fifteen minutes after dropping Summer off, then come back. *He doesn't want me anywhere near her*, he thought. The pervert.

He waited.

Then took the pot. Ten minutes on the dot—then Abdiel's BMW came easing back down the street and paused in front of the house. Lights on in the windows. He waited a minute or two, then slid away.

A few minutes after that, Jackson eased down the street and stopped in front of the house. He stepped onto the porch just as Summer slipped back outside.

Want to go for a ride?" he said.

"Why don't you just come inside?" she said. "Jon Karl's at the Chicken House. It's just me here."

288

He smiled, and shrugged okay. "Let me find somewhere else to park," he said. "Don't go away."

* * *

Summer didn't say anything about Pruet Junior to Jon Karl. She knew the news would get him worked up, and he might really get hurt. Or killed. Plus, he might try to make her quit her job. And that was something she really didn't want to do.

He had gone by Ming's Garden and brought take-out Chinese over for lunch. It was the day he was meeting Jackson for the first time. He said he would come about two.

"It's kind of boring," Summer told Jon Karl, describing her job. "I want to work up to be a guide."

"You probably have to know stuff to be a guide, don't you?" Jon Karl asked.

"They have a training program."

"I think you'd be good at that."

"I think I would too."

"Is Jackson a guide?"

"No. He's just a centurion. And he does something with the sheep."

"I don't like the sound of that."

"Don't be perverted. Anyway, he doesn't want to be a guide. He has another job."

"Besides Scripture Land?" She nodded. "What?"

"He plays poker."

"That's a job?"

"If you win a lot, it is."

"So I'm guessing he does."

She nodded. "He's real good at it."

"How do you know?"

"He said he was."

"Well then."

"He goes to Atlanta every weekend. He made five thousand dollars one time."

"He must be good then."

"You can be a professional poker player."

"I guess you can. Is that what he wants to be?"

"I think he already is."

Jon Karl had formed a mental picture, and when Jackson walked in, and took off his shades, he was just about what he had been imagining based on intuition and Summer's drawings: dark, with blue eyes, hair neither long nor short, he himself neither tall not short, maybe what you'd call good-looking, but something indeterminate about him. And you couldn't really tell what he was thinking. Jon Karl figured that was the poker player in him. Either that, or he wasn't thinking anything.

They didn't talk too long, because that's hard to do with somebody who doesn't say much. And who gives you the impression he doesn't trust you or anybody and is mostly just sizing you up. Afterlife kept an eye on him from across the room.

He reminded Jon Karl of one of those dragonflies that land on the end of your fishing pole. That he would be good for about that long. But Jon Karl didn't share that thought with Summer, who had looked adoringly at him the whole time he was there.

Which wasn't long.

Chapter 59

Redwine Pyle

Who is that man that lives in that little house just as you're heading out of town on Troubleneck Road?

Which house?

That one right past the church that has those poles they lock together so you can't get in the parking lot. He's always got some old car or truck or lawnmower for sale in the yard. And there's a little garden out front. You see him outside sometimes with a walking stick—but you never see him moving. You just come by later and he's in a different place. Like a comet or a glacier.

Oh, you're talking about Gunther Bass. Yeah, he's a little bit of an oddball. And the reason they lock those poles together on the church parking lot is because they got tired of wading through all the used rubbers on Sunday mornings.

I don't blame them. And he's got a wife, I guess, that sits on the porch.

Yeah, she's a little bit of an oddball herself. She would about have to be. I remember one day a few years ago I had some stuff to do and I was running up and down the road and I kept passing the house, and she was sitting up there and waved every time. I'd wave right back. Howdy do. I thought, look at this old woman, living with this certified kook in this little house and she's still as happy as a lark. You just never can tell about people. But about the fourth time, I started to wonder. I slowed down and pulled in the driveway, and walked up to the porch and she said, 'I didn't think anybody was ever going to stop.' That poor woman had been trying to flag somebody down all day long! I asked her what was the matter, and she told me Gunther had fell down. Where? In the garden. I went down there and sure enough there he lay, sprawled out between the rows. He didn't look like he was hurt or having too bad a time of it, so I helped him up, and damn if all his pockets wasn't full of okra. 'Damn, Gunther,' I said, 'what are you doing with all this okra?' And he said, 'I figured as long as I was down here, I might as well do something.'

Chapter 60

Gleams and the Bright House

Jon Karl went by the library and spent a couple of hours prowling the shelves. He thought about all the books, with all their letters, spaces, words, pages. He had read something about the stars, the trillion trillion, ten times more than all the grains of sand on earth, and if all the stars were grains of sand, each one would be six miles from the next closest. He knew he would never find what he was looking for, and that would actually be good, because if you found the answer to everything, or even if there *was* one, you would be disappointed because why would you want to find the thing that left you with nothing else to find? And even if we do arrive where we started and know the place for the first time, what good would that do? Setting out in search of the same thing but this time knowing you're just going to end up right back here?

He stopped off at Racetrac to get gas on his way to the Chicken House. As he was paying, something on the far island caught his eye. It was that feeling that you saw something but it didn't register on your conscious mind—but in some deeper part that knew you saw it but didn't tell the other part. Whatever it was. Usually a snake. Or a flying saucer. Or a face or a shadow where one shouldn't be. But not this time. He squinted—then saw the woman as she emerged from the surroundings, her back to him, tending to her own refueling. He watched her with a desolate feel-ing, and finally she half turned toward him.

Early, mid thirties. Back door of her SUV open, kids strapped in. He stared helplessly, without her seeing him, and his eyes be-gan to burn. What kind of sorcery was this? She was too old. He had the elaborate thought that her life had moved on along a more purposeful vector, faster and more real than the one where he was plodding.

Then she saw him. He knew he was staring but could not look away, and for a moment they held each other's gaze. She tilted her head back, closed her eyes, and let something flood over her. At last her gas nozzle clicked off, she opened her eyes, blinked, finished with the gas, got back in her car, and without looking at him again drove away. And only then did he allow himself to remember that of course it wasn't the first Evelyn-sighting in these post years. More like the fiftieth.

* * *

He could feel the Bright House pulling him—a little rush in the nerves at the prospect.

Shuddering as he crept through the tunnel of privet, he didn't feel any specific emotion, but the possibility of them all. The air, outside the car, likewise shivered with some sense—sight, sound, smell?—then settled into the light fragrance of gardenia and pregnant silence. He knew he was feeling what Summer felt, but in his own key.

The door stood as he had left it, and he stepped inside. He walked down the hall, looking into the empty rooms, and as he came into the back room, with the door, the window, the chair, he paused to watch two old men in a corner absorbed in a board game. He walked over. They seemed as oblivious to him as they would be to someone in another galaxy, which maybe he was. The wooden hexagon on the table between them was carved in inscrutable curves with two translucent game pieces—one lightly rose-colored, the other blue—and Jon Karl knew the game which looked simple, was not, that years might pass between moves, and that the end of it, if and when it ever came, was indistinguishable from the beginning.

He looked over his shoulder, with a vague sensation of something in sly pursuit, like a shadow, or the past, but he saw nothing.

294

Slowly crossing the room he collided with the wavy blotchy mirror on the wall. He didn't recognize the person looking back at him, but knew him.

It was an inevitable motion as he sat down in the chair, with its view over the seemingly endless field. Peaceful. No fears. He hadn't let them in—but knew they were waiting outside, grumbling among themselves, watching the door. Well enough—they could just wait.

Something seductive about the field. What was that? More like music than anything—not music heard in the ears, but felt in the nerves. Not a bad way to spend an afternoon, even if he wasn't quite sure of the wisdom of getting too comfortable there. The red sun sinking toward the horizon brought him out. He left, taking his crew with him, and turned back onto Troubleneck Road.

Like waking up.

Chapter 61

Summer and Abdiel

Summer missed her November period.

"Where's Jackson?" Jon Karl asked her.

"I don't know," Summer said.

"He's not at work?"

No, she hadn't seen him for several days, and when she went by his apartment, it seemed he had skipped out. The people in the office asked if *she* knew where he was.

"What'd you tell him?" Jon Karl asked.

"I told him I might be pregnant."

"I guess that was enough."

By December her breasts were sore and she was feeling sick, and as the first real cold front of winter blew through, she and Jon Karl went together to get the pregnancy test kit.

Jon Karl had actually thought, *why waste the fifteen bucks?* but you needed to be sure.

At first Summer took Jackson's disappearance hard and didn't know what she was going to do. She found it difficult to keep going in to work, but she did. Then one day Abdiel walked in on her in the break room and caught her crying. He came and sat beside her. "What's the matter?" he asked, his hands wanting to do something affectionate, but refraining.

She hadn't wanted him to see her, but it was too late. She squeegied away the tears on her cheeks with the side of her finger. "Nothing. I'm fine."

"Don't tell me it's nothing—something's wrong and I want to help you." He searched her face but she couldn't look at him. "I was coming to ask if you knew where Jackson was."

She looked up, then back down, and shook her head.

"He's just disappeared. Not a word. I'll tell you one thing—if he shows up and thinks he's going to get this job back, he's going to be disappointed."

Summer looked at her hands.

"Hey," said Abdiel, "this is no place to be when you're upset. Come into my office where you can have some privacy."

Privacy from the pecking yard. Summer knew they had figured it out and were relishing their behind-her-back tonguefest.

So she didn't object. She sat down on the end of the leather couch under the grouse hunting print and tried to will the crying away. He took a seat not quite on the other end.

"It's none of my business," said Abdiel, "but—well, I guess you know what. I'm wondering if there's a connection between, you know, you being upset and Jackson disappearing."

"I don't know where he is."

"That's not what I asked you."

She glanced up, then down. "You didn't ask me anything."

He smiled and nodded his head with patriarchal gravity. "All I want, Summer, is to help you. But I can't help you if you're not honest with me."

"I need to put in my two weeks notice."

"No! Don't do that. Don't make a rash decision you will later regret. Don't walk away from a good, steady job just because—" Well, as people sometimes do, he had rushed into the first half of the sentence without knowing what the second half would be. So he just said, "Are we dealing with a situation here that might require—medical attention?"

She looked at her hands, silent.

He exhaled and leaned back against the couch, running everything through his mind. "You don't need to quit your job," he concluded. "I mean, after a certain point we can't—I mean, how would it look?—have you out there with the public, but I think I can find something else you can do. In the office."

She was pretty sure Israelite women got pregnant too, but whatever. She kept her eyes on her hands and didn't say anything.

"And I don't know if you're making an effort to find the young man—but I would offer some advice: don't waste your time. Let him go. I'm sure he's off somewhere, gambling away. He's not the kind of—I mean, he will never be what you need him to be. There are other places to find what you need."

* * *

She certainly had no idea how to take that last bit, but she didn't overthink it. She went home and got a good night's sleep and the next morning it all looked different.

She knew Jackson was gone for good and she wasn't sorry. His image in her mind had completely changed. Try as she might, she couldn't even remember the feeling of being smitten with him. She had bigger things on her mind—like finishing her senior year of high school pregnant, and figuring out how to be a real person.

As the new year came, she went and talked to the principal, and they worked out a plan where she could do her lessons from home. She stopped by the Junior College and had a talk with a very nice lady and got a brochure. And she leveled with Mr. Dawes who asked her if she was sure she wanted to keep the baby, and when he saw that doing anything else had never entered her mind, he said he would help her.

Jon Karl was impressed with her taking control of her life. Then one day she told him she might start going to church.

He was surprised. "Really?"

"I was thinking about it."

"Don't you have to believe all that stuff?"

"I think you have to say you do. But all the people with the good jobs go."

"Not all of them."

Most of them."

Jon Karl tried to read her. "Has that man been talking to you?"

"Some."

And she told him that Abdiel had been very excited about her being mature and listening for the voice of God. But as a new person of faith it might be better to start in a smaller church—he had some suggestions—rather than plunge into the, as it were, deeper waters of First Baptist.

"Goddam, Summer," said Jon Karl.

"You should see his house."

"I don't want to see his house."

* * *

Abdiel was taking advantage of Summer's vulnerability to have some very productive discussions with her about matters of the flesh and spirit. And, frankly, their talks were helping him work out some issues of his own. It was a satisfying feeling for him knowing that God was pleased at his shepherding his young acolyte onto the true path.

He knew she was confused, the oddest blend of inferiority and determination he had ever seen or heard of. She was all over the map, believing one thing one day, and something else the next, as often as not in direct contradiction.

Abdiel's house was indeed spacious, and though he had hired an Atlanta decorating firm to fill it with ponderous furniture and masculine adornments—many of the taxidermist's art, though Abdiel was no hunter, or fisher, except maybe for men, which includes women—an actual bearskin rug in front of the cavernous den fireplace, swords and crossed halberds on the walls, and other things that had nothing to do with him, the house still felt empty. Many of its rooms were closed off. No pets. Abdiel was one of those people who simply couldn't understand the concept of living with animals.

It was in February that Abdiel had Summer over to his house for a dinner he had hired a cook to come in and prepare in his mostly fallow chef's kitchen and which turned out to have absolutely nothing in it Summer wanted to eat, and to lighten himself of some things that had been putting a burden on his heart.

"I look at you and I see a wonderful young woman, who may have made some missteps but has a heart of gold, all alone in the world. "I'm not all alone. I have my brother."

"Well," Abdiel said with a little smile, "of course, but your brother—"

"My brother what?"

"Nothing. I don't mean anything at all. I don't know him, and God won't let me judge him—" smile—"It's just that, he has his own life to pursue, and—"

Summer waited for something after the "and" but it didn't come. Instead, Abdiel said, "Brothers and sisters have a special relationship in God's eyes. I never had a sister—or a brother—" another smile—"so I don't have firsthand experience. But I do have a little experience in the—marriage relationship. I don't know if you're familiar with the second chapter of First Timothy, but Paul lays it out pretty clearly there. Women shouldn't dress like tramps—agreed. Women will be 'saved' in childbearing—well, yes, agreed, that is their role. Women should not take away the authority of the man. She should be 'submissive'—well, some people don't care for that idea—and, frankly, they're mostly women—but you can't pick and choose what you believe in God's word. You have to think and pray deeply to really understand Paul's meaning in that verse. And I *have* prayed deeply, over the years, and I've come to see that, first of all, and this is very important, woman *chooses* to submit to man, in order to lift up God. She is equal in *status*, but different in *function*. I'm talking about the concept of complementarianism. Have you heard of that?"

Summer shook her head.

He laughed. "I know it's a big word. We'll go into more detail another time. I just want to say—" he paused for a long time— "I'm sorry, this is very heavy on my heart. But I've thought about your situation. And mine—" He sort of waved his arm around, meaning—the house? the bearskin rug? the big game staring glassy-eyed from the walls?—"And, well—" he opened and closed his hands—"you're going to need some help raising that child and—" it wasn't coming easy—"well, I've got a lot to offer."

* * *

Thank God for the expression "temporary insanity," or Summer would have had no way to understand what she had done.

Abdiel held out the prospect of security, freedom from money worries, a provision in his legacy for her, and a promising future, secure in the arms of God, for the quiescent spirit soon to be (she didn't know how she knew, she just knew) her son. The transaction, hardly a ceremony, took place on a mild February afternoon on the patio behind his attorney's law office, to the music of a gurgling fountain.

She hadn't told Jon Karl or Mr. Dawes or anybody else about it, because she knew they would try to talk her out of it. She was tired of people telling her what she should or shouldn't do. She was ready to be in control, have things of her own, and not be the mousy little nobody depending on everybody else. The way she was thinking, if she did it of her own free will, without anybody telling her she should or shouldn't, being dependent on Abdiel wouldn't count.

However, neither the "insanity" or the "temporary" was long in asserting itself.

No honeymoon—they just went back to the big cold empty house and Abdiel had his favorite restaurant, The Lazy Crab, deliver their dinner.

After dinner they sat on the sofa watching the struggling fire Abdiel had tried to build in the Viking-sized fireplace, and it was

301

the kind of silence that is filled with a thousand about to be said things that don't get said. At least they didn't on the part of the groom, strangled with embryonic thoughts that constricted his throat and came out only as "That was a nice dinner, wasn't it?" Summer, who had never really eaten seafood and was only then learning that she didn't like it, only managed something to the effect of "I'm tired and want to go to bed," thinking of her own room, but every time the fact that she was this man's *wife* would freeze her and she would only nod.

Then he said, "So, what's your full name?"

"What do you mean?" she said.

"Well, I just assumed 'Summer' was a nickname, and there was a 'real' name behind it."

"Summer is my real name."

"Just Summer?"

"Spring Summer."

"Oh."

"What's wrong with that?"

"Nothing. Nothing's wrong with it. I was just—curious. I—assumed—"

Another silence.

Finally the awkwardness was just too much, and Abdiel said, "Want to watch a movie?"

"I'm tired," Summer repeated, hoping he would translate.

Abdiel smiled. "Oh, you can't be *that* tired. I was kind of hoping for a massage." There. The ice was broken. "A husband has a right to soothing and comfort from his wife. And vice versa."

Summer was horrorstricken. She didn't know which was more repulsive—the thought of rubbing this man's body, or him rubbing hers. The realization that she had just made the worst mistake of her life had been there all along, it was just that now it breached the surface like a sea monster.

He reached over and stroked her arm, then moved his hand down to her leg. "You first," he said. "Let's go into the bedroom." He stood up and held out his hand.

God, she wanted her own room, but here they were in "the" bedroom with its big (but not big enough) zebra-motif bed and somebody's carefully selected furnishings. Abdiel closed the door and turned to her. "You can't get a massage with your clothes on," he said with a feisty smile. "A wife can have no secrets from her husband."

No vice versa. She prayed it was intentional.

She felt clammy. Her face began to sweat. Her prefrontal cortex was considering a shutdown, and as she undressed and lay on the bed and felt his hands pawing over her, her consciousness began to alternate between the execrable sensation and a trip to the ceiling where she watched the two strangers below.

"My turn," he said, pulling her back into her body again. "And there's one area that needs special attention," he added suggestively, as though he were letting her in on some savory secret.

Jon Karl! He didn't even know where she was.

"Like this," he said, showing her how. "And don't be afraid to use your mouth."

She was about to gag. Thank God she hadn't actually eaten any of those buttery insects.

Her special treat had been a little slow getting to its battle station, but at last he was as ready as he was going to be. "Time for the wife to submit to her husband," he said.

Bright flashes of light behind her eyes. "I'm pregnant," she protested.

"There's no risk to the child, if you're careful," he insisted, and tried to move in behind her.

Suddenly her gorge rose at the smell of gravy, and the air went brown.

Later, she wouldn't be sure which had come first—the murderous thought that seared her brain, or the skull she saw as she rolled over to glance at him.

I wish he was dead, the voice in her head had said, and meant it. Then immediately the backlash of guilt. *No*, she corrected—*me, take me, now, God, please*—and just as Abdiel was nearing the peak of the mountain, God obliged.

Only, apparently He liked the first idea better.

"Ehhhh!" drooled Abdiel with a spasm. "Bloo? Blah?" he tried to ask with his rubbery lips, then rolled over with a grotesque grimace.

His eyes were closed, and he went non-responsive.

Oh my God, oh my God, she thought, got dressed, and started frantically looking for her phone. She called Jon Karl but got no answer. *He's at the Chicken House!*

So she called Mr. Dawes, who tried to absorb it all. "Abdiel Eubanks?" he asked incredulously. "Call 911," he told her. "Do you know the address?"

She had no idea.

"Call them anyway. Try to tell them. I'll figure it out and call them too. I'll be there in ten minutes."

Her cross to bear, and all hers: that anguish over the line, if there was one, between knowing and causing.

Chapter 62

Another Wreck

Since the wrestling debacle, for which Pruet's Atlanta lawyer had wangled a simple assault charge and a fine, Pruet Junior's mental state had gone downhill. Even heavier drinking, more fights, public scenes, and his "friends," if people afraid of you can be "friends," had evaporated, as one after another got a job, got married, or moved away, to a small cadre of remaining souls bad enough in their own right, and willing to risk the word or gesture being taken wrong and costing them some teeth. They went around looking for trouble, saturated with hubris, afraid of no one.

It was a Friday night. The drinking had started around noon, and they had long since graduated from beer to Bacardi 151, mezcal, and Rebel Yell. They had scored no women and scared up no fights, and were a menace to society. They were in Danny Trager's Mustang convertible, two in the front, two in the back, with Junior sitting like a Homecoming Queen on top of the seat in between. You could hear the glass packs a mile off as they flew out Bartlett Road, empties and fast food trash flying from them like confetti. Every time the speedometer hit 100, they cheered and took a shot.

There was no deer, no nothing, just a wicked curve and the indifferent laws of velocity, momentum, and angle. The car careened off the road down an embankment toward a serious oak tree with a thick low limb which clipped the windshield, missing them all, but one. The rescuers found the pulverized head before they got to the car, which had ripped through the smaller trees and brush and slammed into the facing bank. They had no way of knowing, at first, whose head it was. But a search through the wallet in the back pocket of the torso, thrown several yards from the car, had identified, and a dental exam had later confirmed, the victim. One other boy—well, you couldn't really say *boy*—the one in the passenger seat which had taken the brunt of the impact, was killed, and the other three seriously injured.

It didn't take long for a memorial, commissioned by Pruet Echols, to appear at the spot where the wreck happened, an elaborate one with goalposts and a general end zone motif and for a while Senior would visit it regularly, replacing the centerpiece pigskin that kept getting stolen. On his next car registration he replaced his vanity plate "Glory" with "27."

And he had put on a funeral, as you can imagine, for the ages. Cabul had shown up, sat in a back pew, interacted with no one, and slipped out after the gridiron metaphor-saturated eulogy.

Pruet had eventually rebounded, but like Theotis, was never the same. He had lost half of himself—how could he be?

Chapter 63

Redwine and the Angel

But when you talk about these roadside memorials, and I've seen some doozies, the one to beat was that one where the angel was hitchhiking.

The angel.

Yes sir. That's their story and they're sticking to it. There's what you might call a trace of that thing left—this was years ago—it was out there on a stretch of Miranda Road. This fella was driving home late at night and he came around the curve—and if you've ever been out there in the middle of the night, which I have, back in the day when I didn't go to bed at eight o'clock, you know it's pretty damn near the middle of nowhere—and there's this hitchhiker standing up ahead looking cool as a cucumber. Now this fella that was driving never picked up hitchhikers—he'd heard all the stories about how they would kill you and steal your car and go to your house and eat your children—but there was something about this hitchhiker that just gave him a good feeling—he wasn't scary-looking or threatening—just a good-looking clean-cut young man like you—

I'm not clean-cut.

Well, two out of three ain't bad—and he just gave him a feeling of peace, and without really *deciding* to, the fella found himself pulling over on the side of the road, like some higher power took over. Was the hitchhiker glowing? He was if you want him to be. Anyway, he picks him up and he gets in the back seat.

That's kind of condescending.

Who's fucking this monkey, you or me? That's just where he got. *Where you headed?* the fella asks him. *Not far*, he says and they just drive along for a while without talking, and the fella keeps feeling that deep sense of calm and peace like nothing he's ever felt in his life, and about the time he gets about a mile down the road, he hears the man say, *Jesus is coming back soon.* Like go on and book him a room, and just about then he sees a flashing blue light in his rear-view and when he pulls over and looks in the back seat, there ain't nobody there.

The trooper comes up to his window, says he pulled him over for some reason or other, taillight out, something like that, and when the trooper asks to see his license the fella just comes out with this story about the hitchhiker he picked up that said Jesus was coming back soon, and then disappeared, and the trooper just sort of smiles and nods his head, and when he's finished, the trooper says, *It was Gabriel. Gabriel who?* the fella says. *No, Gabriel, the angel. Angels don't have last names. Sort of like 'Sting' or 'Cher.' Oh,* the fella says. And the trooper says, *You're the seventh person I've heard that story from today. Well, I'll be blow-dried and battered,* says the fella.

Now, I never heard anything about him finding the other six people, but he lit a fire under enough people when he used that story for his testimonial in church they went out there and built that memorial. I'm telling you, it was top of the line. Deluxe. A pile of rocks they stacked up to look like Jesus, which later they claimed they hadn't built, it just appeared there. I mean, if a bowl of Alpha Bits can do it, so can a pile of rocks—and it had flowers and beads and I don't know what all hanging all over it, and a piece of plywood behind it with sunbeams painted on it, and van loads of pilgrims came there leaving everything from starfish to douche bags—it looked more like where a Mardi Gras party had been, or maybe a plane crash, than a memorial.

You say there's some of it left?

A few rocks if you know where to look.

Did Jesus come back?

If he did, I missed it. I ain't noticed nobody floating up into the sky neither.

That's a good story.

Good enough for Senior Pastor Dr. Malthon Burrell to tell it from the pulpit of Douvale First Baptist Church. You know he was "called" there and they pay him six figures to tell stories like that. Have you ever wondered why you never hear of a preacher being "called" to a lower salary?

Chapter 64

Brenleigh

It was bound to happen.

The vehicle was matching him turn for turn—one of those battleship-size SUVs, the tiny driver obscured on the bridge. Maybe coincidence, maybe not. He went ahead and turned into the parking lot of the Dollar General, where he had come for his weekly Reese Cup, and damned if the behemoth didn't slide in beside him. He got out and could hear the other door open and close. He stepped onto the sidewalk and Brenleigh came around the front of her tank, beaming.

"Jon Karl!" she cried. Like, Imagine running into *you* here!

"Hey," he said.

"Can you believe it—I was just thinking about you! That's some kind of ESP shit or something!" Her dilated eyes were trying to drink him. "Actually, I think about you a lot."

"Do you?"

"I do. Do you ever think about me?"

Jon Karl bobbed his head uncertainly. "Well—"

"You can't fool me! I know you do!"

She was putting some serious strain on the buttons of a cotton blouse, which stopped on her midsection before she did, and asking a lot of her cut-off blue jean shorts.

Jon Karl looked around—no one else out there. She leaned toward him, enhancing the scenery, and touched his arm.

"I was just stopping to get some cigarettes," she said. "What are you doing here?"

"Getting a Reese Cup."

"Cool." She gave him a good look-over. "What are you doing? You're not doing anything. Neither am I. Why don't you come over?"

"Well, I—"

"You're lying! You're not doing anything. Come over—I want to show you something. Her eyes kept their lock on him, then her features turned curious as she dropped her gaze to the asphalt. "Do you see those faces in that puddle?"

He glanced. "Not really."

"Faces. And animals too."

Whatever that meant. She was obviously burning up on something. He knew from Millard about her sweet tooth, how she would make the rounds in town when she was on the hunt—"Let me go in and work my magic," he'd heard countless times, then wait in the car. Some guy she had tamed with a sneak peek, or maybe even let have a taste. On her leash.

Jon Karl knew all that, and had managed to keep his distance so far. Pruet Echols' daughter! You think Zadie was trouble? For the love of God, talk about suicide!

But, of course, it was bound to happen.

A voice was saying, *Don't do it*, and trying to flash some red lights—but it was only the little voice, the one trying to keep order in the asylum. The other voice wasn't even a voice but a flood. *Dry spell. Certain poontang.*

"Who's there?" he said.

"Nobody. Just my roommate." She paused. "And she's about to leave."

Jon Karl stared at her. She turned away for a second and fired off a quick text, and then turned back to him. With that euphoric smile.

* * *

They passed the roommate in the corridor of the apartment complex. She didn't look happy, but her gaze lingered on Jon Karl. Brenleigh didn't seem to notice.

Inside, Brenleigh had no interest in food or drink, and the only thing she had to offer Jon Karl was a Diet Coke. There were no preliminaries. They sat on the couch, and before he even got settled she was all over him.

"I want you to have your will with me," she panted in his ear, then he had to jerk that orifice away from her tongue. Jesus.

My will? he thought. *My will is to not be here.* He looked over at the door—forget that, he knew he was trapped.

"Why?" he asked.

"Just to know what it's like."

"That's all?"

"Isn't that enough?"

The answer to that, of course, was yes, but he didn't reply. He just said, "Does your daddy know what he's raised up under his roof?"

"Not a clue."

Jon Karl knew it didn't matter whether he did or not, and he knew one way or another he was going to regret what was about to happen. That it would be something he would one day wish he could un-do but wouldn't be able to. But by then her hands had found his crotch, and from there it was like something rolling down a hill and over a cliff.

* * *

It seemed the young death trap had not been disappointed. Jon Karl lay on the couch, her screams echoing in his ears, preoccupied with the dread of her hunting him down for more, once he extricated himself from this web. He looked down at her, her face radiant in a smile, her eyes bright and darting about, her hair glistening with sweat, and in a flash he saw himself hanging in chains in a cold dungeon at the thought of anybody seeing them together like this. But how could you hide in this hick town? The goddam roommate better not walk in.

Brenleigh was running her finger over the needlework on one of the sofa cushions, entranced. Of course Jon Karl had no way of knowing she had been up, at that point, for three days, and had no way of knowing that she was ecstatically planning to take everything out of her bedroom and paint it—both the room and the everything—lavender. He just knew he had to get out of there, which came down to his prying her fingers off of him. Bareback, for God's sake. Playing dice with the devil.

Goddam the little head.

Never again.

Chapter 65

Spring Returns, with Vance

With the flowering quince, forsythia, and daffodils reminding the world that spring would return, life went on in Douvale.

In Abdiel's case, barely. He lay tubed on a hospital bed in the coma he had fallen into after his stroke. His two daughters had been located and informed, but so far neither had made an appearance. Somebody said they should try to find Abdiel's ex-wife too, but his lawyer said don't bother.

Summer, swelling on schedule, released from her employment at Scripture Land, and left holding a seventy-five dollar Israelite woman costume, asked Mr. Dawes if he could help her find another job. He reminded her of the importance of priorities: she had other things that needed her attention first, like finishing high school and getting ready to be a mother. He would help her when the time came. She was actually acing her school work and the baby wasn't due till August, but she didn't argue.

Jon Karl turned twenty-one and Spruill signed Mildra's house over to him. "With all the responsibilities," he reminded him. "Maintenance, insurance, taxes."

"Yes sir, I know," said Jon Karl.

I own a house, he reflected. *Who would have thought?* But really, they were already living in it, so the only difference was that now they had some new bills.

That was about the extent of what he thought about it. It was March and he was busy getting all the pots and buckets and implements ready at the growing house for the year's crop. In the off-season he had read a lot more about germinating seeds, which he planned to do in late April. He had gotten one surprise from last year's experience: it had awakened a love of growing things in him he had known nothing about. So this year he was planning a vegetable garden too.

* * *

As before, he had the place to himself. Millard would procure the seeds again, but his wrestling career was keeping him busy. Kid Demon was on the backroad circuit now, and Jon Karl hardly ever saw him. Tamela Johnson had vanished. And when he heard that Zadie had attached herself to some cowboy she had met at one of Millard's wrestling shows, he thought *Thank God*. Brenleigh was in Brenleigh-Land. Jon Karl had started going to another Dollar General—there were, after all, seven to choose from in Douvale—which tells you a lot about Dollar Generals. And a lot about Douvale.

He was enjoying not having any woman around for a while. All he wanted to do was go out to the Chicken House after work, get the seed pots and the garden plot ready—he was building a fence to keep the deer and lesser varmints out—read, sit on the patio, take long walks out in the woods, where he felt more comfortable than anywhere else. He had discovered that trees made far better company than people. Or most people anyway. Being by himself was the greatest luxury of all—even if he never really felt he was by himself.

All he had to do was close his eyes.

And Big and Little Chic still came over regularly to visit.

They loved the walks in the woods more than he did.

* * *

Ninety-seven percent of the seeds had germinated, and now the tables in the growing house were crowded with close to five hundred peat pots of healthy seedlings.

He needed a tiller for the vegetable garden, but didn't want to give anybody any ideas, so he shied away from renting or borrowing one. Instead, he almost killed himself busting it up with a mattock. He had to tone down his plans a bit, but ended up with tomatoes, corn, squash, peppers, beans, and weeds inside the overly ambitious confines of the chicken wire fence.

Otherwise, Theotis was keeping him very busy, but as the days got longer he had more time for horticulture in the late afternoons. He spent most nights out there, but checked on Summer every day. Afterlife would always give him a good smellover, then look at him curiously and Jon Karl could almost hear her asking, *Who are these brutes?*

Spruill had set Summer up with an obstetrician, and sometimes Jon Karl drove her to her appointments, sometime she drove herself and took up two, maybe three parking spaces at the medical center. They went shopping together, as they always had, and still found time to stop in at the library at least once a week.

Of course they drew stares in public, but God knows you can't do anything about what's going on inside somebody else's head.

On one of the library visits, Summer got engrossed in something at a table across the room, and Jon Karl was looking for The Book in the Science section. A thin faded volume caught his eye—could it be?—well, no, but it was about plate tectonics and volcanoes, so he took it back to his table.

Vance was sitting there. He looked ready to hit the disco clubs in his emerald silk shirt and tight white trousers, sitting rather cockily across from Jon Karl's place.

Jon Karl froze at the sight of him, then came and set his book down on the table and stood there.

"Don't let me interrupt you," said Vance.

"What do you want?"

"Oh Lord, I want so many things. And the list grows every day." Jon Karl held his eye and waited. "Sit down—" Vance looked around, no one was near—"looks like we've got some privacy. I've got something to run by you."

"How'd you find me here?"

Vance laughed. "My God, you have no idea how obvious you are, do you? I think you really are as innocent as you look."

"I'm not innocent," said Jon Karl.

"Oh, what a relief."

"What do you want?" Jon Karl asked again.

"Sit *down*," Vance said. Jon Karl sat. "I'm pretty sure you know what I want, and I'm pretty sure I'm not going to get it—at least not willingly—can't win em all—but I do have something else I'll take instead."

"If it has anything to do with me, you're out of luck—"

"I came out to visit you."

Silence. Then: "What do you—"

"I mean I came out to visit you. But you weren't home."

More silence. "You came to my house?"

"Your other house."

Jon Karl tried to digest this. "What are you talking about?"

"Oh, come on. I told you you're obvious."

"What the fuck? You've been following me?"

A librarian walked by. "Sh-h," she frowned.

"Yes," Vance whispered, smiling. Jon Karl just stared. "Why do I get the feeling you're not going to call the police and report a trespasser?"

Jon Karl glanced around to see if anybody was listening, then leaned back in his chair. He waited.

"You've found yourself a pretty remote spot for sure," Vance said. "And you've got some very interesting projects going on out there."

"I don't know what you're talking about."

"Of course you do." He picked up his phone from the table. "Want to see some pictures?"

Jon Karl cut his eyes to the phone, then back up to the half smiling half sadistic expression on the man's face. He found a picture, set the phone down and gave it a shove, never taking his eyes off Jon Karl.

Only a glance—a panoramic view of the scene within the growing house—then Jon Karl looked back at him. "Okay, so what are you going to do—turn me in?"

"Well, obviously, if I was going to do that, I already would have and wouldn't be here talking to you. And I still may." Pause. "Unless—"

"Unless what?"

"Well, we're back to what I want."

"I'd rather be buried alive, so go ahead and call them."

"That hurts my feelings, but I'm pretty tough. I'll get over it. All I'll say is, you don't know what you're missing—and maybe one day you'll change your mind, who knows?"

"What's the something else?"

Vance retrieved his phone, found another photo and held it up for Jon Karl to see. Predictable enough. One of the locker room pictures.

"Impressive," said Vance. "And I really have no interest in putting you out of business, and I don't care what you grow in your little garden—I just want a film."

A flurry of desperate ideas rushed through Jon Karl's head. Grab the guy's phone and smash it under the chair leg—head straight out there and pull all the plants up and throw them in the river—burn the growing house—go to Mexico— "A film," he said.

"That's right."

Jon Karl, nonviolent as he was, now understood how one person could come to kill another person. "I don't do that kind of shit."

"You like prison life better?"

"Yeah. Maybe."

"You *would* go over big there."

"Tell me what the fuck you're talking about," Jon Karl said angrily.

Which made Vance feel his advantage. He stayed cool and smiled. "We make films. You know—grown-up films."

"No way."

"You might want to reconsider. I know a rock star when I see one. Not only will I delete these photographs, never go near your place again, and never breathe a word to a soul, I'll give you five hundred dollars for one ten-minute film. Things get better after that, but that's another matter. One film."

"You're out of your mind."

"Not really. And there's one other thing you should know: we don't show the man's face." Jon Karl watched him, waiting. "Which in your case is a loss, but we don't. And I wish I could say, take your time, think it over. But I need an answer, like, right now. Or I'm making a phone call."

Chapter 66

Impact Media Services

An hour later. Summer safely home and Jon Karl telling her he'd explain everything, but not now. It was easy enough to find the half abandoned strip mall, even if it was the kind of place you could drive by your entire life and never see. It must have known some commerce in its era, but that era was well-past.

Finding the exact storefront was a bit harder: there was no conspicuous sign, but as Jon Karl crept along the row of mostly closed stores, he saw the small sign in the corner of the blacked-out front window.

Impact Media Services.

He parked at the edge of the little cluster of other cars out front, and walked warily to the door. It was blacked-out too, and locked, and he punched in the code Vance had given him. It unlocked with a whirr and some clicks.

Inside, he found himself in an empty reception area—a mostly barren desk, no other furniture, nude walls, and nothing anywhere to indicate what sort of business this was. No people. He stood there, unsure what to do, fighting the impulse to walk out and disappear, but not quite having the nerve. No one appeared, nothing happened. One door seemed to offer access to a back area where whatever was going on here was going on. He walked over and tried it—locked—then put his ear against it but couldn't hear anything. After some hesitation, he knocked.

Nothing for several dubious seconds—then the door opened and a thirtyish woman with some papers was standing there. She looked at him, then down at her papers.

"Jon Karl?"

He nodded.

She smiled. "Come on back," she said, stepping aside for him.

A little group of people, men and women, were working at computers. Editors—and a glance showed Jon Karl what they were working on. They looked as bored as anybody doing their routine job looks.

Weird, very weird, thought Jon Karl. A global billion dollar industry based on watching other people mate. They should have one of people eating—for all the hungry souls out there. Or drinking—big cool glasses of water—to entertain the thirsty.

There was no plumbing the depths of human weirdness. The further you plumbed, the weirder it got.

A hallway was spaced with closed doors. The woman led Jon Karl to the end where another woman, much older, very blonde, very tanned, was arguing with a young guy in a sock hat holding a light stand. Jon Karl knew he had seen her before, and it didn't take him long to remember. At the table in the restaurant that night. Along with leering Vance and Mr. Neanderthal.

She glanced at Jon Karl, showed no recognition, and finished arguing first, sent the disgruntled young technician on his way, then without any sort of greeting or formality opened a door and said, "In here."

It was a fabricated living room with a bar toward the back and a big couch and a few other pieces of furniture in front, and some motel-art on the walls. The front of the room was cluttered with lights and a couple of video cameras on tripods.

"You'll be working with Scarlett," the woman said, and suddenly all Jon Karl could see was the young girl standing to one side in a bathrobe, smoking a cigarette. He knew her at once, and the sight of her came with a stab of panic. She seemed to recognize him too, glanced at him then lowered her eyes. The waitress from that same night at Boca Loca.

"I can't do this," he said, and turned to walk out.

The woman stopped him at the door. "What are you talking about?"

"This is wrong, I can't do this," he said.

He stepped around the woman and into the hallway. Vance had appeared and was blocking his way.

"What's the problem?" he said confidently, in control.

"He says he can't do it," the woman said.

"She's—" Jon Karl sputtered. "She shouldn't be here, doing this—"

"That's enough of *that*," Vance barked. "You don't like the girl, we'll get you another one. What's Velvet doing?" he asked the woman.

"She's already done two today—"

"Let's make it three." He turned to Jon Karl. "If you want to back out of our arrangement, there's the door," he said, "but I fucking promise you I'll keep my end."

I've just got to get through this, Jon Karl thought.

Scarlett, or whatever her actual name was, got whisked away, and Velvet summoned.

"Here are your scripts," the woman said.

Scripts? thought Jon Karl.

She handed Jon Karl and Velvet each a manila folder. "Take about fifteen," she said, then added to Jon Karl, "You need any help getting wood?"

What kind of fucking question is that? he thought. He shrugged. "We'll see."

She scowled. "Be ready," she said, and closed the door behind her.

Jon Karl turned to look at Velvet. Maybe mid-twenties, attractive.

"You look tired," he said.

Just a slight frown. "I'm good." She produced a cigarette from her dressing gown and lit it. "I haven't seen you before," she said.

"I haven't been here before."

Wry smile. "Have you ever *done* this before?" He shook his head.

She nodded, looking him over, and took a drag on her cigarette. "You look okay. Think you can get off on me?"

What do you say to that? He shrugged.

"Can you hold off?"

"Maybe."

"Just listen to the director. Basically a no-brainer—they just want to see the action—keep your arms and legs out of the way. How much are they paying you?"

"Five hundred dollars." No point elaborating.

She shrugged. "Not bad for your first time."

"How about you?" Jon Karl asked.

"A little more."

"Yeah—you're just a dick." She laughed. "What can I say?"

"But people see you, right?"

"Yeah."

"What's that like?"

"I don't think about it." She opened the script folder.

Jon Karl opened his. Only a page.

"You don't really have to follow it," said Velvet. "Only more or less. They don't care as long as things keep moving," Her eyes flicked across it. "Oh good. A scene from *King Lear*."

"What?" said Jon Karl.

Sarcastic laugh. "Same old same old. I'm playing with myself, you come in, I'm surprised, I scold you, you apologize and say how can I make it up to you?, you go down on me, then me on you, reverse cowgirl, down dog, up dog—"

"I guess I'm supposed to know what all that means."

"You'll figure it out."

"All in a day's work."

She gave him a suspicious glance. "That's right," she said.

"So—what? They keep the camera behind me?"

She nodded. "Yeah."

The door opened and five or six people came in. Velvet exhaled and took off her dressing gown. Lacy black underwear. After the shoot, she could get fifty bucks for the panties.

The camera did stay mostly behind him or below the neck and he surprised himself. Once he got going, he got going. Just turn that part on and the rest of yourself off. *Just get through it.* He didn't look anywhere but right in front of him. He could feel all the people back there—Vance, enjoying himself, feasting on him. *Just get through it. It's not me, it's somebody else.*

Neither was Velvet—someone different from the body he was interacting with. He felt sorry for her—this weary girl who just wanted to get a hot bath and go to bed. And the other girl, the poor child, with nothing to sell but her fleeting bloom. And then what?

* * *

As he got dressed and left, he passed Vance. He was wound pretty tight and didn't need to speak. His gleaming eyes said everything.

"The pictures," Jon Karl said more than asked.

Vance held up his hands. "They never happened."

And then Jon Karl saw what he wished he hadn't: Scarlett, in her robe, with her arms locked in front of her, just inside one of the other doors in the hallway, looking helplessly at him. He had never seen such an expression on a person's face in his life.

What after this?

My god my god my god

Chapter 67

The Bright House

As he turned into the privet tunnel, his mind kept circling around the same carrion. Not much different from any other time, really. That dirty feeling. Humiliation. Carrying around that weight in his soul. Love? When had there ever been any love in it? What the hell *is* love? *Who have I ever loved besides my sister, two or three other people, and a couple of dogs*? Well, there was Evelyn. Ms. Quilliam. Those, surely Evelyn, had been love or something like it. Hadn't they? Even if they had evaporated like everybody else.

He parked in the unchanged yard. That was it, what pulled him—the place was *unchanged*. Unchangeable. What people longed for, fantasized about, spent their lives trying to describe or depict—a place fixed in time, like art, though they'd never seen one single example of it and never would. But here, you could feel it. A place of pure *now*.

Where he could regather the shreds of his self-respect. Here where there was no judgment. Nothing good or bad, proud or shameful, right or wrong—everything just itself. Unrated. Un-shelved.

He stepped inside the house—gauging the interior doors, the possibilities. The rodents of his guilty self, his fears shames and regrets, all those things that follow you but you can't touch, waited outside again, a street gang.

A closed door. He opened it and immediately stepped back. No floor. Only a square hole, ten feet deep—red clay sides and bottom. Exuding the moldy smell of a basement, and a man in full-dress military uniform dead center in a chair, sitting upright, hands on the tops of his legs, looking straight ahead.

He closed the door, opened the next.

A woman sat on the floor, eyes closed, clutching a post of the bedframe that filled most of the room.

Next door: A head on a pillow—the body hardly a swell in the bedclothes. A young woman with long straight black hair. Her face in repose, saying nothing. Tubes, medical monitors.

Next door: a girl-child's room. All pink, lacy curtains, stuffed animals and dolls on the canopied bed. And a girl with pigtails sitting in a chair at the window, her back to him, looking into the tangle of junky privet and weeds outside, the head of a life-sized doll resting on her arm. A glass of pink liquid caught the light on a table beside her. When she turned and reached out a dimpled hand for it, Jon Karl had a glimpse of the ancient, over-rouged face. No emotion. Just what it was and nothing more.

A force, like a strong current, pulled him to the back room, and he fell into the chair like a roulette ball. He gazed out the window at the long pasture grass billowing in the breeze. The crimson clover. Gardenia fragrance. The music indistinguishable from the air.

Something on the distant ridge of the field caught his eye, interrupting the graceful curve of the western horizon. Something in his eye? A woman? Maybe not. A tree? Hard to say.

He looked at the back door. Closed. But he knew it would open. Something said follow, something said don't, everything said it didn't really matter. The peace kept him in the chair—the peace, as they who know say, because what else *could* they say? beyond understanding.

Even if the *you* who yearned for it would not survive the fulfillment. *You* never survives anything. Which is why it is beyond understanding.

Again, the sinking red sun brought him out.

He drove away, not seeing another soul, and turned back onto Troubleneck Road.

Back into the other world, everything floating by his windows, seeing the world in a way people before cars couldn't even imagine—the houses, the yards, the fields, shacks, and sheds—each one a saga, an epic—saying something hypnotically simple—so many scenes—drifting by.

Chapter 68

Aftermath

"Five hundred dollars?" Summer asked.

"Yeah."

"You did it in front of all those people?" she went on, not exactly shocked, just wanting to get the facts straight.

"Yeah," said Jon Karl.

"What was it like?"

"Like something you just wanted to get through with."

"You did it because of that creep?"

"Yeah. He could turn me in."

"He still could."

"Maybe he won't."

Summer burrowed into her thoughts. Jon Karl could see what she was thinking. "You're not ever going to do it," he said.

She looked up at him. "Why's it different for me?"

"I don't know. It just is."

"You don't want me to be like all those girls you go with."

"No. Exactly."

"That's not fair."

"It's not about fair. It's about not sabotaging yourself."

"I'm not going to sabotage myself," said Summer.

"I know."

* * *

Millard reacted differently. "*Dude.* You are the *man*, by God!"

"What are you talking about?" Jon Karl said.

"Oh, come on."

"I'm serious. What do you mean?"

"I mean, I'm out here beating my brains out, and I can't even break two thousand followers. You're getting five thousand clicks a day."

"I don't know what the hell you mean."

"Your fuck film, man. Awesome. Velvet Bush! You can't make that shit up. Well, actually, you can. But listen, whatever they're offering you, turn it down. You can name your price. I'm telling you, you're a star."

"Where are you?" said Jon Karl.

"I'm in town. Where are you?"

"About to get off work. Can you meet me somewhere?"

Wal-Mart parking lot. Jon Karl got out and slipped into Millard's Wrangler.

"I always knew you were a walking gold mine," Millard said. "This is fucking brilliant."

Jon Karl had been trying to piece it all together. And he had two main questions.

"How did you know about it?" he asked Millard.

"Shit, man. You're on Bareback. That's an international site. Yes, I check it every day. Nothing gets by me."

Which left the other question. "How did you know it was me?"

Millard looked at him with a puzzled expression. "What do you mean? You think I don't know my best bud?"

"You know me just from my dick?"

"Just from your dick?" Millard's expression turned even more puzzled. "Dude, have you seen it?"

"My dick? Yeah. We go everywhere together."

"The film, man."

"*Shit* no," said Jon Karl. "You think I want to *see* that? You think I even wanted to do it?"

Millard just wasn't following. "Well—yeah. I mean, why else—"

"They blackmailed me. I wasn't even going to tell you. I figured I'd just do it and that'd be that."

"Who's they?"

"Fuck, Millard. I didn't even want to tell you this."

"Tell me what? Goddam, man."

"That sleaze ball guy. He's been stalking me. He came out to the Chicken House when I wasn't there. He took pictures."

Millard's eyes got big. "No shit?"

"No shit."

"Damn, what do you think we should do?"

"I hope I already did it. He said if I made a film he'd delete the pictures and wouldn't go to the cops."

"You think you can trust him?"

"I have no idea."

"God, I would hate to lose the crop. I'm going to get a way better deal this year. But what do you think—if somebody knows about it—"

"I did what I said. I didn't want to, but I did. I couldn't see any way out of it."

"The plants look good?"

"They're beautiful."

"But he's got, like, this permanent nut-grip on you."

"I know," said Jon Karl. He had a feeling like something crawling on him. It echoed in his head, an out of tune twang: the sly shift of pronouns from "we" to "you."

Jon Karl was feeling almost sick, but returned to the question he didn't want, but had, to ask. "They didn't show my face so how did you know it was me?"

Millard just looked at him for several seconds and his expression told the tale. He took out his phone. "I think you need to see it."

When it started, Jon Karl grimaced and looked away. "Jesus," he said. "I can't watch this. It's sickening."

"I just want to show you one part," said Millard, and skipped ahead to a point about three-quarters of the way through the ten and a half minute film. He handed his phone back to Jon Karl.

A primal close-up, and the sight was a revelation to Jon Karl. He had never seen it from that perspective, and it almost made him gag. "Goddam," he said, lowering the phone and trying to give it back to Millard. "I'm telling you, I can't watch this."

"I get it—but just watch it another minute."

Jon Karl exhaled and looked at the screen again. Flesh, close-up of Velvet's faking face, but not his. Then it happened. The camera slowly tilted up, and there he was, eyes closed, behind the girl and in full frame for several excruciatingly long seconds, then the camera tilted back down.

He handed the phone back to Millard. "I've got to go," he said, got out of the car and into his, and drove away.

* * *

"I did what we agreed," Jon Karl erupted. They were in Sensations, which didn't look good with the lights on, in the middle of the day, "—and you *lied*."

"Whoa, whoa," said Vance. "Nobody lied. I can't help it if the cameraman made a mistake. Those things happen."

"Did you lie about deleting the pictures too?"

"No. I'll get around to it."

"You haven't fucking done it yet?"

"I said I would get around to it."

"And the film—"

"There's nothing we can do about it now."

"You can take it down."

"It's still cooking—I can't take it down."

"And you fucking *did* lie. It was no accident—plus, you've got people editing these goddam things—they could have taken it out."

"They must have missed it. I'll talk to them."

"Take the fucking film down."

Something raw came into Vance's expression. "That's out of my hands. It won't happen again. I'll let you review all the films from now on before they go up, how's that?"

"What the fuck? Films? You said *film*, not *films*."

"I meant films." He stared evenly at Jon Karl.

"I'm done. No more films. I did what we agreed. I'm finished."

"You know what?" said Vance. "That's fine. Do you really think little pieces of shit like you aren't a dime a dozen? It was fun, but I'm tired of fucking with you."

He turned and walked back to his office, in the back, leaving Jon Karl standing there.

Fuck you, Jon Karl said to himself.

Chapter 69

After Abdiel

Abdiel died in his sleep just before Summer's graduation. Neither event qualified as dramatic. Abdiel's heart just stopped, along with his breathing, and somewhere in that fuzzy place where he had been, he stepped over a threshold, maybe into another foggy place, maybe into glory, maybe into nothing. Resuscitation attempts were unsuccessful, and everyone involved considered it a blessing. They knew if life hadn't damaged his brain enough, the stroke and coma had, and nothing was to be gained from returning. These things could go on for years.

That Abdiel had remarried was not a widely known fact, and those that knew it didn't see any gainful reason to make it known wider. It wasn't anybody's business—plus, the mysterious and whispered-about wife certainly showed no inclination to step forward. That specter had not been once to the hospital, and had made no move to assert her status. In fact, from where she was looking, about half the time she wondered if she hadn't dreamed the whole thing. And that wasn't just an expression. She was having an increasingly hard time distinguishing dream from reality, or even believing there was a distinction—and though she was capable of the occasional transcendent dream, more often they had a habit of finding some backhanded way to come true. She dreaded them. Plus, she was six and a half months pregnant and hardly leaving the house.

Certainly not to plod in her ungainly state across the stage of a high school auditorium. The principal was a decent, but inherently political man, deeply relieved that she was adamant about not participating so he wouldn't have to smoodge her out of it. Bad optic.

It turned out not even Abdiel's daughters knew their father had remarried. It's the sort of lapse that can happen when people have zero communication with each other. Nor were those two young women exactly on speaking terms with each other. Nor did they know anything specific about their father's finances, except that they had the general idea they would end up with whatever goods there were, probably after a fight, and each hired a money-smelling lawyer. One of these, in his early attempts to access the will, caught the scent of a rumor, and as he tried to track it down, all roads seemed to lead to Spruill Dawes.

Spruill told the lawyer, who had quickly found the marriage license and already knew it, that the remarriage was legitimate, and the lawyer told Spruill what he had found out. Spruill went to see his own lawyer, and the following day called Summer and said he needed to talk to her. And that it would be a good idea if Jon Karl were there too.

Unnecessary though that was to mention.

Afterlife was happy to see Jon Karl and followed him into the den. Jon Karl had his antennae up, trying to detect anything in Spruill's manner or expression, any innuendo, any glancing double entendre, that would imply he had seen an interesting film lately.

But there was nothing. He was all business.

"Now sweetheart," he said, "I'm not here to make any kind of judgment about your actions. You did what you did, I'm sure you had your reasons, but those reasons are your business and they may or may not pertain to the situation at hand. But if I don't ask you, the judge will, so I just need you to be honest with me so I know what's what. Does that sound fair?"

Summer nodded. Jon Karl sat silently, watching, listening.

"Did you have any kind of agreement with Mr. Eubanks?"

An uncertain look came over her. "What do you mean?"

"I mean, did he promise to put you in his will, leave you the house, make you a beneficiary of anything—did ya'll discuss anything like that?"

She shook her head. "A little bit."

"A little bit?"

"It was all a mistake," said Summer. "I was thinking crazy. I don't even really believe it happened—"

"It happened."

"I know. But it doesn't feel like it was me, it feels like I wasn't really there."

"Well, baby, the judge—"

"It was just some talking—he never did anything about it."

"How do you know?"

"I just know." She looked at him imploringly. "We were only married seven hours."

Somehow the humor in that managed to express itself without anybody showing it.

Spruill just said, "Well, actually, you were married to him until he died. And here's the thing: you're his widow and you may have a right to some of his estate."

"I don't want anything of his."

"Well, the fact is, he does have a valid will—ten years old— that leaves everything to his daughters. No mention of his first wife."

"That's how it should be."

"But you might be able to make a case as his widow through the probate process—"

"I don't know what that means."

"It means you could challenge the will and try to force probate—which would mean you might have a right to a share of his assets."

"I don't want anything of his."

"Okay. I hear you. I do have one sort of awkward question though." She looked at him, waiting. "Was the marriage consummated?"

She scowled. "I don't know what that means."

"Did you have relations?"

The scowl lingered. "Sort of. I don't even know why that matters. I don't want anything of his," she repeated. "I mean it."

Spruill almost asked "You're sure?" but as he looked at Summer he saw there wasn't any, not a trace of, uncertainty in her. For a second he thought he was looking at Maryrell. Or Mildra. Or both. He felt proud.

He glanced at Jon Karl and saw the feeling reflected in his eyes.

You could say that a new woman had suddenly appeared, except you knew she had been there all along.

* * *

The principal drove by the morning after Graduation and personally delivered her diploma.

Cum laude.

He wished her all the luck in the world. She thanked him, and of course never saw him again.

Chapter 70

Travis and a Surprise Visit

Everywhere Jon Karl went, people looked at him. They stared, they cackled, they whispered to each other—there was no mistaking it. It wasn't pleasant, but he continued to go about his life. He pushed it away. How could you go around thinking about that all the time?

If Theotis knew anything about the film, he didn't let on. Jon Karl kept going to work, but otherwise avoided everybody. *They're all seen it by now,* he thought, *there's nothing I can do about it. That's just who I am to them.* Whatever—he knew he wasn't really Chamber of Commerce material anyway.

Summer, of course, never watched it—she wasn't interested in the film itself, or Jon Karl's forced role in it, but she was curious about the process, and Jon Karl painted a picture of the inner workings of Impact Media Services that fascinated her. It all just seemed so insane—these people treating it like it was a propane company or something, bustling around with lights and clipboards and cameras making films of people waiting around in bathrobes until it was time for them to do what people do, for money. But when Jon Karl told her about the waitress, she was deeply touched. That poor girl gave you the same feeling a bird that's fallen out of the nest and is flopping around on the ground gives you. Sending out an invitation to every snake hawk and cat in the neighborhood.

Putting the only thing she had to sell on the market. And, of course, when you sell something, it's not yours anymore, it's theirs.

A few days went by after his encounter with Vance and nothing happened. The constant paranoia he was living in eased up a bit.

But only a bit. Every vehicle he met, going to or from the Chicken House, filled him with clammy fear. He'd never realized how terrifying a Ford Focus on a dirt road could be.

Still, the days passed and nothing happened.

Several times the urge to dump all the plants out in the woods passed through him, but he simply couldn't bring himself to do it. They were thriving. Radiant and healthy. His babies. He knew it would have been better if he'd never gotten involved in this nerve-racking business in the first place. Involved? *Shit*, he thought, *I'm not involved, I'm it. And somebody else gets most of the money.*

* * *

One afternoon he was in the growing house working when Big and Little Chic started barking. The sound was like an air raid siren in his ears. He hurried out and saw a truck just pulling to a stop beside his van. It was a late-model gray and red pick-up and he recognized it as the truck of his neighbor. The guy he'd waved to on the road a couple of times—the one he wished lived several more miles away.

Now, speared with fright, he told himself—*don't panic, act normal.* The fellow, of whom Jon Karl had had a hazy impression, got out and approached him. Clean-cut, healthy-looking guy, around thirty, a friendly expression on his face, in work clothes. Not even close to a coot. Big and Little Chic rushed over and fawned around him. "Damn, man, are these your dogs?"

"Well, they showed up a couple of years ago and stuck around so I guess so."

"They showed up here too. I figured they belonged some-where but I didn't know where."

"I hope they're not bothering you."

"No, man, they're good company. If you don't mind sharing them."

"Oh, I don't mind. I'm gone so much. And it's just me."

The guy was disarming. And either genuine or extremely good at faking it.

"I know we've waved a couple of times on the road, but we've never had a chance to meet. I live in the next house down there—" he gestured. "I'm Travis."

"Jon Karl." They shook hands. "You want something to drink or—" The patio was safe. You couldn't see inside the growing house from there.

"No, thanks, I can see you're busy. I was just stopping by to say hello."

"I appreciate it, man. It's good to meet you."

"Yeah, you too. Are you—I mean, is this your place?"

"No," said Jon Karl. "I wish it was but it's not. It belongs to a friend of mine. She's letting me stay here." Travis nodded—waiting for some kind of explanation? "I needed to get away from everything."

"I hear you, man. Most of the crap out there I don't want anything to do with."

"Me either."

"I love it out here. But sometimes—I mean, I was thinking we could maybe grill a hamburger or something sometime if you wanted to. I don't really know anybody out here."

"Yeah, man, sure, that'd be great." At *your* place.

"Do you work in Douvale?" Travis asked.

"Yeah. For Dawes Properties."

"Oh yeah." Everybody knew Dawes Properties. "Do you—"

"I'm kind of a jack of all trades. I work with Theotis Fields." Travis nodded. "All right."

"What about you?"

"I'm a welder," Travis said. "At Barlow Manufacturing. But I do a lot of stuff on the side too."

Jon Karl nodded. "That's good, man."

A few odd seconds passed.

"But listen, there's something I wanted to tell you," Travis said. "Don't worry—" he smiled—"nothing to be alarmed about."

Which Jon Karl heard as *'this is going to be alarming, but—'* and he just let his expression say 'what?'

"I was looking for Buddy and Luckie the other day—"

Jon Karl looked puzzled.

Travis pointed to Big and Little Chic. "The dogs."

"Oh!"

Travis laughed. "Well, duh, of course you wouldn't have any way to know their names."

Jon Karl was just about to tell him what he called them, but thought twice about any reference to the chicken houses.

"I came through the woods and ended up over here. You weren't here. I saw them over there—" he pointed to the woods on the north side of the property—"and I just cut through your yard to get them."

Jon Karl looked at him, hardly breathing.

"I guess that's trespassing, but I didn't mean anything. I was just trying to get the dogs, worried they might be causing trouble somewhere."

"Well, I—"

"And I was hoping we could be good neighbors, so I didn't want to do something like that and not tell you. I just wouldn't feel right."

Jon Karl didn't know how to take this bizarre confession. "Well, I appreciate that," he said, glancing toward the growing house and seeing the path he must have taken.

"And, listen, I wanted you to know—anything you're doing out here is your business. You don't have to worry about me. Not now, not ever. I just wanted you to know."

Jon Karl searched his eyes but didn't detect anything insincere. *This is either the most ingenuous person who ever lived,* he thought, *or the con man from Hell.*

"I appreciate that," he said. There really wasn't anything else he could say.

* * *

A few days later, Jon Karl was working in the growing house, his back to the door. Suddenly he froze. It wasn't suspicion, an inkling, a hunch. It was knowledge: he wasn't alone.

At first he thought it might be a snake, and he checked the dirt floor. But it wasn't that. He slowly turned around.

Spruill Dawes and Ulmer Cubbage were standing in the open doorway, watching him.

PART THREE
2012 -2016

Chapter 71

Strategy

When Ulmer Cubbage led Jon Karl in handcuffs from the sheriff car to the jail, a few spectators in the parking lot watched the scene. Inside, he was booked, mug-shotted, strip-searched, fingerprinted, put in jail clothes. He knew this was rock bottom. The life he wanted had been within reach, but now a chasm had opened before him and it seemed hopelessly far away. People always said, don't ever say things can't get any worse, but in this case Jon Karl was pretty sure they couldn't.

So stupid to get involved in this shit!

And now look: Busted. The whole world watching him in a porn film. Deserting his pregnant sister. Losing the job he loved. Letting Mr. Dawes and Theotis down. Probably going to prison. Would Mr. Dawes take the house back?

And then the ghosts of all the women, crowded in the pantry of his mind, who had taken a bite of his soul then disappeared.

Jon Karl didn't want to die, but he was starting to understand there were certain perspectives on life where you couldn't help but think being dead wouldn't be all that bad.

At least when you were dead you were completely yourself. Being alive was where all the trouble was. Where other people owned you, controlled you, deserted you, hurt you. Boil it all down: other people.

How would you kill yourself in prison? You heard about people hanging themselves with sheets. Filing down a spoon and slicing open their wrists. Maybe he could get Summer to smuggle in some poison.

But resilience is bred into the human soul. Life doesn't know what else to do but keep going. He clung to his mantra: *Just get through this*. And somewhere, beyond the chasm, lay the life he yearned for. He just had to sweat it out and get there. Shake off the last twenty-two years like a bad dream. Away from people. Alone—the way he knew he was meant to live. Do what he wanted. Think what he wanted. Read what he wanted. Cook and eat what he wanted. Grow his garden, take walks in the woods, visit the Bright House when the mood struck.

The Bright House. God, how that place haunted his mind. And right now what he wished more than anything was to be there. He couldn't say why, and didn't even wonder about something so obvious.

Funny, ironically funny, he thought—*I don't even smoke the stuff. I don't do any drugs. Not even Tylenol. I don't drink. I don't bother anybody, I don't hurt anybody. Except for this shit, I don't break laws. At least not the ones that make sense.*

If he could only make them understand that, they could let him go somewhere, sin no more, and melt into the sweet anonymity he craved.

"This isn't about what you might do, it's about what you did," Mr. Dawes fumed when Jon Karl had made the mistake of alluding to the idea.

They were in an interrogation room at the jail, just the two of them. Mr. Dawes was not happy.

"Goddam!" he cried. "Giving you a job and a house wasn't enough? You don't like how much I pay you? I thought it was pretty damn generous.."

"No, Mr. Dawes, it *is*. I—"

"It must not be. And what am I going to tell Theotis? After he's put all this time in you and he's got where he depends on you, and now you leave him in the lurch by doing something so selfish and stupid?"

"I know, I—"

"Don't say anything. Anything you say is just going to make it worse. If I ask you a question, answer me but other than that just don't talk."

Silence.

"Okay, I'm going to ask you a question. Who's in this with you?"

"Nobody. Just me."

"Oh, come on. How stupid do you think I am? Who else?"

"Just me."

Spruill looked at him hard, and his eyes narrowed. "All right," he said. "That's noble and all that, but when you're ready to deal with this like a grown-up, we'll have a talk."

He got up abruptly and left.

Sheriff Cubbage came in right behind him. "Come on, son," he said, and escorted him back to his new quarters.

* * *

Jail gives you plenty of time to reflect on the error of your ways. Even if, as in Jon Karl's case, you already had a pretty good grasp.   After reflecting for twenty-four hours, he was fetched by a deputy for another confab in the interrogation room.

"Everett Gaither will be here shortly," Spruill said. "He'll be representing you."

"Mr. Dawes, thank you—I—"

"Save the thank-yous. Are you willing to do what he says?"

"I guess. If—"

"No, there can't be a 'guess' or an 'if.' Are you willing to do what he says?"

Cornered. "Okay."

"Good. We need to clear up a few things before he gets here. Are you going to be honest with me?"

Jon Karl looked at him. "As much as I can."

Spruill sized him up for a minute. "Were you growing the marijuana for your own use?"

Silence. An impossible question.

At last Jon Karl said, "You said be honest."

"Yes. With *me*. And you know I already know the answer."

"I don't use it."

"So you were going to sell it?"

"Yeah."

"Who was in this with you?"

"Just me."

Spruill exhaled and leaned back in his chair. "Where'd you get all those plastic buckets?"

Pause. "They were already there."

"I thought you were going to be honest with me."

"I said as much as I can."

"That place has been abandoned for twenty-five years. Those buckets were all new. They came from Home Depot."

"Somebody must have left them there."

Spruill nodded. "You know, I asked Millard if he knew anything about all this." Jon Karl raised his eyes and looked at Spruill. They stayed like that for a few seconds. "He said he didn't know anything about it."

Pause. "No. He didn't."

"But it's funny, last March, a year ago, Millard ran up an almost three thousand dollar charge at Home Depot. Do you have any idea why he might have done that?"

"I guess he had some stuff he needed."

"Why would he need five hundred buckets?"

"I don't know."

"Well, I asked him. He said he didn't remember."

Pause. "I guess not."

Mr. Dawes pressed on. "How did you come to set up shop at that place?"

"I just found it."

"And you just decided to squat there."

Jon Karl nodded. "Yeah."

"Without running water or power."

"It doesn't bother me. I like it."

"There's a well out there with a new pump on it." Jon Karl looked at him and didn't say anything. There wasn't anything he *could* say.

Mr. Dawes exhaled. "You know that place belonged to the Johnson family. Aldo Johnson."

"I think I knew that."

"It's still in the family. Do you know their granddaughter Tamela?"

"I might have met her."

"She's good friends with Zadie."

Jon Karl shrugged.

Spruill's demeanor suddenly changed. He dropped the steely front.

"Listen, Jon Karl, here's where we are. You are going to be arraigned day after tomorrow. If you're charged with growing marijuana with intent to distribute, and you're convicted, you could be looking at thirty years. You probably won't get that much, but you could. And your accomplices, which the state will have no trouble identifying, will be just as liable."

"That's pretty tough."

"Yeah. It's pretty tough. Especially for somebody who doesn't even use the stuff." Spruill thought for a minute. "Did you do this last year?"

Long pause.

"Jon Karl, you need to—"

"Yes."

"Did you make money?"

"Some."

"What'd you do with it?"

"It wasn't much."

"Do you still have it?"

"Some."

"Look, Jon Karl. I appreciate you trying to protect Millard. And Zadie. I mean that. I really appreciate it, and I won't forget it. But Everett's going to be here in a few minutes and all he's going to want to know is, were you growing it for your own use? And the answer to that question is going to have to be yes."

"But it's not true."

"It's going to have to be true."

"They're going to know I wasn't growing five hundred plants for my own use!"

"Well, maybe Ulmer didn't really remember how many plants there were."

Jon Karl stared at him. "What's going to stop them from going out there to look?"

"They can go out there if they want to—they won't find anything. You can thank Theotis for that. Next time you see him."

"Theotis? Oh my God."

"Son, nothing gets past Theotis. He's the only one I could trust. The only plants are the five Ulmer brought back as evidence."

"*Five?*"

"That's right. And I know what you're thinking. If we were going to do that, why not just find no plants?"

"I wasn't thinking that."

"You'd have gotten there. But it's more to it—you just have to know Ulmer. He can bend the truth a little—"

"A *little?*"

"A relative term. And so can I and you and everybody else who ever lived. He hasn't got it in him to ruin your life—but he also doesn't have it in him to just outright say something didn't happen when he knows it did. Because here's the thing. It's not like you killed or hurt somebody, or stole their property or kidnapped their children. I know as well as you the laws about this goddammed weed don't make any sense—personally, I can't understand why anybody would want to sit around like a zombie eating junk food but that's their business—and I have no doubt these laws will eventually change in this state. But that time hasn't come yet.

"But here's something else, Jon Karl. You're like a son to me. And I know you as well as I know any of my sons—maybe better—and there's one thing I know about you. Just like your great-grandmother—the finest woman I ever knew—you've got a conscience, and if you just get away with this it will eat away at you for the rest of your life. You may not believe me, but the times I regret the most in my life are the times I *didn't* get caught. And there've been a few. It's like an extra weight you have to carry around from then on because you feel like somebody gave you something you didn't deserve, that you didn't pay for."

"I know that," said Jon Karl.

"I know you do. I'm just reminding you. If the DA gets something, he won't go looking any further into it. A conviction, some time, a fine—that'll be that. And that life you were telling me about—the one you want to live?—and I know you mean it—but you'll never be able to live that life in peace if you don't pay *something*."

Jon Karl could only listen.

"Everett's been practicing law in this town for close to forty years, and I've known him about that long. We've done a lot for each other through the years. And he knows every district attorney, every lawyer, every judge in this part of the state, and he will work the best deal for you. If you cooperate."

"How long?"

"How long what?"

"Will I be in prison?"

"You won't go to prison. Some time here probably, and that'll be up to the judge. A year—or less? I don't know. And then probation."

Jon Karl absorbed that. "Can I ask you a question?"

Spruill nodded.

"How'd you find out?"

"An anonymous tip."

"From who?"

"Like I said, it was anonymous."

"They didn't have a photograph?"

Mr. Dawes' expression froze, and he sat forward in his chair. "A photograph? No, no photograph." Silence. "Was there one?"

"Yeah."

"Who has it?"

"Vance I don't know his last name. He's a boss or something at Sensations."

"The strip club?"

Jon Karl nodded.

Spruill looked at him and gradually his features relaxed into understanding. "Is that why you did it?"

Jon Karl looked up at him, then down. No doubt about what "it" was. And nothing to be gained from acting stupid. "Yeah," he said.

"Well," said Spruill, and sat back. "I have to say, you've left more for the world to remember you by at twenty-two than most people do in a lifetime. Mm. I think the sheriff needs to talk to Vance whatever his name is. They walk a fine line out there."

Jon Karl didn't mention Travis.

* * *

"This is Mr. Gaither," said Spruill.

He looked familiar. Jon Karl had seen him around town, maybe. He absorbed his young client in deep appraisal—a sharp-featured man with surrendering jowls and wire-rimmed glasses, his eyes a little to the beady side and shrewd.

Jon Karl half rose from his chair.

"Just keep your seat," said Mr. Gaither in deep southernese. "We can do without the formalities."

Jon Karl re-sat.

"At the arraignment I'll do the talking. You'll just have to affirm that it's true to the best of your knowledge. You will hear the charges and enter a plea of guilty. Think you can do that?"

At least he hesitated for a few seconds. "Yes sir."

Chapter 72

The Daughtry-Knowles
Management Consortium

As the notoriety of the young porn star's arrest faded, a new item in the *Douvale Daily Record* dethroned it. Despite freshman commissioner Todd Guin's best efforts, the Daughtry-Knowles Management Consortium made the City an offer they couldn't turn down, and assumed receivership of Hargett Realty's financially troubled Hargett Hills subdivision. The condemnation was stopped, and the property changed hands.

Daughtry-Knowles had submitted a plan. More like a vision. The demolition was limited to three houses, which were evidently, in their estimation, beyond salvage, and they entered into a cooperative agreement with Habitat for Humanity and found, after a strenuous interview process and a lottery, three seed recipients willing to put in the sweat equity and set an example for the community. Another competitive interview process identified twenty-five families, a few but not all the original tenants, eager to accept the responsibility of sweat equity in the renovations, and the mortgages for the low-interest loans the Consortium was offering.

Three-fourths of the people in town, when they heard about it, said that it didn't have a chance, it was like putting lipstick on a pig, it would just end up a dump no matter how much money they plowed into it. The other fourth said it sounded like a good idea. As long as the residents held up their end.

Pruet vented the spleen of his bitterness to Bettine. Even so, there was no way he could fully express the depth of his acrimony for, the magnitude of his loathing of, Spruill Dawes.

"Two old white men fighting over money," Theotis had muttered to Jon Karl. "Nothing on this earth you do better getting out of the way of."

If it was possible, and it was, Bettine seethed with even more spite than her husband, and when she said he needed to challenge Spruill to a duel, she wasn't kidding. And didn't even notice the rhyme.

As for that little dickhead, Todd Guin, Pruet should find a way to have him castrated. If there was anything there to castrate.

How do these people find each other?

* * *

Needless to say, neither of Abdiel's daughters was interested in the Gothic monstrosity in Lakeside—they didn't even want to be in the same region of the country with it—each was interested only in seeing it sold as fast as possible, and figuring out a way to get the better of the other.

The stage was set for one of those big legal fights where the lawyers get everything, until the discovery of several old liens filed by cheated contractors on the value of the property dampened the euphoria. And when the inspector came back with a five-page report detailing electrical problems, plumbing problems, mainline leaks, and some serious structural issues, the one-time four hundred thousand dollar house went to bargain basement auction and was scooped up, to everyone's surprise, by the Daughtry-Knowles Management Consortium, a name people were starting to hear more and more around town, for the value of the lot.

Who says you can't make money flipping houses?

And who says it doesn't pay to be on good terms with inspectors?

Pruet Echols had hardly known about the deal before it was over, and then spent three days bitching to the County Commission and anybody else who would listen, to no avail. It wasn't their fault if he hadn't seen the auction notice. He spent three more days slamming his fist into various targets around the house. Goddam Spruill Dawes!

"Are you going to kill that son of a bitch, or are you going to make me do it?" Bettine snarled at him.

Chapter 73

The Rebellious Dwell in a Dry Land

Well, it wasn't prison, that's what you had to keep telling yourself. Only a thousand dollar fine, which Jon Karl, his hair newly trimmed, swore to Spruill he could pay, and did, nine months in Correction Camp, and a year probation.

Jon Karl understood he had dodged a Mack truck, and though he basically already knew it, he learned that it pays to listen to people who know what they're talking about. And even more importantly, to *know* people who know what they're talking about.

Time for *just get through it* mode. He just had to survive till March.

* * *

Jon Karl was processed into the Glorious Light Turnaround Center in mid-June. In an experience destined to be filled with surprises, the most shocking was the first, the one standing in the receiving room in a crisp uniform watching the proceedings with cold bright eyes and a ticking jaw as Jon Karl was stripped, thoroughly searched, and issued his Turnaround jumpsuit.

Barber Balch.

Jon Karl felt something like a javelin impalement. What the hell was *he* doing here?

It wouldn't take long for him to find out.

Balch was also on hand, attentively, for Jon Karl's medical exam—then he disappeared. A guard led Jon Karl to his new accommodations, which he would share with an odd and unsociable fellow named Rilcher Furx, being treated for confusion, which as time went by, Jon Karl would conclude was a pretty accurate diagnosis, even if he had doubts about the treatment—a lot of Jesus, workshops on fighting the temptations of Satan, and some in-depth study of the habits of successful Baptists.

As they walked down a hall they met a young woman with a handful of files. She caught Jon Karl's eye and smiled. A little flutter went through him. Something hiding behind that pinned-up hair, the glasses, the business suit? No wedding ring. No rings, no jewelry of any kind, trimmed fingernails, and no make-up: major turn-ons for Jon Karl, here in this place where the last thing you wanted to be was turned on. But what could he do? What were they thinking letting somebody who looked like that in here?

She passed by, and the guard stopped before the last door on the hall.

He gave the door three short raps.

A voice barked within.

Second surprise.

Pruet Echols, who kept a well-appointed office on-site, was sitting behind his desk writing as the guard let Jon Karl in and left. Jon Karl stood there, Pruet Echols kept writing—at last he finished, gave his pen a little toss, then leaned back in his chair and studied his guest with something like a smirk. Behind him on a table two battle-scarred football helmets looked at each other.

"Well, well, aren't we lucky? We have a celebrity," said Pruet.

Whatever he meant by that, Jon Karl thought, couldn't be good.

"I've heard a man needs to keep his eye on his wife and daughters and hired help around you—is that right?"

Jon Karl met his eye. "No."

"No? Well, you'd better hope not. You know, I'm really not like other men, and if you ever get out of this place and I catch you anywhere near *my* wife or daughter, I'll have your balls in a jar and I don't mean that metaphorically."

That's pretty dramatic, Jon Karl thought, wondering if some things could be grandfathered in.

"And, actually, I don't care how much you love cameras, we don't have celebrities in here. Just cadets. Out of step with God's plan. I just want to make sure you understand that from the outset."

Jon Karl stood there.

"You aren't saying much—am I making myself clear?"

"More or less."

"More or less. Hm. I thought it was pretty clear. Like all the cadets in here, you have made a wrong turn and need to get back on the right track. Is that how you see it?"

"More or less."

Pruet laughed. "Didn't your parents, or whoever the hell raised you, teach you to be decisive? I'm asking if you understand that you are on the wrong path in life."

"Not really."

"Not really? You don't think growing a schedule one narcotic is the wrong path?"

"It doesn't hurt anybody."

"It ruins lives."

"Lots of things ruin lives and they're legal."

Pruet, who apparently had no intention of inviting Jon Karl to sit, gave him a long look. "I had heard you were a smartass. Where'd you learn that—from your shit-sandwich buddy Spruill Dawes?"

"He's not that."

"You're right. He's a crook."

"He's not a crook."

"What the fuck do you know? You're just a trailer trash degenerate with a dick and not much else running around making fuck movies and growing dope. Do you hear that sound? It's the whole world laughing at you. And if Spruill Dawes thinks he's fooling anybody, he's stupider than I thought."

"He's not stupid."

"Stupid and crazy. All this weenie hand-out shit. Free this and free that. Get a fucking job and pay your own way or don't come whining to me."

"I don't know what you're talking about."

Pruet gauged him narrowly. "Maybe you don't. I have to remember you're not the brightest bulb in the box. And that's part of God's plan too."

"What is that?"

"What?"

"God's plan."

"Please don't ask stupid questions."

"I'm serious, what is it?"

"Am I actually talking to this moron? It's the way God designed—yes, *designed*—the universe."

"I don't understand."

"Of course you don't understand, you're a dumbass. God's plan is the blueprint of His entire creation. It's our responsibility to understand and follow the plan. Get it? That's what you're doing in here."

"God wrote everything out like a script and we're just following it?"

"Bingo."

"So why do I need to change?"

"Are you implying it's God's fault when man and Satan get in the way and corrupt His plans?"

"Didn't God design man and Satan?"

"We need to get you on a study plan right away. Who the fuck else? He didn't design their rebelliousness."

"He didn't see it coming?"

"Are you really as stupid as you sound?"

"What about all the different kinds of people—not just all over the world, but over time, as human beings have evolved—"

"We don't allow that word in here."

"I'm just trying to understand."

"You know what? I'm not going to waste my breath talking to you. You think you can just go around thinking whatever you want to? I can see it's going to take a damn big hammer to beat some sense into you. We start at step one: In the beginning God created the heavens and the earth. It was all there. And He gave man dominion over it all. That's God's word. So try to *evolution* your way out of that."

"Can I ask you a question?"

Pruet exhaled. "What?"

"What's that barber doing here?"

"He's the Superintendent of Detention. Anything else?"

"Can you assign somebody else to me?"

"Hell no I can't assign somebody else to you. He's it. Live with it."

Chapter 74

Life on the Inside

Jon Karl didn't see much of Balch during the day—just periodic appearances on the mezzanine of the Activity Center in front of the stained glass window where he would stand in his uniform absorbing everything that was going on in the room—except when Jon Karl took a shower, or relieved himself, all of which took place out in the open, Balch always managed to be nearby.

Doing his job.

That, after missing Summer and the dogs, was the hardest part to Jon Karl as the days passed and he got into a routine: the loss of his beloved privacy and the gaze of those reptilian eyes. The next hardest part was the food—bad institutional food. Like what the schools didn't want.

For the rest—Bible study sessions morning and afternoon, physical training, individual study time in the library, rehabilitative counseling—he developed coping mechanisms. All of which activities were in need of them, and further alleviated by intermittent glimpses of the woman with the files, with whom he had developed a subliminal—was it going too far to say "relationship"? They had never spoken, but those moments of lingering eye contact were the seeds of the deep bond they had formed in Jon Karl's mind. Maybe only there, but Jon Karl knew that look pretty well.

Every cadet in there either leered or hopelessly stared at her, and every now and then one made bold to address her. Especially after the day she walked by and one of the older guys said, "Hey, baby, you and me. I promise you won't ever forget me!" and without breaking stride, and her stride was pure poetry, she said, "Yeah, that's what I'm afraid of," Jon Karl was for once in his life the smitten and not the smittee. He learned that her name was

Twyla Bell and she was a Cultural Readjustment Counsellor, but apparently he wasn't ready for her yet. He was still engaged with his Rehabilitative Counsellor, who was to Jon Karl's mind devoting far too much of their sessions to showing him the extent of Satan's grip on his soul.

Coping mechanism: marveling at how uncannily accurate it all was if you rendered everything he said into its direct opposite.

Bible Study sessions. Coping mechanism: the entertainment value of the session leader, a literal and earnest young man, calling it "study" when he already knew what he wanted it to say, and all the "study" went into making something that didn't say that say it.

Individual study sessions. Coping mechanism: daydreaming about the days of wine and roses in the Douvale Public Library where he had the treasure of an entire afternoon to check into whatever piqued his fancy, here among the dreary shelves that held only heavily-Baptist religious, devotional, or self-improvement titles.

Physical training. The hard labor part—digging up stumps—Coping mechanism: feeling it conditioning him for what he wanted to do when he got out. The exercise part. Coping mechanism: actually enjoying the activities and especially looking forward to the forty-five minutes of game time with the other cadets, where he learned that their initial standoffishness was not because they despised him or had ganged up to ostracize him, but because he was something of a legend among them, and they were in awe of him.

As for his relationship with Rilcher Furx, all he could do was try to imagine what he would say if he ever talked instead of just sitting on his cot looking surprised.

* * *

Saturdays, as they are for most people who live where you can tell them apart from other days, were his favorite day. Visiting time from one to three in the afternoon. Summer had come to

363

every one so far, and by late July, eight months pregnant, she was a favorite among the cadets. "Damn! I'm too late," one of them had said the first time he saw her, and now others were repeating it. Summer just smiled. She always brought cookies or Cheetoes or something.

There had been no sign of Millard.

Summer was due in a month, and looked it. She moved heavily, constantly on the lookout for a chair, wheezed a bit, and exuded general fatigue.

This day she had brought a Piggly Wiggly red velvet cake, and they sat at a table by a window in the Activity Center with a view over the recreation yard. Balch stood overhead, and Summer only gave him one glance, then didn't look at him anymore. Looking at him did something to you. She knew how Jon Karl had to take a shower and do his business where everybody, especially *him*, could watch him, and she felt sorry for him.

The only consolation, though it wasn't very consoling, was that he didn't just watch Jon Karl, he watched everybody.

Summer had some news today. Mr. Dawes didn't like her living alone at such a time and had arranged for Miriam, who had just lost her job at the Spectrum station, to live in and help her now and after the baby came for as long as Summer needed her. She and Reuben had moved into Mildra's room.

"Reuben?" Jon Karl said. "Who's Reuben?"

"Her son."

"Miriam has a son?"

"I didn't know it either. She kept it kind of secret. He's a year old now. He's adorable."

Jon Karl studied her. "Are you sure?"

Summer laughed. "What do you mean am I sure? They're living in the house."

"You've seen him?"

She laughed some more. "Jon Karl—they're right there in the house."

Jon Karl reflected. "Reuben?" he said. "After Billy Reuben, I guess."

"I guess. She didn't say. She's trying to get one of the Hargett Hills houses."

Jon Karl only sort of knew what that was. He wanted to change the subject. "What about you—have you decided on a name yet?"

"I thought about 'Jon Karl'."

"Oh, God no. Don't name him Jon Karl. I've already been Jon Karl and made a mess of it. Let him be who he is."

"That's what I finally decided too."

"That I made a mess of it?"

"No, that nobody could be you. So I thought of something else."

"What?"

"Maximilian."

"Maximilian? You're kidding."

"No, I'm not kidding."

"Where'd you hear Maximilian?"

"I've read it in a bunch of places. I like it."

Jon Karl smiled. "Yeah, I like it too."

"I call him Max."

"You talk to him?"

"All the time. I tell him to stop fidgeting, it won't be long."

Summer's eyes cut upward, and her expression changed. Jon Karl turned around and Twyla Bell was standing there.

"Eight months?" she asked.

Summer nodded.

"I know you're excited."

"I'm excited to get it over with."

"I bet you are." She kept her eyes on Summer. "I'm Twyla Bell, one of the counsellors here."

"I'm Summer."

Now she glanced at Jon Karl, who had stopped breathing for a few seconds. "It must be hard with him in here. But he'll be out soon."

Jon Karl looked up and their eyes met. "Summer's my sister," he said.

"Oh," said Twyla. "Well, that's nice. It's good of you to visit him."

"It's something I look forward to," said Summer.

Twyla nodded and looked back at Jon Karl. "You're fortunate to have such a sweet sister."

"I know," said Jon Karl.

"And I wanted to tell you, I've got a space open now, and I was going to recommend they add you."

Jon Karl looked at her. Summer looked back and forth between them. "Sure," he said. "I mean, yeah. That'd be good."

"Okay, Jon Karl. I'll set it up."

Damn, he thought. *She knows my name. Then a voice said, Well, you know hers. What's the difference?*

Summer watched her as she walked away.

* * *

Visiting Hour ended, Summer left the three-fourths uneaten cake—several cadets were standing around—first-come, first-served—and wobbled out to her diagonal car, and Jon Karl headed back to his room where Rilcher Furx, who never had any visitors, would stare at him in alarmed astonishment. Rounding a corner in the hall, Jon Karl had a near cardiac arrest as he almost collided with the stationary Balch.

"Huh!" bleated Jon Karl, and froze.

Balch drank him with his eyes, his jaw barely clicking. A very odd few seconds passed.

366

"I think it would be better if that sister of yours didn't come here," Balch said.

"Why?"

"This condition she's gone out and got herself in. It's a distraction."

"She's not bothering anybody."

"I said she was a distraction."

Jon Karl didn't respond, thinking, *there's no fucking way I'm telling her she can't come here.*

Neither Balch's head, nor any of his facial features, were moving—only his eyes, licking over Jon Karl. Silence for a minute, as he stood there in his spruce uniform, groomed, his chalk-white shiny hands crossed at his belt buckle, all the secrets of their tendons and nodules and liver spots in view.

"You're the adventurous type, aren't you?" said Balch. "Like to try different things."

The ensuing silence suggested that might have been a question, but Jon Karl wasn't sure and didn't respond.

"Like to earn extra money."

Jesus, thought Jon Karl, afraid to utter a peep. He looked away.

"Popular with the girls. The boys too, I bet. Like to have your picture taken."

At this, Jon Karl looked back, met the steely eyes—nope—looked away again.

"Slide yourself in, don't you? Tell them whatever they want to hear. And you're good at figuring that out, aren't you? Get what you want, then head on your way."

"You must be confusing me with somebody else."

"I know who you are. Little adventurer. That's why you're here. To work that out of you. And you'll be here until it is."

"I'll be here nine months."

A sneer behind that lizard-eyed Mt. Rushmore face? "You'll be here until I say you can go."

That's bullshit, thought Jon Karl, but left it alone.

"It's only for when you're young," said Balch. "And then you lose it."

"You think so?"

Definitely a sneer. "You're a little smart aleck, aren't you? We'll work that out of you too."

Chapter 75

Twyla

Jon Karl was wondering—*Has she seen it?* You'd think you'd be able to tell by someone's eyes—there was certainly no way you could ask. Nothing to do but ignore it. And try to keep from reading something into every glance.

Still, he almost wished she had. Only a matter of time. Get it over with.

Ah, she was Evelyn. She was Ms. Quilliam—which one was she? She was both! No, she was—somebody else. How could anybody be anybody with so many hungry ghosts in your head?

"Do you work for him?" Jon Karl asked her.

"Who's him?"

"Balch."

She made an odd face. "No, I work for the Dynamic Therapy Group. We have a contract here. I don't have anything to do with him."

"You don't know what you're missing."

"Does he bother you?"

"He watches me."

She frowned. "It's wrong the way they take away your privacy. I've told them that."

"Maybe they figure if nobody was watching us we'd kill ourselves."

"*You* wouldn't, would you?"

"Nah. Also, I think it makes the brainwashing more effective."

"Do you think I'm here to brainwash you?"

"I wish you were here to just wash me."

The kind of line you wait for the slap. But she just held his eye. Jon Karl was pretty sure she wasn't the type. Something playful about her. She was giving him a look.

"Just your feet, like Jesus, or a good general scrubbing?" she asked.

"Both." She smiled. "I mean, I'm almost twenty-three years old—you see all these Etruscans and Romans and everything—and I've never had anybody bathe me."

"Etruscans?" she said.

"Yeah."

Now she laughed. "Not even when you were a baby?"

"Well, I guess, but that doesn't count."

"Your mother—you lost her when you were young, I believe?"

"I was four."

"And your father—"

"He died too. I never knew him."

"So that's all you did—grow some weed?" she asked him.

"Yeah."

"Well, you're not the only one."

"What's your counsellor advice about that?"

"When you get out, don't grow anymore. Of if you do, don't get caught."

Jon Karl smiled. "I like you. You're my favorite counsellor ever."

"How many have you had?"

"Just you."

"Well, shoot. You had me feeling special there for a second."

"You are special. Are you married?"

She reared back in her chair. "You know I can't discuss my personal life with a client."

"You don't have to discuss it, I just wanted to know."

The question, apparently, wasn't simple. She looked at him and shook her head. "No."

"I'm not either. And I'm done growing weed, by the way. So they ought to just let me go and live my life in peace."

"Something tells me they're not going to."

"Yeah, they're making too much money from the county off me. But in March they have to, I don't care what Balch said."

"What'd he say?"

"That I wouldn't get out until he said. But my sentence is nine months."

"Don't worry. So if you're just going to get out and be a productive member of society, my job's pretty easy."

"What *is* your job?"

"To get you to the point where you are ready to re-enter society as a law-abiding, productive member. If within a year you've got a job and are clean, I get a bonus."

"That'll be easy. But please don't leave."

The sincere note hiding in his voice touched Twyla. "I'm not going to leave," she said. "You're on my schedule now. Wednesdays at three."

"Thank you."

"You're welcome."

"But I have something else to confess," he said. She waited. "I'll be productive, but I'm not really planning to be a member of society."

Her eyebrows rose. "Oh?"

"I just want to go out and live in the country and stay away from people."

"Even your sister?"

"No, not her. And I'm going to have a nephew too, you know."

"Yes. I know."

"And I don't know if it's possible, but I'd like to get my job back."

"So you *are* going to be a productive member of society."

"I guess. But I'm just going to go to work and then go home."

"Isn't that what everybody does?"

"No, they go to the Lions Club or something."

"You're right. I can't see you there. So, where did you work?"

"For Dawes Properties. I hope Mr. Dawes will let me come back."

"I bet he will. You've finished high school—that's good. But did you ever give any thought to continuing with school?"

"Just long enough to know I didn't want to."

She smiled. "I was just thinking about the opportunities."

"I liked my job. It was perfect for me. That's what I want to do."

"Okay, fair enough. But other than that, you want to be a hermit?"

"Basially, yeah."

"Well, I guess you do seem like the hermit type."

"What's *that* supposed to mean?"

She laughed. "You said it yourself!"

"I'm just joking. I don't deny it. But I try not to think too much about when I get out."

"Why not?"

"Because I know whatever I think of, it won't be that."

"I'd say it's the other way around. Are you going to let anybody into your hermit life?"

He smiled. "I'm going to be selective."

She smiled back. "That's smart of you."

"Of course, I may need additional counseling."

I'm flirting, he thought. It felt like the sun coming out.

She slowly nodded her head, holding his eye. "I think the main problem here is that somebody like you doesn't really belong in a place like this."

"I know what a place like this is like—but what's somebody like me like?"

Her upper body went up and down with a sigh. She had long since laid her pen on the file open before her, and leaned back in her chair. "I'm still working on that," she said. "But I do know one thing: you're not like anybody else in here. Or anywhere."

Jon Karl smiled. He'd heard that before.

Chapter 76

Cleetha Till

The house was the same but seemed more naked—then she realized the big oak tree was missing. One car, a battered Toyota, sat in the yard. The porch felt abandoned, its charm gone with the shade.

Summer stood at the door, doubting her presence would be recognized, and rapped a four-beat knock. After a minute a girl with straight brown hair pulled back the curtains on the door and they looked at each other. Then the girl unlocked and opened the door and waited there in a housedress and red Nikes, staring at her very pregnant guest.

"I came to see Miss Cleetha," said Summer.

"What for?"

"Just to visit her."

"She don't do readings anymore."

"I didn't come to get a reading. I just came to see her."

"She don't do readings."

That seemed to bring the conversation to a standstill, but luckily just then the lady herself appeared in the hallway on a walker.

"Lyla, it's okay, baby. Let her come on in."

Lyla stood back and watched as Summer approached the much frailer looking woman stooped there with still sharp eyes and a faint smile.

"I just wanted to come see you," said Summer.

"I'm glad you did, sugar, I'm happy to see you. Lyla's been helping me—she's my great-granddaughter."

"Nice to meet you," said Summer.

Lyla nodded, watching her a little iffily.

"What does that say about you when your great-granddaughter is all grown up?" Summer smiled. "It says you're right up there with Methuselah."

Lyla disappeared somewhere—a faint electronic rasp surged and died—and they sat down in the living room.

"She's been a big help to me. I had to stop doing readings—it got to where it was too much for me. I let my business license expire a while ago."

"I bet people still come."

"They did for a while but they've about stopped. I would tell Lyla to tell them I just wasn't up to it."

Summer sat there holding her hands in her lap. "I wanted to see how you were doing."

"Oh, I'm doing," Cleetha said with a little laugh. "Looks like you are too. Getting started kind of early. I expect you'll have a great-granddaughter doing for you one day." She smiled.

"It's hard to imagine that," Summer said.

"Just keep breathing," said Cleetha.

"I plan to."

"You're worried about your brother."

"It's just—a feeling I have."

"I know, sugar, but just remember God's ways are deep and part of something we only see a tiny piece of. And He will get you through whatever you need to get through."

"Some of it is real bad."

"It is, sugar, but nothing is bigger than God."

Summer nodded but didn't say anything. Cleetha watched her.

"We all question ourselves sometimes," she said. "It's a dark forest inside of us. I think most people want to do what's right—the hard part is knowing what that is."

"I think so too."

"This man you were with—I'm not talking about your baby's father—"

"I know."

"I'm not here to judge him—but he wasn't what was best for you."

"I know that. But something in my heart wanted him to die. And he did."

"And that's been worrying you."

"Yes mam."

"Well—die can mean different things." She looked at Summer sympathetically. "Nothing on this earth is more ruthless than your heart when it turns on itself. It can go off in a crazy direction. You got to fight that. You have more love in you than most people. Give some of it to yourself."

Summer managed a weak smile. "Yes mam."

"You know what I'm telling you's true, don't you?"

"Yes mam."

"You don't even really know what you're capable of. I'm tired and I don't have a whole lot left in me—" Summer started to object but Cleetha stopped her. "It's just true, sugar. I've laid all my regrets to rest and I'm not scared. You'll know what I mean one day. And I know that whatever I could tell you, you already know better than me. If not in here—" she touched her temple— "in *here*"—she patted her breastbone. "And after all these years I know more than ever it's a gift. It can be a weight on your shoulders, but it's a gift. Use it to help people and keep their hope alive."

"Even when it's dead?"

"Especially then."

"What's left when hope is dead?"

"You'd be surprised." She studied Summer's doubtful face. "You just have a different relationship with what you love when it's on the other side."

* * *

When Summer was in a drawing mood, her dreams got weird. She would work through the night, in a feverish and doomed attempt to keep from falling asleep.

She was walking up behind Jon Karl, as he sat in his patio chair, his head cocked aside, his hands crossed on his stomach, motionless, a dry brown garden below him and the field stretching beyond. S

he stopped—looking at him from the shadows—just about to see his face . . . then she was startled awake, thinking *you could handle Hell itself if only you knew it was real.*

* * *

Jon Karl was disappointed he couldn't be there. He found out later she'd had a pretty rough couple of days, but the delivery had been successful, and Maximilian had come into the world at just under eight pounds.

The nurses made quite a fuss over him.

He was born at dusk on a Tuesday, and that Saturday Summer missed her first visiting day at the Correction Center. But with Miriam at home watching Max, along with year old Reuben, she showed up for the one after that with a German chocolate cake and a phoneful of pictures.

You can't tell much from a newborn baby. Max was still red and still sort of coneheaded.

But he did have a pretty impressive head of hair.

But not as impressive as Reuben's—uncut and curly.

Jon Karl had a vision of those two growing up together.

Chapter 77

Things *Could* Get Worse

It didn't take Summer long to start pestering Mr. Dawes about helping her find a job, but he would hear none of it.

"I'm going to tell you the same thing Mildra told your mother," he said. "You need to be home with your baby."

She knew he was right, and accepted it, but felt guilty for not helping to pay the bills. She couldn't imagine what this experience would be like with a good husband, but she knew she was lucky to have Miriam. Miriam just took care of things as Summer got into a rhythm of nursing Max and stealing some sleep when he slept. And the truth of it was, it all came pretty naturally.

She couldn't say when the feeling had started to bother her. It was like getting a cold—she tried to deny it at first but that worked about as well as trying not to fall asleep so her dreams wouldn't come true. The feeling only got stronger.

It was October and Max was two months old. After her usual Saturday visit towards the end of the month she carried one of those foreboding sensations with her from the Center that sometimes dissipate after a night's sleep and don't come to anything— but this one didn't. It lingered and grew. By Wednesday the feeling had graduated from uneasiness to dread. She stood it till late afternoon, then told Miriam she needed to go check on Jon Karl.

"It's just Wednesday," Miriam said.

"I know," said Summer.

"Is something the matter?" asked Miriam.

"No. I don't know. Something's not right."

The feeling was now becoming frantic. She could feel Jon Karl's fear. She stood in the middle of the hallway, thinking—

seeing an image in her mind as clearly as if it were physically present: hanging all those years on Jon Karl's bedpost, on a belt. She went into his room—yes, still there—except the scabbard was empty. She stared, then cut her eyes up to the shelf in Jon Karl's closet, where she could see it in the same way she could see the milk in the refrigerator where she had left it. She took down the box, opened it, and only glanced at the other keepsakes as she fished it out. She undid her belt and fastened the completed scabbard on the corner of her hip, not knowing or wondering why. Then she put on a baggy sweatshirt and left, an even greater threat to life behind the wheel than usual.

She parked at the Center, more or less, and hurried to the main office. Of course they wouldn't let her into the back, especially if the reason she needed to get there was just a feeling.

"Can I just talk to him?" she pleaded.

"It's against regulations," the young woman at the desk said.

"Can I *see* him?"

"It's against regulations."

A male officer came into the room. "What's the matter?" he said.

"She wants to see her brother. I told her it's against regulations."

The officer and Summer recognized each other from her visits. "Where's Jon Karl?" she asked him.

"He's not here."

"Not here? Where is he?"

"They took him somewhere."

"Who's they?"

"Balch."

"Where?"

"He didn't say. Just said they were transferring him to another facility."

"Another facility? What other facility?"

"He didn't say. He just said they were transferring him."

"When?"

"I don't know. A couple of days ago."

The surge of the electric chair couldn't feel much different from that. So much for uneasy feelings just going away.

"Is that counsellor here?"

"Which one?"

"The younger woman."

"You mean Bell? She hasn't been here all week."

"Why not?"

"I don't know. I don't think she's coming here anymore."

And at that moment she saw him.

She left the building and called Spruill, but she was so distraught he could barely understand her.

"Look," he said. "Just come over here to my office. Can you do that?"

It was only five minutes away. Leaving the car running with the door open, she ran inside, and after he calmed her down a bit, he got the basic facts out of her.

He immediately called Balch but the call went straight to his voicemail. "I think his phone's turned off," he said.

"We need to hurry!"

"Just try not to get worked up. We'll get it sorted out."

He called the barber shop. The other barber said he wasn't there, he was at the Correction Center.

"I can see him!" Summer cried. "I know where they are! Let's go! Now!"

As Spruill looked at her, whatever doubts he may have had disappeared.

"Let me get Ulmer."

* * *

"Pull over here," Spruill told Ulmer as they eased up to the end of the driveway blocked by its metal gate.

380

The last of the Indian summer day had declined to a pink and orange bruise in the western sky through the trees. They got out, and as Spruill and Ulmer stood in front of the car peering down the disappearing driveway, Summer started looking around. She remembered everything Jon Karl had told her.

"There's another road over here," she said, and the two men walked over and saw the barely discernible roadbed curving behind the ridge. There was just enough light for them to pick their way up the slope, and then at the top though the thinning October woods they could see the house—a dark hulking shape, without a light to be seen anywhere. A few late-season croaks and groans sounded from the pond.

"I don't think anybody's here," said Ulmer.

"They're in there," said Summer.

"Isn't that his truck?" Spruill said—and, yes, they could see the back of it, just visible on the far side of the house.

They fell into a silence barely masking their almost-audible individual calculations.

"He's going to hurt him," Summer said resolutely. The franticness was gone.

Spruill glanced at her, then turned to Ulmer. "What do you think?"

"Well—" said Ulmer. "Without a warrant—I guess we knock on the door."

"I wouldn't give you ten cents for him answering it."

"He won't," said Summer. "That will just warn him."

Spruill looked at her solicitously. "You're sure about—"

"I'm sure."

He looked back at Ulmer. "It's almost dark," he said. "Why don't we just go down there and have a look?"

"We *could*—" Ulmer said reluctantly. "I don't think we're going to see anything."

"We've got to do *something*," said Spruill.

Ulmer looked at Summer. She looked back at him with an expression that reminded him of Cleetha Till. He found it hard to look her in the eye. He didn't question her, he just let out a sigh. "All right," he said. "Let's go see."

They tried to stay in the shadows as they stepped lightly over the crunchy leaves, down the slope into the rank front yard. The day was dying quickly, and still the house offered no light of any kind. No sound. Smell was another matter, but no one could say what the almost subliminal odor was. Part pond, part mold, part something else.

Ulmer stepped onto the front doorstep and tried the door handle. Locked. Of course. He leaned down and studied the deadbolt, then stood back up. Spruill wedged his way behind the crazy shrubbery smothering the front windows and tried to peer into the darkness within. Nothing—then a cat face appeared, knocking the breath out of him. Ulmer, startled, came to the edge of the stoop, reached out an arm and helped him back up. "What—"

"Goddam cat."

Summer had ventured around the shadowy southern corner of the house and then, lured by something she thought she saw, disappeared into the darkness. In a moment she reappeared and gestured to Spruill and Ulmer.

As she led them behind the house —yes, a faint glow leaked out onto the ground, just visible through the gnarled trunks of mutant shrubs towering above the back roofline. They crept toward it, and knelt to get a better look.

The light was leaking through the clerestory windows of a basement. Summer slithered through a narrow opening in the shrubs, with Spruill and Ulmer less eagerly behind her. A fetid odor choked the air. The glass of the windows was smudged with ancient dirt and a green patina of algae, but allowed a view into the dim subterranean room. They all three craned to see.

And none of them would ever forget the sight.

Three people occupied that dingy place: His Holiness, and a baldheaded naked man strapped by wrists and ankles to a table. The third was a rigid military man, standing against the far wall, watching. But since he was a mannequin it was hard to say how much he was seeing, and they locked their attention on the other two. The identity of the Pope—because there he was, walking slowly, ceremoniously, holding something—was easier to detect than that of the captive, partly due to the latter's baldness, partly to the angle at which he lay. Neither Spruill nor Ulmer could say for certain, but Summer knew who he was. And as the Pope continued across the room, they could see what he was holding: his dully gleaming, pearl-handled straight razor.

And Summer saw something else: a brown stain obscuring the holy man, as his skull flickered in and out of focus behind his face like a bad TV signal.

A jolt of adrenalin surged through her. She almost felt she could fly through the wall.

They all backed their way into the yard.

"Shoot him!" Summer whispered. "Through the window!"

"I can't just shoot him!" Ulmer protested.

"Then let me do it."

"I can't—"

"He wants to hurt him! He wants to steal who he is!"

"Hurt who?" said Ulmer.

"It's Jon Karl," said Spruill.

"How do you know?"

"Take my word for it," Spruill said. "Ulmer, I know you've got your tools with you, don't you?" Ulmer just looked at him. "Your lock tools."

Ulmer exhaled and nodded. Of course he did. He always did. "But even if I could get in—and I bet you the man's a fanatical locker and has about five locks on the inside—"

"No," said Summer, shaking her head. "He's not."

"—we can't just go breaking in there without—"

"Good God, Ulmer, the boy's in danger!" said Spruill. "Come on."

They returned to the front stoop and Ulmer knelt before the door. Ulmer knew about locks. He had learned from the best, his locksmith uncle, from his high school days working for him, and had found the skills useful ever since. He always carried his little toolkit. With a lever and a pick, he could open a deadbolt in usually ten seconds or less.

"This is pretty crazy," he said.

"It's pretty fucking crazy all right," said Spruill, cupping his hand over his phone light and giving Ulmer some illumination.

Ulmer inserted the lever, then the pick, and felt for the pins. A click. The cylinder rotated, the bolt retracted. Ulmer glanced up at Spruill and Summer, then squeezed the handle and the door cracked open. "I guess not," he said, and they stepped into the medley of odors, predominately feline, with a grace note of rot, in the dark living room, lifeless but for the cats they more felt than saw.

They tiptoed into the room, hardly daring to breathe—they could not make a sound—they simply could not. Spruill and Ulmer stayed close together, not really knowing what they were looking for, trying not to step on a cat, but Summer had disappeared.

As their eyes gradually adjusted just enough for them to make out shapes in the room, Spruill tried to think—where would the basement door in a house like this, even if it was a house not too many houses were like, be? It seemed hopeless. He berated himself—he knew better than to embark on Part A of a plan when there was no Part B, but there they were. He looked around trying to locate the shape that was Summer, but saw nothing.

A moment later, something touched his shoulder. He jerked, barely suppressed a yelp—not a cat, snake, or psychotic cleric—but Summer, standing right beside him.

"I found it," she whispered.

"It" was a door in a short hallway towards the back of the house, with a faint bar of light at the bottom. Ulmer tried it. Locked. Another deadbolt. Spruill shone the light again, and this time the lock was stubborn. They all stopped breathing at every minute sound. Finally, after several frustrating tries, he had it. The bolt retracted, and Ulmer squeezed the handle.

Opening that door felt suicidal, but there was nothing else to do.

Please don't creak, Spruill was thinking. Well, it did creak, but not very loudly. A rush of cool moldy air hit them. They found themselves at the head of a flight of wooden stairs descending sharply into a small ghostly-lit space where another light-leaking door stood closed.

Able to see a little better there, they stood uncertainly at the top of the stairs, listening. Spruill and Ulmer looked at each other with matching "What now?" expressions, but there was obviously only one answer.

Surprise him.

They tiptoed in a file down the stairs, wincing at every creak, and then there was a cat with them, apparently interested in going downstairs too. Spruill tried to shoo it back but the cat didn't pay him any mind. At the bottom they gathered at the door, the cat watching from the bottom step. The door knob was on the left, the door hung to open toward them. Ulmer squeezed the handle—unlocked!—looked at Spruill asking "Ready?" with his eyes as Spruill took a step back onto the tail of the now underfoot cat who let out a bloody screech.

No choice. Ulmer yanked open the door and they tumbled inside.

The Pope didn't surprise easily, but a cat screech followed by the explosive appearance of unexpected visitors in his sanctum did the trick. He stood at the head of the table that held his neck-straining guest, wearing his version of a shocked look.

But not for long.

Quick as thought, vestments and all, the Pope sprang along the side of the table, and clamping a hand over the bound man's mouth, forced his head back and jammed the razor hard against his windpipe.

Ulmer had drawn his revolver.

"If you ever want to see this pretty boy move again, take that gun and put it on that table over there," Balch said in an eerily calm voice, indicating with a nod of his head where he meant.

Ulmer hesitated.

"You think I'm not serious?" said Balch, and then in a movement like a snakestrike he raised the razor and swiped a slice across Jon Karl's left cheek, then returned it back to his throat.

Jon Karl blurted a cry and blood poured down his cheek and throat. Spruill winced, almost feeling it himself.

"Do it now," said Balch. "Hold it by the barrel."

Spruill watched Ulmer, could see he had no choice, saw Jon Karl's terrified eyes and the blood now dripping onto the table, then looked around for Summer.

But Summer had never entered the room.

Ulmer took the weapon by the barrel to the table and set it down, then stood there. "Back away from the table." He did, a few steps.

There was really nowhere else to look, but it was not easy to look at Balch. His eyes were bright and dull at the same time, like a dead fish electrified into life by a pulse of some demonic energy. And something in them as resolute as steel.

"Get out of here and don't come back," he said. "You can't prove anything."

It didn't matter if it was all batshit crazy. There was only getting Jon Karl out alive, nothing else.

"Okay," said Ulmer. "But if we go away and keep this quiet, you won't kill him?"

A gleam brightened Balch's eyes, just as a silent protest brightened Jon Karl's. "That's up to you."

Ulmer gestured to Spruill with his head. "He's got us," he said. "We don't have a choice. Let's go."

Carefully, they backed out of the room, passed the door into the dim vestibule just outside, paused, then clomped up the stairs. At the top, they closed the door with a decisive clunk.

In the two or three weird elongated minutes that passed after that, nothing happened. Except for wounded groans from the table—silence. Everything seemed to be waiting on everything else.

One part of that else stood flattened against the dark wall outside the half-open door, a seven-inch antler-handled knife in her right hand.

She never heard him, only saw his enlarging shadow blocking the light—maybe heard a slight rustle, smelled him—as he approached the door, then stopped on the threshold, his eyes fixed distrustfully on the stairs.

He didn't have time to turn his head, she didn't have time to think. In that lone opportune second out of the eons of the universe, she sprang from the shadows and, missing her mark, sank the knife into his right shoulder, then withdrew it and stepped back. He yowled in pain, brought his left hand to his wound, spun around, saw her, then with a lethal glare brightening his dead eyes, and the help of his left hand, raised the razor in his right, and came for her. She didn't think, only lunged at him again and swiped the knife across his lower right arm. He yelped again, fell back, and his arms went spastic, and in that gap she jumped him again, driving the knife under his ribcage.

The force, the pain reeled him back into the room, just as the upper door burst open and Spruill and Ulmer came clambering down the stairs. Then Balch, with a surprising jolt of energy, raised his arms and made a move for Summer, his chest unguarded, as though he were inviting her. She plunged the knife into the heart of him once more, the razor clattered to the concrete floor, and he staggered back, wavering there stunned, looking her right in the eye with the expression on his face that would remain a riddle the rest of her life, and collapsed like a depoled tent.

Spruill and Ulmer stood transfixed just inside the door. Blood began to pool under the body—and as Summer looked at the sight, ordained and necessary, she felt no emotion. No exhilaration, no relief, no remorse, no horror, no guilt.

She wasn't even sure who had done it—she only knew that person was now her.

Spruill came over and enveloped her in his arms. "God*dam*, girl," he said. "Are you all right?"

She just said, "Jon Karl."

Ulmer, keeping an eye on the maybe dead maybe not Balch, went over and retrieved his revolver as Spruill and Summer hurried over to the table and started to unfasten the buckles.

"No!" Ulmer cried. "Not yet. Let me get some pictures."

And he proceeded to photograph the entire scene. He had already called for back-up and an ambulance upstairs, with orders to cut the chain on the gate.

"Okay," he said, "let's get him loose."

Even up close, it took Spruill a moment to recognize Jon Karl—given his cue-ball head, his missing eyebrows and eyelashes. His blood-smeared face and throat were closely shaved and powdered, lipstick of course. And from there all the way to the once bushy tops of his feet and toes, not a single hair could be found on his body. A blade had slowly, methodically, shaved them all away from every surface and crevice. Hair, the mortal sin. Jon

Karl looked part potato. The little bit of hair the millennia had left on humans, Summer realized, made a big difference.

She went to prepare a wet towel, came back and pressed it against the gash on her brother's cheek, using a corner to wipe off the lipstick.

The poor boy could hardly move once he was freed of the straps. He was so weak he couldn't raise his arms or lift his body or press the towel, so as Summer kept her hand on it, Spruill and Ulmer helped him swing his legs around, then, each with an arm, pulled him off the table and to his feet. But of course he couldn't stand, and buckled to his knees on the cold floor.

"Where are your clothes?" Spruill asked him.

He only shook his head.

"Why don't you go upstairs, find him something to put on?" Spruill said to Ulmer.

"Don't bring me any of his clothes," Jon Karl rasped.

"I know where they are," said Summer, and letting Spruill replace her hand on Jon Karl's cheek with his, she walked over to the corner where the military man stood watch, and where Jon Karl's jumpsuit and underclothes lay tossed.

First the legs, painfully, then the arms, and Summer fastened the buttons. Ulmer brought over a chair, and they eased Jon Karl onto it.

"I don't know what else but self-defense you could call it," said Spruill.

Ulmer nodded. Another phrase was running through his mind, but he didn't say it.

Summer got another chair and sat down next to Jon Karl to press the towel and wait for the ambulance. The bloody lump across the room had no meaning and with the fleeting expression she had seen on its face lingering in her mind, she imagined the transit of his soul from that lump—into—if you could even imagine such a thing—what?

Chapter 78

O, Absalom

"He needed killing," said Redwine, speaking for everybody, "and I will admit I've lost one of my main sources of information, but you know what? I'm eighty-two years old and getting where I don't really give a shit what happened. Things happen, then some more things happen, and the world keeps on turning."

And beyond that, he didn't really have a lot to say about the matter. Neither did anybody else, in public. After the initial thrill, the whole business fell into a thousand private rooms and cafes and street corners, available in case a rival town wanted to argue about who had the most fucked-up crazy guy.

Following an inquiry, in which Judge Ogletree, the DA, and Everett Gaither questioned Ulmer, Spruill, Summer, and Jon Karl, read the crime scene report, looked at the photographs of Jon Karl strapped to the table, and the ones of Balch in a lake of blood with his straight razor lying a foot from his hand, and ascertained that Jon Karl had been drugged and abducted from the Correction Center, and that Summer had acted in self-defense, the DA, with the Judge's blessing, declined to pursue a case.

There was nobody to argue for Balch, or demand further investigation, or hire a shrewd lawyer. This is what happens when nobody gives a shit about you.

Nor had anyone stepped forward to claim his assets, which were, as everybody knew, substantial, even if nobody knew *how* substantial. Then, prompted by whom nobody could say, a few days after the headlines died, a very odd-looking lawyer in mismatched clothes, bald on top with his only hair curling rattailishly around his collar the first day, wearing a cheap toupee the second, and apparently sobered up for the occasion, did appear and located what seemed to be a valid will. But when it turned out that Balch had bequeathed everything to himself, with a provision for the upkeep of his cats, but none for how those services would be effected, that went nowhere. The attempt to find a consanguineous relation was ongoing, with the prospect of the whole business ending up in probate growing every day. The lawyer melted back into the oblivion he had come from.

"Maybe he wanted to cash everything in and have it buried with him," Redwine speculated.

When the inevitable estate sale finally came, it drew a large crowd of townspeople, some of whom were there looking for a steal, some thinking of hidden money, but most driven by morbid curiosity to see the inside of the now infamous house, especially the basement, already a fixture in town legend. Balch's photograph and video collection—which included, among a broad sampling of other unclothed boys and their exploits, Jon Karl's gym shower pictures, several copies of his most notorious performance, and a night vision film of three hazy figures on the ridge across from the front of the house—was seized by the sheriff's department.

Jon Karl was decreed to have suffered enough and, with fourteen stitches on his left cheek, released from the Correction Center into probation. Pruet Echols, being cheated of several months' revenue, vociferously protested, but to no avail.

As time passed, those protests morphed into accusations of a conspiracy against him and a clear case of collusion between the City and Spruill Dawes in the form of his sham front, the Daughtry-Knowles Management Consortium. He was making exactly that case to whoever would listen in the City Hall complex one day when he ran into Spruill in the hallway, and things got heated.

"I'm going to get to the bottom of this," Pruet vowed, "and when I do, you and all the other crooks in City Hall are going to end up in prison."

"Are you calling me a crook?" said Spruill.

"What would *you* call it if somebody stole your land from you?"

"What land?"

"Oh yeah. *What* land. Play dumb. That may cut it for some people but it doesn't cut it for me. Or my lawyers."

"I don't know what the hell you're talking about."

Pruet laughed shrilly. "Just keep on denying until you hit a brick wall. And, believe me, you're not going to be too thrilled when that happens."

"I can't wait."

"Neither can I."

Everyone in the hallway was frozen, captivated.

"What fucking land are you talking about?" said Spruill.

"That third-world rat-infested falling-apart dump that calls itself a subdivision. Do you just have some secret desire to throw away a few million dollars?"

"Oh. You mean I'm supposed to have stolen that land you were planning to steal yourself?"

Doors had opened all along the hall to take in the show, including one on the end where a thirtyish man with black hair and beard, who had been conferring with the City Manager, stood listening.

"And I know you don't really give a shit about whatever socialism it is you're trying to pull off there. You just want to stop *me*. It's pure vindictiveness."

"I think you're about due for a total psychiatric exam," said Spruill.

"Why don't you just admit it and quit lying? It's all going to come out anyway."

Spruill tore off his jacket and threw it to the carpet. "All right, that's it. I let 'crook' go, but nobody calls me a liar to my face. Let's go outside."

Pruet came out of his jacket too. The audience was transfixed. "That sounds like a damn good idea—I've been wanting to teach you a lesson. Daughtry-Knowles Management Consortium," he sneered. "You must think I'm a complete idiot."

"Goddam, you really *are* as crazy as you look."

"It's my company," a voice said.

A hush fell. Everyone turned to look. The black-bearded man, who had made the statement, stood there as calm as a sunny winter day, which it was.

Cabul Echols.

Pruet's jaw fell and he stared in shock at the apparition.

"What?" he said.

"I said, it's my company," Cabul repeated.

"Your—"

"Daughtry-Knowles, yes. It's my company. I bought it and kept the name."

"You—"

"Yes. Me. There's something about running people out of their homes to make some dirty money that I don't like. Mr. Dawes doesn't have anything to do with it."

Pruet stared, his mouth open but powerless to make any words.

Cabul turned and went back into the office, which basically ended the festivities.

Chapter 79

Back to the Chicken House

There had been no sign of Millard since the day the shit hit the fan, and there was no sign of him now.

Millard had moved on.

Mr. Dawes gave Jon Karl his job back, and Theotis, who had survived a revolving cast of incompetents over the last few months, was glad to get him.

"Long as you ain't got nothing to do with no reefer weed," Theotis said.

"I don't," said Jon Karl.

"Good. Ain't nobody but a fool mess with that stuff. I've seen all I want to see of it. It just make people lazy and not do what they got to do."

About recent incidents, they hardly talked. It was all too crazy for Theotis.

"But it just go to show you," Theotis did point out, "how everything work when you in the right place."

"If you're white," Jon Karl said.

"I didn't say that."

"And your name is Dawes."

"I ain't said that neither. Mr. Dawes can't help being what he is any more than I can. He took the white man's path, I took the black man's path. Only one we could have took."

"They're not the same path."

"No," Theotis said. "They ain't. But you turn it around, it'a been just the other way."

He never mentioned it again.

In the months that had passed, Jon Karl's hair had grown back nicely, everywhere but the scar on his cheek, and he was looking human once more, with already a couple of inches sprouting on his head. He didn't *plan* to never shave or cut his hair again, he just never did. Tamela Johnson gave him permission to stay at the Chicken House indefinitely, rent-free. She had floated a hint about him purchasing the place, at a nominal price, but he knew the roof was beyond repair, with new leaks showing up every time it rained, and the idea never took hold.

The terms of his probation were lenient: he couldn't leave the county without permission (he didn't want to), he had to submit to drug and alcohol tests (not an obstacle, though they never happened), couldn't keep a firearm (no problem), had to submit to searches of his dwelling at any time (he had nothing to hide), and must report to his probation officer weekly—in his case, Sheriff Cubbage himself.

What the last stipulation developed into was Ulmer coming out to the Chicken House from time to time less to check on things than to tend to the garden plot he had planted next to Jon Karl's. Sometimes he just came to visit, and they drank iced tea on the patio and, as Ulmer turned out to be of a philosophical bent, talked about what everything meant. Sometimes Summer and Max were there too, and they discovered that they all had different ideas about what everything meant—Max, crawling all over the patio, in trying to persuade no one, being the most persuasive of all.

The garden plots had started when Jon Karl mentioned something to Mr. Dawes about wanting a big garden and told him he had uprooted his old fence and was digging it up by hand.

"Good God, son," said Spruill.

The following Saturday morning just after seven o'clock, as Jon Karl sat on the patio where he had watched the sunrise and was now reading, a truck pulled up. It was Theotis, bringing a tiller. He unloaded it and asked Jon Karl where he wanted plowed.

"I ain't here to do it," Theotis clarified, "I'm just bringing it to you. I'mon do the first row and show you how, and then it's yours."

The sight of the freshly tilled dirt gave Ulmer his idea.

"Man, I miss having a garden since we moved. I wonder if you'd let me come out here and plant a few things."

It was a wide-open spot, with a hose from the well and sun all day. Jon Karl said he didn't mind, and the next morning a deputy showed up in a sheriff department truck with another tiller, and plowed up another big plot.

Now, May again, everything was planted, a fish in each hole, and they sat on the patio overlooking it all, discussing how to keep the varmints out.

Raccoons, possums, armadillos, but mostly deer. The dogs all seemed to understand not to go in there.

"But of course dogs are smart, and they've got somebody feeding them," Redwine would observe. "But I repeat myself."

Chapter 80

Travis Again

Jon Karl fell naturally into a rhythm at the Chicken House. He got up early, tended the garden, took walks in the woods, always with Big Chic and Little Chic, or Buddy and Luckie as he couldn't quite get in the habit of calling them, and often with Afterlife when Summer brought her for a sleepover. The woods were a significant late-life discovery for that urban hound, and eventually Summer just started leaving her there.

"I'm going to get somebody to go to the Shelter and pick me out another one," Summer said. "One of those little fluffy ones."

"You might sqush him," Jon Karl said.

"I'm not going to sqush him."

Summer was living on her own again—just her and Max. She was taking two classes at the Junior College. Miriam had left her husband for good and moved with Reuben to Macon to live with her cousin.

"I think she's got a boyfriend," Summer told Jon Karl.

He was touched. "Really? That's good," he said. "I hope he's a good guy."

"I hope so too," said Summer.

A good guy. You would think that wouldn't be asking too much, but good luck.

Like Travis. Since Jon Karl had come back they'd become good friends. Travis always seemed to drop by at a good time and they would sit on the patio and realize how alike they were in many ways. They laughed a lot. The subject never came up, but Jon Karl realized, after a little mistrust right at the beginning, that it was not possible Travis had turned him in, and never thought about it again.

Jon Karl went down to Travis's house sometimes too—a masculine place of a man of some means, comfortable but a little lonely. Travis, it turned out, like Jon Karl was a good cook. The only thing missing in the whole scene was the feminine, an absence Jon Karl welcomed, except for one floater in his mind, but it was hard to say about Travis. His marriage had obviously left a bad taste in his mouth—but you got the feeling he wanted somebody in his life, just not *that bitch.* You picked this up obliquely: whoever *that bitch* was, there were no signs of her at his place, no pictures anywhere, and next to no information to be had about her. He didn't talk about her.

The afternoon Summer first met Travis was one of those days in early June that make you contemplate the eternal.

Max was ten months old and looked you in the eye. A pint-sized perfect rogue. Summer put him in the book-strewn living room where Jon Karl still preferred to sleep on his inflatable mattress covered in quilts and pillows, and unloaded the car: first, groceries, then Jon Karl's books. When she brought the latter in, Jon Karl was in the kitchen looking through the grocery bags with Max at his feet. With Jon Karl and Miriam both gone, Summer wasn't eating so great at home, and usually ate with him when she came. She had brought stir-fry. She'd watched him do it a hundred times, and he made it look easy. But whenever she tried it, it was horrible.

"I put your books in there," she said. "I saw one glowing, but right when I reached for it, it floated up to the ceiling."

"Damn!" said Jon Karl. "Thanks anyway."

"And here—" she said, and took a pair of reading glasses from her pocket with the price tag still on them. "They're a two— I think that's right?"

"I'm pretty sure."

He put them on, picked up the grocery receipt, and held it at reading distance. "About right," he said. "Thanks."

She smiled at him. "They make you look different."

"How?"

She considered him. "I can't decide if it's smarter or not as smart."

"I *feel* smarter."

"That's not the same as being smarter."

"In fact, it's about the opposite. But who really cares what a hermit looks like?"

"That counsellor woman came by the house looking for you."

"What counsellor woman?"

"From the Correction Center."

A little jolt. "Twyla Bell?"

"I think so."

"What for?"

"She said she just wanted to see you. That you should call her."

"I don't know her number."

Summer dug a crumpled sticky note out of her pocket and handed it to him.

He took it, uncrumpled it, and looked at it. "Well, damn."

He stuck it in his pocket.

And it was about then that Travis drove up.

* * *

They spent the declining afternoon on the patio. Max, after making Summer get up a million times to keep him from putting something in his mouth, finally conked out and she put him in the portable playpen they kept there.

Summer sat down, tired, and they all looked over the gardens and the broad field beyond them stretching to the pond and the line of trees. They had been laughing a good bit and had that feeling you have sometimes with people you've just met that you've known them a long time. Things got a little more relaxed when

Summer let it be known at the first opportunity that Max's father wasn't there for a good reason: he wasn't in the picture, period.

Her attention had drifted to the stones of the patio. "I wonder what it's like to be an ant," she said.

"There's probably something looking at us right now wondering the same thing," said Travis.

"I think the trees," said Jon Karl.

"What I wonder," said Travis, "is why they bite you."

Summer considered that. "Why do you wonder that?"

"Because all it does is make you kill them."

"Then it itches for about an hour," Jon Karl said.

"But they don't know you're going to kill them," said Summer.

"That's what I mean," said Travis. "So why bother? Why bite the mountain you're on? Why bite something you can't kill or eat?"

"Maybe they think they can," said Summer.

"Yeah, I think ants are smarter than that," Jon Karl said. "I can't understand why they don't just walk away."

"Because it takes too long," said Summer.

"Maybe they're following orders," said Travis.

"From who?"

"The queen?"

"She's too busy having babies to give orders," said Summer.

"Maybe they figure the mountain is going to kill them anyway so the least they can do is get in one good bite," Jon Karl said.

"Like that makes them a hero?" said Summer.

"Yes. They have a statue down there in the antbed somewhere."

"They found something worth dying for," said Travis. "How many people get that?"

"Not many," said Jon Karl.

Summer considered that. "How many people die?" she asked.

"All of them," said Jon Karl.

"I meant every day."

"About 160,000."

"Is that a wild guess?" Summer said.

"I think it would be higher," said Travis.

"No, I read it."

"So what does that make you think?" Summer asked.

"What?"

"All those people dying."

"What do you think it makes me think? It makes me think people *are* ants. Except I already thought that so it makes me *really* think it."

Travis laughed. "I've got to get home. Summer, it was really nice meeting you."

"You too," said Summer.

"Why don't you stay and eat with us?" Jon Karl offered.

"No, thank you, but I've got some stuff I need to eat before it goes bad."

"The food or you?"

"The food. But I want y'all to come eat with me sometime. Maybe Saturday?"

"I want to," said Summer. "Can Max come?"

"You know he can. How about you, Mr. Ant?"

"Sure. If you want me," said Jon Karl. "What are you having?"

"Something I killed."

"That's been in the freezer?"

"Yes."

"Your name's not Dahmer, is it?"

"No, we're just good friends."

"That's a risky thing to be."

Travis laughed. "It's venison." Summer made a face. "Have you ever eaten it?" Travis asked her.

"No."

"You willing to try it?"

"I guess."

Travis whistled for Buddy and Luckie, and they came right over. They hopped up into the truck, leaving Afterlife looking bereft in the driveway.

"What'd you think?" Jon Karl said.

"I like him," said Summer. "He's honest."

"I think so too."

"He makes you wonder—what if everybody was like that?"

"Yeah."

And Summer tried not to see what she saw as he turned his head. She had been trying not to see it for a while. Not that there was anything to be gained by denying it.

Chapter 81

A Dream

The field. An endless excursion—he followed the path where he could see it, imagined it where he couldn't. He'd seen only the flash of the person, the woman, and now something wasn't right. His steps were feeling like the impossible exertions of a paralyzed man. Everything grew thick. He fought the growing realization, fought to deny it, but the time came when he knew. He knew the field was not endless. He crested a ridge and had come to the end of it. Ahead of him the air grew moldy and stagnant, the music died, and an infected swamp lay before him, making a much better case for endlessness. Voracious, terrifying things lurked in it. He looked for an escape—but every way was blocked by the same paralysis, and he felt the force—the one that would not let him go back—like an iron gate.

Only two choices: stagnate there, as others had done. A few crude shelters formed an intermittent line at the edge of the swamp, holding mummified remains.

Or go through it.

Jon Karl woke up sweating, breathing hard. *Goddam.*

He forgot most of his dreams.

But not that one.

Chapter 82

Twyla Again

Alone the next afternoon, Jon Karl sat on the patio, thinking. Was love a word, or something real? Or a word and a million things—some real, some not? He knew he loved and had loved a lot of things. He loved Summer, Max, Afterlife, Mr. Dawes, Theotis. He had loved Mildra, Billy Reuben, his celestial mother. And he loved It. Which was the only name he had ever had for it.

He thought about Twyla. Yes, something, maybe—even if in those months she had already become a ghost, her face mingling with other faces, her voice with other voices, and like his mother, like Billy Reuben and Mildra, like everything, she had become sealed by the mental signposts his brain had installed to remember her. He put his index fingers together as he debated with himself. His thumbs balanced out the shape. Then his middle fingers. He let the last two fingers on each hand drop away, and his focus changed from his thoughts to his hands, casually forming the geometry his heart craved. A face could sit there, in that diamond. That doorway.

He knew he could trust It. Because It didn't care, had no agenda, and just was. But out of the seven billion faces in the world, 160,000 leaving every day, twice that coming in, how many could you trust? And could you really trust them, or just decide to take a shot? Could he decide to trust this one?

He mulled that for a moment, then his hands collapsed to his lap, and he thought, "You can't not try," and took up his phone.

* * *

"Well, hello there," said Twyla. "I'm glad you called. I've been thinking about you."

"I've been thinking about you too."

"Good! You've certainly been through a lot since I last saw you."

"You could say that. What happened to you?"

"What do you mean?"

"You disappeared."

"Oh. They terminated our contract. They wouldn't let us contact anybody in there. And then—well—"

"Yeah. I got tied up."

She laughed, then abruptly stopped. "Well, I was just wondering how you were doing. Your sister said you got your job back."

"I did."

"I know you're glad."

"I am."

"And she had her baby."

"She did."

"And now you're living your dream life."

"That's truer than you know."

"I mean—out wherever you are, with your garden and all that."

"Yeah."

"By yourself?"

"Except for visitors."

"How many visitors do you have?"

"Not many."

"You're just a gurgling fountain of information, aren't you?"

"I don't really know what to tell you."

"Well—are you happy?"

"Yeah. I guess. Whatever that means."

"You don't know what being happy is?"

"I know what it is. I just don't know what it means."

She laughed. "You haven't changed."

"Well—I think I have."

"I'm sure. You made a joke once about needing more counseling when you got out. Would you ever like to talk through any of this?"

"No. I don't want to talk about any of it—I can't imagine talking *through* it."

She laughed again. "Is that another way of saying you're not interested in seeing me?"

"No, I—would really like to see you. I'm just not looking for a therapist."

"But a friend?"

"Yeah. I'm wide open to *friend*."

"How about a visit?" she said.

"Sure. If you tell me where you live."

"No, I mean at your place. I want to see where *you* live."

"Well, there's not really an address, and it's kind of hard to tell you where it is."

"I know how averse you are to coming into town."

"I come into town every day."

"So, you're not averse enough you couldn't come get me?"

"No. Not that averse."

* * *

Why there?

Jon Karl knew the parking lot—an odd-shaped one wedged between Camelot Pointe apartments, where Twyla didn't live, and some office buildings. He was running a few minutes early, and as he turned into the half-full lot he saw a man get into a maroon car on the far end. Jon Karl scanned the lot as the man drove out—just a glance—Scandinavian looking guy, sandy hair and stubble beard—any blue Maximas down there? He watched a woman come around the front of an obscured car and get in the driver's side. He circled around—yes, there it was. A woman in the driver's seat. Was that her?

He stopped in front of the car and stepped out. The woman smiled, gathered some things from the seat beside her, and got out of her car.

He still wasn't sure.

She looked odd—dressed down—jeans and a blouse, and carrying a small tote-bag. It took his mind a few seconds to reconnect the face before him with the one his dream chamber had been working on.

"Hi," she said.

Jon Karl stood there awkwardly. "Hi." He waited.

"Don't I even get a hug?"

He shrugged and walked over to her and they embraced. Pat, pat. Familiar smell. "I like your hair," she said. Their eyes met.

"Thanks."

She didn't mention his scar.

"Okay," she said, "you're my chauffeur. Let's go see what Jon Karl-Land is all about."

Out Troubleneck Road, and he only glanced as they passed the drive to the Bright House, knowing he would never share that place with her, or anybody. Except Summer—who wanted nothing to do with it and recoiled from any mention. He understood there are some things that can't be anything but yours alone. Part gratifying, part lonely, like the sun going in and out of the clouds—like being a human at all—part amazing, all doomed.

"So you go to work and come back and don't go out in public?" Twyla asked.

"Yeah, pretty much."

"Don't you see people in your job?"

"Not much. Some. Usually Theotis deals with them."

"You don't go into stores?"

"Not anymore."

"Who gets your groceries and all that?"

"Summer."

"Ah. She's your main visitor?"

"Yeah. She is."

"Her son is cute."

"Yeah."

"How old is he?"

"A year next month."

"I bet he's crazy about his uncle."

"Yeah—we're good."

"You're not exactly the standard nuclear family, are you?"

"I wouldn't think so."

She was smiling at him, and had relaxed in her seat, turned slightly towards him. Jon Karl looked at her and felt a little surge as they made eye contact. The surge went right down the center of him and he almost wished it away. Goddam thing took over. He adjusted himself in his seat.

"So how've *you* been doing?" he said. "Any big developments in your life?"

She shrugged it away. "Nothing of note. We're trying to find some new contracts. I've been thinking about going out on my own."

"That'd be good."

"I don't know."

"Well, you like doing it, right?"

"Yeah, I like it. Some of it. I like trying to help people. People are fascinating, you know."

"Yeah, I know."

"You have to try to find their buttons."

"Hm."

"Yes. Hm."

"I guess we all got our buttons."

"I guess we do," she said.

Has she seen the damn film or not?

She perked up as they turned off the road and eased down the long driveway and the entire canine crew—Big Chic, Little Chic, Afterlife—erupted around the side of the house.

"This is it?" she said.

He looked at her. "You were expecting something else?"

"No. Not at all. I wasn't really expecting anything. It's nice out here." She looked around. "Remote."

"Yeah. If you like remote."

"Are these your dogs?"

"One of them is."

They got out and the dogs came over to check out Twyla.

"They're not dangerous, are they?"

"No. They're friendly."

Jon Karl had cleaned up the grounds a bit. White oaks in the front yard, the spacious view behind. Peaceful, lonely, something.

"That looks comfy," she said as they passed his mattress.

An upturned wooden crate at the head held a propane lantern and several candles. Books everywhere. Three fans on other crates focused on the bed.

"Do you have electricity out here?" she asked.

He shook his head. "The kind from batteries. And a generator for the well."

"You're one of a kind."

"Isn't everybody?"

"Some more than others."

In the kitchen she noted the two-burner propane stove and several jugs of water on the counter—and on the floor the large metal ice chest.

"Is that your refrigerator?" she asked.

"Yeah. Are you going to eat with me?"

"Well—are you inviting me?"

"I am." He opened the ice chest. "I've got some red snapper."

She leaned over to look. A package, among other things, on a bed of ice. She smiled. "Sure." She nodded at the stove. "You cook on that?"

"I do."

She considered the water jugs. "And I'm guessing that's water." He nodded. "You don't have running water?"

"No, I do. When I need some, I run get it."

She laughed. "I see."

"There's a well."

"With a generator."

"Yes."

"I'm going to make some tea," Jon Karl said. "You want some?"

"Well—I hope you won't be mad at me—but I brought some wine." She held up her tote-bag.

"Why would I be mad at you?"

"Well—I know you don't drink—"

"I just don't like it. I never said nobody else could."

"Do you have a corkscrew?"

"No. Sorry."

"Well, let me see—maybe I brought one."

* * *

Early evening—the July heat was starting to ease up as they sat on the patio after dinner looking over the teeming gardens and the mottled meadow beyond. Deep blue sky, the sun behind the house, long shadows, the clouds in the east taking on a variety of colors, looking carved. Their conversation had been easy, eclectic, with some laughs. The wine had made its presence felt.

"Okay, I guess I get it," said Twyla.

"What?"

"You."

"Me?"

"Yes. Your life. You've eliminated the interference."

"I've what?"

"I mean, that's how I see it. And you don't get tired of it, or lonely—"

"Not so far."

She was sipping the wine from a styrofoam cup, which is all Jon Karl had. She had knocked a pretty big hole in the bottle. "You think you'll ever fix this place up?"

"I think it's about as fixed up as it's going to be."

She laughed, and looked at him wine-frankly. "You don't want to, do you? I can tell. You don't want electricity, you don't want running water."

"I mean, people lived without it for a long time—"

"Yeah—they lived without dentistry and good walking shoes too."

"Which is weird, because they walked more."

"You've got a point," she said.

"It just keeps everything simple."

"And that's what it is?"

"What what is?"

"Your button."

He scowled. "I wouldn't think of it as a button."

"I've just never met anybody like you."

"You would have a hundred years ago."

"Yeah. A hundred years ago. But me—you've met lots of people like me."

He caught her eye. She laughed. "I'm not trying to get you to say how unique I am. I'm serious."

"I'm not really sure what you're like yet."

"Do you think you can trust me?"

Jon Karl didn't answer. *What did she mean by that question?*

a. Let's trust each other.

b. Let's pretend to.

c. I don't even trust myself.

"That's what I'm not sure about," he said.

"I'm just saying, I've had more fun talking to you this afternoon than with anybody in a long time."

"Me too."

"I mean, everybody wants a meaningful life—I do—but I don't know if what I'm doing is worth doing. Or if it's just what everybody says is."

"Well, damn, *you're* the therapist."

"What does that mean? Giving twenty-nine cent answers to million dollar questions?"

"You really think that?"

"Yes. No. I don't know. But, I mean, I've really enjoyed being with you." She paused. "I mean that. You put me in touch with—something."

"I don't know what that means, but I hope it's good."

She smiled. "It's good. And if you were wondering if I needed to get back—I don't."

* * *

A week later. This time as Jon Karl turned into the parking lot the maroon car was just coming out, and Jon Karl's and the other driver's eyes met. The Mt. Rushmore stare of another driver. Nordic guy—like a cologne ad—he was gone.

Another timeless afternoon. They took a walk in the woods, and Jon Karl was a little dismayed to notice her not noticing anything. Finally she said, "Can we go back?" and she looked really tired.

But not so tired she didn't spend the sweaty night.

* * *

A week after that. On this occasion, Jon Karl had slipped into the parking lot fifteen minutes early and pulled over to the side among some trucks. Shortly afterward, the blue Maxima came to the entrance—Jon Karl ducked—drove to the far end of the lot and parked. Jon Karl sat up and could see two people in there, talking. Then the blonde man got out of the driver's side, walked over to the maroon car, got in, and drove away. Jon Karl ducked again, and when he looked up, Twyla was rounding the front of the car, to get in the driver's side.

Jon Karl waited seven or eight minutes. Then slipped out the side entrance, came around the block, and drove down to pick her up.

* * *

"It sure is hot here," she said, as they sat on the patio.

"I think it's hot everywhere," said Jon Karl. "It's August."

"Hotter some places than others," she said. "When December comes—I bet it's cold."

"I've got propane heaters."

"Even if December is almost impossible to imagine now." She looked over at him. "You know, that's what it is. I just realized."

"What what is?"

"You. That's what you have. Imagination."

"You mean I live in a dream world?"

"Yeah, sort of. To some extent we all do. But you—"

"Me what?"

"You don't really—need outside input."

"Sure I do."

"Not the usual kind. You know—*reality*."

Which Jon Karl took as, *You're a little too fucked-up for me.*

"You think reality is the same for everybody?" he said.

"As opposed to—"

"Different for everybody."

"How would you know that?"

"Same way you'd know it wasn't. You wouldn't."

They found another subject.

Then they had dinner and spent another sweaty night together. The next morning, when Jon Karl dropped her off at the

413

parking lot, she said, "I know how to get to your place now. Next time I'll come out there."

He shrugged. "Okay. That's fine. When?"

"Saturday?"

"What time?"

"Oh—mid-afternoon." He smiled and nodded. "Bye," she said, and got out.

He remembered thinking he knew—but now he knew he didn't know—who she was.

Chapter 83

Saturday

About one o'clock, as Jon Karl was working in the garden, the dogs perked up and headed for a car coming up the drive. Jon Karl came out of the garden and walked about halfway up the slope.

A yellow car?

A woman got out, and even from that distance Jon Karl could tell it was Brenleigh.

Oh shit! Brenleigh? What the hell was she doing here?

"The movie star!" she gushed as she approached him. *Good God*, he thought. The closer she came, the rougher she looked.

Her hair wasn't the cleanest, and she had some sores on her face and arms, and she had lost weight. Her eyes looked tired and restless, and old. "Hey, little hunk," she said, enveloped him in a bony embrace, squeezed his ass and in a moment of serious awkwardness seemed to want to kiss him, but he deflected her and her nose plowed into his cheek. The cheek with the scar.

"Ooh," she said as she pulled back and looked at it.

Jon Karl was thinking just one thing: *I've got to get her the hell out of here.*

"I heard about all your shit, man," Brenleigh said.

"You and everybody else."

"Pretty creepy."

"Yeah."

"What are you doing?"

"What do you mean?"

I mean, you look like you were doing something."

"I was working in my garden."

She glanced at it, a little jittery. "Garden? Is that what you do out here?"

"Some of the time."

"What about the rest of the time?" She was having trouble keeping the amiable look on her face.

"Different stuff."

She went seductive and stepped in closer. "We had some hot times together, didn't we?"

Jesus, Jon Karl thought. "Yeah—"

"I don't guess you're growing weed anymore."

"Definitely not."

"So what else do you do to get through the day?"

"What?"

"Oh come on. I know you've got some chemistry out here. Something. Anything. I don't even care what it is."

"I don't know what you're talking about. I don't have anything out here."

The smile she attempted didn't quite come off. "I know you do. Look, we had some good times. I'm just asking you to share."

"Brenleigh, I don't have anything. I don't do any of that."

Her look turned confused, as though she had tried not believing him, but that didn't seem to be working, so now all she had was denial.

"Yes you do! I'm going to go in there and look! I'm not asking for a million dollars, I just want a little taste—this is not a good day." A flash of desperation—which she tried to distort into seductive again. She nestled against him, running her hands over his chest and arms. "I'll pay you big time. However you want it. You want to tie me up?"

Yes, he thought, and looked over her shoulder. Jesus, if Twyla drove up now.

He shuddered, and maybe made a noise.

She felt it like a stab, and jerked away to look at him. All the guile disappeared—leaving her raw face like a wound, full of hate.

"So you can make a fuck movie with some skank but you don't have time for me?"

"I don't—"

"And you're not lying—you really *don't* have anything, do you?"

Jon Karl shook his head.

"What are you standing there looking so high and mighty about? You don't have shit, you little peckerhead. You're nobody. And creepy as hell too, with that pervert guy. Like what you've got to offer is hot shit? You know what you are? You're a workout at the gym. A visit to the spa—minus the mudbath—and that's all you are. I drove all the way out here to this shithole and now I don't have any gas—thinking I was going to get something out of you? What the fuck was I thinking?"

"I'll give you some money for gas."

"I don't want any damn money from you, loser!—okay, give me twenty bucks."

Jon Karl went and got the money and gave it to her. She stuffed it in her pocket.

"How do you live in this place? Goddam, it's the end of the fucking world! Nice scar," she said, and walked away.

* * *

When the sound of her car disappeared into the afternoon, Jon Karl had to sit down on the patio. He felt like something had reached its claws inside him and ripped out his guts. The dogs fawned sympathetically around him, then with a cursory pat or two lay down beside his chair. The world had shrunk to the square footage around his head. He dreaded seeing anybody—*anybody*—including Twyla. He tried to prepare himself.

But he needn't have worried. She never showed up.

* * *

About a week later, he got a text from her, apologizing—she'd had to deal with some stuff that had come up. It might not be the best idea for them to keep meeting regularly—what would he think about the occasional confidential tryst—their little secret adventure? He saw Evelyn in his mind, bustling about somewhere to ballet lessons and soccer. And Ms. Quilliam—what if he had been seven years older?

I'm an adventure, he thought.

He never answered her.

* * *

Chapter 84

Jon Karl and Summer

Summer, along with the inseparable Max and Reuben, had spent the brown afternoon with Jon Karl, and now she and the boys were headed over to Travis's for venison chili and Mexican cornbread, both of which the welder/chef did really well. It took him two days to cook the chili. Reuben was a dynamo of energy, whose year advantage made him the head troublemaker, and of course Max wasn't just walking but running all over the place now, exhausting Summer, who also had to keep an eye out for Pitiful, the fluffy pound dog. The big dogs weren't much of a threat—they would just give her a sniff and then ignore her. But there were snakes and hawks and coyotes too.

Miriam had moved back from Macon. The boyfriend had turned out to be not all that good a guy after all, and Miriam was done with putting up with not good guys. She had gotten a good job at Creamer Filtration Systems, and had just closed the deal on one of the Hargett Hills houses.

Summer reported all this to Jon Karl. Very good news. Miriam's transformation from sad person to one filled with purpose moved him deeply. He held it inside and it was enough. He didn't want to know anything more.

As for Summer, she was taking two more classes at the Junior College, toward what end she didn't yet know.

"It's okay if you don't come," she told Jon Karl.

He shook his head. "I'm sorry, I don't feel like it." He looked at her and could feel what she felt. "Summer," he said, "you know I see it too, don't you?"

She nodded. "Yes. I know."

She knew, he knew, they both knew. Talk just muddied the water.

It wasn't him—not really—only his connection to this place. And it was drifting away.

Soulmates.

Summer thought about Cleetha Till, who had been dead a month. It wasn't at all surprising, but inevitable, that everything she said had been right. Summer still felt the relief she had felt when she heard the news. Like, she made it. Safely. The treasure trove of stories and secrets, her life, was wholly hers now, beyond human reach. Hers alone. So it would be for Jon Karl. So it would be for her. So it was for everything.

Chapter 85

Redwine Pyle

I got so drunk one time I went up to this woman and asked her if she knew where Albert Pyle lived. She said—*you're* Albert Pyle. I said, I know who I am, I just don't know where I live.

Did she know?

She was my next-door neighbor so she must have. That was back in the days of the Slag Heap. I have no idea why they called it that since nobody around there knew what a slag heap was and there wasn't one within two hundred miles. It was what they call a *dive*, out in the middle of nowhere by the river where we used to hang out and have a beer or twelve. I'm talking about *back then*, you know. It ended up getting burned down by Ernest Culpepper—everybody called him Moose—because he said he was tired of his wife going into beer joints. He wanted her around the house.

The wife—her name was Faye, built about like a bale of cotton, about the same size all the way around, and the kind of ugly that would back a dog off a gut wagon. If the name hadn't been taken in that family, she could have gone by "Moose" herself.

You're implying she was a big girl.

I ain't implying it. She made the paper for almost drowning getting baptized—out there flapping her arms in the creek going *help! help!*—it took five grown men and a tugboat to get her to shore. I've always said if you can't swim maybe you need to find another religion.

Has anybody ever listened to you?

Hell no. Anyway, the only time Moose didn't mind her going there was when he was there too—the problem was, he was one of these save-it-up drunks and he didn't go enough to suit her. They never could get along—how they got married God only knows, how they *stayed* married not even God could tell you. "When two desperate souls meet" is how Kurly Bobo, the man, not the dog, described it. Anyway, she used to slip off down there, and she got to bringing one of these little red gas containers in there with her and she would set it down on the floor by her stool and start hammering down some Budweisers. Nobody knew why she brought that damn thing in there with her till one afternoon— in August, hotter than two rats fucking in a wool sock—when Moose showed up looking for her, we found out why.

She snatched that thing up and splashed gasoline all over him, then reached in her pocket and brought out a lighter and started trying to light it. He took off out that door and she was right behind him flicking that damn lighter but it wouldn't light. So she picked up a piece of 2x4 laying out there on the ground and whacked him with it and knocked him out, then whacked him again and woke him back up.

It wasn't long after that he burned the damn place down.

His lighter must have worked.

Must have. I had some buddies I used to get in trouble with back in those days. They called us the Three Amigos. Course, there were four of us. But anyway—one time one of those boys, named Eldred, took a tour of the Trojan rubber factory in Dothan and got this tee-shirt that had the Trojan warrior head on it and "Trojan Man" under it. There was this girl he had his eye on at the Slag Heap named Mary Etta—everybody called her Mary Etter— who was in there all the time—missing a few teeth and you could tell she had walked a few miles around a pool table. Anyway, he came strutting in there all cocky wearing that tee-shirt and went over to the pool table where she was separating some country boy from his chore-money and asked her what she thought of his shirt. It's purty, she said—what does it say?

I guess you don't technically have to be literate to mate.

Which kind of sums up the problem of the human race right there. One of my other buddies—who had been Eugene all his life till one day he decided he wanted to be called Ambrose—

Why?

I have no earthly idea—anyway, he had eight or nine brothers and sisters—each one with a different mama. Same daddy, different mama. One would come in just long enough to make a baby and drop it off then get out of the way for the next one. I'm telling you, it was a little bit of everything out there—blondes, brunettes, and redheads—tall, short—fat, skinny—stupid, smart. Most of them stayed right there, but one or two got the hell out.

That would be the smart ones.

At least they got a running start. Then there was Dorphus—Dorphus Traylor—decided he was going to raise some hogs, so he penned off a chunk of his yard. Hogs can't sweat—that's why they wallow, to keep cool—they would get up under the house in the summer—which was no problem until his wife was putting up some tomatoes one day and spilled a big pot of boiling water on the floor and it went down through them cracks and hit them hogs and Dorphus said he thought they were going to tear the house off the foundation. Then in the wintertime he'd let them come in the house. Now, hogs have lice. I don't know if you knew that—

I didn't.

Well, they do and Dorphus was telling that story one day and somebody said, that don't sound none too healthy, Dorphus, with hogs having lice and all. And Dorphus said, naw, son, it don't hurt a thing. I ain't lost a hog yet.

What a relief.

And I know I told you about Gladys—woman that owned a beauty shop that used to cut my hair. Sometimes if I was bored I would go get a trim just to hear what she'd say, because she was one of these you never knew what was going to come of her mouth next, but whatever it was, it was going to be entertaining. I was in there one day and all them women got to talking about bra sizes—how they couldn't get one to fit and how tired they was of this that and the other—and somebody asked Gladys what size she wore. And Gladys said, we ain't gonna talk about sizes, sugar, but it's Something-Long. I'm just waiting for them to get long enough I can tuck them in my panties and won't need one.

Can you fix me up with her?

It might be kind of hard, she's been dead thirty years. About as long as Mama—stuck in that Assisted Living, where they didn't do nothing but drug her into the vegetable kingdom. Saddest thing in my life, and if I had it to do over and could change one thing, it'd be that. I'm going to tell you right now, nobody better think about putting me in no Assisted Living—I've already got Assisted Living, it's called Michelob Ultra.

Cheers.

Damn, I may not have seen it all, but I've seen enough. And here I am, eighty-two years old, still hanging in there like a hair in a biscuit.

Chapter 86

The Bright House

He didn't know where the dogs were. He sat on the patio, looking over the field to the shimmer of the pond and the far line of trees. A familiar scene. Too familiar. He couldn't really see it anymore. He hadn't eaten anything for two or three days, and had the feeling he never would again. No appetite and he was tired. Something more than tired. His heart, another ghost, haunted the Bright House.

There was nowhere to go but there.

* * *

No cars in the yards. Abandoned toys, sagging badminton net. No people. Hardly any memory of people. Had they left? Had they ever been?

He navigated the tunnel, then stood there feeling the weight of the silence. The company he had brought seemed especially surly, desperate even—he stepped inside, turned and looked back through the open door. They stood in a moody huddle off to the side, his worst nightmare among them? Yes—looking dangerously his way, smoking a cigarette. They were all starting to look like crows. He closed the door behind him, scraping it over the uneven floor, and walked into the peace. The intrigue.

He stopped at the first door, and opened it.

A haggard man with sunken eyes, whose age was impossible to guess, sat on the edge of a bed staring at a luminescent bottle of pills and glass of water on a side table, as a woman stood in the shadows with crossed arms, watching. Waiting.

The room next door held the same scene, only with wax figures. Then a room with no people, only a current of bluish energy crackling on every surface.

Then when he opened the door to the room where the woman clung to the bedpost, she was clinging to it more tightly than ever. Looking directly at him. He closed the door and headed for the back of the house.

Some light streamed through the western windows and caught the face of the young woman in the coma. He walked over to look at her. As he leaned over the bed, her eyes opened. She cut them around, her expression baffled, unreadable.

"Who are you?" she asked. "What is this place?"

Then closed her eyes again.

He passed through the gutted kitchen and into the back room. The chair. The window. The door. Then the scent of gardenias, and the crimson clover gently dancing in the breeze outside.

As always, he could have gazed over that field forever—but for the figure, the riddle, back on the horizon. Still impossible to tell what it was. A woman? A tree? Or something in his eye? Then it walked away and disappeared over the ridge.

Well, that eliminated tree.

And he knew he wouldn't be going back. *Better if it had never been.* He felt an old shudder.

One beloved face in his mind, inseparable from himself. But he was tired of thinking. He got to his feet, walked over to the door, paused for only a second, then passed through and closed it behind him.

Knowing the place for the first time.

Again.

Chapter 87

Two Years After

The face. Coming toward her. The bright, dead eyes, intent on the pleasure. He wore surgical gloves and pressed the razor against her windpipe and said, *Be still. Be very still*—as he applied the lipstick. Then he pulled back, his eyes gleaming—a flash of *that look*—then he raised his arm like an orchestra conductor, and sliced it across her cheek. The sudden blaze of searing pain woke her up.

She lay there, recovering her composure, until the daylight found its way through the curtains.

Gardenias. The far-off whistle of an early morning train, echoing over the river valley.

"I had that dream again."

"You sure it was a dream?" Jon Karl said.

"Either that, or this is."

"Or both are."

"You always say that—you don't leave anything that's not dream."

"Neither do you."

"So?"

He laughed. "So don't blame me."

"I don't blame anybody," she said.

"It's better that way. That's all I'm saying."

"But that's not what I want you to say. I want you to say it's all okay."

"It's all okay."

"Because I can't really believe anybody else."

"I can't either."

"And it's not all a riddle."

"Not sure I can do that, but at least it's a something. Looks like you've got a busy day ahead of you."

"Very busy."

"I like it that you're busy."

"Me too."

She knew she had to leave early, to have time to go by and see Mr. Dawes—at home, recuperating, depressed by all the things he was going to have to give up. A mild heart attack, they said. But a heart attack.

A little nauseous, she got up, put on her robe and came down the hall. She stopped at Max's room—of course he wasn't there, he had spent the night at Miriam's—but she looked in all the same. He had taped a number of her drawings to his walls. The ones he was in. Which was most of them.

In the kitchen Travis, early riser, had left the coffee ready, and set out her cup, and a package of muffins.

She was alone in the house.

She sipped some coffee, passed on the muffins, glanced toward the bathroom, then steeled herself, gathered her things, and headed out to get Max for daycare.

THE END